CAPTIVE

♠ TRUTH ♠

A Novel

KAREN STARY

Can't Put it Down
BOOKS

Captive Truth
Copyright © 2019 by Karen Stary

First Edition

ISBN: 978-0-9994623-4-8
Printed in the United States of America

This is a work of fiction. Names, characters, places, and incidents are either a product of the author's imagination or are used fictitiously. Any resemblance to actual events, or persons or locales, living or dead, is purely coincidental.

Published by
Can't Put It Down Books
2113 Stackhouse Dr.
Yardley, PA 19067
www.CantPutItDownBooks.com

Cover Design by Eric Labacz
www.labaczdesign.com

Dedicated to our daughters' legacy

A short while ago, their frenzied desecration was an act of butchery, but now they are spent, like exhausted lovers after a furious rape. They have transformed into detached appendages, sanctioned by an indoctrinated clan. They do not speak to each other, they do not look at each other, for they dare not contemplate the very thought that their carnage may have been only tainted disillusions used to justify an archaic faith.

♠ Chapter 1: The Deal ♠

The Pocket Cards

In the game of poker, gamblers live between two worlds of delusion: the promise of the cards they have, and the fear of the cards they will get. The combination will determine the sanity, for the cards have no memory.

I

AN EARLY MORNING SUN had smeared a soft haze across my windshield as the pall of the work week vaporized into the glass. I followed.

Surprisingly, the miasma first appeared to be soothing, warm, inviting. Well, that is what I wanted to believe. In actuality, it was deceptively auspicious, for this Friday's closure stirred with a tentative promise of the forthcoming evening, in spite of the nip in the autumn air. I recalled how I had shivered slightly as I sat alone in my car, waiting for his call. My cell phone remained indomitably silent on the console, but within reach. Briskly, I stroked my upper arms, trying to chase away the chill inside the car.

I waited, glancing out the side window, staring at nothing in particular. Shifting my attention back to the console, I feinted reaching for the cell as my hand veered downward, flipping the knob for the seat warmer instead—a more prudent choice. Once more, I sat aimlessly trying to discount my apprehension and the silence. Finally, I could no longer ignore the unrequited urgency and snatched the cell from the console. I hesitated momentarily, then fervidly punched in his number. An exhaustion of rings collapsed into a "hello." I was relieved that I didn't have to speak to voicemail. After a rambling of hollow pleasantries, I charily asked, "Are we getting together tonight?"

Later, I would chastise myself for the unrelenting replay of the exchange that followed. It was to be the beginning of my fall into the mirage.

"So, tonight…we're still getting together?" I repeated because there was no response the first time I asked. After too long a pause, he blurted, "I think we should cool it for a while."

In the subsequent hours I could not quell the thought of how easily he had said those words. Although our relationship had been recklessly skeletal, it had been elusively nourishing. No, not just that. It had been passionately intimate. These words were a violation of that intimacy, and from the spit of a cliché, that fulfilling bond had become a naked uncertainty. I do remember how I had not wanted him to say anything else after he had said the words, "cool it." But I didn't tell him that. I just remained silent, like the indomitable cell phone. I rationalized that if I didn't provoke him to go any further, his words would not pass the point of no return. But, to tell the truth, I already knew that it was past that point the moment he spoke. I could only think about how the warm car seat was incinerating my rear end. I guess when I didn't immediately respond he felt obligated to continue his reasoning. "It's just that I can't handle three women at the same time anymore."

That was when I fell into Alice's rabbit hole. Oh, I was well acquainted with that little ditch. As I tumbled past the stumps of legitimacy of our intimacy, I tried to soften the crash. I convinced myself that perhaps some humorous remark might negate what he really was attempting to tell me. "You've been seeing three women besides me!" I playfully snickered, but I think that it came out more like a snip.

"No, no, three women including you," he clarified without reservation. Yes, he was quite adept at shutting down a surly female!

His caustic response stung my concocted sense of humor. Yet, in the darkening absurdity of the moment I still wanted to revise the intent of his words. My thoughts continued to fester. Oh! That was a relief! Only two others! I thought he was going to recover from his delusion and admit that I was the most wonderful woman who had ever touched his life! Of course, he didn't say those words, and I didn't either. Perhaps I should have. It's not that I cowered before the unforgivable. I had always considered myself a resilient woman. It's just that I doubted even then that by vocalizing those words the direction of the discourse would really change. So, instead of a rebuke there was another pause, an implicit pause this time, for my turn to speak. However, I refused to say the words that would make the severing more palatable for him. In a lame way it was my own voiceless coup d'état.

Finally, he retorted more ruthlessly, perhaps to prod me closer to that inevitable. "You knew I wanted to see other women!" He punctuated "other" to disembowel further quirky bantering on my part. It was obvious that he was uncomfortable and wanted closure. However, neither of us spoke. Neither of us said anything. It was not the words but the silence which finally jarred me.

"Yes...the other women...yes, I knew about the other women." I hadn't liked being his backburner girl, and I had known that I was for some time in spite of my need to negate it until now. I'm sure he digested that thought, too, for he cleared his throat as if he had just read my mind.

When he spoke, he tempered his voice, whining like the "wayward son" petitioning clemency. "It's just that I can't handle the guilt anymore."

Oh yes! The convenience of guilt is always an appropriate resolution for civility. Nevertheless, I was moved by his effort to finally make an attempt to sound less standoffish. We both knew this justification was just another white lie, like all the white lies he used to build our relationship because he was…a kind person…a meticulous man with a tidy closet who could not live with clutter. Somehow, I had become the clutter in his life, and the reason for this exchange was to clean house, so to speak. Usually he cleaned on Saturday morning. However, my phone call prompted an early jump on cleaning day. I took a deep breath for I knew that, in spite what was unfolding, I had to make an attempt to harness my cynicism. The intimacy of our relationship deserved better than that…I was better than that! And besides, I actually was able to empathize with his struggle about letting me go. Like the other men, he always had this thing about "letting go" throughout his life.

I told myself that I should be angry about what he was doing, not just tell him the hollow words… Let's talk about this, or I'm sure we could work this out. After all, we were old enough, educated enough, compassionate enough not to be prosaic, predictable, or scripted. Weren't we a man and a woman of substance, midway in making an irreverent mistake? It's just that, perhaps foolishly, I had always believed that we would be forever companions of the night, so that we would have meaning of day.

Instead, I lost my will to defend those words. I just gripped my cell phone tighter to stop it from trembling and tried to arrest any traceable quivering in my voice. I always like to appear in control. He knew that about me. He knew that I would present the front of an undaunted lady and not fall to pieces in his presence like a glass doll. However, as I pressed my mouth closer to the cell to speak, the cold metal numbed my diminishing breath even further. The conversation lagged. It was time for him to fade away into the distance of the morning, just like all the others had faded into the distance of the night. His breath wilted. "Maybe…I'll see you around." Trailed by a tired afterthought, "maybe…we could get together some…"

I cut him off to recoup that shadow of fraudulent dignity by finally releasing the words that he wanted to hear. I exhaled back, "I don't think so!" And that was that.

Unfortunately, that type of finality has a face of betrayal, like allowing sand to easily slip through frail fingers while clenching a fist. The duplicity lies in the surrender of deceitful pride and pining hunger. Sure, "letting go" might be an altruistic definition of love, but its residue lingers in badgering doubt. I remembered that I was so afraid of how I would live the rest of my life. I was not prepared for the fall...not again, not again...

In the weary minutes and callous seconds after that exchange I tried to figure out why and when the breakup really began. Did it loom within our silences months before when I had denied that our quiet contentment was really having nothing to say to each other? Did he want to say those severing words even then? Perhaps the most telling evidence of the forthcoming separation existed even earlier in the relationship. Was the evidence there when he turned his back to me in bed after he had too vigorously fondled? Was that the first snub? Even then, in spite of an uneasy inkling, did I too easily dismiss his indifference as I sank in a sweet flush of my own?

I wrestled with such thoughts as I gazed into the harsh glare, embedding the cell into my ear. I finally eased my grip on the phone and closed the exchange with another futility, "You know...that I love you."

His last words were, "Yes, I know." And I knew that I would never see or hear from him again. I was embarrassed. I was old. I was alone once again.

I clutched my cell tighter, arduously begging it for empathy, but its cover thoughtlessly snapped shut. Reaching beyond the steering wheel with detached bravado, I replaced it back on the console, my fingers refusing to release from its casing. I held this pose as if I had expired into some still life canvas, a solitary female in a silent world of a Wyeth watercolor.

The ticking of the vehicle's clock pelted the silence within the car like an obscene metronome. Incongruent thoughts continued to throb. How utterly confused I was. I began to worry that I had forgotten to go somewhere, wherever one goes after a breakup. I worried there was something I needed to do, whatever needs to be done after a breakup. But the "wherever" and "whatever" only ricocheted like vacant moans within the unforgiving timepiece. I remained in that pose for some time until I thought I'd better go. I moved my hands onto the steering wheel, but I did not start the engine.

The sky darkened. At first, it was just a sprinkle. Then the rain dribbled tender droplets against the windshield before pelting into a raging downpour. The glass was tainted in smeared invisibility. I thought that I better just stay put for a while, at least until the cloudburst let up. Besides, I really was in no condition to drive away as if nothing had happened. I lay my head against the headrest, closed my eyes, and drifted into another windshield from a distance evening, decades ago…

Lightening flashed in wicked onslaughts within the darkness, concealing the boy and girl inside the truck. It was close to midnight, and hopefully my father would not awaken. The pickup was parked at the far end of my driveway. The boy might still have been in high school, but he wasn't stupid. Arousing my father would not be a good scene. We had been drinking cheap beer while parked off road by Old Man Mackey's rabbit farm for the last couple of hours, ever since we left the CYO dance, which was over at nine. Even though I was under age, it didn't seem to matter to the boy. He was eighteen, so in his mind it was okay for him to drink. I took the offered sips from his flask. Although the ignition was off in his truck, he kept the panel lights turned on in the cab and made sure that the radio was on low. The soft music was a soothing calm in sharp contrast to the harsh elements battering the vehicle outside. Whichever direction I looked, sheets of rain painted the windows into portholes of obscurity. We could not see what was beyond, but even more pertinently, no one could see what was happening within. We were cocooned in a haven of endless possibilities.

Reeking of stale beer, tobacco, and body odor, he leaned into me. I was repelled by him, but I didn't move away; I was expected not to. As if to remind me of that deafening tenet, lightening flashed, Zeus' thunderous boom. It was a forewarning…as a female, I was expected to submit. Clumsily, he continued to press his weight against me, anchoring my left arm. I tried to assure myself that this was not rape. It was just that interlude from innocence into becoming a woman. He said that he was a man of experience, and I need not fret. He said that he had everything under control. Yet, to be honest, I wasn't convinced. When he lunged into me his lips missed mine, his sweaty cheeks were way too sticky to be in control. But the misstep would not stop him for he was a boy about to proclaim his manhood. His lips were moist, mushy, and vulgarly aggressive. They pried mine open without asking permission. He invaded my mouth and ransacked my sensibilities. He thrust his tongue deeply into the cavity in cadent darts. I was uncomfortable, and there was pain. Fearing that the sides of my lips would split, I brought my hand up to his chest to push him back; he palmed the back of my hand into his. Just like his cheeks, his touch was clammy. Another lightning bolt ripped the darkness and illuminated his face. His glassy eyes were wild with anticipation. Yet, before the light dissipated, I saw his moist lids drowse in begging neediness. I instantly knew that this tower of strength was a sweating fool of incompetence, but in my naïveté I tried to convince myself that I was the one chosen to fulfill this deficiency. "I will truly be the only girl in his life," I kept reassuring myself. "He needs me, and most importantly, he adores me." Obviously, this was the onset of other delusions as well! But, what did I know then? Over time you would think that I would no longer fall for the sweet sensations, which delicately lift the tiny hairs on my skin into delirium. But I swooned then, just as I swoon each time I enter the mirage. I fell into the rhythm of his tongue and became that captured butterfly, frail, submissive, green to what was about to happen.

"I want you, Christine. I want you, Christine, Christine, Christine..." The repetitive words were hypnotic. I liked the way he pronounced my name. His voice drew me deeper into him, and I sank into what I wanted to be true. There was no longer any space between us. The thunder continued to thrash against the outside of the truck, but it seemed so far away. I was safely wrapped within the blanket of his body. He began to knead my hand like it was soft clay. Then, in a symbiotic embrace, he moved our hands downward as if they were on a mission. I knew what he wanted. I had read about these moments in the cheesy romance novels I sequestered from Walt. They had saturated my teenage curiosity with lucid descriptions of tittering foreplay and salacious orgasms. But this was different; this was real. What I was doing was not mere words. His mouth swallowed my ear in a guttural plea, "Take me, Christine, take it." Then with his other hand, I felt its nudge against the back of my skull as he gently but firmly pushed my head into his lap.

It was over very quickly. And when it was over, I really wasn't sure it was over. I just remained very still. I didn't quite know what to do, or what to say. He turned away from me and quickly rearranged himself as if nothing had just happened. I still did not move. I was afraid to move. Shame flushed through me. He must have realized my awkwardness because he briskly rubbed his hand over my shoulder blades. I heard him say, "You did good...Christine, you did good." Then he, too, sat very still.

When I finally looked up, I saw that he was fixated on something outside his side window. He had the appearance of a wax mannequin, expressionless and hollow. A pungent bitterness seeped into the fraudulent music. Deception pitter-pattered in the rain. I moved back up into the passenger seat, and for some time we sat in the drunken fabrication of our own truth, under the spell of low music and dim lights.

"I hope I wasn't..." I stuttered.

"Not at all; it was quite all right." He cut me off. It was then that I realized that words really don't matter after all.

The thunder had stopped. There was a soaked, clean, crystallized world on the other side of the beaded window. Inside everything seemed dim, muddled, no...more than that, imperceptible. Severing the moment into obscurity, he abruptly leaned over my lap and turned on the ignition. The motor barked a piercing whine followed by abrasive rumblings. It was my signal to leave.

When I spoke, the words sounded flat, even to me. "Well, good night."

"Night." His voice was quiet, clipped, empty.

I left the truck and my first sexual encounter—quiet, clipped, empty.

Remembering that interlude so long ago, I draw down the driver's side window to rethink the latest intimate situation. A whiff of damp air brushes my cheek. The mist brings a relief to the stuffiness within the vehicle and my mind. I start the ignition. Turning my steering wheel in the opposite direction from which I am parked, I head south for the Garden State Parkway. My destination is Atlantic City. I needed a sympathetic shoulder, and Walt will be there. My bag had already been packed for the weekend. It was prepared with another man in mind, but I will make adjustments.

It is a two-hour, tedious drive in Friday's rush-hour traffic on the Garden State Parkway. The road is damp and visibility compromised. I keep tight fists on the steering wheel as the countryside streams past my window.

Endless questions from former split-ups whiz by like pesky flies. Where did I go wrong this time? What did I say or do? Or not say or do? Was it my breath? Yet, in hindsight maybe it was his breath! After all, I am a modern woman, an adherent to equality, whether it involves intimacy or halitosis.

These are the familiar questions which had followed prior breakups, silly questions: obsolete ghosts never completely fading. Nevertheless, regardless of the misgivings, the answers always lead me to misconstrue that it must have been me, the earmarked jaded lover, who has misled her man down that road to discontent. The breakup had to be my fault! It had to be something that I missed!

Traffic has come to a dead stop. It must be because of some accident, I think, as police cars zip by on the service lane. Through my windshield, an endless row of cars amass, a graveyard of cadavers. Various pitches of sirens wail in the distance, forecasting that it will be a long wait.

Boredom coerces me to turn on the radio and stare into the vast terrain of the sinking day. As Sinatra croons, a specter of my father's countenance imprints itself through my side window. I try to blink the image away. But it refuses to dissipate. I address the eyes in the rearview mirror…

"Papa, could you make the music louder?"

"No!"

Papa always played the music low when I rode in the car with him. There wasn't much I could do about that. I had little clout, sitting too far from the controls. Besides, I was a girl and well aware what that meant, even at seven.

Slumped in the back seat of the old Chevy I would stare into that rearview mirror and watch my father's eyes as they slow danced with Old Blue Eyes in some weird duet. He seemed to be having a personal conversation with the singer, probably unraveling why he was widowed at such an early age.

"Could I ask you a question now, Papa?"

"No!" That was the defining 'No!'—the one that meant I dare not question further, even though I wanted to, even though I needed to, even though I knew his answer wouldn't matter anyway. It's just that it was so hard growing up in a house without a mother to answer a young girl's relentless questions. Absurdly, I thought if the volume of the music was louder, maybe he would answer all my questions.

Unfortunately, the answers to my questions about being female would remain elusive. Even at eleven, shortly after the first spotting, I never was allowed to openly discuss what was supposed to be hidden. I was shamed into believing something was wrong with me. This self-inflicted inquisition usually ended with the notion that I must have some innate flaw, a flaw perhaps of being born female, like Eve, born second, without a soul, as postured in the Holy Book. Old Eve didn't know what the hell she was getting into, and invariably, it seemed, neither did I. Each month throughout my teen years I became ashamed again, acutely aware of my nakedness, like the first female. That shame was like what I felt after breakups, the shame that a man no longer wanted me in spite of the intimacy we had shared.

I revealed none of this to anyone except Walt, and he didn't count because he took none of this seriously enough to warrant serious attention. He was always wrapped up in his own miasma. Besides, he was a man! Would he truly be capable of understanding any of "this female stuff" as he called it?

Another siren, another police car, and then an ambulance…yes, this traffic will not ease up. I shut the engine, but the incessant clock's ticking within the silence of the car propels me to switch the radio back on. I play with the station dials thinking I might be able to catch "my song." That would help the time pass. I am only half way to A.C. and even further from home.

Yes…my home…my lovely townhouse situated on a mountain ridge overlooking the Hudson River. It has a captivating view of the river with its backdrop of the New York skyline. It is so picturesque and comfortable that many mornings it is difficult to leave, especially during the fall.

In my early morning commute to work I would search for the "song of all songs," the song that would be "my song." And when that day came, I was determined to capture this butterfly, never allowing it to fly away from me. That was when I would sink into the deluded promise to myself that perhaps another day, another place, another lover, another song would make my life different. The music beckoned me further into the mirage, a deception for impetuous fools deluded by the songs of the sirens.

Finally, it happened, quite unexpectedly. On one of those mundane mornings, I picked up the unfamiliar melody. I was immediately drawn to it, much like a deaf reptile to the swaying flute of the snake charmer. I could not catch the title in its debut, and so had to wait for it to be played again to retrieve it. Well, it did play again, and again. With each daily commute to the city I would surf the dials, neurotically attempting to catch its lyrics from various stations.

Of course, I was not the only one attracted to this song. It zoomed up the charts and quickly became the copious darling of the airwaves for other female dreamers like me. Nevertheless, it was "my song." I had adopted it, allowing it to seep into my subconscious. This obsession escalated, and when I snagged the tune in my ongoing quest, I would become so caught up in the lyrics that I would unabashedly sing aloud, making voice and melody mingle throughout the cavity of my sedan in my own glorious opus. Sometimes, in the zeal of this private performance, if I became conscious of other commuters glimpsing sideways from their cars, I would tone down my fervor and just slightly move my lips to mime the lyrics. Surely, I didn't want anyone to think I was another crazy female. When you live close to New York City sometimes it is prudent to embellish pretense. Passion often comes with callous cynicism.

Inevitably the song remained in my head. It would begin with a soft melody, which would swell into a crescendo before the release of the lyrics. The verse would mist over me in a peculiar miasma:

> *Strange, when you come to doubt your sanity,*
> *When vision makes the tangible translucent,*
> *And you can only focus on indiscriminate haunting;*
> *When hearing makes words stutter,*
> *And interim pauses collect meanings of incongruities;*
> *When speaking only makes billows of breath,*
> *Lovers' lies,*
> *Lurking within mirages of truth.*
> *Doubt is a forsaken promise;*
> *Passion is its deluded quest.*

Empty-headed mutterings chanted with the repeated refrain, "Doubt is a forsaken promise; Passion is its deluded quest." Sometimes I would quickly turn off the radio, spooked. Better to remain distant than to reveal that the song was about my life. I feared that if I understood the meaning I would be impelled to take ownership of its message. Perhaps, in this particular libretto skulked another haunting, a more sinister haunting, ticking closer to where doubt and passion would bring about my demise.

I was faced with a dilemma. Should I detach myself from this song and have a lobotomy, which I obviously needed, or should I embrace the song and believe that I should enter the deluded quest? I had always seemed to struggle with the residue of the tattered threads in my life. Regrettably, I was to find that there was more than one way to deflower a female.

Enough of the backstory. Tomorrow I will finally have to deal with the song, for I have tickets to attend a concert at a casino in Atlantic City where the singer and his song will stir the muses to do their mischief.

It is already early evening, and the traffic jam shows that it will be awhile before I arrive in A.C. After this morning's rejection I entertain the thought that maybe I should not attend the concert tomorrow at all. I want to cancel the entire weekend! But, arrangements were made weeks ago when Walt had secured the concert tickets to coincide with some poker game at the same casino. I knew that he wouldn't join me and my date during the concert, or for that matter, probably any time during the weekend. Typically, we would separate on such jaunts, giving each other our respective space. From past understandings, Walt was well aware of how much I insisted on privacy when I went out with my men. Besides, it was not a problem since Walt would be involved with the poker action. However, the morning's phone call had changed the dynamics of the weekend. Perhaps I had better get in touch with Walt to tell him the latest situation. Fortunately, he answers on the first ring.

"Yeah?" Walt sounds preoccupied.

"Walt, this is Chris."

"Yeah, kid, What's up?" He really wasn't expecting a call from me until tomorrow.

"Well, Walt, it's this way, I'm on my way down, now."

"Really! Cool! I got the room for you guys tonight as well as tomorrow night."

"Well, that's just it. I'm coming alone."

"Yea. I thought the guy was coming with you."

"Well, he's not!" I sharply snap. I really am not mad at Walt. I am mad at the world…no, not the world. I am mad at myself! There is a second or two before he responds.

"Yeah. What gives?" Walt is good at picking up on unspoken details, the obscure discourse that revealed the real intention behind the words. It is a skill he probably cultivated from the subtle exchanges during poker. However, I do not want to be coy with him; he deserves better from me.

"He bailed out, Walt."

"So, he's coming tomorrow?" Walt was still not clear what I was attempting to tell him.

"No, the man has dropped out of the picture…for good!"

"The bastard!" Walt hammered pejoratively.

"Walt, he's not a bastard!" For some reason, I feel I have to defend my former lover. Don't ask me why. Maybe I am still caught in the rabbit's hole. "He's just another guy who had his own problems. And…well, things just didn't work out, that's all."

"Listen, Chis, forget about the bastard."

"He's not a bastard!" I am more insistent.

"Yeah, yeah. Whatever you say."

"Look Walt, I'm pretty wrecked about the whole thing. The breakup just happened this morning. And I'm still hurting."

"Got it." A more sympathetic Walt responds. "Just forget about him, Kid. You were too good for the…" He catches himself.

Walt is always on my side, making sure I am okay, making arrangements that are good for me. It is Walt who got the "comp rooms," so that I would be set for the weekend with my date. I had told Walt about the guy whom I had been seeing a lot lately, a man of interesting possibilities, as they say. I told him that I thought this might be "the one," and wanted to believe that this outing in A.C. would further that relationship. Walt had reacted indifferently at the time. But, of course, that is Walt, always the poker face.

Still, I didn't want Walt to now feel that all his plans were for nothing. I wanted him to know that there was something to be salvaged. "Walt, don't worry. I'm still coming down."

"Good…good. That's good." Walt sounded relieved. "So, where are you now?"

"On the Parkway, just past Point Pleasant exit, and I'm sitting in traffic…actually vegetating with the engine off… just sitting here, stewing. Walt, I'm really sorry I snapped at you. It's just that I'm a bit messed up."

"Yeah, yeah. Okay, okay. Listen, Chris, you're staying with me tonight. Okay? I'll cancel the other room reservation. I got a nice room here at the hotel, a real nice view… overlooks the beach and all. Don't worry about tomorrow."

I would rather stay with Walt than be alone. He knew of my strange affliction for this elusive song and its hot singer. It was Walt, not the so-called "man-in-my-life" who purchased the hard-to-get tickets to the performance. That should have given me a sign of a brewing breakup. Besides, that was just like Walt, never waiting around for someone else to do the right thing.

"Walt, I hope I'm not interfering with your plans." Walt sometimes liked entertaining the finer sex on his little excursions.

"No worries. You will probably have the room all to yourself most of the night. I'm playing cards with a bunch of guys right now, and it'll probably go on for a while."

"Oh, so you made the final rounds in the tournament!" I finally was able to channel my self-absorbed agenda into interest in my friend.

"No, not exactly…may have a better gig."

"Oh?" I am confused. This tournament was all Walt talked about for weeks. "So, you are not in the main poker room, anymore?"

"Well, I'll tell you all about it when you get here. Just look for me."

In fact, about a month ago, Walt had told me about the poker event in Atlantic City. He was to go a week before to check out the competition. It was one of those process-of-elimination competitions, "best man, last man standing." And, of course, Walt would probably be in the final rounds by this weekend unless he decided to bow out early to keep a low profile for some future "Game of all Games!" as he often said. However, this week he hinted about rumors of some high rollers being there.

With that kind of crowd, he would never leave the tables. I tried asking him about these so-called "big wigs," but Walt, being Walt, was evasive. I wasn't offended. He usually was vague about particulars, especially when it involved "the cards." In all truthfulness, I think that he doesn't want to burden me with details. He has been like that since our childhood, and I long ago accepted the fact that he was not going to change. He has that uncanny tenacity to remain mum when he wants.

"I'll leave the key at the front desk. Let yourself in, freshen up, get something to eat, and then get some rest, Chris. You probably need a good night's sleep. Tomorrow you'll be ready for the concert." Just like Walt. He knew I would not want to miss that concert. And he always was able to say the right words to get me out of my funk.

But, then there was silence, and I thought we got disconnected. "Walt…Walt, are you still there?"

"Yeah, still here. Listen, Chris, I know how upset you get from these…incidents in your life."

"I really don't want to talk about it! At least, not now, Walt, not over the phone…not now."

"Okay…okay, Kid. So, it's this way…You don't need to look for me. I'll probably mosey into the room sometime in the early morning hours. Give me some time to close my eyes a bit, and when I get up, we'll take a walk on the boards, get some Philly subs, and then we can talk. You'll be okay, Chris. I'll take care of you, Babe."

That was how Friday night and the next afternoon were supposed to be before I attended the concert on Saturday night. However, the fates had something else in mind. Friday night would turn out to be quite differently.

II

AT THE CONCERT, AS I WAIT in my designated seat for the singer of "my song" to enter the stage, I know that I, too, am beckoned to a stage. Certainly, Friday's painful rejection has once again dragged me down into the unforgiving rabbit hole of sunken memories. Nevertheless, I refuse to allow that bleakness to ruin Saturday night. I want the music to pull me out of the hole, as it has so many times before. With undivided attention I lean forward in my seat and await the song. It is seven thirty-four in the evening. The performance is about to get underway. I inhale a deep breath to silence my thoughts, and I silence my cell phone.

Unfortunately, silence cannot quell the distant sirens that chant inside my head. It is just my overactive mind! I remind myself that it is only my imagination, and not some psychotic fixation. I justify my thinking by reminding myself that I am as sane as any other female who has undergone rejection. Defining my condition as insanity only undermines my credibility.

If you are to understand the message of my story, it must be understood that it is being told by a woman of sound mind.

As I lean into the concert seat, extinguishing a flailing breath, it is not a breath of submission, but a little more challenged. What else can a rejected female do but hope that there are different possibilities left in life? Is it not within the pause of breath that we are lured into the anticipation of new breath?

Maybe that is the reason I love those moments before a live performance when I can arrest the onslaughts that seem to continuously invade my femininity. I draw in another deep breath and use my restless hands to smooth away the wrinkles on my black taffeta skirt. I am ready to begin...again.

Doesn't it always seem that no matter how hard we try to obliterate those damn wrinkles they still remain, our unrequited desires? I admit that I have given too much attention to my appearance. I like to have some type of control over something in my life, even if it is only superficial. Being conscious of my appearance satisfies that need. That is why I am so compulsive about wrinkles. This vanity has been a fixation of mine since childhood when so much seemed out of my control. When I was seven, Walt would often scold me to stop fidgeting with my clothes, following up with a comment that this self-conscious twitch showed my insecurity. "Never show what you're feeling!" he warned. But I never was able to let go of this frivolous quirkiness.

I kink my neck to see if Walt, next to me in the place where my lover should have been, has noticed my insecurity. I try to ignore him and focus on the concert. To distract my hands, I gamely open my purse and withdraw a petite mirror and lipstick. I smear its color back and forth over my lips. As I realize the redundancy might appear strange, I stop, but, still continue to stare at the reflection. I cannot ignore the little creases beginning to form around my eyes. Sometimes I raise my eyebrows in an exaggerated attempt to smooth the lines, but they still return. I snap the lid shut and convince myself that I look good enough. "Oh, vanity, vanity, comrade of unremitting time!" Do I equate my dwindling looks with the loss of possibilities? Finally, I am able to settle myself enough to wait for the song. I blink, but wandered aimlessly again…

Throughout the concert hall, discordant notes mingle with expectation. Musicians hidden deep in the pit tune their instruments in a prelude to the evening's magic. Random violin plinks and plunks stammer like timid rain droplets. As impending darkness drapes over us in an imperceptibly slow fade, I sense the audience restlessness. A solitary trumpet scolds in the obscurity of the hall and thins into the undertone of "hushes." I blink again. During this pause I try to arrest my inner chatter by focusing on insignificances. Suddenly, brazen floodlights assault my senses, screaming out into the music hall, momentarily blinding me, but, I dare not look away. I want to embrace the lights. They shift their round moon eyes, emitting bright beams that resemble ghostly triangular megaphones through the darkness, floating searchlights that collide swiftly over each other's paths. With an impulsive gasp they halt in midair. The performance is imminent. I cocoon myself deeper into my seat, burrowing away from any offensive intrusion.

But this can never be; I am precipitously disturbed. To my right is some commotion…something concerning the holder of the ticket stub for the seat next to mine. I simply ignore what has no relevance to me and instead resume gazing into the stationary strands of light now dissipating above my head. I can almost reach up and touch them. As I sit transfixed, I see the hint of dust particles in senseless disarray drifting through the diminishing light.

Once again, I am encroached upon…once again, to the immediate right, the bustle of covert activity continues. I shake my head in haughty dismay; this type of occurrence seems to be a frequent imposition in our society. Intrusive rudeness has unfortunately replaced courteous deportment. The seated man tempers his voice to some disheveled older teen who believes that he is in the correct location.

"But, I'm sure this seat is mine!" the lad retorts abrasively, providing a ticket stub as proof.

The exchange flattens into a tone which, obviously, suggests something that I am not meant to hear. More whispering ensues.

"I'm sure…work out…let's see…"

Once again, I strain to ignore this disturbance. What could possibly be the problem? My curiosity has been tweaked. I inconspicuously brush my chin over my right shoulder to snapshot the scene. In a blink, I catch him handing the young man back the ticket seat stub, folded in such a manner so as to conceal a hint of buried cash within. *Yes, Christine, obviously, there is some impropriety taking place!* But, I repeat to myself, *this business certainly does not pertain to me.*

I redirect my attention to the stage, barren except for the petrified instruments in readiness for the dance. A solitary guitar leans slightly askew on its stand like some deserted lover forlornly awaiting its sweetheart. Close by, the lady in waiting, a microphone, limps off a slender stand, bowing her head in penitent prayer. A vacant stool stands in rigid, staunch chivalry. The audience waits; the darkness waits; I wait. The silence wafts with indiscriminate, muffled coughs. I sink further into the dim.

Yet, the scent of his aftershave can no longer be ignored. It is sweet without stickiness. I sink into that, too. Within my tight seat I try to reposition myself in a futile endeavor at unassuming posture, for I am quite aware that sitting to my right is an attractive man...a seasoned man...nonetheless, a very attractive man. As I shift to get comfortable, I inadvertently brush up against his sleeve. Although my shoulder only slightly grazes him, it is abrupt enough to warrant a response. As a warm flush sweeps over me I scold myself, *Oh no, Christine, you cannot allow yourself to fall this easily again, especially after yesterday! Do not engage this man, Christine! Ignore him! Do not utter a sound!*

But I cannot harness the customary decorum of good manners that dribbles out of my mouth, flowing out of like unruly drool. "Excuse me!" *So much for fortitude, Christine!*

The words are slushy, and my attitude is obviously a bit too edgy. I quickly rationalize that my attitude is justifiable. Perhaps some violation has been committed by this beguiling man, who may have been involved in a shady deal obtaining his seat next to me. However, rethinking the matter, maybe I am overcompensating because he is too, too attractive. Perhaps my cantankerous demeanor stems from this evening's uneasiness about myself. Whatever the explanation, certainly the residue of some precarious ghost seems to hover above me within the pesky overhead dust particles! *He probably will just ignore me.* I am wrong.

"Quite all right." He delivers his reply in a more civil tone than perhaps I deserve. "We certainly are packed in here."

It is obvious that he is attempting polite conversation, just as I am engaging in unwarranted mistrust. I silently chastise myself for my snooty attitude.

I turn and smile, wanting to retrieve a more appropriate sense of courtesy. For if we are not civil to each other, especially in the confines of artistic arenas such as this concert, where else can we replace those rigid formalities that keep us further from each other? I assure myself that this is the reason why I need to turn and smile, "for art and truth!" I smile and nod, nod and smile, and linger a bit more than a respectable nod, a synthetic doll with a plastic smile on a bobbing head.

And with that, his face folds in on me. My overactive imagination has gotten the best of me. I continue to stare. Framed under slightly graying temples, his features are embedded with crevices that tell of histories of living. It is a face that quivers with interest, revealing perhaps too much too quickly. I am embarrassed that I have somehow transgressed into a place that I have no right to be without invitation. I pull myself away from looking at him with the pretense of committing my attention to the vacant stage. The senseless dust continues to float aimlessly in the light, but, the image of his face does not dissipate. Rather, it coagulates into a ghostly mirage in front of me. It haunts me. I cannot let him go. And therein lies the calamity, not to let go of what should be let go.

In spite of a possible fiasco, I brashly continue to reconstruct him in my mind: A firm chin cast with the darkened hue of a long day's unattended growth. Does this indicate he was consumed with something more pressing prior to attending a Saturday night concert? I have often been offended by the lack of attention to one's personal grooming. However, there is that curious feature of his face that compensates for any earthiness. He owns a sagacious smile that punctuates his thoughts. His mouth twists upward to one side, almost a sneer, revealing a smidgeon of upper teeth. His forehead complements the grin by tilting his eyebrows above cavorting eyes. It is a disarming smile. I consider how it would be very difficult not to fold under his charm, for I suspect it is a countenance that probably has come to his defense in many ticklish situations. As the mirage of him decomposes in the dust I wonder if he, too, is drinking me in. It is, of course, just wishful thinking; he is attractive, after all. Surprisingly, I do not want to release this rambling image that is sheathing me in a longing warmth.

III

SUDDENLY, LIKE A POP from a fizzing soda bottle, the image siphons to invisibility as applause thunders through the hall. Show time! She shudders as if from a chill.

Embracing their instruments, the musicians rise in the pit for their bows. A renewed ovation surges as the singer struts forth with deliberate conviction onto center stage to retrieve his waiting guitar. Unabashedly, he lifts it from its stand and flings the strap over his shoulder. He straddles the stool and slouches momentarily as if clutching a cherished lover. He bows his head in a brief, silent prayer, the reverence noticeable and quite intimate. The applause dwindles to a residue of irreverent, solitary claps and hoots. Finally, all sound subsides. From the hidden pit a distant trumpet blares. He strums his guitar. His lyrics launch from some distant land. The intent crystalizes in the dust and drapes upon her…

Strange, when you come to doubt your sanity,

A halo of light frames the singer's face as he continues to play her song. The soloist seems farther away than before, shrinking on the distant stage as the melody looms and his sultry guitar draws her inward. With each enveloping strum a tenuous connection forms between the singer and her. She squints for she can no longer see him. She has been kidnapped by the lyrics...

When vision makes the tangible translucent,

Her body swoons with the beguiling song. She rises and withers in the rifts and surrenders to the hypnotic notes. Time is suspended; she is only slightly aware that there is some hasty rustling across her, some lost playbill, picked up and returned to its rightful owner. She ignores the inconsequential activity as she melts back into the music...

And you can only focus on discriminate hauntings,

She drops back into the realization that her right shoulder is again pressing indiscreetly against his upper arm. She shifts away, too quickly, in a movement that suggests repulsion, certainly not her intention at all. She rushes her apology, "Excuse me, I hope I wasn't..." this time, she is not able to finish the thought since she really doesn't know how to complete it, just a hesitant pause, groping for some appropriate courtesy...

When hearing makes words stutter,

"Not at all... it's quite all right." His reassurance salvages her rambling humiliation. His voice is inviting, and she falters, trying not to be drawn into him again. She gives her head a quick shake in a paltry attempt to clear her mind. But the melody is such a slow, sad song. It pulls her to its sadness. She descends into a foreign land, a place where she does not belong, but fears she will eventually be. No! She cannot stop the plummeting! In desperation, her fingernails press against the armrests, gripping the edges tightly. She cannot stop the plunge! She realizes that her nails are not on the chair but embedded into his arm. She quickly opens her fists. Without looking at him, she mumbles, "I'm so sorry!" He does not respond...

And interim pauses collect meanings of incongruities,

She is sure that he is now looking straight at her, even though his head, like hers, has not turned away from the stage. *So much for being cool, calm, and collected, Christine, you are certainly the embodiment of poise! Well, there is no retreat for fools!* She wants to say something but cannot form the words. She is just another paltry fraud...

When speaking only makes billows of breath, lovers' lies,

Anxiety drizzles like a curtain of mist; she cannot release her feeling of inadequacy. Beads of sweat trickle down her forehead, downward, past the back of her neck, downward, between the crease of her breasts, downward, over her belly, downward, and into the most intimate folds of her being, where the sweet rain lingers in warm puddles...

Lurking in the mirages of truth.

"Sexiest song I ever heard!" His voice is deep, dark, delicious. He leans into her. The warmth of his breath braises her earlobe and the passion of yet another deluded quest begins. Her heart pounds wildly.

"Yes, indeed!" she quips, trying to smother her forbidden thoughts and recoup any residue of composure. "If you think that is sexy, you should check out the video!" Her words sputter back with bohemian acumen. Surprised at her newfound wit, she smiles at him, slightly raising her eyebrows to punctuate some intended nuisance. He responds with a suggestive grin to reaffirm what is now understood only between them. His scent seduces her even more.

"That good, huh? I didn't know he had a video!"

"Just search his website!" She lewdly pokes the flames. "I'm sure you will be impressed!"

"Really...that good!"

"That good!" She echoes back, nods again, smiles again. But, it is his signature smile that finalizes their flirting. Fortunately, this intimate exchange is quiet enough not to interfere with any other "patrons of the arts." And if there was ever a singer to stir the Muses to do their mischief, this singer has just done that! Her fervor suddenly cools. Could there have been some misunderstanding in encouraging this stranger on her right, certainly a man of receptive possibility, if not a man of questionable credibility...

Doubt is a forsaken promise;

This precarious situation certainly has been fostered from yesterday's musings. She has become that skeptical woman desensitized to possibilities, for...

Passion is its deluded quest.

She remains paralyzed for the next hour and fifteen minutes until the second encore is completed, and the houselights have flushed the hall. The show has ended. It is time to depart.

Rising, she is careful to conceal her countenance, which may reveal forbidden thoughts. She is unsure of his intentions. In the unforgiving illumination of the houselights, she turns her back to him, hoping never to meet up with him again.

However, *the best laid plans do go astray*. As the sluggish patrons stutter between the row of seats toward the main aisle, she continues to avoid him, yet, is keenly aware that he remains directly behind her. His presence blankets her as his warm breath feathers the tiny hairs at the back of her neck. His aftershave has lost its freshness and mingles with sweet sweat. She is not repulsed by this, in fact, she does not want to let go of his scent.

"I'm not sure we are really getting anywhere." After a pause, he revises the statement into a scintillating question, "Do *you* think we're getting anywhere?" He delivers this more as a defining statement than a question, possibly to engage her in some more repartee. She helplessly shivers for she knows that it is a question that she should ignore, but will not.

She turns her head slightly over her right shoulder and replies, "No, we certainly do not seem to be going anywhere. Perhaps the Muses have not finished with us yet." Even as the words spill from her lips, she fears they sound vulgar. What might those fates design for her and this stranger? Would they try to ensnare the two in their treacherous mischief? This was one of those moments when she wishes to possess some superpower to retract one of those sentences that periodically fly indiscriminately from her mouth. Something like Superman's power to turn back time by flying against the earth's natural rotation to erase the past to replay the present. As always it is too late; she has been here before and can predict the next move. *He probably thinks I am some ridiculous woman, not to be taken seriously, and will snicker under his breath, if he recalls me at all!*

He laughs, not really a hearty laugh, more an affirming grunt. *Maybe, Christine,* she continues to silently narrate, *he's not what you think he is!* They continue to inch their way between the narrow rows of seats. As they draw closer to the aisle, where all pretense may finally dissipate, they remain pensively silent. It cannot be denied that some connection has occurred between them, and in such a pause the difficult decision that can change the very course of lives lies before them. It is the decision that has plagued relationships between men and women throughout time. Songs are written about it; singers mourn in agony over it. The decision whether or not to enter the "rabbit hole" and roll down into the unknown, or to stay above on familiar ground and just safely peek into the opening. One path is right, the other is frightening. The struggle is to determine which one is which. Should she turn around and give this stranger her name, rank, and cell phone number, or should she deny that this person ever existed at all?

When her deserted date had dropped her off the side of the last rabbit hole, Walt had decided that he would become the auxiliary for this unrequited lover by being her replacement throughout the day and night. She makes her decision. As she continues to shuffle ahead, she pretentiously places her palm on the shoulder of her date in front of her; it is a defining grip of choice, that gesture that solidifies the final severance to the stranger. She never considered herself a fickle woman, in spite of her recent craziness, but suddenly she regrets her decision. As the queue spills out into the aisle, she realizes that she can no longer draw in his aftershave, and glances back. Frantically, she scans the multitude of faces, searching for the stranger. But he is gone, becoming yet another puzzle piece to forever float aimlessly in the dust particles of her life. He has vanished into the floodlights. The haunting refrain resonates in her head...*Doubt is a forsaken promise...passion is its deluded quest.*

IV

TO CAP OFF THE EVENING, the man that I had shouldered faithfully out of the aisle, had made reservations to dine at the restaurant in the same casino as our concert. The eatery is an acclaimed Zagat-rated bistro noted for its upscale New York style cuisine and extensive fine wine offerings. To get to this celebrated establishment we just need to take the glass elevator from the concert hall corridor to the second level spiral staircase off the main concourse. This is the same level that houses the private poker rooms. The main gambling tables are situated at the far end of the casino on the first floor. I had heard that private area was reserved for the high rollers, secure places for those special patrons, cloaked in shadowy innuendo, who expect a more reclusive space, cut apart from the first floor riffraff.

Walt and I ascend the coiling stairs edged by a curled iron railing and mosey through an extensive corridor of closed doors before arriving at our restaurant. It seemed to be worth the effort. Ornate double glass doors frame the entrance to the bistro, suggesting that a world of elegance and privilege await within. My curiosity is, of course, tweaked.

We are escorted to our table in high-brow style. As we move through the maze of linen covered tables, I am captivated by how the soft, mellow light shimmers off the cut-glass stemware filled with sparkling spirits, and how the cutlery accents the setting with its gold-leaf handles. It is a restaurant draped in plush fanfare and dripping with intimate sophistication.

Reaching across dressed tabletops, young delectable males adoringly lean toward elegant women, insipidly stroking slender arms, speaking in romantic undertones with their eyes and touches.

Conversely, stretching backwards in cushioned chairs, older seasoned males arrogantly lean away from elegant women, smugly stoking their own self-righteousness, speaking in insidious whispers with their eyes and touches. I quickly realize that I am not in Kansas anymore, and these are not "my people." This is a place of pretentious dualities, a scene that I fear will further disturb my already unsettled humor. Tenuous desire is like an unrefined palette tasting fine wine. The fledgling sips without judgment, swishes for hopeful gratification, but in the end only gulps down wavering doubt. The amateur always seems to be unsatisfied, embarrassed to admit inadequacies, but fretful of being hoodwinked. So, it is with dishonest exchanges between men and women.

I need to buckle up and keep my thoughts to myself. My last-minute-pinch-hitter date, Walt, had taken great pains to secure these last-minute reservations, and he obviously wants the evening to be special. I do not want to seem ungrateful for his efforts. However, dualities have drifted throughout the day, and I have been badgered enough! My day has been spent solely with Walt. It has been very different from the regular jaunts we usually shared together. This Saturday had a strange feel to it, sprinkled with touches of explicable quirkiness from me, tumbling with inexplicable quirkiness from him.

Perhaps the most annoying oddities throughout the day came in the form of uncomfortable flirtations from a man I have known my entire life. Now, it is not that Walt ever had any trouble with flirtations; it's just that I was never the target. Yet, today it was as if Walt had received a new bow and arrow "Cupid" set, like the Indian bow and arrow set I had given him for his eighth birthday. And, he decided to try it out on someone, namely me, who would not ridicule his incompetence in using it. I just figured that this was a kind of warm-up before he zoomed in for the real kill later this evening with some other unsuspecting squaw after our dinner. If you haven't figured it out yet, Walt is a "ladies man." And there were many ladies within his teepee. Even though Walt and I have been lifetime cronies, his was a teepee I never wanted to enter. Nevertheless, he had no reservations about telling me the most savory and intimate particulars of the goings-on within his teepee of ill repute. He would retell each of his escapades with infinitesimal attention to detail, until I would have to stop him in mid-sentence because he had gone beyond the need-to-know point, or crossed the line of my sensibility to digest further embellishment.

So why do I hang out with the Playboy of the Western World? Because he is not just a crony with whom I share life's escapades, but also my friend, my best friend; someone who needs an individual like me to keep him in one piece to see another day, so to speak. But today I have become the one who needs to be kept in one piece.

Tonight, I am still grappling with latent sexuality, and I am not up to sparring with any more of Walt's remarks, which had agitated the shit out of me in our afternoon stroll on the boardwalk. I try to be polite. After all, he is trying to pick up my spirits. However, as these same asides spill over into the evening in spite of my indifference to each sexual innuendo, I can no longer shed my annoyance. I suspect he has finally noticed my discontent because within moments of being seated, Walt begins an incessant questioning about my health. Am I okay? As I look across our table, I mulled over how to fabricate an answer to fend him off indefinitely. Unfortunately, we have known each other for so long that it is almost impossible to conceal anything from one another. Maybe long-time companions share the same intuitive DNA, perhaps because they are usually breathing the same air, or drinking from the same straw, or using the same towel to wipe off each other's sweat after a game of tennis. Or maybe this connection was sealed between Walt and me during a sweltering summer day shortly after a special birthday of mine.

We were both eight and voracious cowboy and Indian groupies. We dressed, spoke, and moved like these icons in our pretend play. I always was the cowboy, and Walt was forever my faithful sidekick Indian brother. It was during that summer we made our pact and swore to be "blood brothers" forever. (Our different genders mattered little.) In a simple but reverent ceremony we drew blood by slicing our thumbs and pressing them together in solidarity, thus confirming a pledge to be in each other's debt, promising to protect the other even to death. Certainly, a rather heavy contract for two eight-year old's, but we took it quite seriously. Ironically, that contract had shaped our lives, and I wonder if it would have any impact on us this weekend as well.

So when Walt stares back at me across the restaurant table and asks for the third time this evening if I am not feeling well, I shuffle my response to him for a third time, deciding that I had either better tell him the truth or else quickly depart the premises to collect my composure, for I can never outright lie to him. I decide to have some needed space. Now, where can a woman retreat to rethink her life, or at the very least, to find refuge to take a momentary breath to collect herself? Clutching my handbag, I excuse myself and ask which way is the Ladies Room.

With resolve to stall confronting him again too soon, I take the longest route to my destination. I leave the confines of the Bistro and venture out into uncharted territory to some far away ladies' powder room. I turn toward the expansive corridor beyond the restaurant with its gold leaf glass doors of grandeur and my inquisitive date.

After meandering through relentless twists and turns of the casino's corridors, I finally arrive at a door garnished with a petite silhouette of my gender. Depleted from my aimless drifting, I enter. A demure lushness unfolds inside a welcoming lounge. Like the restaurant I have left behind, this respite resonates the best of what a reputable establishment has to offer its female guests. Glancing just beyond the lounge, I see an inner alcove housing the water closets and basins where an unsullied sheen is cast off the mottled marble from recessed lighting. I remain in the sitting lounge, a suitable refuge designed to idle, a place to replenish a frazzled female back to a state of grace. Here I might possibly regain my mislaid sensibilities. Relieved that the sitting room is vacant, I postured myself upon a luscious settee adorned in vibrant lime green accented delicately with gold threads. The tautness in my stomach gradually releases, and my tattered thoughts dissolve into a serene blindness.

My breathing dozes to a gentle lull, allowing me to contemplate the area. Directly behind me is a massive, ornate beveled mirror, encompassing almost the entire wall. I smiled over how prudent it is to place "Alice's Looking Glass" behind where a female will sit, so that she is not forced to judge her reflection if she does not wish that. However, considering feminine egotism, she probably will eventually surrender her vanity to the smaller mirror placed pretentiously on a gilded pedestal frame on the gold-leaf dressing table. Narcissism never allows Medusa to escape the obsession to see her image. Around the table mirror are sundry toiletries, necessities furnished for a needy female: soft tissues, super hold hairspray, fragrant, apricot hand lotion, faux designer perfume, and of course, tampons. I linger on the tampons and recall all those inopportune times I had to use them. A slight pang of loss sputters in the deep recesses of my loins. I redirect my attention from such matters and resume perusing other areas of the chamber.

My browsing is arrested on the far wall across from where I have been loitering. An immense watercolor has been painted directly onto the wall surface. Adhering to the plaster in spite of a flawed nick here and there, the faded mural depicts a seashore scene. I am transfixed.

A vague image of an older female figure sits on a sand dune. Her legs sprawl out from under a floral printed sundress. She is in a slight backward tilt, leaning on her slender arms for balance, and the ribbon that pulls back her vivid auburn hair drizzles down to the sand. She appears to be casually watching the undulating ocean waves as they caress the shoreline. They are breaking not far from her. I squint and descend further into the settee. My mind blurs; I am mellowing. I become so mesmerized that I began composing a scenario to accompany the painting, allowing myself to be gently pulled into it. The scene begins to shimmer.

Movement lags at first, but then quivers like a tossed penny wobbling on its side. Finally, the tremble becomes a steady flow of solidity. The painting moves. The foamy lace on the water's edge seethes into a ribbon of whiteness and begins its approach. Like a charge to battle, the jagged line reaches for the seated figure in a fevered pitch, pauses momentarily in some decisive thought, and suddenly retreats, like a prostitute snatching her fee. Intuitively, it expires back into the belly of a blackened ocean. Captivated, I descend further into the mural, embellishing the storyline. The mature woman stands, brushes the sand off the cotton folds of her sundress, and saunters toward the shallow rim where land and sea converge. There, tender rifts continue to fold over each other in a dance of impending tenacity and receding timidity. With bent head, she walks barefooted, slowly but unfalteringly, on the wet sand, for she is on a mission; she is in search of the perfect shell. Suddenly she catches a glimmer of possibility. It is deeply embedded in the suctioning sand. And with each passing wave it melts further from her grasp—in an irretrievable instant it will be gone, swallowed by the sea, lost forever. In this precarious moment she must act quickly if she is to redeem the vanishing shell, resurrecting it from its fate, so that its beauty will not vanish. With an outstretched arm, she pinches her thumb and forefinger to retrieve the find of the season. However, as she snatches it from its realm and inspects its innards, she realizes that she has been deceived, for the shell is no longer whole but has unseen broken parts. It is quickly discarded, tossed like an infected animal, lest it linger too long in her wrinkled fingers. I cringe under the guise of such a scenario, for like the once exquisite shell, I shudder at the thought that eventually I, too, can be imprudently chucked away because of broken innards.

V

I PULL AWAY FROM THE MURAL, slouching further into the chaise, wishing no longer to look at the wall. Glancing at my watch, I know that my absence from my date is becoming too long for any viable explanation. I move from the seat, mosey over to the dressing table, and gaze into the beveled oval mirror. I fumble for my lipstick buried deep within my purse and smear the glossy ruby back and forth over my lips until there is no more reason to continue the process, a familiar insecure fixation. Taking a resigned breath, I turn and leave the lounge to return to the inevitable: Walt and the tired world to which I no longer want to belong.

My languishing shuffle back through the twists and turns of the casino's corridors only further substantiates my diminishing will to revisit the restaurant. I walk in a trance, moving as if I am being towed by an invisible portent. I proceed onward sluggishly through the embroidered corridors, drinking in the golden pretentiousness. On my left I move past oversized Grecian urns placed on top of weighty marbleized end tables. They stand with formal rigidity as authoritative sentries next to opulent, striped, lime green settees with golden threads. Opposite the string of overstated furniture is a wall of double-hung doors. These thresholds line up neatly along the corridor like tin soldiers. Their closed entrances suggest that although they may be fundamental to the casino, they are also firm statements of exclusion to all others. Just ahead of me, one of these restricted doors is ajar, open just enough to tease my rambling curiosity. What could possibly be within? Was it left open by some frazzled server overwhelmed while tending to an urgent request from some celebrity inside? I slow my pace and stop just before the breach. Whatever the reason for its being left opened matters not. It taunts me to look, while alerting me not to enter, making the spying even more enticing. I lean around the door's edge for a peek and adjust my sight to accommodate the rather spacious, yet subdued interior. Cast in a shadowy stain, a lone oval table is strategically placed under a suspended Tiffany lamp in the room's center. It illuminates the downcast heads of eight seated men. Their backs are hunched as they hover over the wooden lip of the green felt-padded table top. The sobriety suggests that these men are engaged in a serious game of cards. Close at hand, but certainly detached from the game, men in dark suits with folded arms stand in firm stances, invincible structures, like cemented lion statues guarding the gates of a fortress. Their presence is both peculiar and ominous. I have seen enough and would gladly be on my way, when in a momentary blink, I snatch onto something familiar. The recognition grabs and pulls me back into the belly of the whale. It may have been just a brief encounter, but I know for certain who it is, and I freeze long enough for him to know me, too. As a lark rising from the misty morning dew, he raises his chin from the green felt and stares back in my direction. Then as if affirming my right to exist, the man at the table gives a slight nod.

Suddenly, like a disquieting cloud shrouding the sun, a meticulously well-groomed but massive figure covers the entrance, cutting off my view. It is one of the invincible structures. At first, the figure smiles cordially enough, but his demeanor quickly changes to a vulgar smile of impertinence. His eyes sliver into two razor-sharp knives. I am taken aback by his presence. Delicately the massive structure closes the door, cutting off my vision from the scene as if severing me in half.

I stall in an indecisive stupor. I do not know whether to move on or to remain. There really is no choice. It is time to move away from the door and the man within. I briskly turn and resume my trek down the corridor back to my aimless existence, forlorn with the thought of what could have been but always seems to be denied. About twenty paces later a tenuous sensation brushes across my right shoulder. It is a subtle touch, haphazard, but enough for me to stop moving. Even before I turn to digest its meaning, I already know. Something inside jolts with fear, perhaps bolts with desire. I turn.

He stands facing me, inches away, his feet spread in a commanding posture. His jacket is gone, and his white, wrinkled shirt sleeves are rolled up accentuating the dark hairs on his forearms. His hands rise, clutching my arms like two unrelenting vices. I stare into his chest. The top two buttons of his shirt are now undone, revealing a hint of wired strands of chest hairs; some are gray. His necktie hangs slightly askew, and I cannot decide if it looks like an elongated limp fish or a not quite spent penis. Slowly I lift my eyes to his face. His upper lip slides into his sideways smile. He speaks. "We seem not to be able to remove ourselves from each other. Do you think it's those fickle Muses dancing for us, again?"

I have no breath to respond. My eyes sink. I'm staring once again at the necktie. I open my mouth to say something, anything, but quickly back down. Instead I raise my eyebrows to answer him, and instinctively he seems to understand. I relinquish my silence to his presence, allowing him to speak freely. He accepts his role to lead the dance.

"Well, I cannot have you just turn your back on me, again, without at least knowing who you are." And the music plays on.

I have heard this song before. It is that same sad song in which the melody drowns out the majesty of the words. The guitarist plucks the strings and passes his pick downward in a strum that lingers. The singer moans and holds his voice in a high whine like some dying animal fading into the night.

He wants to know who I am, and I am not so sure that I can answer that question myself. It is the very question that has lately been strangling me. His eyes squint. I try to command my heart, *Get hold of yourself, Christine!* I immediately look at the floor; why am I such a coward? I know my worth! I have lived long enough to know this! Why do I allow these predictable regrets to dominate my life? *Why?* I raise my eyes and force them to fix on his.

I'm sure it is the pause that signals him to continue. "So… don't tell me your name." This is not so much a sign to end the conversation, but a lull to allow me time to gather affability. His hands loosen slightly, and I think that he is about to release his grip on me. Instead, he reconsiders and glides his palms up and down my bare forearms in a suggestive, intimate rub, finally placing them in a firm grip upon my shoulders. He bends his forehead toward mine, appearing to delve into my thoughts, perhaps trying to provoke me into speaking.

It works. I lambaste him defensively, "Well, it's this way, I have my date waiting for me in the restaurant, and..." attempting to be that sophisticated woman with acidity, "perhaps some other time and place."

He quickly removes his hands. I have mistaken his intention. His eyes fall, "Yes, well, I really have to get back," he says, flinging his arm carelessly back toward the open door to the forbidden room. But he still doesn't move, pinned by some mysterious grip himself.

"Really!" I voicelessly fume. "What does he expect? That I am that easy?" Placatingly, I say aloud, "As I said...I have a commitment tonight, and if I'm not being too..." the stuttering dwindles with indecision, "and...you look like you're also... engaged," and then I repeat, "...perhaps some other time and place." But we both know this is only a formality, like saying, "We'll get together sometime," when meeting an acquaintance whose name you have misplaced forever; it is just a courtesy with not the slightest intention of being acted upon. However, my words repeat, "...some other time and place..." Suddenly, I am concerned that he is construing something more solicitous than intended.

Does he see through this see-sawing? He does not respond for an uncomfortably long time. Then he raises his eyebrows as if understanding the situation, turns and takes definite steps back toward his lair. Suddenly he stops as if realizing that he had forgotten something of importance. Pivoting, he charges back at me, raising his index finger to punctuate his point, "I hope that you didn't think that I was coming on to you...I just thought you might...want to get together sometime."

His remark is innocent enough. I am out of sorts, and perhaps displacing my inner turmoil on him. I smile back. He picks up on my receptive demeanor. His smile slides to the corner of his mouth. "So... maybe that 'other time and place' could be...let's say...next Saturday night... right here...nineish?" And raising his eyebrows into his charming manner, "We will meet again! Is that not so?" He does not wait for a reply, but brazenly turns and walks to the open door. With his back to me, he pauses before entering, almost as if he is continuing a bold commentary. Then without looking back, his fingers hook the door's edge; it closes deliberately. He slips back into a world beyond my understanding.

I try to decide whether or not I am agitated by this flaunting exit or relieved. He pranced away like some haughty peacock abrasively self-assured of my reaction. That very arrogant attitude hardens my resolve to never make the next Saturday rendezvous a reality. I whirl away from the closed door and jut out my chin ratifying my decision. Another man is still waiting in the restaurant. However, like a fleeting shadow in a subtle whiff, a fragrant question emblazons my emboldened attitude, "Am I actually sinking deeper into the belly of the beast?"

VI

AS BEFORE, THE BEVELED GLASS doors of the casino's restaurant lie before me like two sentries eloquently affirming that beyond is a gentler land of fine dining and soft voices. Their heavy glass adorned with gold leaf metallic vines is similar to the vines twisting inside me. I pass through their golden gates and apprehensively walk back into eloquence and pretentiousness. As soon as Walt sees me, he pops up from his chair like a jack-in-the-box. With unbridled flamboyance, bracing himself in an elongated stretch, he frantically hails me as though I am a New York cab. I maneuver between the tables, walking deliberately toward him in an attempt not to be as obtrusive as he is. Unfortunately, when I finally make it to our table, things get worse.

"I thought you got lost or somethin'!" His words have become a bit more affected than when I had left him.

"No! No! I was never lost." I stutter, maybe because I'm not so sure this is true.

"Good, good," Walt smothers his words in winded puffs, pauses and then resumes his disjointed thought, "...because this is such a large place, and I thought you were..."

"No!" I clip his words, trying to quell any further inquiry. "I was never lost!"

"Good, good," But his dubious inflection and impulsive shudder of his head suggest that he is not totally satisfied. Silence again. I look toward the fringes of the restaurant to suggest that I have nothing more to say. More silence. I want to believe he has been satisfied—he is not. He construes the pause as permission to continue prying, flicking his words loudly into the silence like sparks of an afterthought, "I was almost ready to go lookin' for you..."

"No! No!" My stuttering obviously needs an alibi if I am to end this aimless inquisition. "I just needed some time in the ladies' lounge, that's all." Walt twists his head sideways to digest this, and I want to believe, again, that this has finalized the dance.

"So...you are sick, then!" Walt drums again. It is only the refrain.

"No! No! I'm fine!" My voice has ascended marginally to his, and I am acutely aware that I have drawn attention to our table. The patrons swivel their heads with demure yet derogatory glances. I lean toward Walt with the intention of dodging our impropriety. I am about to justify my prolonged absence in the ladies' room by fabricating some half-truth when I am cut off at the pass with Walt's next bushwhacking.

"...because you only nibbled on the appetizers, and then, I was so concerned that maybe you weren't feelin' well, and that's maybe why you were away so long."

This straggling wordiness seems to be some conscious attempt on his part to prevent me from tweaking the truth, which by the way, I was about to do. Walt has known me a long time. However, I have known Walt a long time, too, and I am familiar with this type of behavior, usually when he has committed some unspeakable offense and drowns himself in guilt under the guise of babbling innuendos and self-absorbed intoxication. The babbling is quite evident; however, I'm not so sure how inebriated he is. Walt has always held his liquor pretty well, so it is hard to tell. I am exhausted from the evening's driveling absurdities and embarrassed by his uncouth manners.

"Walt, I'm fine," I concede in spite of his dribble, to prevent any further display of coarse decorum under the restaurant's ceiling of refined civility. It's only just another concession, it isn't my first, and indubitably it will not be my last. He knows this, too, for he bows his head in shame. Once again, we surrender to the silence. I collapse backward onto my cushioned chair, one extended arm sprawled across the top of the table. I want to be rid of the exchange, to deny it even occurred. With my thumb and forefinger, I flick a couple of bread crumbs off the tablecloth as if flicking away the previous words. The crumbs sally off their launchpad and onto the floor. I look up and detect a tinge of disdain from a female patron adjacent to our table. My behavior is as crass as Walt's. I wittingly bring my forefinger to my brow, shadowing my indiscretion behind my palm and away from this woman's glare. Walt and I have become two vagrants in the restaurant. I want to leave, but we have not even ordered, and I am famished. I remain in this position for some time trying to figure out what is wrong with Walt. I conclude that it may be fueled by something beyond my control. However, whatever the reason for his inane questioning, I know that if the remaining evening is to be salvaged, I had better take the reins of this insanity and steer this swaggering stagecoach back onto the path of rational thought. I change the subject and address Walt in a guarded tone.

"Have you ordered dinner yet?"

He quickly rebounds from his petrified trance. "No, I thought I would wait for you, and because you were so long..." This is exactly what I hate about Walt; he just doesn't let go! He is about to resume his craziness, "...and you were away so long..." he repeats, but suddenly pausing long enough to notice my detached attitude as I become fixated by a smudge on the ceiling. He gets my message. He twists his lips this way and that, squinting his eyes into a quandary of what he really wants to say, but dares no longer. He wiggles in his seat, struggling over something. Finally, he takes a deep breath. "So, what do you think. You wanna' eat?" The face-off has finally ended.

Nevertheless, I hear the elongated vowels, and I know that they weren't for emphasis; the "so's" are becoming increasingly slushy. I think, "Great! This is all I need now, a smashed date!" I abrasively grab the plush red velvet menu to punctuate my annoyance. However, I truly doubt he knows how peeved I am. I rear my head back and forth, up and down, in exaggerated comportments appearing to scan the entrees. I only see a blur without meaning. I am exasperated, not by Walt's drunkenness or a stranger's rudeness, but by my own ravaging wretchedness. I curtly spew out, "I'm not sure I'm hungry anymore!" *I am more famished than I have ever been.*

"You are not well!" as if to confirm an earlier point and missing the present one completely!

"I'm fine…I'm fine…I'm fine!" I flair back! This time not only heads turn, but there is a muffled, disgruntled buzz throughout the establishment.

His voice sinks into a resigning wheeze. "I should have tried to find you because you were away so… long, and I just waited here, drinkin' and…"

Finally, Walt has lost his will to parley any further, perhaps from dousing himself "sooo long" over the rim of his Jack Daniels. It is a fade into a diminishing evening, crestfallen, barely audible. "We can leave if you want to."

Suddenly, I see what I have done. I feel like a slug, a narcissistic bitch slug. I should expect better of myself. Here my best friend, my proxy date, is grasping for straws to please me this evening, to cheer me up, to pull me out of my mire of rejection. Was it not Walt, two weeks ago, who with exuberant enterprise, waved the two concert tickets of my favorite singer inches under my nose? Was it not Walt who with tenacious "wheeling and dealing" obtained the hard-pressed restaurant reservations to "top off" the evening? And why? So that I can share the weekend with not him, but the latest fling of my life, the fling I endlessly flung about like endless dust particles in our endless conversations. "Walt," I would profess. "Walt, I think this is the one. I think this is the man, finally, a real gentleman!" Walt would just stare at me…just stare. I knew that stare of doubt. I didn't care about that stare because I had been waiting so long for a real gentleman, and, maybe if I believed that this man was the true gentleman, then it could be the truth.

Now the fling has flung back into the shadows of dust particles which endlessly have floated above my head since my childhood, and now I am the one staring. I have joined the callous shadows in the egotistical mire, the jilted woman who thinks nothing of decimating the gentleman before her, half soused, but nonetheless, a truer gentleman. This is the gentleman who would unselfishly lay his new Ralph Lauren jacket over the muddy puddle of that mire as I exited my narcissistic carriage. On second thought, this is the very gentleman who would go so far as to lay himself face down in the mud puddle as I pressed my spiked stilettos into his lower spine. How can one associate with a person like me, never mind consider me a friend? I do not want to be remembered this way when I die! I do not want to be remembered this way right now, either.

"Look, Walt, you were right, I do have a slight headache." *Oh, is this original, or what?* "Maybe it's because we haven't eaten since noon. I think we should eat something now…okay?"

His filmy eyes twinkle, or at least, I want to believe they do. I want to believe that I finally said the right words. "Well…if you wish…" he drawls as he simultaneously signals our waiter, who has been watching this little soap opera from the wings, waiting for his cue, or perhaps just waiting for the dust to clear. With flawless panache, he sashays over to Walt. "May I be of some assistance, Sir?" he asks with a touch of nasal haughtiness. I instantly despise this man.

Walt rotates his shoulder blades, a reflex, which may be called "squaring one's shoulders." He does this physical gesture only when he has to recoup some faltering prowess. Without looking at the server, he swaggers, "What is the best…," he now has an undeniable slush. "What is the "bestest"…steak you have in the house?" He is obviously trying to impress me. I, however, cannot move a muscle. I want to just disappear. I am incarcerated in a humiliating gaze as I watch a smashed friend beat his chest like the Beast of the Jungle! I brush my chin over my right shoulder to see if the indignant woman next to us is still glaring at our table. She is.

Not missing a beat, the insipid waiter smells the weighty tip of an inflated bill from this spongy customer. "May I suggest…" The waiter immediately sees my threat, for I am quite sober and see that he is steering Walt toward a pricey selection, clearly taking advantage of my vulnerable drunken friend. The server pouts disdainfully to disquiet me and snaps his intimidating itchy fingers inches before my cynical face as if lassoing my focus; my eyes crisscross. To further clarify who will dominate, he offensively presses his body against my shoulder and points his bony middle finger suggestively to the entrée on the menu leaflet.

"Keep your composure," I sizzle to myself. "For Walt's sake, keep cool, girl!" So, imitating my friend, I square my shoulders in a smidgeon of dignity, feint a smile, avert my eyes, and with a dampened lilt respond, "That will be quite all right…" He better get that obnoxious pointer away from me! "I will have the same as the gentleman." Walt nods, quite pleased over my choice, and so does Puckered Lips, who stiffens with an overly erect spine and snorts a pronounced sniff to punctuate, again, his self-importance, if not his forthcoming prosperity.

When he leaves, I sink back into my chair, once again beaten down by this little drama. I am saddened that the light-headed grandiosity which Walt is presently exhibiting will have him paying heavily later. Like some majestic eagle, Walt fans his outstretched arms as if he is embracing the entire restaurant. Slowly he collapses his wings behind the back of his chair in a retired wrap; his chest brandishes. He is a satisfied kingpin looking over his subjects. However, his fickle subjects deceitfully lower their heads with subtle shuns. It is only Walt and I who sit in that contented grace often shared by friends who accept each other in spite of their inadequacies. I look at him for quite some time with love and resignation. Although Walt is slightly older, he still has retained his boyish features, defying age.

Suddenly he is aware of my stare and straightens his spine as if summoning a dormant thought. He peers at me as if getting ready to send some clandestine communiqué. He twists his eyebrows in a strange manner. It is the same unsettling expression he had during the afternoon whenever he gazed in my direction. He was unaware then that I picked up on this behavior, peculiar even for Walt. Throughout the day, I just let it go and said nothing. Now sitting across from me, he resumes that same bizarre glare.

"What?"

"What you, Christine?" he quickly rebounds. His eyes knit. In spite of his drunken stupor, he appears cognitive enough to snag that fleeting question within my thoughts. "Christine," (He only calls me by my formal name when it is serious), "Christine, is anything wrong? You seem, I don't know, distracted. Lately you always seem so distracted."

I really do not want to address the recent churning within me. I'm not sure how to explain it. I scrutinize the intricate patterns on the silverware as if some cryptic answer to my life can be deciphered in these inconsequential items. However, if I don't say something immediately, Walt will undoubtedly resume his haranguing.

"I guess I'm tired."

He grunts. But after considering my remark, he diminishes his tone. "We don't have to eat here...we could eat in our room...that is...if you want to." As we both sink into silent indecision, I am aware that I have wounded my best friend.

"No, no, I really want to stay here." I'm back to stammering. "I'm, we're, both of us are hungry, and we need to eat. This is fine, Walt," and half-heartedly I add, "I'm sorry, I never had a chance to thank you for the wonderful evening that you had arranged for me and my date." (But I had no date! Walt has become my date! And I am being so thoughtless again)! I quickly paste a pardoning smile on my face.

In spite of my blunder, the forced gratitude now seems to have brought some succor back into our restaurant wingding. He smiles at me. It is evident that he, also, wants to revive the evening. His smile once again becomes cryptic. He twists that right eyebrow to suggest some deeper meaning on my "wonderful evening" comment. He tilts his head and with pronounced slurring responds, "The 'wonderful' is not over yet...There's more to come..."

I am uncomfortable about where this conversation is heading. "Yes...yes, that's true." Avoiding his licentious implication, I divert my eyes and shift slightly in my chair. "I can't wait to sink into that steak!"

Of course, I got the implication of his not-so-subtle remark. We are sharing a hotel room, an arrangement that never has been a problem. We are friends, never lovers. Don't get me wrong. Walt is definitely attractive. He has always been a meticulous traveling companion. His dress is contemporary and rather hip for a man in his forties. But to bed down with Walt was never in the picture. Our platonic relationship had allowed us to go on many jaunts together without any hitches. Why go astray tonight?

Because tonight Walt's demeanor is different, in fact, different all day as we strolled on the boardwalk discussing "the one who got away again." Throughout the afternoon there was Walt's wacky behavior, an offhand wink here, a ludicrous smirk there, sprinkled with "crossing the line" remarks everywhere. I stuffed the blatant innuendos into my denial pocketbook. I had not instigated such conduct. I chucked it off to Walt stewing sensual ingredients in his male crock-pot. I often had to turn a blind eye to Walt's playboy antics. Perhaps it was this broadmindedness on my part that had solidified our friendship for so long.

Alcohol seems to have stirred the pot tonight, and I have a limited tolerance of such bawdy behavior. A pattern is unfolding. The men I have encountered lately must have been lined up in some celestial arrangement, like moons in a cosmic design within the universe. They all seem to have that same one-track mind. I cannot ignore the growing glint in Walt's eyes; eyes that keep slithering downward from my face to linger languidly on my cleavage. And now in his drunken state he is coupling such action with drool. How do I handle this situation with Walt, who seems to be fanning some newfound desires with his longstanding platonic friend—me?

Perhaps, I need to redirect that question to myself. It's not just how do I handle my lecherous friend, or another misplaced love, or a stranger who has reawakened my yearnings. Perhaps the most significant question should be: How do I handle the seething insecurities of defining myself as a female? I no longer can bury that question; I am not so sure that I will be able to accept the answer. Should I make love tonight? Will it be with my life-long companion, or an overnight tryst with some stranger? Or should I live out my life devoid of true intimacy? It is a dilemma of fractured desires.

Walt continues to grapple with his own pestering demons as he grips his glass of Jack Daniels. He peers into the golden liquid a long time, sips it gingerly, and then gulps the entire contents in one heave. I watch with annoyance. He looks up and grins, and I think, "Oh, this is not comforting!" He detects my displeasure because he pulls away from my stern countenance and scans the restaurant in search of some more sympathetic soul who may extend a bit more compassion than I am giving him. He pauses as he peeks over my shoulder. I twist to see, too. He has snatched a prospective candidate. His "friend," our haughty waiter, is leaning smugly against a gold leafed pillar, cagily watching our table. Walt gives him a nod and a feeble smile, raising his empty glass to ask permission for another. The waiter glares back but does not move. Sucking in his upper lip, Walt pouts over the fact that he will have to wait awhile before that refill. Walt is not a heavy drinker. He wants to remain sharp while playing cards. His livelihood depends on maintaining an edge over his opponents. Yet, I am quite aware that Mr. Walter has been indulging in the spirits more than usual since early afternoon. I don't mean to suggest that I have never seen Walt smashed.

VII

JUST LAST SPRING when we were on vacation together Walt had no problem swaggering in this inebriated state. I did a bit of swaggering myself. We had secured a furnished two-bedroom bungalow in a secluded wooded area on Cape Cod for a week. As in our past outings, we shared the expenses. During our stay, our platonic relationship would allow us to occasionally part to pursue other pleasurable diversions. However, a glitch occurred when the endless torrential downpours of five consecutive days put the squash on my sightseeing excursions and Walt's girl-seeking opportunities. We wound up spending lots of time together, which really did not turn out to be the horror I had originally envisioned. We idled away the hours playing chess and engaging in long-into-the-night discussions. I sipped my Pinot Grigio, and Walt his Jack Daniels. We nibbled on cheese, fruit, and nuts for nourishment, not so sleek, but very bohemian. In our ponderings, we covered a hodgepodge of topics from the intelligence of whales to the stupidity of sharks, from the intelligence of women to the stupidity of men (however, I might be slightly biased here), from the intelligence of love to the stupidity of love…We took turns reverently speaking and patiently listening to each other across the chess board, sipping slowly enough to make the evening last. And when the king fell over, or one of us fell over, we would call it a night and respectfully retire to our designated and quite separated bedrooms. There was never a suggestion of anything else. Somehow it all worked.

It was an unusual week, an enlightening week during which I had learned a lot about Walt, as I'm sure he learned about me. We spoke poignantly about our childhood together. Perhaps it was the alcohol that loosened our tongues; perhaps, it was the confinement that gave us the opportunity to listen so intently. Perhaps, it was just a time in our lives that was overdue, to delve into the raw fabric of our most private thoughts where our deepest desires and our worst fears lay in state. By that week's end, we finally spoke about the secret that had been left unspoken throughout our years together. Could that intimate exchange of last spring have anything to do with his outlandish behavior on this autumn night?

Certainly, something is amiss this evening. I mull over whether I should give Walt time to work through this male mid-life crisis. As I watch him down two more Jack Daniels, I have an uneasiness that his problem might well be beyond quirky. I fear that things are about to get out-of-hand. And in the midst of all the lewd dust with which he peppered the day, this thought is not reassuring. *Well, Christine, the time has come to nip this in the bud before it blooms!*

"Walt, I think we need to talk. I think we need to understand something." Of course, I am speaking to his fragile Freudian male psyche.

"What's up, Babe?" His groveling is overstated. Now I know things are definitely blooming.

"Well, Walt, this is the very heart of the matter!"

"What's that, Babe?"

"That's it!"

"What?"

"Babe!"

"Uh?"

"Babe...I'm not too thrilled that you are calling me Babe!" I try to deliver my intention gently enough to preserve that fragile male ego.

"Oh...why not?"

"Because!"

"Because?"

"Because it suggests something more than what it means." The hell with placating his fragile ego!

He is relentless, "Maybe, I might want it to mean more than what it means." For someone with impaired judgment, he certainly delivers this declaration with crystal clarity. I cannot determine if his fragile male whatnot is too intact or completely out of whack!

All I know is that this precarious situation presses me to just get up and leave. Unfortunately, we still haven't eaten yet. Besides, how could I just get up and leave? That would mean abandoning the man sitting across from me, now tilting "three sheets to the wind," or more like a sailboat ready to capsize. He would have to fend for himself, alone. In his present condition, could Walt really handle that shark who is presently smacking his lips in the distance, still leaning sideways against the gold pillar and glaring his haughty glare? I remind myself that this drunk is my friend, my best friend, and can't give up on him. I remove his hand from his drink and cradle his palm in my hands. I lean across the table placing our faces eye level to help him focus on my words.

"Walt, you know we have known each other a long time…"

He shakes his head in exaggerated affirmation, and then stops his bobbing in mid-stream as he becomes fixated on the crevice between my breasts again. I have to give up the ship; he is not going to hear any words regarding his offensive vulgarity, and "capsizing" at this moment doesn't seem so bad anymore.

"Okay." I release my hands, flinging them over my head, surrendering in an impasse. A second later, our sizzling steaks are placed in front of us by you-know-whom! Our friendly waiter curtly plunks the dishes onto the table with disapproval, and, as if we have not picked up on his implied commentary, he discharges a snort to punctuate his point. Wincing, I try not to look at this despicable creature with the pronounced nasal infirmity. With his job requirement satisfied he moseys away, slightly swiveling his chin over his shoulder, pressing me not to miss his haughty glare. I wince, again.

I am demoralized. But the aroma of steak is inviting, and it revives what little is left of my self-worth. I pick up my napkin, drape it across my lap with contrived etiquette, and poise my fork and knife delicately in my fingers like a gracious geisha, in spite of my raging hunger. I am sure that Walt is just as famished. Maybe the food will appease his other ravenous yearnings, too. Yet when I glance over at him, I see that he is just sitting there like a zombie. His head is bent over the steak in a transfixed state. His clutched fists grip the table's edge as if trying to maintain his balance. There seems to be a malfunction between body and mind. He is too fucking drunk! I slide my chair close to his, so close that our thighs are pressing against each other. Still holding onto my own knife and fork, I contemplate whether or not I should use them on him. Instead, I cut his steak into manageable bite size chunks. He watches the slicing intently, like a young child waiting for his turn in a game. When I finish, I place his fork in his hand and squeeze his fingers around the silverware, trying to get them to adhere to the utensil, "Can you handle this?" I inquire, sympathetically.

He lifts his head and gazes at me with a moronic smile, "Yes…" he pauses slightly, and then, as if to himself, he gently whispers, "Thank you." Allowing my friend the dignity to solo on his own, I remove my hand.

We do not need dessert. I know this when Walt's forehead smacks into the sweet potato soufflé on his plate, and it sticks to his eyebrow as he raises his head. Of course, the grimacing waiter rushes toward us with fluttering cloth napkins. Agitated, he flaps the napkins inches from my nose and snorts his notorious snort, "May I be of assistance?" When I don't immediately respond, he releases the cloth into my lap, swivels his chin over his shoulder in his sidewinder snub, and wheezes, "Would the gentleman be needing his check?" Looking Walt up and down, he sniffs, conveying that Walt is done for the evening. I really hate this person!

"I will take the check!" I say with audacious clout. I clearly want to convey that I am the one in charge now, and if he doesn't change his demeanor pronto, he can forget about that handsome tip he had been drooling over from the very moment we sat down. In fact, if I have my druthers, he can forget about any gratuity at all!

However, our dining experience is still not over, for when the waiter picks up my date's empty glass, Walt grabs his wrist, "I would like another." With another sniff, the waiter leaves, then promptly returns, clutching in one hand the filled crystal, the final request of a condemned man, and in the other the billfold, the explicit edict of our expedient departure. He plops down the drink in front of Walt but keeps the billfold in his hand. Well aware of my sentiments, I'm sure that he has taken the liberty to include his tip. He poses next to me, erect in ridged insolence, and sinks his eyelids sideways. The billfold drools from his elongated fingertips like the lapping tongue of a slobbering hound; he wags it up and down before my face. He need not say aloud that our dinner is done. Snatching the check to stop the motion, I snap back, "We are staying in the casino's hotel and will charge this to our room." I wanted him to connect that we are paying guests of a more far-reaching entity than his little restaurant, and that he better watch his step.

He is not impressed. Withdrawing a pen from his breast pocket, he swings it in an exaggerated arc and halts it directly in front of my face, intentionally pointing it upwards in the same lewd manner. I pluck the plume from his fingers and scribble my signature. Then, to return the courtesy, I hold the folder and pen up in the air, mirroring his vulgar gesture. Snobbishly, he takes it and slips both sleazily back into his breast pocket.

"Can I be of any further assistance tonight?" he asks, sneering at me and then glancing over at Walt, who, surprisingly, is sitting quite erect in his chair. Unfortunately, his eyes are closed; life is not perfect. The waiter glares back at me with a what-are-you-going-to-do-now expression. And I get the memo loud and clear that he has no intention of assisting. With one more lingering leer at Walt, he smirks at me and moseys away, swaying his jeering head. I really, really, really...detest this man!

But, this is not the time for reprisal. I stand up, wedge my shoulder blade under Walt's armpit, and hoist my proxy date from his seat. Surprisingly, he regains some cognitive awareness and rallies to my efforts. However, just as we are about to depart from the table, he reaches for his glass, and doing that squaring-of-his-shoulders action, pulls himself up as if an imaginary thread is hinged to the top of his head. Then with one limp arm dangling down his side, he raises the other, clutching the Jack Daniels high above his head like the Statue of Liberty, and decisively salutes the restaurant. The patrons gape back at him. He brings the glass back down to his lips and chugs it in one gulp. He emits a lugubrious burp.

I smile at the fitting gesture. Walt and I might be trudging out of the elegant restaurant, but we are certainly departing in our own style. Leaving the pretentiousness behind, we pass through the beveled, metallic gold leaf glass double doors, held open by the maître d' who flaunts a pasted smile and gives us a not-so-cordial nod. I smile back amicably, in spite of laboriously clasping the cumbersome Walt. I want to believe that we are still displaying some evidence of politesse.

VIII

SOMEHOW, WE MAKE IT to the glass cage elevator that pulls us up from the mire. The sludge of the restaurant shrinks below us as the birdcage rises to the floors above. On the fifth floor we trek down a long corridor before getting to our room. When we finally arrive, I wedge Walt up against the wall, jut my hip into his stomach and brace him firmly with an outstretched arm against his chest. His eyes are still closed, and I think that maybe he is not just very intoxicated but on the verge of dying. I attempt to determine if that should be an inviting thought or not. With my other hand, I fumble through my purse in frantic maneuvers to retrieve the card key. I am about to lose the embalmed deadweight when I finally extract the prized item and slide it into the slot. The door snaps open, none too soon.

Guiding him into the room becomes the easy part of the mission because I just tilt him toward the nearest bed and release my grip. He falls like a deck of cards, his limbs sprawling in every direction. He lies on his back with his eyes still shut. I am confident that he will remain in this spot for the remainder of the night. Yes, he is definitely out for the count! I gently remove his shoes and stealthily turn away so as not to arouse him from his slumber or those misplaced desires.

"Christine, I have to ask you..."

Oh, no, here it comes! "Walt, listen. I'm sorry, but there is no way that I am going to make…"

"Chris, I have to go!"

"Go?... Go where?"

"You know…go!" His intonation is at a higher octave than usual.

I got it, all right. Oh, no! I repeat to myself with a much different intent than I had initially. I thought he wanted to make love to me; he just needs to make it to the bathroom. Unfortunately, there is no way for him to do this on his own. Once again, I slide my shoulder under his armpit and hoist him to a sitting position, and then, on a count of three, begin to raise him, something like raising the Titanic. He is immovable, not even slightly budging off the bed, and he still has not opened his eyes.

"Walt, you are going to have to help here a little bit more." Although Walt's eyes remain shut, I can tell that he still has some auditory acuity. He stirs, places his hands on his crotch and attempts to fiddle with his zipper.

"No! Not now! Not here! Look, Walt, you have to hold it until you get to the bathroom!" If I keep talking to him, he may follow my commands and somehow this nightmare may pass. I get him to stand and inch him toward our target. "Okay, we're doing fine, pal…just around the corner." I hold onto him tightly, pillaring him under his armpit. As we move along slowly, I have a reoccurring phrase in my head, "…and they call this the pits!"

Finally, we reach our destination. Unfortunately, I have not the slightest idea how I can maneuver this man into the proper position so that he can relieve himself. I face him in front of the toilet, standing behind with my palms flat against his back for support. Hopefully he will be steady enough to complete the task at hand.

"Are you able to handle this from here, guy?"

He nods in his usually exaggerated bobbing affirmative, and although I am behind, I know that his eyes are still shut. Hoping that I have done my part, I cautiously step backward, keeping my outstretched arms frozen with flat, upright palms, like some mystic trying to connect with the spirits from the underworld. Unfortunately, these spirits must be out of town because Walt's knees begin to buckle, and the magnetic conduction of the spirits severs. "Oh, no!" I shout!

I grab his shoulders and give him a hard twist; it's a maneuver like yanking off a soda bottle cap. Gravity does the rest. Walt sinks and plops his buttocks directly into the opened seat. Impressed by my reflexive ability to salvage the falling giant, my good feelings quickly dissipate as I realize that he is sitting on an open toilet, fully clothed and intact. There is obviously a problem here. I bend over and place my face inches from his, "Walt, listen to me, if you have to go, you need to adjust yourself. Do you understand me? You need to do this by yourself!"

He nods again, still with closed eyes. And then, like a horse drawn to water, he instinctively knows what to do, unzipping, positioning to relieve himself into the appropriate spot. To prevent him from falling over, especially at such a delicate moment, I move close to him and brace my body against his side and place my palm against his back. I feel his body constrict as he releases a strong steady stream. Pulling against the urge to look downward, I avert my eyes toward the ceiling. His back muscles relax. He is done, but he doesn't move.

"Look, Walt…Walt?" I repeat his name to confirm that he is still in this world. "Look, Walt, straighten yourself up, and I'll help you back to bed."

Now, it's not that I have not seen a man intimately, or for that matter never touched a man intimately. It's just that in Walt's vulnerable state, I am trying to give my friend some sense of dignity. Perhaps in my own vulnerable state I am trying to give myself that sense, too.

He regains his privacy and I go about the task of raising the Titanic again. I am determined to get him into bed. He rises, sustains his balance enough to make it to bedside, and then falls onto the cover sheets like a tired, ancient monolith. I survey the situation. Once again, he is on his back with wild displaced limbs hanging off the sides. I check to see that nothing else is hanging out. Yes, he is intact, and like a boulder, he is not going to move, thank goodness! I retrieve a soft blue velour blanket from the hall closet and drape it over him, pulling the ribbon edge up to his chin. I study his face. I am so close that I inhale the alcohol on his breath. I do not turn away. He looks so peaceful, far removed from his agitated state in the restaurant. He gives a slight grunt and I know that he will be fine for the rest of the evening.

I don't move away but continue to peruse his face. Throughout all these years I have known Walt, I am drawn once again to his youthfulness, in spite of the receding hairline and subtle, peppered graying. Sweeping some stray hair wisps back into place, I guide my fingers across his forehead. From out of nowhere, I have an urge to kiss him. Maybe it is a delayed sensation from our recent bathroom "close-encounter-of-I-don't-know-what kind," or perhaps it is the hint from all those lame attempts to seduce me throughout the day. Somehow the memory of those flirtations is not as offensive now. What should a woman do in a situation like this? Is it in the very composition of how we define ourselves as female that should determine that answer? Should we maintain the inhibition that restrains us from base lust? Or submit to the pining within our circumstances and embrace passion? Sometimes, a girl just must commit to life. I lean gently over him, and cupping his head with my hands, tenderly place my lips on his. I feel his quiver as I kiss him.

In a trance, I back away until the back of my knees fold on the adjacent bed. I'm sure that my eyes do not blink for some time. Perhaps I do love Walt in some obscure way. I had known him a long time, and there has always been some comfort in that, like not trying to reinvent yourself to fit unpredictable scenarios. So, after all these years why do I not desire Walt? And perhaps more perplexing, why, in an arbitrary impulse, was it some stranger, not Walt, who caught my fancy instead?

Suddenly, I am exhausted; the overstressed muscles of my emotions are shutting down. Whatever broken puzzle pieces were scattered in the strangeness of this evening, I have no more energy to sort them out. I replace my day clothes with my negligée, pull back the covers on my bed, and retire the night.

IX

I SQUEEZE MY EYES ATTEMPTING to block the sun's rays slithering through the venetian blinds, invading my sleep. I keep my eyelids glued; I refuse to release the night. But the light is more persistent. My lids lift, and I gaze into the brilliance from the sliding glass door. Dust particles enlarge to flat pictorial screens, like floating puzzle pieces of memory. I squint. Within one of the imaginary panels, I see the arm of the singer strumming downward on his guitar. Another pane holds the stranger's side-angled smile. On a still larger leaf, Walt's back heaves as my open palm lies flat against it.

I twist away from the dust beams, turning onto my side facing Walt's bed. It is roughed up. I squint again. It is definitely vacant. I sink back into the pillow and stare at the ceiling. Maybe he died last night, and the coroner took pity on me and just quietly wheeled him away on a stretcher so as not to disturb my slumber. Maybe he has amnesia and is presently groping about in the maze of the hotel's corridors trying desperately to find his way back to our room. (I hope he does not have anything hanging out as he asks the maids which way "to go"). Of course, the most logical explanation is that he is looking for some place in the lobby to purchase aspirin for the very unpleasant hangover I'm sure he must be sporting. Yes, that's the most plausible explanation for my man missing in action.

So, what can a friend do but wash up and search for her friend in need before he gets into another uncompromising situation? If he returns to find me in my scanty negligée I am not so sure that I will be able to handle that scene. I recall his recent indiscretions, not to mention my disconcerting kiss last night. I sit back on my bed to assess the situation. What I need is a mystic to help me find my friend in need. Because my mystic might still be out of town, I survey the terrain through the glass elevator on my way down to the lobby.

As the glass transport sinks through the innards of the hotel's vast hall, I view colorful floral arrangements. The morning's sunlight flickers on the greenery, and I wonder if the flowers are natural or just plastic. I cannot tell. Finally, the glass cage slows on a cushioned puff of air, and I vacate the cubicle with a hesitant step. The lobby has lost the clutter of bodies from the prior night, and in the morning light, I feel displaced. After scanning my surroundings, I see last night's restaurant. It evokes the sobering swan song of Walt saluting his flock with laborious panache. I wince and try to reassure myself that there is certainly no one at this early hour to attest to that episode. In spite of the unsettling memory, I mosey over to the gilded restaurant entrance with the rationale that like lost wounded animals that drag themselves back to their lairs to die, perhaps Walt, too, is dragging back to this vicinity. As I press my forehead against the cold glass and peer through it, I only see a darkened room. I am relieved that it is closed in spite of feeling like a lost soul, too. However, adjacent to the bistro, hidden among more greenery, I spy a sunlit alcove that opens onto a courtyard eatery. Perhaps all is not in vain. This breakfast retreat looks inviting enough for a lost soul in desperate need of a cup of strong coffee. Maybe, like me, it is the very place into which a wounded friend has wandered.

Just like last night's restaurant, a sentry is posted at the door, probably to keep out the riff raff. In Walt's disheveled state, he probably would not have been able to pass. However, this hostess does not seem as foreboding as last night's sentinel. She projects a demure, sweet manner with a cordial smile. So, I think, "Give it a try, Christine!"

I approach her and inquire. "Could you see if a gentleman with slightly graying hair is sitting by himself inside?" I assume he is alone. Even Walt could not pick up a dame in this time frame, at least, not in his present condition. The hostess is amenable to my request and leaves her post to look.

I wait by the entrance, not wanting to venture further into the restaurant. I am concerned about Walt's appearance if she does discover him. If he is in his rumpled state, would she return trying to figure out what kind of woman would associate with such a man? Maybe, before she returns, I should leave and preserve what little pride I have left. Of course, if she did find him, I could always deny any connection to him. At least I would know where he is.

I hear the precise clip-clop of her heels against the stone flooring. She wears an affirmative smile; I have hit pay dirt. Trying to devise an alibi to save my waning self-respect, I smile back. She waves me to enter, and I follow her and the aroma of morning coffee. I have difficulty staying even with the punctuating heels as they snip over the uneven stone flooring. Concerned over the quick pace, I cast my eyes downward, fixed on the stone terrain for any irregularity that would cause a vicious fall. I dare not look ahead. She abruptly stops before a red leather high back chair with the back toward me. I do not have a clear view of its occupant, but I spy a protruding man's pant leg. It looks familiar. Another identical empty high back faces the occupied one with a small square table between. In the center of the table a petite, cut-glass vase holds a single fresh flower, a slender daffodil delicately drooping sideways over its rim.

With the hostess's mission completed, she turns, and with a sweeping gesture invites me to sit in the empty chair. She gives me a subtle wink and sallies away. I do not sit. I just remain standing, slightly drooping my head much like the daffodil and trying to look sideways to the man in the chair. Annoyed that Walt has once again imposed upon my good nature, I bring my voice up an octave ready to take my firm stance over his antics.

"I have been looking for you throughout this entire hotel, and you could have at least…" Too late, I try to swallow my trailing words but can only salvage the fizzle, "Excuse me. I thought you were someone else!"

Somewhat relieved, I focus my attention to the newspaper spread open, concealing its reader. I stand in staunch silence, smoldering a hole through the newsprint to envision who may be behind it. The sprawling trousers and the manicured fingertips really do look familiar. Maybe it is Walt! Time drowses as the edges of the paper collapse. Its reader sits in languid deportment. A pair of haggard eyes peep over rimless glasses positioned low on his nose. His eyes squint matter-of-factly and then open with recognition. His eyebrows rise, the corner of his mouth lifts. It is his inescapable smile that once again draws me. He gently nods, the same gesture with which he greeted me last night when he spied me from his poker seat inside the private room behind the forbidden door. Finally, he accordions the newspaper, folds it twice and places it neatly on the tabletop, suggesting that he is ready to engage.

"How fortunate I am to have such attentive Muses!" He is, of course, mocking my allusion from the concert again. He pokes at me further. "Whatever brings you here to me…I hope you will stay awhile this time." He rises smoothly and places an inviting hand on the back of the empty chair, a polite gesture to join him. The touch of frivolity underlines a suggestion of possibilities. Moreover, so that his intent will not be misunderstood, he reiterates. "Please, join me." He returns to his seat and awaits my next move.

Wanting not to be considered even more daft, I bow my head in exaggerated consent and with overstated, graceful femininity swing my body, sweep my hands beneath my skirt, and sit. I want to convey that I, too, am ready to spar. Once situated, I continue to play along, elongating my arms across the tabletop, intertwining my fingers in a defiant clasp, staring directly back at him. Yes, I am quite good at playing emboldened pretentiousness. If it is going to be a showdown of the sexes, I will oblige him, if not with a display similar to gunslingers of the Old West, then at least with the emotional muscle to get me through the few couple of seconds!

He doesn't blink. He resumes hedging with another punch. "I thought our date was for next Saturday. This seems a bit premature on your part, don't you think?" I grunt to hint at this truth. Of course, there would have been no way I ever would have met him on Saturday! My eyes wander upward dubiously.

He picks up my disposition. "Well then, perhaps we both know that the Saturday date would never really have come to pass." He pauses, allowing me to appreciate his candor. "So, maybe we can think of this morning as a brief interlude to a different scenario." He pauses. "What do you think…perhaps?"

This question wisps about my head like fleeting shadows of indecision. I muse over how "perhaps" has been haunting my recent insecurities. Perhaps I should? Perhaps I will? Perhaps I already have? How about it, Christine, perhaps it is time for another perhaps. There is no doubt that he is interesting. The deep resonance of his voice has drawn me into wanting more of his subtle wit. It is obvious that he possesses depth on many levels; I like that. I have grown tired of mundane conversations, babblings of shallow insignificance. And, his quips are raw layers of frankness that tickle my fancy. Across the tabletop the alluring electricity of repartee churns. I am not sure if I want to let go of that just yet. I smile; he smiles. No longer is it an indifferent truth.

Suddenly, the congealing energy is broken by an intruder, a waiter has invaded the beguiling space. Flushed to protect this fragile link from any alien invasion, I flippantly wave my wrist, trying to dismiss the waiter as if he is a pesky fly. "Just coffee, please."

The extraterrestrial departs to unknown lands, but quickly reappears cradling a coffee carafe. I pull my hands onto my lap, resigning myself to the unbridled reality of the present. Pressing my shoulders against the back of the red chair, I draw in a faint scent of leather. I glance down at my hands. I cannot believe they belong to me; they look not just foreign, but ancient. I become fixated on them. The stranger clears his throat. His suave body bends toward me. He picks up the carafe and pours its contents into my coffee cup and returns to his chair. We sit once again in silence, perhaps to rethink what suddenly seems irrelevant. The dark liquid emits its hearty aroma as its vapors rise from my cup. Our interchange is like the swirls of those steamy ghosts, embracing us in some seductive dance. I lift my eyes through the hazy urn's breath and still see him staring at me. Our eyes linger a bit too long, and I command my sight to release me from this trance. Panic seethes, and I quickly look back down to my lap.

He clears his throat again. I look up. His head gives a slight tilt as if to suggest, "Why not?" His eyes squint, inviting me to have faith in the unknown. Charmed by the smile in those eyes, I relax and take a sip of coffee.

He speaks. "So…let me, at least, introduce myself…my name is Cameron Dawson…and your name is…?" His pause leaves the question dangling over a precipice of foreboding. I retrieve the answer before I plummet.

"Christine…Christine Ledge."

"Now, that wasn't so difficult, was it?"

He seems to know me too well. I cannot release the shadow of familiarity about this Mr. Dawson. I had this same sensation the moment I first pressed against his arm at the concert. I had ignored that feeling because I had thought that I probably would never see him again. But like a relentless itch, it is a thought that aches to be scratched. So, I take a breath and scratch.

"Have we met before?"

"Last night at the concert and then later in the hall!" a bit too quick and a bit too tidy. I am not satisfied.

"No, before last night. I feel that we had met before last night."

No response. He sips his coffee. I sip my coffee and allow its warmth to appease his evasiveness. Obviously, I had just trespassed over some line. Because there is no need to ruin this moment, I allow his hesitancy to pass. After a moment he stirs in his seat.

"Did you enjoy the concert?" It is obvious that he wants to change the subject. But, I am a female. And his abrupt shifting is troubling. I disconnect from my unfounded hunches.

"Oh, the concert…well…yes…of course, I enjoyed the concert."

Last night's images block any coherent reply. Fractured conversations interfere…caressing words serenaded by the music opened wounds as I recall pressing up against him. And so, I stare at him now and think about how it would be to lie naked next to this man, to physically be touched by him. I harangue myself over my intimate urges. I flip my head back trying to shake off the irrational desire. However, I cannot let go of last night's encounter between this Mr. Dawson and some young man in a questionable financial exchange to obtain the seat next to mine. Suddenly, I am wary of how much I should trust this man seated across from me.

Watching me carefully, he tilts his head as if to pardon any past indiscretions. He seems able to read my misgivings. This veil of deception must dissipate to have more clarity. And for that to happen, I must be more forthright, too.

"No, Mr. Dawson, to be quite frank, I did not enjoy the concert last night. I really struggled to sit through it." Then to continue this openness, "Was that obvious?"

"I did sense you were a bit uncomfortable." His polite delivery seems sincere enough.

Trying to inject some humor to lift the heavy tone: "You mean since each time I banged into your arm, you got a new 'black and blue'?"

"Actually, I rather liked the banging in spite of all those black and blues."

"You did, did you?" There is a pause; I am more comfortable with this exchange. "I'm really sorry; I didn't mean to be so abusive."

"No, no…no apology needed. What I meant by the banging was not because of that… but, yes, because of that, too…More because I found you quite intriguing as you squirmed about like you had hemorrhoids or some serious itch in the seat of your pants." His humor releases any lingering veiled suppositions.

"Oh, I hope it wasn't that annoying…I should have gotten up and left so that you would have enjoyed the show better."

"No, no, really don't feel put off…because…to tell the truth… I rather enjoyed watching you watching the singer."

The lurking ping returns. He found sitting next to me more engrossing than the singer! Could this be the intent of the covert money exchange? Was there some other reason for him to sit next to me? I need to address these flickering dust particles of doubt.

"Can I ask you a question, Mr. Dawson?" Deliberating over my intent, he stares and then nods. "How could you be more interested in me when the singer was so good?"

He does not respond immediately, but when he does, his answer is softened and uncomfortably intimate, "…because so are you."

The conversation is too raw. He is a surgeon deviously cutting into my most vulnerable parts. Can he know that I find him so delicious? I remember another delicious time and place: Walt lying on the bed with the wisps across his forehead and the numbing of my lips in a kiss. Conflicting emotions flush over me; they are not only embarrassing to a woman my age, they are beginning to spook me into doubting my sanity. I have to get a grip on myself!

"Look, I know this may sound like I am putting you off again, but I do have to go."

He scrunches his mouth in lighthearted dismay; his brows twist.

"However, I really would like to meet with you again…that is…if you also want to?" Oddly enough, I still want to retain a possibility for this stranger and me, just not now.

His disappointed grimace slides into a cornered smile, and I know that whatever had begun here is that seed of trust needed to sustain the potential of a possibility.

He buys into this potential, too. "Yes, I most certainly want to see you again." And resurrecting my own words, "…some more convenient time and place, perhaps?" I could tell that he is enjoying this repartee. He relaxes his voice back to its deep resonance, "I recall we do have a tentative engagement for next Saturday?"

This is more of a question than a statement. It is a question of "perhaps," a "perhaps" that we all blindly long for, which when presented seems beyond our reach. Should I once again back away from this unknown stranger and head for the hills? Maybe this was why I never sustained any significant relationship throughout my life. I never allowed myself to be vulnerable enough to embrace "perhaps." Every choice I made was analyzed, calculated, reassured. I look down at my hands folded in my lap. They look so foreign; they look so ancient. Perhaps, it was time to open Pandora's Box.

"Yes, I will meet you here next Saturday." And with that resolved, I rise from my chair. Yet, after taking only a few steps, I stop and turn. There is no way to reseal the nymph's lid, so I might as well flip it completely off.

"I saw that the concert seat was not yours, but I am glad that you bribed the young man to sit next to me, anyway. But beware! Perhaps those commissioned Muses are still dancing around us, making us dizzy!"

He doesn't even hint a response. I leave without looking back.

X

I WALK OUT THROUGH THE ALCOVE and directly into the caged elevator, which lifts me from the lobby like the steam from my morning coffee cup, rising toward the skylight where light penetrates through the glass shaft and bathes me in warm grace. I am returning to my room in a different state than I left.

When I open the door, I find Walt sprawled in his now signature position, this time not on the bed, but on the cushioned chair before the sliding glass door. His back curves in a slouch within the contoured chaise. The drapes are pulled back, and light permeates the room, painfully revealing everything. His legs are prostrated in front of him like a wounded bird; his arms hang lifelessly over the sides of the chair. Across his eyes is a terry cloth towel, probably heavily saturated, but neatly folded, very much Walt's pristine style.

"Walt, are you alive?"

"No...but please don't walk so loudly."

"Walt, the floor is covered in plush carpet, and I just removed my shoes."

"That's why I want you to be very...very... quiet."

I stare at this pitiful creature and try to stifle my cynicism. "You really must not be feeling well. Could I get you something for your..."

He cuts me off, as if he really doesn't want to engage in any dialogue, yet also suggesting he absolutely must. "Had that...done that...just like you!"

"What?" His cryptic remark irks me. "What are you muttering about?"

The wet cloth slides to his shoulders as he props himself up to take a good look at me. I cannot deny the obvious severe hangover in his sunken eyes. He hasn't shaved, which is highly unusual for him, perhaps because of an unsteady hand. But, he has showered. Thank God! Knowing Walt, he probably remained languid under the soothing steam until the warmth numbed every cell in his body. Those wispy hairs are smoothly flattened down in a combed sheen over to one side to minimize the receding hairline problem.

"So, you washed up. Good…good. But you still look a little green around the gills, buddy." He really needs some TLC. I try the solicitous question, again. "Can I do something for you?"

"Yes…yes, you can…yes…you see…" he seems to be tripping over his tongue. "You see…I think that's where we left off…last night."

His stammering prods my latent insecurities. How could he know about last night…about the kiss… he was out cold? I walk over to the side of his chair and pick up the wet cloth, which is lying on the armchair's cushion. If I replace it on his forehead, maybe he will not be so obnoxious. Suddenly, he snatches my wrist and squeezes it more aggressively than his usual manner.

"Walt, you're hurting me. What's the matter with you?" Although, to be quite honest, he really isn't hurting me at all. It is just that he momentarily stunned me. Nevertheless, such aggression has to be confronted. "And what did you mean, '…just like me…' and '…left off last night…'?"

It is obvious that he is hesitant to reveal what twisting snake is squeezing inside him. I decide to say nothing more until he comes to terms with his wrath and returns to an acceptable level of civility. But he continues to spittle.

"I remember saying the same thing to you, girl…'What's the matter, Christine?' I asked last night. 'How do you feel, Christine?' and all…last night in the restaurant…and I don't think you ever answered me…and…" In his stringy sentence, he seems to be tightening his grip on my wrist, not out of anger, but tugging to bring me closer to him, wanting me not to leave until some important question is answered. He continues the string of thought in one held breath, "…and I remember coming back to this room…and I remember something being released in me…and when I woke up this morning, I was on the bed…and my fly, unzipped…and I was damp…and I just need to know if you and I…"

In a jolt, I desperately try to muffle my silent laughter from my clenched wrists to his clenched teeth. Walt thinks that we engaged in some tryst last night! Something he probably longed for the entire day. And when it finally came to fruition, he missed it! I shake loose from his grip. I turn my back to him so that my amusement is not revealed. Behind me, I hear the desperate plea in his voice.

"Well, did we…or…didn't we?" I glance back. His expression is so forlorn, and this uncertainty causes him to sink even deeper into the chair. I try not to react to the irony, for he does seem quite dismayed. But this is way too delicious to dismiss quickly. Some Machiavellian mischief seethes inside me. And why not? Yesterday I put up with all those ridiculous flirtations. Maybe he needs some impetus to rethink our relationship. I pucker my lips and blow out the punctuated words.

"Walt, dear, now that it has come out into the open, I just want to tell you how...wonderful...you were...last night!"

I watch his lower jaw drop slightly as his sunken eyes widen. I try to interpret his response as he digests my remark. Is it, as in my initial analysis, that he had missed out on some salacious moment in his life, never to be experienced again? Or is his response about the reality of another irreversible situation? For the moment he doesn't say anything. His chin drops to his chest, and he seems to be making subtle grunts as if to reprimand himself.

How long should I have him remain in such a state? I'm really not a vicious person, just someone who delights in the incongruity of appearances. Yet, I am beginning to sense that this little scenario might be a bit more significant than my off-handed frolic and deserves a more thoughtful approach. Walt is still holding something back. There is more going on than he is willing to admit. It is time to stop this charade. Friends must rise to a higher moral compass, or else true meaning becomes just a mirage of truth.

"Walt, listen to me...last night...nothing sexual happened between us."

I wasn't so committed to those words, but I said them carefully as not to give Walt any inkling of any other intention. Besides, it's not that I was completely fabricating. It's just that I wasn't sure what end it would serve to tell him about the kiss. To do so would make something out of nothing.

"What...what are you saying?" At first, he seems relieved, then disappointed. "Oh," he says like air seeping slowly out of his deflating balloon of desire. Suddenly, he perks up with some enlightened realization of what I had just done to him, and his tone is fortified with curtness.

"Look, Chris, that was not very nice of you, especially in my fragile state."

He is right. I had been deliciously bad. Maybe my boldness was empowered by the attention I had received from that intriguing man this morning. I have a renewed sense of self-confidence. Yes, this possibly might be the reason for my roguishness with Walt, a combination of the wry repartee with Cameron, and the struggle with my femininity, sprinkled with the embarrassingly inebriated scene with Walt, notwithstanding the upshot of his not even being able to pee on his own. Rethinking my naughty playfulness, I don't feel that remorseful.

This misunderstanding between Walt and me must be resolved. We have always made the effort to protect each other. It comes from raw honesty forged from a lifetime of words captured in heart-rending midnight discussions. If we deny those words were ever spoken, then we lack the courage to validate our existence. Perhaps this is why Walt and I were never really alone, even in the most vacant moments of our lives.

I sink to the carpet besides his chair, draping my cheek on his lap, I wrap an arm around his torso. His hand brushes over the top of my hair in a soft caress. I have no more words to violate his deflated spirit. We are just two friends wanting to convey that enough bad feelings have been exchanged. Sometimes gestures have enough meaning, a wordless language, but perhaps a better language, for words cheat our thoughts, too many nuances and variations of interpretation warp the true intent.

"Walt, let's go take a walk on the beach." Walt has something important to tell me, and maybe a change of venue will allow him to open up. Maybe a change of scenery will be good for me, as well. I am not so sure that we should remain in this room any longer. Actually, I am not so sure that I can handle any situation that leads to where last night's kiss left off.

"Yes, I think that's a good idea, too." His voice has mellowed, and some gentle grace brushes over us. He wraps his hands around my head, drawing me to look at his face; his moist eyes hint at concern, and I detect that whatever is bothering him somehow involves me. I twitch in inner panic and he hugs me, reassuringly.

"Chris, you know that I would never hurt you?"

These words are not what I expect. This strange comment does not fit the moment, especially because it has always been understood that we will never really hurt each other. Why bring that up now? I look back at him. His eyes sliver in search of my response, but I just do not know where to go with this. I turn my head and gaze out the sliding glass door. The last twenty-four hours have taken their toll on me, and I don't know what to think anymore. He brushes his hand over my hair again and helps me rise.

"Please, Christine, trust me. Okay?"

I nod and mosey to my suitcase pulling out something a lot warmer for the morning beach than my flimsy skirt and top. In the nearby alcove, I strip off all my clothes so that I will be more comfortable on the sand in my sweats. After the exchange I go to the glass sliding door and step outside onto the concrete balcony to pick up my sandy sneakers.

XI

THE TERRACE IS JUST a small overhang with a sturdy black iron railing guarding against any irreversible fall from the fifth floor. I take a deep breath of sea air and look beyond the water. The sunshine has dissipated into a mist that blankets the sky in a vast gray and casting the same somber tone onto the ocean. The distant horizon separates the expansive sky from the endless water with only a vague thin line, a good indication that it is not going to be a good beach day at the Jersey Shore. Such an inhospitable beach will fend off those idle morning sunbathers. On the other hand, this gloominess also provides isolation, the very harbor for any lost soul at sea to return home safely within the redeeming embrace of a friend. There, on that sand, perhaps I would become the listener for Walt's sad song, even if it is not a place for me to sing my own.

"Are you ready?" Walt has been pensively waiting for me. I slide back the glass door and follow him faithfully out of the room, the hotel, and onto the beach where we remove our sneakers, and sink our toes into the loose sand.

The sand has always been most inviting for me at the water's edge where it squishes erotically between the crevices of my toes. Walt and I stand quietly next to each other, facing the ocean in a mystical trance as its white noise summons us, like a tribal ritual passed down by distant ancestors.

We stand like minuscule grains of sand on the vast beach of the human race. I try to grasp the incomprehensible design in the natural order of life. Is it not the function of a man and a woman to both procreate and to preserve this natural design from those intolerable forces that try to annihilate it? Perhaps the challenge lies in determining how resolute one's courage is to face that preservation. Any misunderstanding between Walt and me is sinking away with the undulation of each frothy wave. We are ready to talk and to listen.

"Walt, what seems to be the problem?" Although my tone is encouraging, he remains silent. I prod further; I will not allow him to slip away into that inaccessible place again. I up the stakes.

"Apparently, something has been on your mind that made you think it was okay to indulge yourself in more than your customary limit of the spirits last night!"

Still silence, I forge onward.

"And I think you had the intention of not just drinking yourself under the table but consuming enough alcohol to make yourself so blind as to never see 'the table' again!"

In all the hardships Walt had to endure throughout his life, I never worried about him contemplating suicide, but now I am worried. I place a consoling hand on his upper arm. Whatever burden he is carrying, he should not do so alone. Still, he remains distant. He becomes deeply engrossed in watching the activity of a sand crab, desperately trying not to drown as it claws its way to the surface; inevitably it will be swallowed back into a collapsing sink hole. Perhaps this is what is happening to Walt.

I apparently am getting nowhere fast, and I fear that if I don't do some quick maneuvering Walt would follow the sand crab into the depths of no return. Perhaps this is connected to his weird behavior and lewd comments throughout Saturday.

"Walt, does any of this have to do with your hitting on me yesterday?"

Oh, I hit pay dirt. He jerks his head up and glares back at me. "Okay, now that I have your attention…let's talk!"

He nods his familiar nod, and then turns, moving to higher and drier terrain away from the tenuous water's edge. Yes, I sensed this is going to be a serious talk. He plops down on the sand ridge. I follow his lead and sit next to him, both of us facing the ocean like the seagulls in their ancestral positions staring straight ahead toward the faint horizon.

"You're throwing me down a rabbit hole of limited information. How can we have a dialogue here, buddy, if I'm the only one talking?" I slide closer to him and give him a shoulder nudge.

"Okay…Okay…" He hesitates just long enough for me to give him a discerning grimace. "Okay! Let's cut to the chase, Chris! Have you ever wondered why you don't hold onto a man?"

"What are you talking about?" This comment is out of the blue. "Look, Walt, you better have something relevant to say. And, what kind of a question is that, anyway?" This 'switch and bait' is getting to me."

"I'm just asking you a simple question. Why don't you have a guy?"

"I have had lots of guys, and you know that!"

"Yeah, but only guys who are not the stick-around-type-of guys; I'm talking about the stick-with-it-kind'a guys."

There is a twinge of truth in his insinuation; I have never had a significant other. But, since he finally decided to open up a dialogue, I will let this last comment pass. Maybe this direction will lead to his problem. "All right…all right, but what does all that have to do with anything?"

He seems pleased that I am yielding to whatever game he is dealing. Walt has always been a good poker player, and you can never really be certain what is up his sleeve. I wave my hand lightheartedly in a poker gesture, egging him to go on.

"Look, Chris, did you ever wonder why you never got married?"

"Never found the right man."

"Why you never allowed the right man to become the right man?"

"Never found the right man."

He tilts his head to halt the circling, and then he pouts with his notorious smirk of impropriety. "Or never found the right woman!"

"Maybe I never found the right woman…yet!" I decide that I will have the last word. "So, pupil mine, you better make your point, and very soon!"

"You have a man problem because you have a breakup problem!"

"Where did you get the idea that I have a problem with men?"

"We sleep in the same room!" Walt raises his eyebrow playfully.

I know what Walt is referring to. Whenever I go through a breakup, I invariably find myself calling Walt. I need his comfort as I pour over the sad details of the goodbye kiss. Moreover, Walt and I are certainly strange bedfellows! Sometimes we just talk on the phone. Sometimes, if I cannot bear being alone, I knock on his townhouse door and stay the night. There is never any hanky-panky, just a friend consoling another friend from the arrow wounds of Cupid, providing a safe haven from unrequited love. This is the reason I have crashed in Walt's hotel room since Friday. I admit this last breakup threw me for a loop. I really thought this lover was different from the others. I wanted to believe that forever could be a possibility this time around. That, in spite of early telltale signs, that I could change the end game. I thought that maybe if I didn't hold back, physically or emotionally, but remained honest to the relationship, it would work. But with boundless passion comes persistent doubt. Did I give too much; did I give too soon; is it infatuation or real love? Am I worth it to this man? The subtle pangs of doubt bled into the final trickle of denial. After all, can a woman who can no longer bear children really give something substantial to a man?

I shake this thought back into the archives of lost affairs, and I look at Walt. He has not diverted his eyes from me. My cryptic kiss from last night rises out of this mire of uncertainty.

"Look, Walt, forget about me; I'm more interested in trying to help you with your problem."

"That's just it, Chris; my problem is your problem."

His poignant remark scares the willies out of me. Does he know about the kiss? I cannot tell. It has always been difficult to read what is stewing in this man's head. He usually leaves out the pertinent facts.

"Walt, just spill it, or I'm gonna' stick my hands down your throat and strangle it out!"

He knows I really wouldn't do such a thing; I'm a willy-nilly pussy. He slouches into the sand dune and rubs his eyebrows with his thumbs, struggling over a reply. I have seen this body language before, and I am worried that he might follow the old sand crab he is intensely staring at downward into the sink hole. I lower my voice and gently prod him out of it.

"Walt, just speak!"

Forming brushed arches in the sand, he glides his fingers back and forth as if formulating a decision. He stops halfway through one pass and speaks. "When you sleep over, you have terrible nightmares."

I'm not sure how to respond. Lately, it is true. I have had nightmares, terrible nightmares. But I have tried to keep this to myself. Unfortunately, I never am able to recall the specifics in the morning. I just know I had them. The evidence was in the soaked nightgowns and my racing heart that would wake me in the middle of the night. I chucked this recent phenomenon off as quirky hormonal changes.

Unfortunately, from the piercing look in Walt's eyes, I detect that he has no intention of allowing me to pass on this issue. "So, what about the nightmares?"

"Those nightmares that I overheard…you were reliving that night…that night in grandma's bedroom. We never talked about it. But I know what the old man was doing. And I didn't do anything to stop him!"

"Look, Walt, let it go. Don't judge yourself so harshly! Just let it go!

"I'm not so sure that you have let it go, Chris."

I shake my head in denial. "That was a long time ago." I feel a need to repeat this. "To be honest, it's all forgotten."

The scent of the salt water mists over us. Walt digs into his pocket and pulls out a photograph. Gingerly, he hands it to me.

I gaze into the black and white photo. Do answers loom within the faded images steeped in shades of gray? It is the scene that was snapped years ago in grandma's kitchen on my eighth birthday. I look at Walt to question him, but he has disengaged. He remains in a muted trance, fixated on the distant horizon. What did this photograph capture when it was snapped so long ago that has any connection to me now? And why did Walt hold onto it throughout the years? I never knew he had it until he just resurrected it from his pocket. I stare at the snapshot that captured a lost moment within the frayed, yellowing edges.

"No, it isn't forgotten, Chris! No, it's not! Last night, I heard the moaning again. Just like all the other times I heard you moan in your sleep! And I know why you are having these nightmares." Walt's hedging spooks me. I no longer want to listen.

He blurts out. "Chris, you're going crazy!"

I have heard enough of his nonsense! I snatch nearby wet jetsam off the sand and fling it toward the sea. I snarl, "Crazy! Who said I'm going crazy?" Exasperated puffing punctuates my annoyance of his sidetracking the real issue. But I do not confront him. I do not look at him. I dare not look at him! In the gap created by his denial, the coldness of moist sand seeps through my clothing. I sniff the heavily salted atmosphere. It stings my throat. Could Walt be right?

I whisper a plea for him to be more lenient with me. "You really think that I'm crazy? Walt, listen! I know I've been absorbed in my own thoughts lately, but I know what reality is!"

He softens his tone. "I'm not saying that you're insane. I just know that you are worried about something, and I think it has to do with what happened to you a long time ago in Grandma's bedroom. I wasn't there to help you then, but that's gonna' change." He pauses as if too unsure to continue. "It's time, Chris."

"Time…time for what?"

"To have a meaningful relationship, and I am going to make it happen."

"What!" Oh, this is reassuring! I think that I'm losing my mind, and Walt thinks I need a man! And after Friday morning's drama with my cell phone in my car, I'm not sure I can handle any more of that! I still have no inkling what Walt's problem is, and I can see that our discussion on the beach is going nowhere. Perhaps I should not take him too seriously. He has always managed to get out of scrapes throughout his life, one way or another. If he wants me to help him, he knows where to find me. I never am really that far away from him.

I stand up on the embankment and brush off the loose sand from my sweat pants, much as I wanted to brush off this strange dilemma between Walt and me. It is time to return to our hotel room. The harsh overcast drifting in from the sea is making the morning too chilly to remain on the beach. I know that there is still more to be said, but that will have to wait. He promises to explain more when we get back to our hotel room. However, as we are leaving the beach, Walt broaches an unusual request.

"Chris, will you do me a favor?" I twist my eyebrow in a "what now" expression. "Will you stay the week, at least until Saturday? By then, I promise I'll explain everything. By then everything will be worked out."

I am not so convinced about his pledge. However, there is that so-called tentative date with another man, a man who has loitered into my world, tweaking my curiosity. Maybe hanging around until Saturday will not be so bad! Perhaps I should take some time off from work. I really do not need to report to anyone about this. Yes, a week in A.C. could do the trick.

"Sure, sure, Walt, Saturday." I guess I will have to just let go of Walt's problem, or whatever else is in play in that poker mind of his.

We walk silently for some time before he finally speaks again. "I'm in trouble."

"Well, that's a start." I look down at the photograph. I sense that the dragon slayer has reemerged to right a wrong once again. Perhaps he has kept the photograph all these years because he has become the trustee of my frailty. I would have destroyed this long ago. Instead I hand it back to him. He pauses as if having a second thought. His tenuous courage seems to be receding much like the waves a short distance from us. However, I knew if I could be as patient with my fractured friend as nature is with man's folly, Walt will return to me with the next wave. He moves toward the hotel; the photo drops from his hand. As I follow him, I snatch it off the sand and bury the image of the past into my pocket.

As the morning mist continues to siphon the light from the day, she is unaware of another occurrence. Absorbed in uncovering Walt's strange dilemma, Christine fails to see the distant figure leaning against the iron rail balcony in the hotel room next to the one they had just left. He has been scrutinizing their movements since the moment they removed their sneakers and stepped onto the beach.

♠ Chapter 2: The Flop ♠

The First Community Cards
The Dealer has drawn three cards from the Poker deck and places them in
the center of the table, face up. Three exposed cards challenge each player.
Should they "Check" and stay in play, or "Fold" and discard their cards.
Perhaps it is already past the point of no return; the illusion of possibility is
too tempting to leave the game at this point. The gamblers remain.

I

HE GRIPPED BOTH HANDS on the rim of the railing and peered down. The iron was clammy with dew, but all he had to do was wipe his hands onto his dark navy trousers. He was never that particular about technicalities, and wet marks on his clothes were the least of his concerns. He watched the two figures perched like two seagulls, on a sandy embankment near the shoreline. He folded his upper lip over his teeth and made a smacking sound, affirming a thought. He knew what they were discussing, and he knew how the plan would play out. He knew because it was not their plan, it was his. Satisfied that all was in place he returned inside, assured that there would be no hitches. After all, it was business...his business.

He finally returns to the hotel's bedroom, glances over the queen-sized bed, and the haunting begins. No matter how much he denies his desires, they seethe through his empty days and vacant nights. It is recent, this weariness of being irrevocably committed while remaining forever unattached. Even excessive alcohol cannot smother this affliction. He swallows hard now, a couple of times. Sometimes this deadens the sensations for a while. He must get a hold of this problem; if he doesn't, it will be his demise. He shakes his head. Never would there be any debate about whether he was the wrong man for this job, that he was getting too old, or getting too soft! He must carry out the operation and be done with it. But why is it becoming so difficult? Why is it more difficult this time? He knew this answer. No matter, years of detachment have groomed him to clear his mind of these side noises so that there will be no collateral damage. This time, with this package, the mission must be pristine.

On the bed his opened suitcase waits, his clothing judiciously belted to prevent slippage; he has always been scrupulous over business details. Closing up the suitcase, he yanks it upright next to the bed and scans the room: the console, desk, shower area, closet, until he is satisfied that nothing has been forgotten, no evidence that he was ever here at all; he remains a man without existence. He leaves the room, one hand firmly gripped on the suitcase handle, the other gently closing the door behind him. This two-fisted exit is a reflection of his own duality: resolute but cautious.

In the hall, as he fixates on the indicator signal just above the fifth floor elevator doors, his internal monologue returns. He watches the intermittent gage move—a sporadic indicator of doubt. *This time is different.* The nagging is irregular. *This time it is different because of her.* The harassing is predictable. *This time it is because of this particular woman.* The torment is definite. He is drawn to her, yet intimidated by her, captivated by her, yet impeded by her, truthfully wanting her. Yes, he has a problem.

"Just get on with it!" He harangues himself aloud. Another shake of his head, and then, as if flicking away fiery embers at the end of a cigarette, all dithering ceases. He exhales and turns his back to the elevator. He glances back down the corridor of closed doors and fabricates what licentious scenarios might have unfolded behind them. He continues to scan farther down the hall until he isolates the door to her room. Its silence reminds him that his plan has been set in motion, and that his job is nearly done. He just needs to be alert to any obstacles before wrapping things up.

In spite of forewarning, he ignores the rising elevator behind his back as it transports a cargo that will sabotage his plan. With blind callousness, the elevator arrives on his floor and destiny taps him on the shoulder. He turns and immediately notices the locked elbows.

They are causally standing with rolled up pant legs. Wet sneakers drip from their hands. Processing each other's presence, the three freeze. Walt and Christine are captured inside the elevator, Cameron outside it. No one is prepared to address this moment. But Cameron, mistrusting what might be unfolding, speaks first, feigning an upbeat tone.

"I thought bare feet were not allowed in an exclusive hotel like this one!" Although his nimble remark is accompanied by his signature smile, a slight discordant stammer is evident. The door begins to close, finished with its business, ready to resume its journey, indifferent to human pretense.

Walt, however, is not about to be controlled by either mechanical or human apathy. He slams his right hand against the door's edge, causing the slide to halt and back off, like a thought recapturing a poor decision in flight. Walt's other cradled palm tightens under Christine's elbow. It is a signal both to guide them out of the enclosure, and to affirm their solidarity before an adversary.

For Cameron, this precarious scenario has occurred before: other faces, other places, other similar predicaments. He is a professional, after all. Although this is a blunder, he is confident that he can resolve it. To get back on track with his plan, Cameron quickly scans his rolodex of expressions and conjures up which façade to apply. Will it be the quizzical knitted brow, the wide-eyed startled expression, the all-knowing smirk? Will any of these pretentious smokescreens hoodwink this woman? His teeth gnaw on a dumbfounded lip. This hedging needs to be addressed immediately; his tightly-knit plan is unstitching. He was never to see her again, and now here she is, in front of him, disarming him with her "I-am-so-pleased-to-see-you-again" innocuous smile.

When he doesn't react, she delicately bends her head in that charming manner of hers. Her right eye slits on an inquiring note trying to revive their morning tête-à-tête. However, there seems to be some inconsistency. She flips her head attempting to shoo away that impetuous fly of irregularity, which fans her insecurity. She straightens her spine to regain the courage to appear as a woman who has the fortitude to handle any situation. Taking the reins of this runaway wagon, she believes she has the remedy.

"I'm sorry for being remiss," she enunciates as if the perfect hostess. "Let me make introductions. Walt, this is…this is…" But, she halts in mid-sentence after snagging the grimace on Walt's face.

The stranger swallows, but quickly saves her incomplete introduction by chiming in: "Cameron Dawson…Cameron Dawson." His voice trails from a positive to a punctuated lilt as he snatches Walt's irritation. Actually, Walt is the true recipient of Cameron's capricious reception, for Cameron needs feedback from this unexpected assembly—and feedback is not happening because Walt averts his eyes to the flowered rug, then raises his head and throws a dagger-like stare at Cameron.

Christine does not miss this exchange. Although she tries to deny Walt's rudeness, she mumbles.

"Yes…yes…that's true…Cameron Dawson." She braces herself, forever a woman of grace, attempting to retrieve a semblance of politeness. "Mr. Dawson sat next to us last night at the concert…and…I met him again this morning in the café."

She peers at Walt in a what-the-hell-is-the-matter-with-you stare. Trying to shake him out of his stupor, she drives with a poignant sting. "You remember…when I was looking for you…earlier!" Walt turns away and resumes his examination of the carpet. Christine composes herself and says in a more cordial tone, "That's when I met Mr. Dawson."

The silent interchange between both men is stiffening. In a faltering voice she gropes to make whatever this underlying indiscretion right again.

"Mr. Dawson, this is Walt Mitchell, a good friend of mine." She punches the word 'friend' to imply that they are nothing more than that: friends, just a friend. Her encounters with this stranger earlier have developed into a desire to know him better, and she is not about to ruin that possibility. Punching her words, she clarifies her relationship further.

"Walt is an old friend who knows how much I like music, so he escorted me to the concert." She realizes that she is rambling, grappling for words to extend the conversation since no one else seems to be engaging in it.

Cameron is uneasy too, for he is missing vital information. An immediate concern is why Walt is so mum. He watched them from his balcony where he assumed his directives were being followed. But now, he is not so sure about that. He cannot read Walt's expression. If those directives were not implemented on the beach, and the plan compromised, then he must get it back on course immediately. He must risk some transparency, so, he glares at Walt and sharply asks, "Did you tell her?"

Walt abandons the carpet and barks at Cameron, "Shut up!"

Christine's pallor bleeds. Walt's tone has finally thrown her. "Walt?"

But Walt continues to glower at Cameron.

Christine is confused. "What is the matter with you?" Although her question is emphatic, Walt still does not move.

"Walt, tell me 'WHAT'!" Christine studies Walt's face. His deadpan expression has been cultivated during the edgiest poker moments, and she knows that an answer will never come from Walt first. She swiftly turns to Cameron. "...Tell her 'WHAT'?" she says, repeating his own words.

Cameron surmises that Christine is still in the dark and that Walt might be having second thoughts. He must control the damages now! Too much is at stake. Blatantly ignoring her question, Cameron attempts to pull back on the harsh tone to divert the conversation. With an incongruent gesture, he extends his hand toward Walt.

"Yes, I do remember you. Sorry, I seem to have confused you with someone else." Cameron continues this exchange with cordial affirmation, "And how did you two enjoy the concert?" This, of course, is a question completely out of place. Yet, it jolts Walt from his zombie state. Altering his demeanor with exaggerated bravado, he punctuates his response.

"We enjoyed it very much."

Letting go of Christine's arm, he extends his right hand toward Cameron in a seditious shake of truce.

Christine's eyes widen. She glares at Walt who holds onto his matter-of-fact expression, making sure he doesn't look at her.

If some passerby had witnessed this last exchange, they would have given it only casual attention. But Cameron cannot be that blasé. Walt is obviously disgruntled, and Christine appears not only baffled, but peeved. His plan is being ravaged by this unforeseen moment that can no longer disguise the terrifying hook from this unsuspecting catch. Christine is not biting the line. Cameron lingers in the subversion of truth. He smiles his infamous smile, and stares into her questioning eyes to stoke the early morning candor and expectation of a promised Saturday. Unfortunately, he is outclassed by her astute eyesight as she detects the suitcase next to him. Christine realizes Saturday was just another ploy from another disingenuous lover.

The stranger studies her face. He compares it to the one that was so alluring in the early morning light. He recalls that woman. The moist lips were full and ruby, inviting a kiss. But, before him now he watches a different woman, her lower lip protruding and quivering. He accepts his role in those tense lips. He wants to look away from her, but cannot. He wants to gently bend over those puckered lips and tenderly kiss the quivering away. Her flawless complexion was fair and full of life this morning; now it is ashen. He reminds himself how her cheeks blushed as he flirted with her across the table, how he had wanted to brush the wisps of reddish hair back from her face and touch those flushed cheeks. Now, under the harsh light of the elevator corridor, the crevices around her eyes have deepened, tugging her lids in repentant shifts as they grapple for answers to unspeakable questions.

As this paradox links the two moments of time, he sinks deeper in love with her. Unfortunately, she now stands at the apex of an unforgiving triangle completed by these two men: the sentries of her future. Cameron must contend with Walt, whose betrayal will leave the deepest scar. She scans Cameron's face, and then twists her neck to view Walt's, and both men immediately know that she has caught onto the duplicity. With a desperate denial of truth, she shakes her head in disbelief as she feels a pinch on her upper right arm. A quick rivulet of fire burns up her limb and into the deepest recesses of her eyes. Her last sight is that of four outstretched arms reaching toward her as she sinks into the darkness.

II

SHE DRIFTS DOWNWARD into Alice's rabbit hole. It is a crater of passages of time where doors remain ajar and boxes beg to be uncovered—doors she had refused to open and boxes into which she dared not peek. It was thirty something years ago in grandma's kitchen when the older man bent over the young child, chastising her with his insidious whispers…

Grandma's kitchen had a homey presence with abundant sunlight and walls papered in petite spring flowers and watering cans. It was also a place of dualities, comfortable with an undercurrent of neglect. So, it was with the diminutive child and the titanic man. The two were like the insignificant refrigerator in the corner of the room, overpowered by the massive wooden credenza that hovered beside it. The fridge had a slight tilt giving it an abandoned appearance; for all practical purposes it was just something to be taken for granted, much like the young girl. It was not that the child could not be seen, it was just that few cared about goings-on involving a child. Sight was filtered through adult eyes, like the sunlight that filtered through the sheer kitchen curtains that hung from large double-paned windows. Objects and forms could obviously be identified, like the credenza, just sometimes their worth became obscured. Duality unfolded in other ways, as well.

One curtained window, which brought too much warmth during summer, hung above a raucous radiator, which remained coldly unreliable throughout winter. And then there was the small backyard porch just off the kitchen. During warm evenings the family would retire there, clutching coffee cups like security blankets, and drift in idle discourse. Memories rose within the ephemeral cigar smoke and dissipated into the distance of the night, lost forever. But sometimes memories would remain, lodged in the fabric of the kitchen like distinctive aromas or tainted yellowing on the sheer curtains. Over the deep porcelain washbasin was the other double-paned window. Its sheer curtain would flutter nervously whenever the window was cracked open, the breeze a welcome relief when preparing meals or washing dishes. The deep sink was where her mother would bath the toddler. Invariably, as her mother washed the child's hair, came the familiar comment, "Such red hair…the neighbors will think you belong to the milk man!" The inference was beyond the young child's grasp at that time, but the color of her hair would become quite significant later in her life. Such moments within the soapy caresses of her mother's hands were endearing, yet ephemeral, for the toddler outgrew the basin washings just prior to her mother's demise.

Yes, grandma's kitchen was a time capsule in duality, a passage of the loss of childhood defied on the day of her eighth birthday. As the older man continued his guarded whispers, he tightened his grip on the young girl's forearm.

Because it was her special day, Grandma allowed her to dress in whatever she wanted. The party would not begin until later that afternoon when grandma invited a couple of distant relatives and neighbors to show up for a bite to eat, a grown-up drink, and a slice of birthday cake. It would really be a gathering for adults even though it was her birthday. After her mother died, the youngster's attachments dwindled. Her grandma handled the household chores, leaving little time for mothering. Her father remained distant, trying to come to terms with his wife's death. Uncle was the only one who tried to keep an upbeat atmosphere in the grave house. And then there was Walt, Uncle's son and her best friend—her only friend.

So, on her eighth birthday, to fortify her diminutive stature among the crowd, she outfitted herself in her tomboy Western style gear, not the usual garb for suburban New Jersey young females. But she had an affinity for Western films, and often would emulate the rugged good guys in those Westerns. She might not have owned a white cowboy hat, but she still epitomized virtue over evil. She was fastidious in how she portrayed her heroes. Her stiff blue jeans might have been faded, but the fashionable red plaid cuffs were neatly turned up, the rawhide belt ensuring they would not fall off her slim waist. Furthermore, so that the jeans would not sag, she would tuck the Western shirt snugly into the waistline. Keeping the neckline open by unsnapping the top two buttons gave her a sassy cowgirl flair. The rolled colorful bandana tied to one side of her neck added the final touch. Her body was still innocently proportioned. However, it was a frame that would develop into a voluptuous beauty someday when the snap buttons would stretch apart over fuller breasts, and the slim waist would become alluringly accentuated by shapely hips.

The older man, always near her, was her father's wartime buddy. And, because he was considered family, he often sat in the kitchen, the heart of this massive two-family house. It was really grandma's house, but the girl lived with her dad on the second level. She loved her father, of course, but she adored her father's friend, whom she was told to address as Uncle even though he was not kin. She trusted him as if he was family. He would entertain her with his jokes and magic hand tricks; she knew that she was his favorite because he even had a special name for her, Smooch.

She loved being in Uncle's presence. She would observe his mannerisms as he weaved his anecdotes of conquest. The storytelling was even better entertainment than watching TV. Listening to the salacious vernacular of the adults introduced the young innocent to a world of stimulating adventures as well as the spicy language. Childhood became a time of imagination without limits. It was supposed to be a time for a child to frolic though piles of crisp autumn leaves and fling handfuls skyward toward unreachable clouds, and then to collapse onto the innocuous foliage. That would be the natural order of growing up. Unfortunately, she was exposed to other unsettling developments.

Her eyes would move from speaker to speaker, hypnotized by the dance of the discussion. And in the fray, at the pinnacle of the punch line, "…And then he unzippers his…" Uncle would suddenly stop in mid-sentence, aware of the wide-eyed young girl gaping at him. Her father would immediately reassure his friend with an offhand flick of his wrist, "Oh, she's too young to know…it's okay…just go on. What happened next?" And the storyteller would resume his tale with more embellishments and exaggerated gestures. She loved these moments. She giggled over how silly he looked, and he would turn and giggle with her. These stories were about human conquests and human frailties, delivered in unabashed truthfulness. And if she was too young to understand the off-color content, she certainly understood at least that much. It was a truth which would draw her into its mirage later on in life.

"But I want to see what's in the box!" she blared out in childish temperament. Uncle was shocked. She had never been so mulish, and the remark was not only abrasive to him but quite embarrassing to her father, who seldom had to reprimand her. She was a child who never disrespected his wishes or challenged any adult for that matter.

In the center of the grandma's large kitchen sat the eight-year-old girl, her father, and Uncle. Uncle's son was off to the side, slouching against the refrigerator, as forlorn as it was. There was a dour pall over the scene. Grandma hadn't noticed any of it because she was getting preparations ready for later that day. In fact, the only indication of a forthcoming celebration was the twelve-inch square box with silky red ribbon placed in the center of the table. It was, however, unreachable. And, in spite of this birthday gift, the girl was out of sorts, quite unlike her usual sweet demeanor.

Uncle just bent over the unruly child emitting strings of whispers into her ear so low to make sure no one would know what was being said.

"But I want to see what is in the box!" she was insistent in trespassing beyond tolerance and leaned across the kitchen table to grab it. Even her father's subtle, unmistakable glances would not quell her doggedness. The enclosed box was her birthday gift from Uncle, who now was noticeably irritated. Finally, banging his fist, he snatched the box off the kitchen table and placed it on top of the tall wooden credenza, a blatant statement that its surprise was to be beyond her reach for now, perhaps forever. However, the truth of the matter was that box was beyond her reach even before the day of her eighth birthday.

She was aware of behaving badly, talking in a manner similar to that of his son. The difference was that she was always considered the "good" child, not at all like Walt, the "bad seed." Uncle's son was so bad that his reputation exceeded the word "notorious." He was so bad that all the neighborhood dogs would cringe whenever he crossed their path. It was one strange sight to see the "big, bad, and ugly," be it man or beast, cower before this eight-year-old skinny chap, Walt.

It must be understood that his father, the man she affectionately called "Uncle," was not a bitter man. He just wanted his son to be a disciplined boy who would not grow up to be like the very monsters he had fought in the war, "those undesirable elements," he would often declare, "who would ruin the very fabric of American society!" So, his wayward lad had to be taught how to behave, and that often involved his father's belt.

The girl cringed when she heard the phrase, "I'm getting my belt!" Uncle never said this as an idle threat. He always followed through. His justification was that it was his duty as a father to whip the boy into shape. The girl, however, never understood this manner of discipline. It seemed too harsh, barbaric, and most of the time unwarranted. She liked Walt…liked him a lot. She was able to see a side of him that no one else saw, especially his father.

While their fathers engaged in repetitive reminiscing, relentless poker games, and drinking binges, Walt and she spent time together, engaged in activities that brought out the best not only in him, but also in her. They learned to appreciate each other's hidden talents, and to appreciate themselves.

She liked those moments best when they would retreat to the attic of grandma's house, far away from the adult world. The house was old, and the contents in the attic were richly primal and propitious to two curious children. The attic was the storage area for grandma's family heritage. There were histories of generations lying beneath spider webs and years of pristine dust. It was a land of the lost and forgotten. It was here that the children reverently opened heavily belted chests and sagging boxes and explored the multitude of treasures, which only young eyes could envision. There were chests with an array of pastel Easter bonnets netted in veils and sequins. They would wear them sumptuously with the imitation furs in "let's pretend" scripts, composed out of the webs and dust. Walt would place a bonnet on his head and prance about in some alluring wiggle. He didn't make a beautiful woman, but he made up for his clumsiness with his sweet melodic falsetto voice. It was first class entertainment!

Then there were the piles of boxes that held assorted postcards and black and white photographs with strange names and addresses, the images so remote that they took on a ghostly quality. It was the war photographs that captivated the girl. She would peer at them, mesmerized by their hidden stories, trying to connect how the distant lands had emboldened the bare-chested young men to pose in cocky stances. And when she would look up from these glossy photos, she would find Walt staring intensely at her.

And, of course, there was all the "stuff" scattered in disarray throughout the attic, nameless objects that to children were wonderful things. There were long, twisting wired things, and metal hooking things, and rusted flat sheet things, sometimes punctured with holes that lined up in strange patterns. They would collect this "stuff" like wandering prehistoric gatherers and construct great inventions and masterpieces. The magic of the attic with its low ceiling was the perfect place for a child to stand up in, both literally and figuratively. It became the place that forged the fabric of not only who they were, but who they would become as they moved through the minutes there with unabashed and saturated wonder.

A kind of brotherhood and sisterhood emerged between them. Although only a child she was committed in her love for him, not a sexual love, after all, he was her best friend. Although, there was a moment in her early teenage years, when she saw Walt not as a young boy, but a young boy in a man's body. He had stayed overnight, not an unusual occurrence. They had done this ritual ever since childhood when it was just more convenient for their parents to have them sleep over during nightly poker games. The parents would imbibe copious amounts of alcohol and carouse to the wee hours of the morning. The children slept in one of their parents' beds until they would finally "call it a night" and retrieve them to be taken back home. The kids always slept in the same bed because, being so young, they were too scared to sleep alone. It was a time when they would talk quietly for hours about whatever came into their heads. It was a time of innocence; it was a time of eight-year-olds.

However, as teenagers, something changed. They had been hanging out in the privacy of the girl's tulip bedroom, lounging in their pajamas, as always, talking endless talks about what they wanted to be when they were all grown, when she realized something was out of place. Walt was not talking, nor for that matter was he listening. He just stared at her, and not at her face; he was staring at her chest. "How odd!" she thought, and glancing downward, saw that her pajama buttons had come undone and that one very developed breast was sticking out—the nipple a directional signal. In an unassuming movement, she drew her pillow across her body and pressed it firmly against her chest, cradling it like a baby doll. And that was the end of it. They never spoke about the incident. It was whisked away like some fleeting thought. Yet, she recalled the arousal she felt from a boy's stare. It was the first time that she knew that she was attractive, that she was a woman. This moment became the prelude to her first sexual encounter with another chap the following summer. However, when Walt glared at her in her tulip bedroom, he was probably remembering the incident of her eighth birthday. Her obnoxious behavior over what was in the birthday box was not because "all children are born unruly and need to be disciplined," the principle upon which Walt's father based his parenting skills. It was the residue of what had occurred the night before, the night Walt was recalling as he glared at her breast eight years later…

The night before her eighth birthday there had been one of the nightly games of cards held in grandma's house. Walt's father was visiting as grandma prepared the ongoing funnel of food for the evening. As always, Walt and she were to sleep in grandma's bedroom at the end of the hall so that they wouldn't be too far away to be checked on, yet, far enough not to interfere with the night's grownup activities. Although they were only down the hall, they were close enough to hear the voices becoming louder as the grandfather clock pinged out the late-night hours. Apparently, there was more drinking than usual, indicated by the escalating commotion. The voices also seemed more unruly than usual. Walt's father bellowed in some hopeless whine that held a hint of aggression. He was probably losing heavily, and drinking heavily, too. Her father was winning because he seemed to be more upbeat and taunting.

Struggling over the faint-hearted attempts to sleep through these sporadic outbursts, Walt and she resigned to stay awake. Actually, they were quite satisfied doing that. Lying next to each other on grandma's double bed was peaceful. They stared into the darkness of the room, watching shadows dance on the walls from flickering moonlight that weaved through branches outside the windowpanes. As they viewed the dance, lying on their backs, they conversed quietly about how they would never grow up to be like their parents; they would be different. They would look for all that was beautiful in the world and embrace all that was good and natural. They promised to defend "Truth and the American Way" together, just like the good guys in the Westerns. Yet, with each sudden outburst from the kitchen down the hall, their bodies quivered in unsettling response. And with each quake, their resolve was shaken by the thought that perhaps they lacked the courage to fulfill such promises and sank into a resignation of silence.

Suddenly, there was a jarring, intruding rattle from the direction of the bedroom doorknob. It was one of the parents coming to check up on them, probably to see if they were asleep. It was late, very late. They should be asleep. If they weren't, there would certainly be some form of reprimand. They were eight-year-olds with vivid imaginations. Their worst fear was that it would be Walt's father. If he found them awake, she, of course, would be released from any scolding, but Walt's father would unleash a fury of wrath on his son. How unfair it was that Walt would take the brunt of the punishment for both their sins. So, to save him from such a fate, Walt and she had developed their skills at playing possum, pretending they were sleeping, hoping to ward off any confrontation. They pulled the sheet up to their chins, lay on their backs, and remained very, very still.

The door opened and closed. They heard the clink of it being locked. Walt grabbed her hand in his, welding them together by their conjoining hands and hips. She felt the intertwined pressure of fingers. Even from across the room the reek of alcohol and sweat was nauseating. The labored breathing was that of a man so drunk that he stumbled shamefully around the furniture through the darkness, clawing his way toward them. Her eyes slivered and fixated on the bulky shadow swerving within the layers of darkness. When he bumped the edge of the bed frame and wheezed a muffled curse, she squeezed them shut so tightly that her temples began to pulsate. Her stomach twittered. She commanded it to stop shivering; it obeyed out of fright. The only understanding of what was happening to Walt was the degree of pressure from his hand under the covers. His fingers tightened, conveying that the intruder was indeed his father. If Walt's pretended sleep was discovered, he would certainly get the belt. She knew what that meant. She had seen too often the wrath of Uncle's whippings. And had witnessed Walt's reaction. Walt refused to cry. He would not even give out a slight whimper but stood in expressionless resolution. The more unflinchingly Walt would stand, the more Uncle would bring down the belt, harder and harder, trying to break his son. Finally, from sheer exhaustion, Uncle would stop; not one tear would trickle down Walt's cheek. So, when she realized that this was not only Walt's father, but Walt's drunken father swaggering in a volatile state on the brink of unleashed fury, she plunged deeper into the mattress, apprehensive over Walt's fate. Walt might get hurt. He might get hurt very badly from a hand that could not control itself.

Although her eyes were still cemented shut, she sensed Uncle's closeness, felt each putrid whisk of breath against her cheeks. He was very close to her face. The bed sank sideways, and she tensed so as not to drift into the tilt. There was a pause. There was no movement within the hollow room. Her body flushed with panic, and she wasn't sure whether or not she still was visible. She remained paralyzed. Nothing happened for a while. Then she felt the sheet that covered her to her chin begin to slide away. It slipped into a bunch on her left side, the side on which Walt lay. The bunched-up sheet concealed Walt's clutching, frozen palm. She felt Uncle's cold, clammy hand move under the waistband of her pajama pants and rest on her tummy. It slithered downward. His palm rubbed over her thighs a few times, then moved upward. His cold fingers wiggled over her pee-pee. He pressed his fingers harder against her. He began to sway back and forth and pressed harder, vigorously rubbing her. Her eyes flicked open. His broad back was to her; it moved like a snake, swaying from side to side. His breathing was louder, like some laboring machine. The pressure of Uncle's fingers and Walt's intertwining fingers built with the same intensity. Finally, Uncle graveled a low breathy growl, which seemed to suspend in the air. His body seemed to deflate, and he collapsed forward over his lap. He didn't move for some time. *Was he dead?* He moved back his fingers, sliding his palm over her belly in reverse, like a wave tenderly retreating from the shoreline under the folds of a returning ocean. After a few moments, he shifted about and rose off the bed. He stood straight above her. He saw that her eyes were open as she gazed back at him. He continued to look indifferently but didn't speak. He turned, walked to the door, unlocked it without looking back, and left the room, closing it quietly behind him.

She couldn't move. Walt's hand was so tight that her fingers were numb. Then deep inside, her stomach wobbled, like jello, from some distant vibration. The tingle dilated outward into ripples in a pond, which became waves with sharp crests that seethe into violent gesticulations, and her body shook in an uncontrollable seizure. She didn't know what had just happened, but she felt she had done something terribly wrong, that she should not be allowed to ever breathe again, as if somehow, we can control breath!

Walt turned and wrapped his arms around her body, holding her tightly. He whispered in a cracking voice, "It's okay, Chris...You're okay, Chris...It's okay...I'm here." His voice was so calming that he was drawing her into a trance. She began to lose all sensation of feeling, as if her body was losing its weight. She became a feather drifting off the bed, moving into the light shadows on the wall, dancing in the darkness. The shadows finally melted into black, and she did, too...

And so, that following morning, she sat next to the blurry eyed man, who leaned into her ear and whispered a sizzling string of words. But they seemed to be foreign words; she could not make out their meaning. And in her confusion, he gripped her forearm and squeezed his palm harder, digging his fingernails into her skin. She did not move away. She did not even flinch. Even though she knew there had to be pain she did not feel anything.

After tossing the box high upon the top of the credenza, he stamped to the massive kitchen sink. He placed both hands firmly on the edges of the porcelain in a grip that reddened his knuckles and stared out the glass panes over the basin. The morning rays of sun steamed through the double hung windows and illuminated the beads of sweat on his forehead. He hunched over it as if he was about to be sick. No one moved. Suddenly, Uncle whirled around with indifferent eyes, the same indifferent eyes she had seen the prior night in grandma's bedroom. But his apathetic stance quickly changed. He raised an aggressively pointed finger in her direction. Uncle was about to eject his reprimand at her when he was suddenly cut off by the unexpected. Like Saint George slaying the dragon, Walt blurted out, "Leave her alone!" With a little more hesitation, he stammered, "Just leave her alone!" The two glared at each other, father and son, in some final standoff. Tears welled in Walt's eyes, "Leave her alone, or else I'll tell."

The moment expanded into deafening stillness. She suspected that is when she finally stopped breathing, even though she remained alive for the rest of her life. From that very moment, the two young comrades shared the residue of that moment, never to be far apart from each other. That was the only time she ever saw a tear on Walt's cheek.

To break the strange tension, grandma perked up with, "It's your birthday…let's forget about this…whatever it is. Let me get my camera…I want to get a picture of all of you before everyone gets here for the party. I'll be too busy later on to get a good picture." And with that she opened the credenza and extracted the black box camera from the drawer. She directed them to move in closer to set up the shot. Christine sat to the right of the table; Walt stood behind her, placing his hand on her shoulder. Her father stood behind the table, in the center in the vacant space, alone as he was for much of the rest of his life. After some coaxing from grandma and her father, Uncle shuffled over to the left side of the table, remote from the rest, slumped in the chair. When the picture was snapped, it captured him looking away from everyone, his chin cradled in his closed fist.

I never found out what was in that birthday box that was placed on top of the credenza by Uncle. Somehow it didn't matter anymore. In fact, I'm not sure if Walt and his father spoke any meaningful words to each other ever again. If they did, their communication was brief or only a series of grunts or nods. Uncle died within the year, and Walt had to learn to raise himself. This time to be disciplined by "the code of the streets." He was not totally abandoned, for he lived with us until he was legally old enough to be on his own. During this time, he learned how to skillfully play poker, drink excessively, carouse with hoodlums, and develop the fine art of wooing the gentler sex. In some ways, he had become the very man he had despised: his father. I guess that it is true that the sins of the father are passed onto the son…

When grandma snapped that photograph, I instantly snapped the memory of the incident from my mind, until decades later when Walt and I, as adults, sauntered along the Jersey shoreline in the early morning after the night of the concert.

III

WHEN I FINALLY SEE LIGHT, it is only a sliver as I climb out of Alice's hole. It is like emerging through the folding shutters inside the black box of a camera. I blink. Seeping through the aperture there appear more slivers of light, perhaps moonlight slithering through blinds in a blackened space. I blink again. The highlighted crevices form slats of shadowy bars as in a jail cell. This seems to be the only light source. Otherwise, I am entombed in blinding darkness. I command my eyes to remain open. *Where am I? Why am I here? What time is it?* These are the questions sizzling in through those shafts of moonlight. I dare not move until my eyesight becomes acclimated to the dimness.

Slowly I make out the contours of a room. The shapes are recognizable: the defined edge of a corner wall, the bureau with the high console which holds a DVD player. Yes, I know this room…it is my hotel room. In the stillness swishes the familiar white noise of ocean waves crashing in the short distance beyond, a confirmation of my whereabouts. My breathing becomes more regular. However, there is a ping of incongruity. My feminine sense of survival cautions me not to be so confident. "Whereabouts" has been resolved, yet the "when" and the "why" remain to be unraveled.

Suddenly, I know that I am not alone. It is only a slight stirring, almost imperceptible unless I concentrate on it. Yes, something is definitely inside the room. It is the sound of breathing, deep breathing, like that of an animal killing time with a hushed pant. But this is no animal; it is the rasping of a man. It could be Walt. But I am not sure. Should I confront whoever is here, or I play possum until I know more? I am no longer that small child who has to surrender to veiled assumptions. *Try, Christine, to remember how you got here.* I recall a hotel elevator. I remember elongated arms pulsating toward me as I sunk into the rabbit hole. Yes, something was definitely wrong at that elevator, and something is definitely wrong now. I want to believe that the truth is not clouded in some insanity. *Is this my insanity?* My body shivers with that possibility, and I cannot command it to be still. The bed's restless creaking gives away my presence. I can no longer play possum.

"So, you finally have awakened."

I'd hoped it would be Walt's voice. It isn't.

"Who's there?" I try to forcibly confront the specter in the darkness, but no reply resounds from the dimness. "Who are you?" I embolden my words even more for I know who it is not, and I am a seasoned woman who no longer will be intimidated by a charade. I have encountered a ghost like this before, one that a seasoned woman fears, the ghost of the unknown. *Chris, you're losing it! Get it together, girl!* Forbidden questions return. Why is Walt not here protecting me? Have I been abandoned again? My stomach wrenches. I speak up even more emphatically than before. "I want to know where Walt is! Answer me…now!"

"He's on an errand." Within the darkness the brooding cobra is in striking distance, probably looming upon the very chair on which Walt had slouched before our morning talk on the beach. I squirm. *Is it the same day as this morning? Certainly, it is now nighttime, but what time of night, what day? And why am I in this vulnerable state, lying on my back in my hotel bed?* The questions vomit inside my head as I try to ignore the possible answers spewing closer to the surface. *Walt was on an errand for this unknown voice. The voice knows Walt. How does Walt know him?*

Slivers of moonlight continue to pierce the darkness. In the rays I recall two anxious men by an elevator facing each other in some posturing inane banter. An afterglow shadows the reason for their awkward behavior. Certainly, a predisposed gambit was already in play prior to that encounter. One man by the elevator was Walt, the other a voice in the dimness. Yes, I now know this ghost. And I can surmise why. My present compromised situation must be connected to Walt's warped ramblings on the beach...something to do with some concocted notion that the right man would be the antidote for my nightmares. *Is this the man Walt had in mind? Is Walt trying to set me up?* Walt is fucking crazy! When I get my hands on him...I'm going to...But, then again, where the fuck is Walt? Oh, forget it, Chris! Wherever he is I am going to put a stop to this, now!

"Look, Cameron, I don't know what arrangement you and Walt made, but I will have no part of it!" My disclosure is absorbed into the anonymity of the darkness, and I fear that perhaps I have gone too far. My pretense buckles. "Why are you here? What do you want with me? I know who you are, Cameron!"

"So...you have recognized my voice."

"What do you want, Cameron?" I ask again.

He clears his throat but still does not speak, as if he is having second thoughts on what he is about to say. And in that uncertainty, I wonder if he is going to tell me the truth or compose some fabricated response.

"What is all this about, Cameron? What do you want with me?" I decide I will say nothing more until I get some answers.

He gets the message because his tone conveys that he is ready to address something of substance. "So...Walt didn't tell you when you were on the sand?"

On the sand...he had been watching us this morning. "Were you spying on Walt and me when we were by the shoreline?"

No answer.

"Why?"

Again, he delays. "I thought I would never see you again."

Thought that he would never see me, again! Now that is a strange comment. "Never see me again. Cameron, didn't we have an appointment for Saturday, or were you just playing me?" No comment. But this is too strange for me to keep silent. "And by the way, what was all that commotion by the elevator?"

"I thought that Walt changed the deal." This slithers from him with sinister overtones.

"Deal? What fucking deal?" *Could this be Walt's problem, the one he couldn't coherently talk about?* "Cameron, what does this have to do with Walt?"

"…thought he lost his nerve. But he doesn't know what scared is, yet…he'll find out soon enough." He inhales to convey a more ominous implication. "…and so…will you!"

Ancient moonlight shadows flicker on the ceiling and ghostly figures from a frayed photograph sway in provocative dances. I gasp for breath, "Oh no…not again. Not again." It is only an utterance, one that would not penetrate through any walls, but it is enough of a shriek to trigger him.

In seconds he is on top of me, like scaffolding collapsing without warning. His body drapes over me and I am helplessly pinned. His palm aggressively smothers my mouth. "Shut up…be quiet!" I struggle to be free of him. His tenor changes from aggressive to insistent, "…please, be quiet!" I realize that if I do comply, I could set up a ruse of submission, which might deter his assault. My body becomes limp and he removes his hand from my mouth. This, however, is only a deception. Like a relentless ocean wave retreating in temporary reprieve, a menacing swell dispatches to the complacent shoreline, and I sense that the stakes have just intensified. He presses his fingers over my lips and begins to sensuously glide his forefinger into my mouth. I want to breathe, but there is no more breath. My eyes flood, however, the frozen tears of memory will not permit it. As I stare into his face it becomes a blur.

He extracts his moist finger and pencils it down my throat. Spreading his fingers around my neck, he grips me in a chokehold. I dare not move! His other arm wraps around my back. He draws me into him. His probing fingers snake off my neck and slither to the center of my chest. They have their own agenda as they move under my bra. His palm cups my breast. Slowly he begins to rub my nipple with his thumb. I sink into the mire of his desire relinquishing myself under a veil of terror. His offensive hand eases off my breast and flattens out in the middle of my chest. I can feel the pump of my heart as it pulsates against him like a maddening drum of some distant tribe.

Suddenly, he withdraws his hand as if snatching back an indecisive thought. It moves to his abdomen, and I know what is about to happen. I am no longer that naive child playing possum in grandma's bedroom. I am about to become just another female rape victim. There will be no one to stop this from happening. I am that pathetic fish floundering against the violent turrets of an unforgiving fate, desperately dashing myself against the jetty, seeking refuge even if under a guise of pretense. It is a legacy that has been passed down to our daughters throughout time.

Strangely, something changes. As I brace myself for the inevitable, his body language alters. With a punctuated shove he pushes off me and quickly dissolves into darkness. I am released, tossed out from the belly of the whale muffling a pathetic, silent scream. Instinctively, I roll sideways, fling myself from the bed, and clunk onto the floor. I scurry on all fours over the knotty carpet to the nearest wall, my kneecaps burning as my sweat pants ride up above my knees. Blinded by obscurity and panic, I slam into a barrier. The abrasive stucco chafes my palms as I haul my body upright. My arms whip, frantically groping for anything I can use as a weapon. They brush against cool metal. I clutch it. I am familiar with its shape. "Shit!" It is the DVD remote. *Okay, okay, Christine, it will have to do!* And with my expletive comes a click, and brazen light flushes the room.

My eyesight returns through a film of moisture. I will not allow tears! My resolve stiffens. I scan the surroundings to find him standing by the sliding glass door. His back is to me, one arm stretched under the shade of the pole lamp. How could he still have his back to me after my commotion? He is like a fossilized redwood hardened to the calcified cries of humanity. I grip the remote so tightly that my fingers drain into weakness. I point it toward him.

He slowly turns around. He has no response, almost as if he had been stung by some wasp and the pain had not yet connected. His eyes follow down my extended arm to my hand, which is gripping the remote like some Jessie James six shooter water pistol in the O.K. Corral.

Suddenly, the Muses' hypnotic fingers snap, and he bursts into laughter. Its obtrusive vulgarity stutters in waves across the room. The mirth splinters within my spine, vibrates down my outstretched arm, and shivers into my fist. I try to grip the remote tighter to stop the wavering, but it is a grip of futility.

"You don't want to shoot me with that, do you?" he says this through his familiar crooked smile. It is a smile that once again disarms me. As his laughter mounts, he becomes the swaying snake charmer luring me from my fear of the unknown to his flute of possibilities. My attention glides down to my hand, and I peer at the remote as if I am seeing it for the first time. In that instant, I, too, catch the lunacy of the moment. I snap into a gush of nervous laughter. My hilarity swells about me making the remainder of my sensibilities disoriented. My knees buckle, and my back oozes down the stucco wall. I flop like a rag doll on the carpet, legs twisted like broken straw, convulsing into a frenzy of madness, finally releasing my corralled tears.

He saunters across the room, still chuckling, and plops down next to me. He, too, leans against the wall and our shoulders press together. The contact fuses us and fuels us back into synchronized laughter as we move like two hovering hyenas, rising and subsiding in ebbs of irrational hysteria on the edge of something beyond our understanding. Finally, the last of the lingering puffs of mistrust drain into a quiet bond of faith.

He glides his hand down my arm and gently extracts the device from my grip. Hoisting himself to his feet he replaces the remote back on the console. He looks down at me, assesses the situation, and takes a deep breath. Perhaps he does not know what to do next, or perhaps he is worried that I have lost too many marbles and might never recover. I, however, worry that he must think that my frazzled appearance is repulsive. I might have lost a few marbles, but I still pamper a few vanities as a female, even in the disheveled face of adversity. He answers my concern by extending a hand of camaraderie to affirm the ceasefire. I answer his concern as I slide my hand into his. He raises me out of the mire. We stand face to face, inches apart from the potential of our destruction or our salvation. And in this tenuous moment, the right choice can fall on either side of the line drawn in the sand.

"Well, what do you think we should do now?" His voice is still deep and resonant, yet no longer aggressive. It is certainly a question intended to ease the situation. The stakes are probably just as high now as before, but the pretense is gone. He bends close to my ear and lowers his voice to just above a whisper, "I'm sorry." I feel his breath against my neck.

I hear the sound of ocean waves kiss the shore. Questions weave within them as they tumble over each other trying to retain a semblance of distinction and coherence. But in spite of the present dance, the doubt returns. I have to know what is going on. I back away a few steps. My eyes are still on his, still steadfast, looking for answers.

"Let me ask you the first question." My voice sounds unfamiliar to me. Obviously one question will not make it, but I need to release the mounting doubt before I return to the mire. His eyes wince as he prepares for the inevitable, and I worry he will hedge his response. I must have faith, perhaps even blind faith, that he will do the right thing. He nods.

"Would you have raped me?"

"Yes." This succinct answer jolts me. I wasn't quite prepared for such raw candor.

But I would be just as terse, "So, why didn't you?"

"Perhaps I still might!" The back of my neck stiffens, and I grip my sweat jacket tighter about my torso. I examine his eyes for the truth. His smile broadens, and I ease into its charm once again. Shuffling backwards, my calves bump into the chair behind me allowing my uncertainty to collapse into a soft cushion of security. Persistent in my quest for a more complete answer I slosh deeper into the mire and repeat. "So, why didn't you?"

He mirrors my movement, shuffling backwards into his own chaise on the other side of the room. We sit in opposite corners like two prize fighters, our gazes unwavering, trying to stare each other down for some advantage. I remain mute; it is his turn to speak.

"Because…" he hesitates, "because I felt your panic."

I take a second to digest this remark. It is not a comment from a rapist, nor a response from someone who wants to remain a stranger. He pulls away from my confused eyes, scouring the vertical blinds that cover the sliding glass doors next to his chair. "I want you to believe that I would never hurt you." I take this not only as some abbreviated comment to arrest whatever might be pending, but as a committed promise to assure me about what might be forthcoming.

IV

AS I STARE AT CAMERON, processing what he just said to me, I recall another man who had said those same words to me, "You know that I will never hurt you." The juxtaposition of those exact words and their intent is uncanny. Are both men inadvertently forecasting some underlying fate for me? *And by the way, what has happened to my old friend, Walter?* If he is party to this nasty business, he will answer to me, but good! Perhaps what scares me even more is why he would place me in this situation to begin with. These thoughts converge into my next question.

"Where's Walt?"

He shot back an uneasy squint. I pick up the disapproving vibe. "As I told you, I sent him to do something for me."

My honed feminine skills smell blood. Although the answers I receive might be unforgivable, I need to shark around in these waters.

"And he knew that I was here…with you?" No response becomes a clear response. "And he left me alone with you?" Cameron still does not answer. "Why?"

His smile is a grimace intended to ward off further curiosity; it doesn't. I am not only an inquisitive woman, but also a prudent woman, one who is quite aware of the questionable situation in which she presently finds herself. If I drop the haughty tone and show this man that I am sincere about knowing the truth, maybe he will be more forthright.

"So, Cameron, even though I find you quite charming, I believe that I deserve to know why Walt left us alone."

"He left you with me," he sucked in his breath, "because he had no choice." I am taken back by his answer. This sounds a lot more foreboding than I care to hear. It is obvious that my presence with Cameron in this hotel room has something to do with Walt's problem. And I am not so sure that I want to poke into Pandora's Box anymore. I ask an arbitrary question.

"What time is it?"

He glances at his watch. "It's close to one in the morning. You've been out almost the entire day since your collapse by the elevator. That's when I realized that I had to change my plan and take charge."

Plan...*His plan!* I snatch those words and reexamine the situation. Whatever happened to Walt's plan for me, the one that was to resolve his problem by Saturday? I scan Cameron's face, realizing he is unaware that Walt was formulating a plan of his own. Even more crucially, he also does not know the grit that emboldens Walt. I do! After all, we have history, Walt and me. I decide that I will tuck Cameron's hazy feedback away until I have clearer insight into what the hell is really going on. One thing for sure, when I finally meet up with Walt, he's going to do a lot of explaining!

Cameron hunches his shoulders, a subtle suggestion that he is no longer approachable and wants to sever further discussion. Perhaps he thinks that he has said enough...or too little. I decide to switch directions.

"Look, Cameron, I'm sorry for your inconvenience...Let's talk about it tomorrow...over lunch tomorrow. So, maybe you should leave now...so that I can get some rest."

His eyes scrutinize me. "Sorry, Christine, I can't do that."

A sudden flush of alarm hits me. Something is amiss here. However, I smile and resume with a cordial tone. "Cameron, we're both very tired; let's call it a night, okay?"

Without a word, he rises from his chair and walks across the room to the door. Judiciously, he checks the bottom dead bolt and locks the top security latch, which would prevent anyone from the hallway from entering the room. Of course, this would prevent anyone from leaving within as well. I stare at the deadbolt.

"So, you are going to rape me?"

"No. I'm not going to rape you."

I stare at the deadbolt.

"Don't worry. I told you that I'm not going to harm you."

I stare at the deadbolt.

"Let's say that you are my guest...in your room...for a while."

I stare at the deadbolt.

He is kidnapping me!

Now, this is crazy, not only because I don't have the kind of money to satisfy any sufficient ransom, but because I don't even know anyone who would even care to pay any ransom for me! What in the world would be my worth? Cameron watches my reaction.

When Walt lived with us at Grandma's house after his father's death, he taught me some "street smart" tactics from the treacherous alleys of Newark where survival was guarded by cunning. "Chris," he would say, "whenever you find yourself in a bad situation, don't ever show 'em your hand!" He was, of course, using street poker vernacular, but the advice was far-reaching. So, as Cameron waits for my response, I silently mull over my options. "Chris, what would a savvy poker player say to her kidnapper?" Walt would have said that she would need to "play her hand" even if it was not a good one. "Go with what you got in your hand, Chris. Just wear your poker face and show composure. Never show 'em that you are about to crumble." I never was able to play poker very well, however, I am definitely in the preliminary stages of crumbling. But, I am not a woman without innate feminine resources. So, where could a kidnapped female retreat to within the confines of her hotel room to compose herself? Of course, the old reliable ladies' room, the very place for this wayward lady, right now!

"Cameron, is it okay if I use the bathroom?" I think that if I deliver this as a question it will not be interpreted as scheming. Apparently, no alarms are set off because Cameron nods, "Okay…" Then, he adds, for good measure, "but don't try to leave this hotel room on your way to the powder room…" and attempting to regain our former humorous connection, "or else you know I would not like to get the remote out of my holster to stop you." He pauses as he reads my concern about how dangerous a man he might be. He softens the warning. "And I don't mean my metal gun." He caps this statement with the suggestive rise of his right eyebrow.

I gracefully smile the charming smile of a female in total control, letting him know that I get his lewd comment." With feminine poise I briskly trot around the corner partition, which separates the bathroom from the rest of the room.

As soon as I switch on the bathroom light, I become unhinged. I grab the knob of the door and lock it. I don't really know why since the small room is devoid of windows or any chance of escape. He must have entertained the same thought because I hear his distant voice from the other side of the door, "I got a key!"

I keep it locked, deluding myself into an illusionary sense of safety. I stagger to the marbleized sink and peer into the vanity mirror above it. The image reflects an unrecognizable woman: fragile, lost in the confusion of this situation, a deflated woman drained from some mislaid loss in her life.

V

HE RECHECKS THE HALLWAY DOOR even though he knows it is secure. Then he nonchalantly walks to the far end of the room by the sliding glass door and sinks into the cushioned chaise, seeking a sense of consolation for his previous actions. However, the chair's wraparound armrests only provide a cold embrace; he shivers. By placing himself far away from the bathroom will he appear less threatening when she emerges? She is overcompensating for her apprehension. He has gone through this process enough to read those telltale signs of fear. However, those victims were girls, just young girls, not a woman, and certainly not a woman like this woman: poised, self-assured, accomplished. But her eyes betray her pretense. Yes, she is scared. And he was deeply moved. He had wanted to rush to her, throw himself before her, bury his face in her lap. But when she asked what had happened at the elevator, how could he tell her that he had drugged her? She definitely was making the connection between the two men. Yet, did she know all the ramifications?

It is obvious that Walt is having second thoughts in a plan that does not allow for second thoughts. Walt was to deliver her without complication, and Cameron was never to see her again. But at the elevator it was obvious the plan was coming apart at the seams, and he'd had to take charge. Of course, he was equipped with the backup needle for such a situation.

When she collapsed both Walt and he thrust forward to catch her in their arms. Together they tenderly drew her down onto the carpet. As she lay there like a delicate wilted flower, Cameron gazed into her ashen face and was overcome with regret. He had never reacted this way before. He always was able to retain a sense of distance. Walt shoved him aside, and Cameron caught him in a chokehold—years of training had cultivated this involuntary defense.

"What the fuck did you tell her?" Cameron lashed out as he squeezed harder. "What does she know?" This was more displaced frustration from his own faltering rather than Walt's incompetence.

"Let me go, man, let go! I can't breathe!"

Cameron released his grip and Walt tumbled backwards. "What did you tell her?"

Walt had not followed the instructions written unambiguously on the folded paper placed inside the playbill at Saturday night's concert. Ordinarily, Cameron did not become personally involved. But this time he wanted…no, perhaps needed…to come face to face with the package after noticing her the night before. He had to look at her again to satisfy a hunch. As the music oozed into the concert hall, Cameron could not take his eyes off her. That was when he knew for certain that this job was going to be different.

Walt daggered a chilling stare back at Cameron, recouped his wits and scurried across the carpet to Christine, cradling her in his lap. His eyes softened, his head dropped as he murmured, "Nothing…she knows nothing."

Cameron shook his head. "Then why did this shit just happen?" Cameron did not trust Walt. "Let me tell you something, buddy, you don't know with whom you are dealing. These people play rough. You better not be screwing with me because I'm the only person who will stop them from screwing with you." He looked down at Christine, "…and from screwing with her."

Suddenly, Cameron realized how easily those words flowed from him, and he felt nauseated.

Walt quivered. He stood up and gently lifted Christine. He pressed his best friend's head into his chest, and her legs dangled over his arm. "I'm bringing her back to our room."

Cameron paused to assess the situation. He knew where this was going. He knew he was about to break protocol. He shook his head in resignation and followed behind. When they entered the room, Cameron shut the sliding door vertical blinds, concealing the outside innocuous world from the insidious one inside. He turned on the pole lamp as Walt carefully placed the fragile woman onto the bed, maneuvered the pillow under her head, and removed her shoes. Then both reverently stood above her, like mourners paying respect to the dead. Somehow, they had become her guardians.

Walt was the one to speak aloud the sentiment Cameron silently echoed. "I don't think I can go along with this anymore." Cameron remained mute. Walt continued, "I must have been crazy...I must have been fuckin' crazy...what could I have been thinking... to do this to her?"

"Well, Buddy, you damn well weren't thinking...now you've got to pay..." Cameron was steaming over Walt's wavering, but he knew that he was more incensed by his own vacillation, "...we all got to pay."

Walt didn't understand the stakes. He might be an adept poker player, but he had played a bad hand. Cameron had to pick up the slack.

"Listen, Walt, I'm going to help you. Don't ask me why, because I personally think that you're a piece of shit."

Walt didn't respond; he had no more fight left. He continued to look down at Christine lying peacefully on the bed under the soft light.

Walt muttered, "I'll do anything...anything...to make it right. Call the man. I got to call it off."

Cameron placed his tongue against the inside of his upper teeth and made the familiar quick, sucking snap. "It's going to be a 'no go.' I'm tellin' you. There's more here than just the original deal. The man won't be too thrilled to hear this!"

"Hey, make the call!"

Cameron paused, then walked directly to the sliding doors and onto the balcony. He punched in the numbers on his cell.

VI

APPARENTLY, I have been in the bathroom too long, certainly an ongoing practice since I arrived in Atlantic City. Cameron is now banging on the other side of the bathroom door, even though he supposedly has a key!

"Christine! Are you okay?" This is more of an affirmation for him rather than a question by him. *I really am not okay.* "Christine, if you don't answer me, I'm coming in!" Some anxious buttons must have been blinking within this man for I can hear the thinness in his voice. I bet his distress is over the need to know if his cloak-and-dagger plan is in jeopardy, rather than any real concern for my welfare. I, however, need to stall so that I can devise my plan, which is getting the hell out of this hotel room in one piece! I holler back, "I'm going to take a shower!" That certainly sounds plausible under the circumstances. There is no immediate response. "Okay?" Toning down my audacity, I meekly ask again, "Okay?" Perhaps if I express this in a form of a permission, rather than a threat he will be satisfied enough to just go away—preferably far, far away!

Still no response. Maybe he thinks I have figured out his precious plan, and I am building up my militia in the cubical of the bathroom for a counterattack. Because he does not answer I amend my approach. I turn on the spigot in the shower as a statement that whatever frailty of woman is in this bathroom, she is in control of her own hygiene, if not her own destiny. However, when the stream of water sloshes recklessly onto the tiled floor and saturates the bottom of my sweats, I grasp the definition of "inadequacy." I punch the frosted plastic shower curtain back into the tub to catch the overflow, then throw a hotel towel onto the floor in frustration. The unrelenting insult continues as the water beads thrash senselessly against the plastic, making loud abrasive pitter patter like war drums trying to intimidate the minion. It is a sharp disparity to the silence on the other side of the door. My apprehension merges with my humiliation. If he has read such activity as something to keep me engaged for a while, he might buy into the ruse and all will be justified. He shouts back, "Okay, that will be fine…enjoy yourself!"

He bought it! I bought time.

"Enjoy myself!" Now, that's a kicker! He has a strange perception of enjoyment. This is exactly what I fancy about him because there is something strange, interestingly strange, about this man. Ever since the concert his absurd wit has beguiled my curiosity. Nevertheless, it is a new day, and I will not undermine the situation on this side of the bathroom door. The upshot, of course, is that I have no intention of undressing to get into any shower, especially with Mr. Sex-Crazed lurking so near. I stare at the door, daring it to renege on its promise of privacy. It doesn't. I decide that by allowing time to lapse, the water flow is my convenient ally, at least for now, perhaps a valuable comrade later as well.

The mist within the room is steadily thickening. My clarity becomes hazy as I stand before the door. I do not want to open it and return to the other side, not yet…not just yet. It might give me the space to unravel what has led up to this absurdity. I glance at the mirror above the expansive vanity. It is now a foggy blur. I entertain the thought that maybe I could evaporate into it and escape. That would be a wonderful absurdity! I move closer to the glass, inspecting the image to see if I still have substance, or at least, a woman still in touch with a smidgeon of sanity. I swish a section of it with the sleeve of my fleece and peer at my reflection. The deepened lines in my expression reflect the misplaced threads of condensation drizzling on the mirror's surface. I study the splintered likeness; the image fractures. Certainly, there is something very misplaced with my current situation. I have experienced this unsettling doubt before. As the pitter patter of the shower pounds against the plastic, it reiterates that thought. I drift deeper into the misty mirror to another unresolved moment not too long ago.

VII

IT WAS JUST THIS PAST WEEK when rain beads had prattled against the windowpane of my bedroom. Throughout that afternoon, I had been conscious of the constant rhythm. It was soothing, hypnotic, intimate, a moment suspended without time or place. I recall the reflection I viewed inside the pane when I stood before that window. The lines on my face commingled with rivulets from broken rain droplets. A fractured depiction of a woman stared back at me, a hint of what I had become, what I had conveniently negated for so long. I worried that he saw this misplaced woman during the heat of our passion, for I was older than he and didn't want my lover to think of me as that old.

I pull away from that memory and look back at the bathroom door. It remains mute. I try to ignore the concern of whatever tomfoolery Cameron is thinking about on the other side. Although quite aware of the importance of remaining vigilant, I am also drawn back to the distortion in the vanity mirror.

Fragmented phantoms sway within the glass like smoky whispers. I am spellbound. The images court me with a ghostly dance where screens of layered vapors crystallize and dissipate. Is there some connection between this misplaced present and that misplaced window reflection in my bedroom last week? I am standing again before the fractured window of my bedroom, however, this time I am gazing beyond it.

The rain had eased. From the bedroom window a sinking sun filtered through fine mist and drizzled over a herd of undressed saplings gracing the endless slope at the back of my townhouse. The land seemed to be slipping into the distance of the late autumn afternoon, beckoned by the Hudson River far below. All life hung in the stillness of the frail vapor. Suddenly, behind a darkened cloud, a latent sunburst invaded the serenity. It was the falling breath of light. Delirious vagrant rays threaded the wooded skewers, indecisive of appearing or disappearing. I felt that way, too. I tightened my robe and turned to face him, still contentedly dozing under ruffled bedcovers, I knew that he would hear me. "Are you awake?" I spoke loudly enough to rouse him.

He mumbled, but eventually pulled himself onto his elbows and pried his drowsy eyes open. His slightly graying hair was puffed out like hay fluff. I was amused by the scruffy man before me, so different from his usual fastidious appearance. He propped his torso higher, sliding his rear onto the scattered pillows. The blanket draped lower about his waist, slightly exposing the line of darker, coiled hair running downward on his flat belly. I could not avoid thinking how delicious he looked. He tilted his head playfully, and I raised my sight to his imploring smile. Okay, his muted grin said, you got my attention, so speak or I'm going to finish my snooze…unless you had something else in mind?

In spite of my trepidation his approachable demeanor allowed me to finally verbalize what I had been silently rehashing in front of the window. I bravely began. "You know why I like you?" His eyebrows knitted in a fortuitous leer of where this might lead. I arrested his rising desire and ignored his innuendo. "I like you because you're an interesting man." Although his suggestive grin broadened, I remained steadfast in what I wanted to discuss. "You must know that you are different from other men!"

"Huh!" His grunt became blatantly lustful. "How am I different from other men?" This time he punctuated his promiscuous response with a not-so-subtle, upward hip thrust beneath the covers.

And I could see the challenge before me, to harness this one-track-mind lover boy who was no longer a boy, but an experienced lover purposely slanting the intent of each of my comments. I had wanted a serious discussion, not a prelude to foreplay. I was attempting to hold onto something consequential in our relationship. With other lovers, inevitable partings always seemed to linger under interned uncertainties long before the actual finality of the affair. I often considered if I had only taken the initiative to address pending concerns before things got out of control, perhaps the lost loves of my life might have been rescued. My friends often reminded me that losses are only part of the game between men and women. "Just enjoy the ride, Christine, and then move on!" they would say. And for the most part, unfortunately, I had found this counsel to be true.

That would have been the end to it, except that the yoke of doubt would invariably tailgate the failed relationships and shadow the ones to come. In the past I would waver and not say anything. I assumed that whatever I said or did would have little impact to change what was destined to be. I would hesitate to speak up, and, of course, the depiction of lost lovers and their unspoken uncertainties would dissipate into other wearied afternoon rains.

However, I was convinced that this time I could ward off another loss if only the truth were spoken. I often thought of myself as the impetuous fool attempting to defy fate. So why not chance it? This time, I told myself, was different, because this man was different. He might want something more, something more substantial. He was accomplished. So, when he asked how he was different from other men, I stalled momentarily trying to prepare the right response.

After an uncomfortable silence, he grumbled, "Speak to me, Honey, or else I am going back to finish my beauty rest!" His "hot-to-trot" was quickly fizzling to "lukewarm-to-not."

I drew in a breath. "You're different from others because when we speak I feel that there is a lot of talking going on…but,…" However, as soon as the words were spoken, I knew this was the wrong approach.

He yawned. Wrong approach! "Yeah, there does seem to be a lot of talking going on…huh!" He leaned over the side of the bed and took a swig of water from a plastic bottle on the night stand. After a few moments, surprisingly, he piggybacked on my comment with a question of his own. "Yeah…yeah?"

"Oh, just forget it!" I blurted out. I don't like it when men undermine what I want to discuss; that's when I bail out.

"No, no!" He too quickly responded, attempting to soothe the inadvertent unpleasantness of which he obviously had little understanding. "I'm listening. Go on!" he prodded. He was trying to convince me that he truly wanted to rectify whatever the misdemeanor. Yet, I was wary that this was only a front to placate me. "In fact, why don't you come over here under the covers next to me, and we could talk some more." He patted the bed sheets propitiously and my misgivings were confirmed; his placating indeed had an agenda. I did not move from the window.

I often have watched grown men grovel for pleasure. In fact, I have cultivated that technique quite well over the years; it gives a tryst its timbre. However, this was not my intention. Although this type of playful repartee comes with the territory, his mischievous pouting came at an inopportune time. What I had to say was too important. I tightened my arctic stare to clearly convey that his proposition had better be moved to the back burner, and if he didn't give me some serious attention, pronto, it would be taken off the stove altogether! His sulk simmered, however his eyes wanted to barter; he wanted to negotiate a compromise. *The main course of the afternoon will be placed on hold as long as the feasting comes later.* I got it.

"Good enough!" I agreed aloud to harness further digressions for a while.

"Okay…okay," he vocalized, toning down his drool. "Now, that was talking all the time, huh? That is a feat! Yes, we do talk all the time, don't we!"

Struggling to curtail my edginess, I spoke rapidly to cut off any more of his sidetracking. "That's true. There is talking all the time. You talk to me about your daily activities all the time. You tell me how you make the sauce for lasagna...how you grow the chives in your garden...how you can determine if the wine is not quite right...or if the bed covers fit. You describe the etiquette of golf...the endurance of racket ball...the touch of fly fishing..."

"...Gee, I hope that I don't bore you all the time!" he interjected lightheartedly, perhaps to slow me down.

"No, not at all!" I steadied myself. "You know that I love listening to you!" And I meant it. I was amazed at how easily he expounded on these things with meticulous expertise and devoted passion. And I wanted to convey that as a compliment, not vacant flattery. "In fact, this is why I find you so interesting. Without a doubt, you are an accomplished man!"

"Well, this is who I am!" he boasted, conceitedly.

"Yes, I know. You tell me that, too, all the time! But..."

"But? Well, although I do like butts...I'm not fond of those kind of 'buts'."

He was diverting the discussion once again. In spite of that, I continued. "But...your accomplishments come with a condition."

"Condition...what condition?"

"...That you never push aside these activities for any man!"

"You got that right, Honey!"

"...or woman!"

He caught my quip, and then followed it with his signature pout. I was not so sure about this playful brooding anymore. I was quite aware that when a woman challenges a man's space, she is treading in precarious waters. I turned my back to him and gazed out the window.

After a pause he cut into the unresolved uncertainty. "Hey, Honey, what is it that you want to say?"

I did have something to say. I thought that by this point in my life I would have the uncertainties under control. But this man was special, and our relationship was at a crossroad. I expected the truth, not just from him, but from me as well. I looked back at him. Yes, indeed, he looked delicious. I really never liked the term 'Honey.' I let it go.

"Okay...Okay." His tone mellowed. "So, speak to me, Honey." His softened voice released what I had suppressed. I dove into the precarious waters.

"You have never asked me to join you in these activities. Do you realize that I have never actually shared in any of them with you?"

His eyes slit, digesting what I had just said, filtering some innocuous comeback. "Certainly, we do fit quite nicely with the bedcovers. A good fit, No?"

I nodded, halfheartedly. "We both know that the sex is good." This was a half-truth—my half. He never suspected; I am expert at pretending gratification. "It's the other physical involvements that are lacking."

"I'm sorry, Honey. I'll be more conscious of spending time with you in the future. I guess I have been insensitive to your needs. Sorry."

The conversation lagged. His eyes glimmered with the insidious question, 'Now?' It was a crafted inquiry of whether the time had come to retrieve the meal off the back burner!

I smiled back. *Cute, but not yet, buddy.*

He yawned in spite of his patience. More guarded, he returned to the discussion. "So, is that all?" He had deduced that the more expedient we were in resolving my agenda, the faster we would get to his.

"Well, these exposés exclude another side of us, a more 'up close and personal' side.

"Yes, I do like your 'up close, personal side,'!"

"Yes…yes, I know…I know. He grimaces. I better fan the discussion to be more upbeat, or else he will sink back into those lukewarm waters. "You often talk about what inspired you to be the person you had been. What impacts you to be the person you are now, and what you foresee for yourself in life. And I am deeply moved. This is when I feel close to you."

"Well, I do want you to know all of me!"

"But…"

"There's that 'but', again!"

"But…I don't. I don't really know you. And what's more, you don't ask about me." His perplexed eyebrows knit. "We have been seeing each other for three months, and you still are careful about how much you say to me. It's on a need-to-know basis. There are broad gaps left unsaid. You never have asked me about my past, how I feel about myself today, or what I want in the future. And the problem is… the problem is…" and indecision choked my words.

"The problem is what?"

"…the problem is that I am in love with you…and..."

I wait for him to respond; he doesn't.

My thoughts press the sides of my head…*and I don't know how I fit into the rest of your life. I have become a female of irrelevance to a man of indifference.*

I try to read his expression. Although he is staring back it is obvious that his eyes are attempting to harness any vagrant thoughts. That is when I caught the blink. It was only a fleeting tick, almost imperceptible, nonetheless, evident. And I instantly recognized that I was inside the mirage of what I wanted to be true, but never would be.

I turn my back to him, seeking the refuge of the window once again. There was so much more to say, but sometimes words must be left unsaid if it is evident that there would be no more dialogue, the unspoken dialogue usurped by a silent monologue. I gazed out the window, following the slope of the terrain as it sank into the distances of the late afternoon, But the muted words continued…

When I am excluded from sharing days with you, we lose the possibility of exploring who we could become together. I feel cheated. But you have been cheated, too, from the very best of me. By not allowing me into your life, we lost the promise of forever. It's not just about me—that I wanted more from life than I had. It's that I finally cared for someone to whom I wanted to give more of myself. As your lover, I would have been very gentle with you. You taught me how to be gentle. And I have been waiting for you to realize that I love you. But I will not wait forever, my Love, because we do not live forever.

His silence revealed the returning pangs of doubt, like sour discordant notes, teasing and provoking. Had I misread the truth again? His head had slightly drooped, fixated on something on the covers. I had seen that fixation before, and I could no longer look at him. I returned to the reflection in the window. I had crossed the line, the one that is not allowed to be crossed by a female. We were only supposed to be lovers, companions in the afternoon rain, and nothing more. The pitter patter of the rain anesthetized the uncertainty. I wanted him to reply that he loved me, too. Instead, I heard his muffled words as if from a distant drum. "I guess that I don't feel the same way as you do."

These were the words I had dared him not to speak. Now they dangled on the window, rain droplets like displaced teardrops. I placed my palm on the glass to comfort them, but they were untouchable.

"I just want to know if you would give me a chance…can you give me a chance?" I was embarrassed that my voice sounded so frail.

He whispered finality in an expired huff. "Well, I have a lot going on in my life right now."

And I had my answer. Sometimes there is more legitimacy conveyed in the falsehood of words than can be genuinely spoken. Truth only comes in the acceptance of that reality.

I turned, slipped off my robe; it dropped to the floor. Naked, I went to his bed.

Kisses flickered like sunlight weaving through a forest of saplings in the sinking afternoon. Lips were soft, warm, moist. Lovers whispered to each other in the tides of the ebbing light. The dance quickened. His fingertips glided over my body in feathery shadows, like movements in a symphony's crescendo. I became aroused. I pressed him into me and felt the cushion of spiral chest hair against my breast. We wrapped each other in ropes of arms and legs. I no longer knew where I ended and he began. Gently, he coaxed me to release any resistance that I might still harbor from any past regrets. I did. He hunched over me. And there we tangoed, endlessly, in a frenzy of lost time until the sweet nectar came for him. I remained only a paltry fraud.

When slower caresses dawdled over moist skin harsh reality returned. We would embrace each other in the consoling thought that we were lovers in the wrong time and place; you lived too far away; I lived too long. Our differences could never justify the promise of further possibilities. I was just a woman of convenience.

Tomorrow there would be the phone call from my car. Tomorrow, you would say that we had good memories. But memories would never be enough. Where would the touch of memories be in the middle of the night... the breath upon the neck...the feathery breeze from your fingertips...the rush of passion with the sweet moan of release? I suspected you always knew how this would play out. I would hold onto a thread of pride and tell you that I would never bother you again. Then I would backstep and mention that if you wanted, you could call me. I hoped that you would miss me enough to do that. Yet, in truth, I knew you never would. To bring closure to the call you would gingerly convey the soft reassurances that everything would be all right, and the concerned departing words, "Will you be safe to drive home?" In a last ditch effort to salvage the defunct love affair, I would say that I didn't know what to do. And then I would just hang up in spite of not wanting to.

I am so afraid that I will never allow myself to love. But, this, too, is duplicitous for I am old enough to know that the residue of lost relationships always lingers in subsequent ones. It is only in poker that the cards have no memory. Will I forget you? Or is it the desire for the extraordinary grace of intimacy that keeps lovers forever captive in a contrived truth?

VIII

AND THERE'S THE CONNECTION! The rain beads, which prattled against the windowpane of my bedroom, resonate in the pitter patter of this bathroom. It is the bleating threat of my demise, a female too fragile to save herself. The obtrusive echo reminds me of the pending threat on the other side of the door. I draw my mouth up against the vanity mirror and puff. My breath clouds the image; the specter evaporates into the fog.

I am aware of how oppressively warm the confined cubicle has become and that I am still wearing the sweat jacket from the beach yesterday morning. Instinctively, I pat down my fleece and dig into the pockets; the cell phone is gone. Cameron must have attended to that little detail when I was out cold on the bed. I am disheartened. My cell could have come in handy right now. The realization of my situation intensifies. *I might never return from where I am going.*

I recheck the pockets, hoping I have overlooked the obvious. In the cavities of the jacket my fingertips fidget on the jagged edges of stiff paper: grandma's kitchen photograph. Departing the sand embankment yesterday morning, Walt had trudged ahead of me, as if towed by some imaginary tether. He had made a decision on the beach, and it seemed urgent that he return to the hotel. That is when the photograph fell from his hand and I picked it up, slipping it into my fleece. I figured that I would give it back to him when we got to our room. As we shuffled over the sand I wondered if he didn't drop it on purpose, for I wasn't really sure he wanted it back. He had been the keeper of it all these years, and maybe it was time to be released from its bondage. Perhaps, he couldn't carry the burden of its memory alone anymore. I, too, understand the burden of memories.

And by the way, where is Walt? Did he split, leaving me with this stranger in a locked hotel room? Why would Walt do this? I look down at the photograph cupped in my palm. I refuse to believe that the slim eight-year-old boy in this photo, standing so resolute as my protector, would abandon me now. I do not know what this is all about. The truth is elusive. Yet, there is one aspect of this mysterious truth I understand; Walt had said it on the beach. He definitely was, and perhaps still is, in trouble.

My problem is embedded in Walt's problem. The ocean's mist of the morning had shrouded Walt's hidden agenda, which has brought me into this bathroom. Walt definitely was keeping one significant puzzle piece in his pocket—a habit of a good poker player: Never show your hand! However, I do know one thing; Walt is not here. I'd better rely on my own resources.

The sustained alliance with the shower has provided enough time for me to strengthen my frailty; further complacency will not provide endless immunity. I need answers and I don't even know the questions. I must look outside the cubical. I pin my ear against the bathroom door and coerce my willy-nilly spine to stiffen up. *Christine, it's now or never!* Timidly, I twist the door knob. It splits open. The gap widens just enough for me to slither through. Barefoot, I inch through the opening and gingerly close it. I check over my shoulder; no one will suspect that the bathroom's occupant has vanished.

Unfortunately, my getaway quickly begins to unravel when I realize that

I have no idea what to do next. In uncharted territory, I slouch in the enclosed alcove. It houses a small vanity with running lights framing its mirror. Thank God, they are not lit! Although it is nighttime, my concealment is compromised; distant illumination filters from around the corner. It casts enough visibility for me to spy the exit door to the hall and my freedom not that far away. *But, where is my assailant?* Although I do not know the whereabouts of Cameron, I hear his voice. He could be in striking distance! If I can only peer around the corner undetected, maybe I will know his proximity and devise an exit strategy. Or, then again, I could just play it safe and return to the bathroom, wait, and see what develops. After all, Cameron has basically been cordial to me, and maybe whatever is happening is some kind of misunderstanding, which we will laugh about over a cocktail. Yet, is this just another delusional desire? There isn't any other choice but to take real action! I continue my surveillance.

Bent low, I peek around the corner, my head slightly askew. I see my adversary on the other side of the balcony door. His back is to me as he leans over the balcony's iron railing. He is engrossed in some conversation on his cell phone. His voice has a professional, rigid demeanor. I am irritated that I cannot understand what he is discussing; he is audible enough. Then I realize that he is speaking in a foreign language. The intonations are not even vaguely familiar. However, in mid-sentence I snatch the isolated words, "Christine" and then "Walt."

I jerk backward. My body, like my resolve, retreats from the edge of the wall to the haven of the dim alcove. He is discussing me—but with whom? I am overwhelmed by this thought and what the unknown might suggest, and my willpower surrenders upon the plush carpet as my back presses into the wall. The structure behind me slithers as if it is an awakened monster! My heart skips! But I quickly reassure myself that this conveyor belt motion is only a sliding door to the empty confines of a coat closet. Annoyed that I was spooked, I chastise myself; I am on borrowed time. If I am to escape, then I better make my move now!

I stare at the exit door, and my anxiety, like sour bile, rises in my throat because the door, about eight feet from where I presently am cringing, is so close, yet so far away. The door is not only closed and locked, but it is secured with a double latch. These bolts would certainly take time to unfasten, as well as create who knows what commotion! Furthermore, as I fiddle by the door, I will be quite visible to Cameron if he glances back into the room. This vulnerability adds to my indecisiveness. If he catches me in the act of leaving, a blatant defiance, will he abandon all sense of control as he rushes to ward off my escape? He hinted that he had a gun. Maybe, he would try to keep me quiet in a different way. Would he become that irrational animal I had witnessed on the bed, pinning me down in an indomitable hold? Like any man, he has that potential. Would he be driven to the madness of lust in retaliation for my insolence? Like any man, he certainly would not take a woman's defiance well. Would he snuff out all breath of life, suffocating me under some possessed sexual climax? *No, get a hold of yourself, Christine! Take the chance!* Stiffening my resolve I prep myself for escape…

Suddenly, harsh pounding blasts from the other side of the entrance. The blows vibrate through my body and whip me backward, like an unexpected gale. I fall, fanny first, into the open closet. As I cower inside, I draw my knees to my chest, seeking cover. Using my exposed toes, I glide the closet door closed. I am now camouflaged in absolute darkness, entombed in real helplessness.

The banging escalates, or so it seems…could it be that in darkness, noises intensify? But the next clamor demands no further clarity. "Dawson, open up the God damn door…open the door…for Christ's sake!"

I hear the balcony door click shut, and the heavy hurried footsteps. It is Cameron trying to quickly address the racket. The latches rattle impertinently.

"Open up, Dawson!" I hear the exhausted whine of a desperate man. "It's Walt!"

My first impulse is to break out of my tomb and fling my arms around his neck. But the jarring at the door snaps my will and temporarily zaps my thinking. I don't move.

"Where is she…Where the hell is she!" I envision a frantic Walt ricocheting off the walls and furniture as he enters the room.

"She's in there." Cameron must have flicked his thumb toward the bathroom door where the steady stream of the shower continues my charade.

I am more than ready to burst from the closet because Walt is now here to rescue me, that is, until I hear him stammer, "Can she hear us…I don't want her to hear this!" I recoil further into the abyss of the closet.

"Man, you're so fuckin' concerned now…You fuckin' blew it, Man! Now I have to pick up the fuckin' pieces." Cameron's voice is callously infuriating.

"I…I know…I blew it." Walt's voice chokes in resignation.

There is a long pause. Neither speak, and there is no movement. I wait for words to follow, any words that make sense. However, the reality of those words would be deafening as Cameron tones down his voice and says, "Listen, man, get out of here, I'll watch over her 'til Saturday. You're out of the loop, man. I'll take it from here."

I stop breathing. But it is Walt's reply that finally sucks out all of my breath. "I just don't know what to do…I don't know what to do…Maybe you better take over."

Did I hear what he just said to Cameron? Walt is handing me over to this monster! This is mind-blowing! How could he! My thoughts collide in incoherent denials. *Walt's distorted problem has become my distorted problem! I am to stay kidnapped until Saturday...Saturday! And why the hell Saturday! What's happening on Saturday?*

Then as if in a second thought, Walt blasts, "And if you lay one hand on her, I'll..."

"You'll...what?" Cameron spikes back. He is apparently as disgusted with Walt's liver-bellied weakness as I am. Walt's obscene silence provokes Cameron to intensify his taunting... "You'll what? You're in no position to tell me, 'What!' And besides," he adds slyly, "I already had a handful, and all I can say is that she's up to snuff!"

It is an intentional comment to goad Walt, and it does. The outburst is violent. Bodies fling against the wall with grunts that terminate in one hard pounce onto the carpet, followed by stillness of heavy breathing.

Abrasive shrills from the room's phone drift into the pause. Finally, Cameron stops the incessant ringing.

"No...everything is all right...just a little rough housing...that's all...sorry for the disturbance...good night to you, too." The click of the phone sends a shiver through me.

Then I hear a sound from Walt, which I had never heard before, not even when his father beat him senseless with the belt. He is whimpering like a wounded animal. And as he cries, tears stream down my cheeks. I want to squeeze the hurt from him, instead, I squeeze my knees with my arms until they are numb.

"Give it up, man. You've got to let her go." Cameron's tone is now solicitous. He, too, must have been moved.

"No!" Walt aggressively snaps back.

Cameron barks at him, to snap him back to reality, "You have to...I know you saw the film!"

There is a long pause. Then, like a dying animal crying into the distances of the night, Walt vomits, "No...No...No."

"You have to...you have no choice...I've been there, man, plenty of times...I know...I've seen it happen...give her up." Cameron's voice is still commanding but now expresses empathy.

"I couldn't believe it was real; how could they do that...how can anyone do that to another human being?"

Delicately, Cameron prods, "If you care about her, give her up."

"I just need more time... to make it right," Walt pleads.

"Man, it's beyond time. Besides, you thought it was a good idea in the beginning. And it still may be."

No more words are exchanged. The heavy breathing subsides into long drawn breaths that release the moment. Time passes in silence. I hear the door open and shut. Apparently, there is only one man left in the room. He walks over to the glass door and slides it back. He probably is on the balcony again.

There is no way I can pull myself together to make it to the exit door. My will has drained from the exchange I just heard from the darkness of my coffin. I begin to hyperventilate. *I have to get out of this closet, and I have to get out of it, now!* I haphazardly shove back the sliding panel. I reopen and close the bathroom door, immediately locking it behind me. I press my back against it. The cubicle is meshed in sweltering steam as the spray continues its steady beat against the plastic curtain. I cannot see anything in the thick mist. I am disorientated.

Suddenly, there is pounding on the bathroom door; it vibrates against my backbone. I throb with it. My panic increases. If he sees I didn't take a shower, he will know I heard everything!

Pound, pound, pound…the drum beating on my back pulverizes into the…pound, pound, pound!

Then the twisting sound of the bathroom door handle begins clicking back and forth. Ancient words resound inside my head, "I have a key!" A key that is always placed above the door's ledge. The door knob is jarring in its cranking...pound, pound, pound!

*He must not know that I heard…*click, click, click! *He has a key...he'll see that I'm not wet!*

I fan my arms over my clothes, frantically, tearing them from my body; they fall onto the tile in a heap. The door clicks open as I shove myself through the slit in the curtain and immerse myself under the stream of abuse. The battering spray stains my body.

Aggressively, the shower curtain is yanked back, gripped by a clutched fist. I lift my head within the steam and turn to look at him. The water bleeds into my eyes blinding them. I squint to refocus. I am looking at Walt.

He does not move. I cannot move. We are two human beings polarized by a force that is beyond our control. Our eyes become hostages, transfixed in lost time and space. His eyes move, and I follow the path of his focus. They ride upon the rivulets of water flowing downward over my body, moving from my eyelashes, downward, over my lips, downward, over my breasts, downward, and linger intimately on me. Strangely, there is no shame. Like gentle smoke rising, his gaze returns to my eyes. His eyes want to explain, but they speak an alien tongue. He breaks from this trance and reaches for the spigot, giving a quick turn on the valve. The stream of water suddenly halts, and I, too, shut down. Removing a large towel from the rack, Walt tenderly drapes it over my shoulders and guides me out of the shower.

The tiles are cold under my soles. Chills explode up my legs, and I surrender to uncontrollable shudders. He embraces me, wrapping his arms tightly, drawing me into him. I bury my face into his chest. I hear a deep gulp within him like a moan of regret. Then Walt moves me out of the bathroom.

IX

MY FEET SHUFFLE over the plush carpet as I lean on Walt's arm. He directs me gently toward the nearest bed. My head hangs, and I see my bare legs sprinkled with beads of wetness. My feet seem so far away that I doubt they even belong to me. I sway with them in some floating dance.

Strange when you come to doubt your sanity; when vision makes the tangible translucent, and you can only focus on indiscriminate haunting; when hearing makes words stutter, and the pauses collect meanings of incongruities; when speaking only makes billows of breath that gasp into lies, lurking within mirages of truth.

This is what my reality has become: strands of lies intertwined with sinews of truth, twisting in unspeakable muscles that strangle Walt in his humanness and Cameron in his inhumanity.

I feel Walt's open palm pressing on my back through the heavy, white terrycloth towel. It hangs loosely on me as its edges kiss my thighs. I sink into his touch. It is similar to the way I touched his back when I held him in his inebriated state last night in the bathroom. Do such touches give testimony to our humanity, those invaluable touches of grace when we can no longer endure unbearable pain alone?

He releases his grip momentarily. I sit in a folded slouch. The draped towel slithers from my shoulders and bunches about my waist. He whips off his sweatshirt and slips it over my head. At such an incoherent moment I can only think how this is his favorite article of clothing, how I was harshly reprimanded last summer when I was about to wear it over my bathing suit. Now he is lifting my arms carefully within its sleeves. He grips the shirt's edges and gives a slight tug, pulling it over my bare breasts. It is damp. I shiver. He rubs my back briskly as if trying to chase away the residual chill and lingering anguish.

He scurries back into the bathroom and returns with my sweat pants, also slightly damp. Crouching in front of me, he kneels and cups each ankle, guiding them through the leg opening, first one ankle, then the other. He shimmies the sweats up to my knees. His arms surround my waist, and he lifts me off the edge of the bed, drawing me toward him. The towel slips to the floor. I am fully exposed to him. He pauses for a second, and I can hear him snivel. He yanks the pants up to my waist.

There was no shame in that second, only some intimate caress of regret from a friend taking care of another friend. This moment breaks me from my stupor, and I am finally able to look at his face. His eyes are dark and sunken. Yes, he is hurting, and I know that I have to give him the opportunity to explain what he is doing to himself and to me. But for now, the haunting incongruities need to be silenced. And this will only happen when Walt and I can talk without pretense or shame. I stand up and face him. He stands, too, directly in front of me.

"Walt, we have to talk."

A slight pause, "I know...we will...later...," then to clarify further, "...after we get some rest." He is right. We both know that we are asking for unforgiving fortitude from each other, the very fortitude obviously lacking in our present tattered state. Yet, I cannot let this go by so easily, no...not quite yet. I cannot release the thought of Walt's irreparable statement. "Walt, I need to know something right now...something that cannot be put off for later."

He stands in silence and then gives a nod.

"Would you have left me with Cameron?" The words flow from me like a string of pearls.

"Yes." The string severs, and irretrievable pearls ricochet through contradictory hallways of confirmation and disbelief, of relief and anguish, of empathy and anger.

And in the flight of the shattered pearls my fists rise up, pounding senselessly against his chest, my arms waving like frantic batons. And a resigned Walt stands staunchly, absorbing the blows. Finally, my arms become weighted and drowse lamely to my sides. My head tilts, and I press my cheek into his chest where it longs never to leave. His arms cradle me. "Do you realize, Walt, how devastated I was...how abandoned I felt?"

He strokes the top of my head with trembling fingers. "On the beach I thought everything would be okay." He stutters. "I didn't tell you everything...I realized that I made a mistake...I thought I could fix it. I've been trying to change the outcome because..."

My tears feel warm, and I try not to blink. I finish his thought, "...because of what would become of me?"

He mirrors softly. "Yes, of what would become of you." It is almost as if he is saying the words to himself. I realize that this must be what Walt has been wrestling with because he whimpers a muffled noise, an ache, followed by, "Christine, how will you ever forgive me?"

This is not a question, but a statement of apology. Yet, I am gripped by the presence of another apology, a forthcoming apology, one that Walt is still harboring, one that might be more foreboding, inexcusable, perhaps even more sinister. However, this would not be the time or place for that secret.

"Walt, take me home…I want to go home."

X

THE SCUFFLE HAD BEEN BRIEF; Cameron had easily overpowered Walt in a choke hold. Although Walt was over ten years younger and attempted to lash back, he was no match against Cameron's prowess at martial arts. Cameron's enmity intensified as he continued to vent his frustration by chafing Walt's cheeks against the nylon carpet fibers. His fury certainly could have snapped his adversary's neck like a dry twig if not for the piercing sound of the hotel's phone. The shrill ringing arrested the two into groans of labored breathing and brought Cameron back to sober thinking as he shifted his awareness to the shower beyond the alcove. It was a beacon reminding him of her presence and quelled his will to kill. Cameron released his grip. Walt collapsed and withered into a fetal position. Walt was spared.

Emotionally staid, Cameron moved toward the phone. At first, the voice was high pitched, "Sorry to call you at this time of night, but there was a complaint of loud banging coming from your room…" The female voice subsided to a lower nasal and more apologetic tone, after all, she was regretful that such a phone message had to be given in a hotel that made every effort to accommodate all its guests, even the unruly ones. "Is everything all right?" He knew how to handle this situation; he had been here before. He reassured the speaker and apologized for the disturbance. His compliance conveyed normality. He cradled the receiver with a departing click, signaling the end of the altercation as well.

Walking over the Walt's motionless body, he moved to stand next to the closet and stared at the bathroom door, unaware that she was no longer there. The noise of the shower was steady and apparently unaffected by what had just occurred. Taking deep breaths, Cameron tried to envision what was happening in the bathroom. She was probably under the stream of warm water flushing out the fear that he had instilled in her. He wanted to open the door using the emergency key that rested on the ledge above the door frame and enter the small room. He desired her. He envisioned stripping off his clothes and standing behind her in the shower, embracing her, kissing her neck, asking for forgiveness. Instead he rubbed his chin, considered his options. The spell was broken by groaning from the adjacent room. He would have to return to that potential killing field to resolve that snag. But, not yet.

He scrutinized his palms. They appeared to be stained crimson. Reddened by his altercation with Walt, or streaked from haunted slaughters?

He never touched the scalpel himself, but he was guilty. Throughout the unforgiving decades, he had tried to convince himself that it didn't matter how he felt. He had given up believing in the existence of a heaven or a hell long ago. Those delusions were for those who needed to justify their failures in the search for a forgiving God. He knew how to capitalize on those lost souls. He had blinded himself to his inhumanity. So why be moved by these two now? He thought about Walt writhing in pain. They shared a similar agony. Each had become a fragment of what a man should be, the ideals of youth dissipated into an empty vessel of a man.

Earlier in the evening, when he had stood by the balcony door, clutching the lamp, he recalled his youth. He had frightened her; she believed he was about to rape her. And he had wanted to. The moonlight had slivered through the slats like slender flames from the mission candles in the church's niche. But he could no longer relinquish affirmations of goodness, which was her; he needed to renounce evil, which was him.

XI

"DO YOU RENOUNCE SATAN and all his works?"

"I do." The congregation droned in unison. Kneeling in the side pew, Cameron bowed his head and kept silent. Even as a young altar server, he wondered if he would ever need this entity in his life, so he just kept silent. He didn't realize then, in the dark shadows of the church, that later in life he would have intimate contact with the "renounced."

This early morning Mass was always given in Italian, reflecting the ethnic profile of the Newark streets "Down Neck." And, when the affirmations were completed, he would rise from his knees and carry the vessel of Holy Water behind Monsignor, who sauntered down the aisle flicking droplets over the sparse multitude of bowed heads; heads hoping that some singular pellet of the blessed liquid would not miss them again this time. Whenever Monsignor left the altar to walk down the aisle, the congregation would twitter with anticipation, for it was understood that God was being brought to the people. The young Cameron knew that walking behind the Monsignor graced him with status, and this became his blessing. As his robe clung to his black school pants, he worried that he might trip over the clutter of the layered garment. He did not care whether or not the blessed water spilled; he cared that he might make a fool of himself and lose face. Making sure that he retained respect was a matter of neighborhood survival. At fourteen Cameron had learned how to position himself above weakness by walking in the shadow of the powerful. And Monsignor Tomas was the most powerful man in this Italian neighborhood.

How had he become the "chosen one," the monsignor's boy? Monsignor never diverged from the rituals of the Mass, and the ridged Catholic education had been ingrained into Cameron so skillfully that he knew exactly what was expected of him during each Mass ritual. His skills surpassed the other boys.

Monsignor took him under his wing, a fledgling in the inner sacristy of Monsignor's hidden world. His subtle street smarts and ear for languages allowed him to enter into clandestine dealings with Monsignor that would eventually culminate into a profession of criminality.

His early initiation into this vile profession occurred one evening after the last weekday Mass. He served this Mass alone with Monsignor. When it was over, the caretaker extinguished the candles as the parishioners trickled out. No one was left in the building except for Cameron and Monsignor. Within the dim shadows, Cameron went into the sacristy off the altar to retire his robe and tunic for tomorrow's Mass. Although it was past confession hours, the holy man had made an unscheduled arrangement with a parishioner in the confessional booth at the back of the church. At night, the high, rafted ceiling and smooth stone walls reverberated with the slightest step upon the marble floor. As he carefully adjusted his server's garments on the wooden hangers, Cameron noticed the sound of footsteps but brushed it off. It was not unusual, particularly after this Mass.

He put on his jacket, emblazoned with his school colors and embroidered Catholic school name on the upper left breast, and exited the small room. As he passed the sacristy, he quickly genuflected in a half knee bend, crossed himself absentmindedly, and walked down the long side aisle of pews toward the outside doors at the back of the arched hall. Car lights flashing from outside gave occasional life to the scenes depicted in the stained-glass windows adorning the side walls. He had memorized each Gospel scene as he drifted through the repetitive sermons he endured during the Masses he served each week. He continued his retreat, moving past the simplistic wooden relief figures portraying the Passion of Christ suspended below each window. Even their sacred morals could not penetrate his detachment. Bowing his head, he surveyed the cold marble floor, more impressed by its workmanship than the religious icons. He did not falter as he lifted his head and stared straight ahead at the confessional structure at the back of the church. It consisted of three slender doors. Over the doors tiny lights perpetually remained lit. The center door and the one to the right reflected small but distinguishable red lights over the top ledges. The door to the left had a solitary green light. Behind the right red-lighted door someone was confessing his sins and receiving penance. Monsignor, of course, would be sitting in the center cubicle.

Cameron was only a few pews from the confessional when he heard shouting from inside the booth. He recognized the Monsignor's voice, but the other man's was unfamiliar. Both voices escalated in Italian aggressiveness.

"I don't a care if yous' a man of da' cloth, yous' a no God damn good. That is a my'a son…my'a flesh and blood. He's maybe not the good of boys, but what yous' a do wis' him is a wrong…and yous' agoin' fry in a' hell."

"You listen to me, you God damn greenhorn. This is America…and I can do whatever I want to any God damn greenhorn's son!"

"Yous' make of a mistake wis' me, Padra…I was a big a' man back in a Italy…and yous'a goin' pay…and paya big."

There was silence. For too long a time, there was silence. Cameron didn't move, not because he was scared or wanted to know what would happen next; he felt that he should be available if needed. And as the events unfolded, his destiny was forged. A quick clap shadowed a sudden flash of light in the center booth, and then a thud. Although he had never witnessed someone getting shot, Cameron instantly knew who was shot and who had pulled the trigger. He remained where he was, the obedient servant. Slowly the center booth's slender door cracked open, squealing on its hinges. Monsignor skulked out of the darkness. The religious man's eyes were sunken with dark circles on an elongated face embedded with deep crevices. Those eyes captured the boldness in Cameron's. They stood there silently, peering into each other's souls, and read the dark waters from which both would drink.

Monsignor growled his orders, "Go get some cloths and holy water, get a couple of sheets from the linen closet; don't let anyone see you. Come back here immediately!"

Cameron neither spoke nor tried to reason but went about his tasks with efficiency and stealth. By the time he returned, the other door to the confessional was ajar. A distorted figure slumped in an irreverent position, his legs sprawled apart, his arms hung downwards from deformed shoulder blades. But it was the lopsided head with the wide, glassy eyes that was the most gruesome. A splattering of crimson peppered the entire interior of the confessional. The young fourteen-year-old just gave a glance and readjusted his focus to his task of eradicating all evidence that something had happened. It took both of them the entire night to restore the confessional, obliterating the remains of blood and guts using consecrated cloths and holy water, and concealing the body in white linens. Finally, the drive to the dump a couple of towns from the church brought closure.

Staying the night with Monsignor was never a problem with Cameron's uneducated parents, who would never question the integrity of such a revered man of the cloth. From that night forward, Cameron spent endless nights away from his home, taking up the cross of the dead man's son, who was no longer available for the monsignor's insidious businesses. It didn't take much time to train the new recruit to the ways of the buying of human flesh or the sale of human souls. Cameron exceeded even Monsignor's own expectations.

When Cameron quietly closed the hotel door, the bathroom shower still droned. He knew he had to leave them alone; when she finally emerged from the spray, it would be into Walt's arms that she would fall, not his. However, Cameron conceded that if she was to survive, Walt had to become the instrument of compliance. Cameron retreated from their hell; his hell awaited him on the beach just outside the hotel.

XII

PERHAPS WHEN TRANQUIL DAWN surfaced on the ocean's eastern horizon, Cameron would be able to release the disquieting thoughts of this woman. But such serenity is only afforded to those who know when to renounce evil. He unfortunately could not...not just yet. He had unfinished business on the beach. But before moving onto the sand, Cameron hesitated. Exhausted from lack of sleep and the hotel room ordeal, he was concerned that he was too impaired for discourse with his perceptive adversary.

He scans the beach. Still vacant. In the darkness the shore was cast in gray-peppered shadows, like day-old growth on a man's beard. He rubs his chin, the prickle indicating his own day's growth, measuring the passage of time. Within the last few days a different passage has taken hold on his life because of this woman. Time is no longer a commodity, nor is she. She must be placed at a safe distance from those who see her as such. That is why he has left her with Walt, who will take her home, and why he is now secluded on the beach far removed from her hotel room.

He waits by the water's edge. Under the cover of waning night, there is time to galvanize his options, or at lease to resuscitate his floundering grit before the rendezvous. Sprinting over the sand dunes, he moves closer to the shoreline, so apprehensive that he stumbles, losing his footing on the shadowy ruts. His thoughts waver before the immense, hypnotic black ocean.

He squirms his shoes deeper into the wet sand as he stares at the frail moon glimmering over the frothy white crests and receding tide. The repetitive swells were like the faltering ebbing between this woman and him. Sinister waves rise in suspended claws before griping into the next avenging surge, like the impenetrable claws of the unknown mercilessly clasping their lives.

The operation has disintegrated, and he has no solid plan to change the situation. He shivers. Pivoting his chin slightly up, he looks for solace from her balcony on the fifth floor. There is no movement. What is done, is done, and hopefully, they were gone by now. As daylight hints over the horizon, a sprinkle of lights from other hotel rooms wink at his foolishness. Cameron, alone, is left to defy the merciless claw.

"Well, Mr. Dawson, what is the status of the situation?"

The sudden intrusion jars his thoughts. Cameron camouflages his vulnerability, remaining stationary for a few seconds before responding, the sand slipping under his soles. Finally, he moves his head to address the voice.

"Hello, Jewels, nice evening for a walk on the beach…huh?" Cameron is always able to convey calm in the face of brewing tempests. He commands himself to remain composed before this man, who certainly is not like the others with whom he has dealings. He turns his back and faces the ocean— an act of defiance as well as a dodge of truth.

Jewels is not only a polished politician, but an accomplished skeptic, an attribute Cameron possesses as well. However, Jewels is also a businessman who will not take having his time wasted lightly. Cameron is aware that this small talk is an insult, and that is the very reason he engages in it now. He is vying for the upper hand against this formidable nemesis. Because Jewels is a man of perception, he immediately catches the virtual slap across the cheek. But he will not easily yield. He simply moves beyond the insurgent and stands closer to the swelling tide, a retort of dominance as well as a taciturn statement for Cameron to stop wasting his time.

Jewels should be totally out of place as he stands on the beach in his Italian black cashmere suit, but he is never a man out of place in any environment, especially the harshest ones. He moves through the world with an aura of such self-confidence that his surroundings mold around him like aerodynamic, sinuous waves. He walks through the waves of life like a graceful antelope, his body slim yet rigorous, his movements delicate yet alert, all complimented by deliberate refinement, untouched by severity. He holds a posture of a cosmopolitan gentleman who never understates his attention to detail: the 14k gold cufflinks, Cartier white diamond watch, meticulous silk pocket square, black, laced Italian alligator shoes. There was also a formidable duality to this distinguished-looking man in his fifties with tight brown curls framing the deep skin tone. His countenance is weathered in profound, defined lines that foretell grim histories and hard-pressed triumphs. It is a duality of intimidation: not just of polish, but of foreign polish, not just of wealth, but of extreme wealth, and certainly, a demeanor of not just not American, but arrogantly not American. Turning one's back on such a man and dilly-dallying with his time is an insult testing grievous ramifications. However, the implied threat from Jewels emboldens Cameron, who knows he holds the upper hand. He has what Jewels wants, or at least what Jewels believes he wants. That mirage of truth is enough.

Cameron understands that he must quickly modify the agenda for this rendezvous. It was originally scheduled for mid-morning. It is apparent from Jewels' personal presence, as well as this early arrival, that this stakeholder is eager to hasten the operation. But the original plan is unraveling, and Cameron is painfully aware that such news will not be received well by a man who believed that failure is never a matter for consideration.

In his resiliency cultivated by the Monsignor's training, Cameron composed an improvised plan. "The package is being prepared as we speak."

Although Jewels still has his back to him, Cameron catches the reflexive flutter of the cynic's shoulders.

"Is that so?" Jewels' tone is menacingly skeptical.

"I will notify you about the arrangements."

"Is that so?"

"You will be personally involved." With that, Cameron turns and walks briskly away from the water's edge and any follow-up questions, which he definitely is not prepared to answer. Just before he stepped off the sand, he looks back to scrutinize Jewels. The moonlight still shimmers under dawn's shadows. Cameron squints harder. Doubt seizes his senses. Before the glistened white froth is a questionable reality, not of a powerful intimidator, but of a ghostly figure hunched before a dominant ocean. The phantom slumps in resigned defeat. Cameron shakes off the image or its possible impact on him, leaves the scene and the ocean's portent. He has more immediate business to attend.

Prior to this trip Cameron's competency had been above reproach. The two have known each other for over twenty years. At their first meeting, Jewels immediately recognized that Cameron would be indispensable. Jewels had to prove to his father that he could someday walk in the old man's shoes. Therefore, he saw in Cameron such a man who would be able to facilitate that approval, a man resourceful in uncovering whatever was hidden, a man particular in managing whatever was supposedly insurmountable, a man unquestioning in following whatever was uncontestable. Throughout the years, Cameron had become essential to Jewels' operations. But also, Jewels foresaw that this mercenary was an unfettered truth-seeker, a romantic visionary, a modern-day noble savage. Such a person would not adhere to indisputable loyalty over a personal moral code. So, in spite of their unique business relationship, Jewels often filtered some of the delicate particulars of his life from Cameron. Certainly, the particulars surrounding Jewels' immediate urges were difficult to justify even to himself. Ironically, presently Cameron and Jewels are entering deeper into the mirage where truth can only be surmised, for both are on their own deluded quests.

Jewels' life like the flip of the cards had begun in as unpredictable a way as Cameron's. Jewels was an unknown player on the circuit. Few knew the depth of his gambling aptitude; he was the best kept secret in Pakistan, a place that frowned on such behavior. Nevertheless, he was bred on poker at an early age when his father took his young son, his only son, with him during the old man's questionable business dealings. The youth, of course, was placed safely at a nearby location under the auspices of his father's loyal, yet quite unsavory henchmen, his father's personal guard. Under their charge, Jewels spent endless hours preoccupied in card playing. These menials were both adept card sharks and unscrupulous in their methods, giving the impressionable youth unorthodox coaching in the game of bluff. To round out his education, they also exposed him to the sultry life of the opposite sex. Before Jewels had finished his teenage years, he was an apt gambler under the guidance of debauched men and a ripened lover under the tutorage of decadent women.

Yet, his father had grander plans for his son. Poker and womanizing were too frivolous for a boy in the profitable world of powerful men. Furthermore, in the old man's world, "acceptable" women were to bear more sons to secure the legacy of the family's jewels, and nothing more. This wealth and power were endowments to be passed down from a wealthy, influential father who would never allow his only son to squander such a heritage. Jewels' carefree lifestyle was quickly curtailed, his days smothered in constraints so that he could be groomed to the life that his father had designed for him.

Jewels also possessed an innate passion for life, inherited from his mother's side. He yearned for romantic love and had an unquenchable thirst for a challenge. But his father's law was immutable. Very early on in this arrangement, Jewels realized that he needed to contrive a means to appease his father's expectations and yet chart a life that addressed his own untamed desires. He was about to woo a different love: concealment. Romance was conducted under a veil of contracts, and poker under cover from his father's scrutiny. Jewels nurtured his poker acuity in the back rooms of gaming parlors with unconditional confidentiality. He surrounded himself with men who could maintain that secrecy. He matured into a daunting man leading a double life: one half carried on his father's questionable but very lucrative business, the other on his own questionable but lucrative lifestyle of loose women and unrestricted gambling.

With the sudden death of his father in the early part of this year, the winds of change placed demands on this self-indulgent son that he had not encountered before. Jewels was expected to continue his father's reign to secure stability within the tribe. Unfortunately, he had never understood that his father's power resided not from embracing the loyalty of his constituents, but from curtailing the sedition of his enemies. Treachery might not have been outwardly evident, but it was never privately extinguished. And with the demise of his father, Jewels, the playboy, had little understanding how the hounds would nip at his heels of incompetence in governance until they would weaken him enough to usurp his power.

But Jewels was not a man without sensibilities. He never missed subtlety, a language, perhaps, cultivated through the innuendos of poker, a discourse of the "poker face." In his court, duplicity was everywhere, caught in side glances and muffled in cupped whispers. Jewels had no stomach for it. This was not the existence he had envisioned for himself, especially when finally liberated from the dominance of his father. Instead of addressing the insurrection head on, Jewels reverted back to his recreational activities, ignoring the brooding storm and avoiding making major decisions. He continued in some of his father's illicit business practices, however, he was more interested in seeking out adroit competitors of the cards.

It was the event of this past month that pushed Jewels into a political decision. It would topple his house of cards and drive him into madness. The ensuing days brought him into such secluded depression that Cameron arranged for him to board his yacht for an extended journey. Cameron went ahead by plane to set up the appropriated arrangements for Jewels' arrival. He knew that Jewels needed a month at sea alone to recoup his deteriorating lucidity. Jewels, too, was aware that his vulnerability was becoming greater each day, and the vultures were drooling over his imminent downfall. It would happen either by them or by his own hand unless he could demonstrate that he was indeed his father's son. He knew how to appease them by using the tricks of his father's trade. With Lady Luck, his despondency might turn from madness to possibility. If Jewels could prove that he was a man to be reckoned with, not just to others, but to himself, he might regain his acuity. But he had to get as far away from his homeland as possible. Cameron charted the coordinates for the other side of the world, the coastal areas of Atlantic City, New Jersey, and its poker parlors.

In this early morning on the Jersey shore, Jewels wanted to finalize the operation. His early arrival was interned by gnawing angst, and disquieting uneasiness about his subordinate. Cameron's demeanor has been strangely distant since his arrival in Atlantic City. It piqued this intolerant man. However, Jewels was aware that he needed Cameron as he had always needed him, perhaps, more now than ever in his life.

The foamy white on the dark water is cold to the internal plight of the lone disbeliever as the waves continue their relentless sway. Jewels is unsettled before the immense dark seascape. He has been wounded by the onslaught of recent events. He cannot lie any longer to himself. He is merely a grain of sand in a waning world under the eyes of dubious men. The dark waters moan in consolation. How easy it is to stand on this division of life and death, a shoreline where a desperate man can contemplate his demise. He advances toward the water's edge. The sirens' chants cast their melodious pall over him, luring him to disappear forever in the wake. A renegade wave sloshes upon his black laced shoes and saturates his socks, jerking him backward. He turns and hastens from the ocean, indifferent to the vulgar shrill of the ladies' voices. But he does not leave unscathed. This is only a deceiving reprieve for a drowning man already descending under the inevitable, for even the most intimidating sovereign is humbled before the ocean's unbounded ascent.

♠ Chapter 3: The Turn ♠

The Betting Increases
Another card is placed face-up on the felt, next to the exposed flop. Four cards tease each gambler. The players are at a crossroad in the poker game. Will the bets be raised to weed out the bluffer or the faint of heart? At this point the win or loss begins.

I

THE PETITE WOMAN IS CURLED in her queen size bed, reawakening to the sensory evidence of her room. The pillow-soft mattress squeezes her into its puffiness as her favorite blanket hugs her shoulders. She returns the embrace by wrapping the light cotton around her fists tugging at it, almost as if to be reassured that it belongs to her. She is affirmed.

During the twilight of morning awakening, we drift between two worlds of being and becoming: Should we command the course of our lives and awake to forge our day, or do we relinquish ourselves to the drift of fate's hand and remain asleep until the prince's kiss? When I awake each morning, I pause and push away the impulse to rush the day. I would rather linger for a short time in my bed to ponder that very question. If wondering about the fabric of life is too heavy for a gentle morning there is something innately comforting about waking to the familiar smells, sounds, and touches that are extensions of my very being. Hence, I pause to embrace the moment and sink into the breathing of my bedroom with its clutter and histories of my life.

I open my eyes. Streams of fragile sun rays flutter over the sloping terrain of my blanket. The morning light filters through the six-paned window on the eastern wall of my townhouse. Washed in a mellow honey tint, each glass panel depicts a Native American design from the early frontier era. The legends lull me back into a gentle repose. A spike of illumination pierces through the window, demanding me to address the day. Yet I am not ready to be released from the sanctuary of sleep. I hide from the sun and bury my face into the softness of my pillow, captured in the scent of lavender. The morning light is insistent. Turning into the rays, I command my eyelids to lift. They are obstinate but eventually acquiesce.

On the wallpaper the honey sunlight glazes over the drooping yellowed daffodils scattered among golden fields of wispy straw. Presently an offensive intrusion sweeps over the straw fields and flowers with an intermittent greenish specter. I know the source. I turn my head to my nightstand where the green-eyed monster lurks; my indomitable cell phone flashes its incessant emerald signal, its black rechargeable wire snaking onto the floor. There it is, my lost cell phone! It is a reality and not a mirage. I do not recall plugging it into the outlet. An inner haunting squirms inside me. But the green light is not just an inconsequential annoyance. I twist my upper body with an unnatural reach and snatch the hard, cold intrusive mechanism, bring it within inches of my face, its message screen darting before my defiant eyes...*It's Walt*. I read no further but immediately return it to the nightstand. I am not awake enough to address his call. I rather sink back into the tranquility of my bedroom. I lie on my back gathering the blanket's edges again, wrap my arms into a pensive fold, and glower at the silent oak ceiling fan. I thought I had lost my cell phone forever, and now it is on my nightstand beckoning me to action. Walt must have recharged it. Walt must have been in my bedroom last night. Yes, the implausible nightmare must be over. I try to convince myself that I just had a bad dream and nothing more. Then, I clench my chest. I am wearing last night's sweatshirt, Walt's favorite sweatshirt, its edges still slightly damp. Last night, in fact the entire weekend, could not be a dream!

I toss the blanket back and whirl my legs down the side of the bed where they hang pathetically. Bracing for the onslaught, I straighten my backbone like a bird of prey. I try to reassemble the weird weekend. Nothing makes any sense. I'm spooked. No, numb. I sit rigidly at the side of my bed, blocking out the cell phone and its implication and seek solace inside my bedroom.

The warm honey continues to flush over every item in the room. On the side wall, scarves drape at irregular lengths from wooden pegs, retaining a sense of softness in their array of colors. I peer into the mirror on my closet door. Some woman imitates my movements. Could that woman be me? She sits in some untouchable world. I shift my head away from her and guide my attention to the oak dresser where two bisque lamps, like opposing sentries, guard each side. Their lampshades are printed with yellow humming birds singing to the approaching day. Scattered about are forlorn trinkets, reminders of distant places, experienced sometimes with friends, sometimes alone, sometimes with Walt, testimonies that I did exist somewhere at some other time.

Among the overwhelming array of photos I gravitate to one on the far left: two children hold hands in a wooded grove. The small girl is outfitted in her favorite cowboy getup. The white-brimmed cowboy hat, slightly tilted back, is a stark contrast to the scattered strands of wild red hair. Her six-shooter belt rides low on her hips, slouching to accent her courage. Her sidekick is a young boy, slightly thinner, slightly taller, slightly older. He is scantily dressed in Native American garb: A kidskin vest over a bare chest with fringed leggings and moccasins. In a full array of colorful feathers, his Indian headdress lies lopsided, wrapped around his shaggy, muddied hair, the feathers scatter in unruly directions, suggestive of whom he would become as a man. The scene was captured that afternoon when Walt wanted to seal their bond as he withdrew his pocket knife.. He asked if she could trust him. "Of course, I can!" she responded without hesitation.

"Don't be afraid," he said, placing the blade on her thumb and dragging its edge across it. The burn stung, but she refused to flinch. He did the same to his, and pressed their thumbs together "Indian style," according to Walt. They pledged to protect each other forever. It might have been only a moment in the innocence of childhood, but this alliance would test their fortitude the following night, the night before her eighth birthday.

A more recent photo frame vies for my attention: A professional photograph taken on a cruise last spring when Walt and I decided to take a break from our mundane lives and sail around some Caribbean islands for a week. I needed to detach from office chauvinistic innuendoes; Walt needed to bask in his womanizing urges. Although we boarded the ship together, we have a mutual understanding that we always allow each other space. So, I sat alone in formal dinner attire at my designated table, wearing my low-cut black dress, accessorized with small golden earrings, a gift to myself. My fingers delicately embraced the stem of a half-emptied wine glass of Pinot Grigio; the sallow gold on the earrings glint in the pale, yellow sparkling liquid. As I peered at this photo, I catch a subtlety I missed in prior viewings. My expression suggests a question about my life. Is my life fulfilling? Do I want to embrace the future? The vacant gaze and plastic smile answer.

After that photo was snapped, I had returned to my stateroom. Somewhere on the ship, I was sure, Walt was carousing. There on my single bed I gazed up at the ceiling. I never realized how closely Walt's and my life were intertwined. It was just an unspoken understanding that we would never be far away from each other. Aren't these photographs our testimony to that? And just like that commitment of the past, I cannot turn away from him now.

The algae-colored ghost continues to sweep intermittently off the glass that preserves each photograph. I must pick up the insistent message emitting from the cell phone. I roll to the side of the bed and listen to my voice mail, *"Chris, it's Walt. Call me as soon as you get this…I'll wait for your call."* His tone is serious with a hint of impatience. Finding some reserved strength, I draw in my breath and tap his number on the speed dial.

There is only one ring, and then silence. Walt is most certainly listening on the other end. Is he too anxious to speak first, or too timid about what he has to say? Does he believe that someone else is on the other end beside me? No matter, I am impatient. "Walt, is that you? This is Chris."

"Yes, Chris, it's me." He is still hesitant to speak.

"Walt, I'm okay." I know that he needs to hear this before he can continue.

"Chris, did you sleep well enough last night?" This is not the response I had in mind, and I am not about to engage in idle chit-chat. Whatever he is struggling with must be addressed sooner or later, and because I know that I, too, am somehow placed within this struggle, sooner will be the way out of it!

"Walt, listen. You and I are going to talk about this…whatever is going on…I want to know…I deserve to know!" I have reached my limit! He still hesitates. He is side tracking again. I need to use language he cannot cast off easily. "And if you are to continue with these mind games… then…we must never see each other again!" I hear a muffled ache of disbelief through the line. Never have either of us ever stated such an ultimatum, even as teens when we would tease each other to the raw limits of trust.

II

TO TELL WALT THAT I WILL sever our relationship is a provocation to his recklessness. He must have the courage to tell the truth and accept that his problem might be beyond his control.

"So, Walt, what's it going to be?"

He does not answer, but I know he heard what I just said, and that he understood the intent of my words. He always takes his time thinking through his decisions, and I gave him his time now to think through his answer.

"Chris, I can't come over there. I'll meet you at Dante's in about two hours."

Now why not at my townhouse…why meet at our regular eatery? Is it because he has to be in a public arena? Is he that apprehensive over my reaction to his secret? Maybe a public rendezvous is better than a private confrontation—it will be impossible for me to wrap my arms around him and make passionate love with him. I am beginning to fear this, and perhaps he is anxious about it, too.

Then Walt asks a strange question. "You didn't call the police, did you?"

"No." I answer quickly. But he certainly heard the concern in my voice.

"Good. Don't contact them." Almost begging, he repeats, "Please don't call the cops."

I remain silent.

"Listen, Chris, I'll explain everything to you when I meet you at Dante's."

I do not know what to say. I'm still having difficulty digesting the question about the police.

"Chris, don't worry. I promise I will tell you."

"I'll be there." I end the conversation. Strangely, I thought I detected another voice before I hung up. But it might have been just an echo in the phone.

I twist my torso and stretch flat across my bedcovers, staring at the daffodils in my wallpaper; they look so delicate, so receptive, so peaceful. Yes, I will go to Dante's and listen to Walt explain what happened in the hotel room, and what else is going on. Then we will be back on solid ground, where all will become right again. *It can't get any worse that this!*

III

IT WAS OFF-HOURS, mid-afternoon dining at Dante's Restaurant, and customers were sparse. In a few hours the evening crowd, mostly locals, would mosey in, first gravitating to the bar for happy hour, then when hunger summoned, retiring to the dining room for something more substantial. Many would, of course, return to the bar to be entertained by the jazz quartet until closing. I had done this often with Walt, sometimes with other men.

Now, I sat alone in the dining room, forgoing the bar scene, very much immersed in the solitude of my own happy hour. I'd arrived about an hour earlier than the designated time, but two hours had passed and still no Walt. I could leave, I should leave and just lambaste him when he finally catches up with me. But I am committed to this meeting. It is imperative that whatever is going down is no longer put off. So, I will endure the inconvenience in spite of the interminable wait.

It isn't uncomfortable, waiting here, as I justify my predicament. I'm in familiar surroundings, sitting at our preferred, square table in the dining room, positioned next to the immense window wall, the best view in the house. Yet, why then, with each passing second, does uneasiness squirm inside me? Maybe, just maybe, he won't show. He has—finally—lost his nerve and figures that if he doesn't come, I'll just leave, and he won't have to confess.

My conviction wilting, I nervously finger the stem of the wine glass, filled and refilled throughout the afternoon with my vino of choice, Pinot

Grigio. I sip again before sending another text message, the tenth one of the afternoon.

Am I too conspicuous, remaining alone at this table for so long? Yet, who really would care in this almost unoccupied area of the restaurant…the management, the waiters, the sparse clientele? No, I've been a good customer, never caused a problem. I reposition my body, stretching my flattened buttocks so it will become less numb, and once again focus on the mundane.

On the table two place settings are still tightly rolled up in cloth napkins, the butter dishes still pristine, the melted ice almost imperceptible within the tumblers. I envision myself as the portrait of the perennial rejected woman, and the scenario draws me inward. I turn my head and gaze out the window. Perhaps the serenity beyond the glass will bring some solace.

The splendor of nature's palette saturates my senses. Splotches of greenery layer into the distances of a wooded maze. Subtle shades of lime greens overlap deep forest greens. Olive hues contrast with variegated emeralds as the sinking afternoon light kisses the moist darkened leaves. Elongated boughs lace the tableau like feminine limbs shamelessly intertwining in suggestive embraces. A slight stir from the wind and the montage sways in a slow sensual dance to distant ghostly melodies. As I watch the hypnotic waltz, it beckons me to join in. How easy it is to succumb to the mystic woods. I become fixated on an overgrown deep green pine in close proximity to my window seat. Embedded in the spiny branches is a thin sapling of vibrant orange and red foliage, the pinnacle of Nature's palette, it's premature onset out of place before the deep sleep. I reflect on my imminent passage of life and turn from the window. I bring the cold edge of the wine glass to my mouth and allow the liquid to flow over numbing lips. Suddenly, I break from my daze to peruse the restaurant for Walt. His baffling desertion defiles the moment. I shrug off the offense and try again to refocus on something else…anything else!

In spite of my frequent attendance at this refined bistro, I've never paid any attention to its décor. The linen-covered tables are surrounded by contemporary Swedish chairs. Their low, thatched wraparound backs give a slight cluttered congestion. However, there is still an airiness in the room. In the afternoon the stark whitened walls and the earthy tableau beyond the expansive window gives a sense of infinite dimension. This boundless perimeter continues through a set of glass doors for outside dining. The transparent exit leads to a series of wooden decks, also vacant now, which cascade downward beyond my sight. If not for the massive, darkened wooden beams raftering the lofty ceilings, the restaurant could have drifted away into some unhinged cosmos.

I canvas my surroundings and steal another momentary glance toward the eatery's reception area: still no Walt. At some point, I cease peering back to the entrance of the dining room and allow my head to slightly droop into unalterable resignation. It is the voice of my server, Dale, which finally prompts me to lift my chin and resume living. "Ms. Christine, why don't you order something, perhaps some soup?"

When I look up, the face is fuzzy, but it comes into clarity and warm recognition. "Oh, Dale, I'm not hungry."

"But you are always hungry when you come to our restaurant! So, how could this be so?"

He is attempting to humor me for he intuitively understands the needs of customers, especially his regulars.

"Ms. Christine, I will not take no for an answer! When was the last time you ate?"

I muster the image of the Atlantic City restaurant with the gold leaf glass doors and insipid wise-ass waiter. I smile, for I recognize that he is offering me something more substantial than just food. "Okay, Dale, you win. You can bring me a burger...ask Mendez if he could throw some veggies on the plate, too. I'm in need of some good ol' solid American nourishment."

"Don't you worry yourself. I'll take good care of you!"

His thoughtfulness gives me renewed resolve to tackle Walt's desertion. I withdraw my cell phone from my purse and hit the speed dial for Walt's number...again! When once more there is no response I poke at the screen in repetitive raps before tossing the cell across the tabletop. Its screen remains black. I wrap my fists about my forehead, squeezing my temples, then snatch the cell again and redial, this time waiting long enough for voice mail.

"Walt, where the Hell are you!" This is not a question any longer, but a threat. "I'm still at Dante's. Call me...now!"

Surely, he will finally respond. He never shuts off his phone. Even in my inebriated state I know that this seething exasperation is only the fading denial of my real apprehension. I put the cell down and stare at it, commanding it to break its silence. I no longer know what to do with it, much like Walt's absence. He should have known better than to do this to me. Being stood up is not only discourteous, it violates a basis tenant of humanity, especially between lifetime friends. He should have been more sensitive to the ordeal I endured the prior nights, especially because he was party to it.

Yes, I have always overlooked Walt's self-absorbed quirks, but this is just plain rude, perhaps unforgivable. I must release myself from this inane vigilance. Still, I will not leave, at least not until I finish eating what I just ordered.

IV

AS TIME TRICKLES INTO THE DISTANCE of the fading afternoon greenery, the throb remains. I can no longer witness the splendor beyond the window, for I am stuck inside the glass, unable to pass through it. That is when I detect an image embedded within the pane. At first, I try to deny that it exists at all. It must be only a figment of my fragile mind. But as I study the ghost, carefully inspecting the lines and shadows, I acknowledge that it is indeed, corporeal. It is a face, a very distinctive face…of a man…quite a distinctive looking man!

My initial response is that I have seen this face before. Yet, I am not able to recall when, so I shrug the thought away. Perhaps curiosity, boredom, and an inebriated soggy mind give this reflection more magnitude than it deserves. As the backdrop of branches and leaves slowly fade into the distances beyond the glass, the face becomes more lucid, its features breathe with life. A firm forehead dominates an angular chin, made more pronounced by the slightly receding hairline cropped into dark, tight ringlets. Deep crevices line sunken cheeks in sharp contrast to the subtle, thin lines at the edges of his eyes. It is a face of urbanity, empowered through hardened experience, that exemplifies a rare sense of intelligence demanding both serious deference and unquestionable allegiance. Yes, the ghostly image smolders with contradictions. Plump lips soften the harsh demeanor, inviting sensuality. The penetrating eyes fires with passion. Devoid of color, they pierce through me, probing into the most intimate recesses of my thoughts.

I swivel around to verify that the face is indeed attached to a body. He sits gentlemanly erect with one leg draped over his knee in a posture that is receptive.

"It certainly is a magnificent setting, isn't it?" The voice is deep, carrying a slightly cultured foreign accent. It matches the entire disposition of an extraordinary man of means.

I do not answer immediately, but reposition my elbow onto the table, slightly bending my head and cradling my chin in my palm. It is a feminine posture conveying confusion over whether or not to engage. The wine makes the choice for me. Normally I would remain polite, give a slight nod or a half-hearted smile. But now I am unbridled from the flush of wine, displaced by the absence of Walt, and slightly infected by the deliciousness of this man.

"Yes, it is splendid."

She is obviously unaware that he has been sitting there for over an hour, watching her, drinking in her every anxious mannerism. And with each shifting pose, he attempted to delve deeper into her thoughts. It was a dance without touching. Now that a vocal touch had been made, he fans the flames.

But he will not be reckless in his pursuit lest she slip back into her fixation beyond the glass. Perhaps an unassuming question is safe?

"Do you come here often?"

"Yes!" She responds too quickly, immediately unsettled that her vulnerability has been exposed, and that she may look like an easy pickup. She tries to cover up with a pleasantry.

"The food is outstanding…you know…it's quite a comfortable place to just get away…you know…from the hustle and bustle." Her voice trails off "…you know."

An uncomfortable silence follows. Although both want to speak, they remain polite strangers executing appropriate protocol for an initial encounter. She snatches a deep breath and is emboldened again. "Yes, yes, I do… come here, often," she repeats.

He sees her discomfort and is apprehensive that what had been gained might slip away. He replies with gaudier firmness. "Yes, it certainly appears to be a curious place." In spite of his effort to engage her, his tone comes out garish, a foreigner with incongruent inflection, and he is ashamed of his linguistic inadequacies. Both defer back into their detached postures, yet much aware of the other's presence. He resolves to close this impasse and initiate a leap of faith. "May I join you?"

It is not an unexpected question. Perhaps she wants it to be asked. She is about to say that she is waiting for someone, but quickly retracts that thought. This is not the man she had wanted throughout the afternoon, but he is a man, and a rather beguiling one, at that. He will at least fill the void of the other. Throughout the endless hours, she has been dissolving like the golden liquid in her empty wine glass. Chit-chat may refurbish the void. Any chit-chat will do. No, not just chit-chat. She is desperate for conversation, and exhausted by Walt's ludicrous absence. She slips her palm off her chin and waves an overly exaggerated gesture toward the empty chair, inviting him to her table, graciously beseeching him, "Please, you will be able to appreciate the view better from here."

He executes the switch to the chair across from her like an unruffled breeze, almost as if he is returning to where he should have been in the first place. His confidence is that of the able fly caster proceeding into the river's current rapids.

Sitting closer, both inhale a whiff of each other: alluring fragrance and pursuing scent. Both harness their composure: she to conceal her yearning and he to disguise his trawling.

However, he is not concerned. He has always been a patient fisherman. Without rushing the moment, he will reel her in, delicately probing, swooshing the line just above the water's surface to tantalize the unsuspecting fish below, whipping the rod over and over again, coaxing, delicately coaxing, patiently waiting for the defining moment before dropping the hook. He glances out the window. He glances back to her. He smiles. A slight curiosity flutters in the outskirts of her eyelid. Whip! Swoosh! The line swirls and hovers in its ballet with each flick of the wrist. His smile dances. She squirms in her seat, a subtle but responsive shift, a nibble of desire that only a man of fly-fishing dexterity can detect. Flick! Whip! Swoosh! Perfect execution. She smiles. He has snagged his catch even though she does not realize she has been hooked!

"Here you are, Ms. Christine, an American burger with nourishment!"

Dale's abrasive intrusion cuts the fisherman's line, and the catch is gone. The server's usual upbeat tone is razor-edged as he brazenly addresses the intruder at her table. "Good afternoon, Sir. May I get you a menu…now?" It is an emphatic "Now!" Obviously from the riverbank, Dale has been watching the stranger wading the shoreline becoming increasingly leery of the foreigner's motives.

"Yes…yes…you may bring some cheese and fresh fruit…and a bottle of wine…the label the lady is drinking."

"Oh, not for me! I'm afraid I had a bit more than I should have had…"

"Please, allow me…it is my pleasure."

Dale is uncomfortable at this request. He knows she has already overindulged this afternoon, but it is not his place to speak openly. Instead he hesitates, giving Christine a moment to stand her ground, but she folds under the fisherman's enticing line and accepts his offer.

"Thank you, that's very kind of you."

Against his better judgment Dale departs, obligated to remain blind to a different culpability. The fisherman sternly watches the server until he disappears behind the swinging doors to the kitchen. Then resuming the cast; swish, snap, he smiles amicably at the woman across the table.

"So, your name is Christine, is it not? Isn't that how you were just addressed? 'Christine!' Allow me to make my introduction. I am known as Jewels Khan." His vernacular suggests formal British education mingled with a Middle Eastern accent. He pauses to give her time to respond.

"Jewels?" She squints for she cannot connect such a name to this man.

He sees her bewilderment. "It is just a name that I go by." He is succinct; he does not go any further. He is more interested in directing the conversation to finding out more about her. He examines her flawless complexion. Earlier, he was not able to appreciate such beauty. Her milky skin is exceptionally fair, almost translucent, with a hint of pink flushing her cheeks, from the alcohol, or perhaps her natural glow. She smiles, and he is surprised at how easy it is to smile back. Usually his words and actions are premeditated, uncomfortable, not spontaneous. He reflects on the incongruity of his unaccustomed behavior.

"Would you like some of my burger?" He is jolted from his musing by her gracious voice.

He shakes his head, repelling her entrée before realizing that she is only being courteous. His face reddens by his coarseness. "Please, eat. Do not wait for me."

"Then how about some fries... some veggies?"

"You are most kind. But I have a restricted diet."

She looks down at her plate; suddenly it doesn't look so appetizing. The good, old American food no longer looks heathy!

He suspects that he has somehow offended her. "I'm sorry." Again, he is spooked by another absurdity in his behavior; he never apologies.

With a cordial smile she picks up her wine glass and finishes its contents. He watches her with amazement. Never has he known a woman to consume this amount of alcohol. Alcoholic consumption was always forbidden, not for him of course, for he considered himself one of the privileged, defining his own code of behavior over religious doctrine.

For Christine, the buzz has been increasing in a slow swell, sapping her clear-headedness in miniscule moments. Walt's absence has wreaked havoc on her judgment, yet it doesn't seem to matter anymore. Without Walt, she just needed to connect with something familiar: the restaurant, this table, the greenery beyond the window, and perhaps now, this man. Although it is just a chance meeting, she cannot dismiss that ping of familiarity. She tries to explain this to herself. Maybe it is just that he has replaced the soon-to-be cadaver of Walt she periodically has been envisioning throughout the interminable afternoon. She fingers a strand of hair, trying to remember if she has met this man before. There is, of course, no answer. In the silence she says his name to herself, *Jewels!* She still has not told him her last name.

"I'm Christine Leger. Nice to meet you, Jewels Khan." She extends a hand to formalize the greeting, but he keeps his tightly folded and just nods. She brushes this reception aside in spite of its oddity.

Dale returns with the platter of cheese and fruit, a crisp white linen cloth draped over his forearm. The bottle of white wine is snuggly pinioned against his chest. Retrieving a corkscrew from his side pocket, he goes about the ritual of wine opening, carefully uncorking for the sniffing, selectively pouring for the tasting, patiently waiting for the consent. Jewels is not impressed, nor is he about to participate in such ceremonial pretentiousness. He remains aloof, focusing his attention only on the woman sitting across from him. Dale stalls, winces, and proceeds to fill only Jewel's glass. Christine's glass purposely remains empty. "Will that be all, sir?" he sniffs, and places the bottle down.

Jewels, who never misses any indiscretion, wants to forcefully answer this intruding man. However, he is not about to sully the moment, especially over such a minor infraction, and especially not in front of this volatile woman. He does not directly address Dale's conspicuous intimation. Instead, he peers into the server's eyes to drive in the intended point. "Thank you, I do believe that we are, and will be, fine without your assistance." Jewels picks up the wine bottle and fills Christine's glass. Although his delivery is amenable enough, the understated pouring clearly conveys that Dale is not just dismissed, but also is not to interfere any further. A punctilious pivot and snappy exit broadcast that the server "got the memo."

As late afternoon dissipates into early evening shadows, sparse customers meander into the bistro. The occupied tables are at enough of a distance for the two to dawdle, however, not for too much longer. A larger evening crowd will be a problem. Soft music wafts about them, concealing malicious intentions.

"You know, Jewels, I often come to this restaurant just to sit by this window." He detects in her voice the yearning to come to terms with some deeper thought, her need to talk ripened by Walt's unforgiving offence and her now well-lubricated tongue. Jewels has been waiting for this moment. He knows her anxious confusion from the weekend must be addressed. His function is to defuse that anxiety so that he can determine if she is worth the imposition Cameron has imposed on him.

V

WHEN JEWELS WAS TOLD that Cameron had allowed Walt to take Christine back to her townhouse, he was livid, concerned that she might go to the police, thus compromising the operation. She should have been secured in the hotel room until decisions were made to proceed. Cameron had messed up!

Cameron knew that, too. In the hotel, unexplainable feelings had unfolded between the woman and him. The operation unraveled with his unravelling desire. Of course, Cameron needed to obscure this from Jewels, but he had to be cautious. When he suggested that Jewels take over the operation, Cameron was not only placating a disgruntled man, but shifting focus away from an insecure one: himself. He devised the notion that Jewels, who was privy to all the particulars, would be better at assessing her qualifications. Jewels was amenable to that idea. Therefore, Jewels was now sitting across the table from Christine, not Cameron.

Without a doubt, it was a more judicious maneuver. Jewels had more experience in such delicate details. This was not the first time an Eastern client had wanted an American woman with specific qualifications. However, this time was strangely different. Never had Jewels needed to find a female of this age, a substantial female, not just some mindless juvenile. Furthermore, she had to be healthy enough to have vitality, suitable enough to be intellectually sociable, acceptable enough for doctrine. She must be sexually receptive in fulfilling the demands of an older client, but most important, she had to be beautiful: slender and shapely, fair and flawless, and hair, long silky burnt red. It was the perception of an American Beauty defined though Eastern eyes.

There was a lucrative incentive for such services rendered. However, that was not the reason for Jewels to take on this affair. He was already affluent. His primary rational was embedded in deeper trenches. Since his father's death, he had been aware of his faltering dominance in his community. His sovereignty was slowly deteriorating, especially among the Elders. If he could appease the restless old men, not with concubines, but with substantial women who could be paraded off their old flabby arms, maybe he could calm the archaic seas of the discontented.

He would not waste his time; if a product did not meet the requirements, he would take a different course of action and find another package for his customers. If too much was expended and it did not work out with her, all remnants of the operation would be sanitized. Jewels hesitated in facing such a decision, but would if needed. That is why he was carefully assessing this commodity now, because he might need to be callous in terminating her later.

So, as Jewels sits across from this woman, he wants a timely closure, but not a rushed judgment that will jeopardize significant information. He certainly does not want to alert her or anyone else to any impropriety. He has already lost some ground with this waiter, Dale, who seems to have some considerable connection with her. And in spite of her intoxication, she still appears to have enough presence to detect any hidden agenda in this hasty friendship. Whip! Flick of the wrist, and his fishing line whizzes unobtrusively over unsettling waters. He must keep her talking.

"I can understand how someone would want to sit here among this beautiful setting. It must mean something important to you. Is that not so?"

She tugs on the silken line. "It is beautiful, isn't it? From this window, I have watched the changing colors of seasons. I have always been moved how the trees become more dazzling with each passing year." She pauses and stares at him to see if he is still interested. She had expressed these thoughts to other men, so called admirers of beauty, believing their false admiration until she realized it was only a pretext to get her to bed them. The first signs were polite aloofness under muffled yawns, and then the remark of finding a place to lie down. That was when she would lose the will to discuss nature's beauty. But his eyes are unlike the others. They are riveted on her, coaxing her with a smile. Whip! Flick! She resumes her testimonial.

"Sometimes I look into the distances of the woods. It's as if they are permitting questions to enter...that hidden answers lie dormant out there in nature, answers to all my questions...out there...you know...questions that gnaw at you...the ones that you can never let go." These last words unsettle him. She catches a subtle tick in the corner of his eye. He quickly recovers and nods. Flick! What she does not comprehend is that he is becoming concerned with where she is going with this imagery.

"As a young girl I had so many questions, and there was never anyone to help sort them out."

She reflects on distant thoughts. He considers recent ones. Could this be a different fish than he had believed she was wrestling with when he watched from the other table? His initial suspicion was that she had figured out what had been planned for her. But time is dwindling, and he can no longer allow this uncertainty to interfere with his preparations. He must find out exactly what she is thinking, even if the risk exposes him.

"Christine, there seems to be something troubling you. If I could help in any way, I would be more than willing to."

His stare is unwavering. She can no longer look away, captured by the pale pallor of his eyes, a vacant canvas awaiting her words. Has a lifetime of pain drained those orbs of their vibrancy? Could these eyes be the very ones that can grasp what she needs to say? Or are they just colorless indifference? She sips her wine as wooziness detaches her further from discretion.

"Jewels, how old do you think I am?"

Now, under the circumstances, this is a bizarre question. Jewels is puzzled; he is not a stupid man about the sensitivity females have about their age. But it was asked with sincerity, and he needs to address it if he is to follow her thinking. He knows the answer to this question, but he proceeds diplomatically. "I would say that you have the carriage of a woman who has lived a seasoned life."

She, on the other hand, hopes that her appearance does not suggest a haggard life. She sighs, "I am over forty, you know." She lingers on that thought before proceeding. "And I really feel that old...oh, not physically...I'm in good health, have a job that stimulates my mind. But I feel weary...you know...in spirit. Somehow, I have lost my way; my desires....are gone..."

Concerned that she is veering into obscurity, he attempts to finish her thought by redirecting it to his agenda. "Is that what saddens you, Christine, that you have lost out on missed desires?"

She bows her head and replies an exhausted "yes."

He is about to say that he could fulfill her desires but remains silent. He is momentarily moved by what was delivered so simply. He scrutinizes her expression, and sees not just a vulnerable woman, but a beautiful woman of sincerity. Perhaps he had known her somewhere else in his life, not just from Friday night. However, these are not the words he was prepared to hear. He thought this would be easy when he took over the operation, that he would be able to expedite the arrangements. Repeatedly, he looks away to the splendor beyond the window and then back again to her. And with each returning glance he is drawn more and more into her own splendor. She is indeed alluring! He is enamored by her gentle beauty and soft voice. And there is that faint moment of familiarity he cannot shake away.

"So, I sit next to this window and search for some ancient words of wisdom. But you know what has happened instead, Jewels?" She is stirring up his own suppressed questions.

"What's that?"

"I just got older waiting for answers that probably will never come!" She lets out a snicker as if she had just made a joke. Jewels doesn't laugh. Not being an American, he often feels that he misses Yankee humor. Christine continues, attempting to be more upbeat. She grins and uses a more comical tone, "Yes, I admit that I have wasted my life... and that I certainly have passed the point of no return!"

Point of no return. The phrase underscores the uncertainties in his mind. His back becomes ridged. *What does she mean?* He reconstructs all the pertinent facts concerning her situation. She is a single woman in her forties without family. Her associations are sparse and impersonal. Her independent lifestyle allows for unpredictable routines. She often makes impulsive travel plans without leaving any information of where she is going or when she will return. No one is ever concerned by these irregularities. No one will miss her until it is too late. However, he was uneasy about what "point of no return" may suggest. Does she suspect? How will he be able to deny that at the end of the week? How will he be able to deny it now if he doesn't ask?

Christine has no inkling what is going through this man's head, so when he leans toward her to confirm his suspicions, she has trouble following his next question: "What do you mean by 'point of no return?'"

Her back straightens as she squints. She had forgotten where she left off in her narrative. "What? What? Oh, yes...point of no return...Well I guess I mean...that I have no children." She lifts her eyebrows as if to punctuate... *and that's the way of it.*

Silence follows as if she is awaiting approval for not having any children. His thoughts sink back to his agenda...*Certainly being childless is an asset. The client will be pleased! Now if only if he could redirect her to his agenda!*

"Were you ever married?"

"Nope...Nope...Never married...And probably never will be! At least not at this rate," she quips, haphazardly, thinking over her last rejection on Friday. "It seems that I will remain alone the rest of my life because there will never be anyone to share those children with me." She drifts back into the window of greenery.

Trying to bring her back to reality, Jewels repeats his question. "Christine, so what does 'point of no return' have to do with children?"

Not facing him, but continuing to stare through the window, as if addressing what lay beyond it, she responds, "All these years I thought of nothing but to immerse myself in my job...my townhouse...my indulgences. I saved myself from childbirth, thinking that I had plenty of time left...waiting...for the right man to finally come along...well...it looks like now that will never happen." She turns to him and takes another swig of wine. She attempts to initiate a twisted smile to convey that she is only joking.

Jewels is beginning to see through her twisted humor. There is something more deep-seated than playful bantering. He drops his head in deference of her vulnerable state.

Christine is sinking fast, but she is coherent enough to sense that his silence might mean that she has embarrassed him. Truly, not her intent.

"Sorry, Jewels, I am...It's just that it's been a tough couple of days. I'm not myself. I'm really sorry. Just babbling."

"I understand. It's fine. I have bad days, too."

He tries to make his voice consoling, but she is on a roll, and suddenly remembers Walt and his present desertion, and Walt's familiar comeback whenever she brings up her familiar aloneness remarks. "As I've been told...so many times from a friend...the problem is...that I just have never lost my virginity to the right man!"

"Really!" Once again, Jewels is confused, something has been lost between Eastern and Western vernaculars.

"Oh, just babbling."

Was it just babbling when Walt had uttered those same words to Jewels last Friday night? Could such a statement be taken literally? Certain specifics were unrealistic to expect from a forty-year-old, but absolute confirmation would come later. As long as she had never had a child she would be intact enough. And if there is a problem, he has enough audacity to physically reconstruct the truth. Jewels has often had to filter information like this before. Even half the truth can become a mirage of truth to a client. He has enough information to proceed. He makes his decision. Jewels turns sideways toward the window in quiet meditation, hoping she will do the same. When she finally rotates away from him and drifts back into the distant landscape beyond the window, he seizes the moment. Pouring her another glass of wine, he covertly swishes it before offering it to her. "Christine, this is for you."

She turns back and takes it. "Thank you." Gracefully, she brings the rim to her lips. He watches intently as she swallows half the contents in one gulp. Shortsightedly, Jewels did not realize how inaccurate his assessment was of the situation, or how resilient this woman is in spite of her present brittle appearance.

He must have her drink a little more before the final closure to the afternoon, and so stumbles into the next thought, "Christine, you can still live a fruitful life...with or without children."

"But what does fruitful mean anymore for me, Jewels? I always wanted to know how it felt to hold a life within my body, conceived from the passion of love, and to nourish that innocent life against my breast." Christine could not distemper the longing. She inhales deeply and shifts to a more upbeat tone. "Oh well, that's life!" She takes a swig as if to punch the thought.

Suddenly, he is ashamed. Here is a woman who has poured out her soul to him, and he had only been concerned about her as a lucrative commodity. As he watches her, he grapples under a feeble residue of guilt.

"Men often marvel at that miracle, too." His words are even more banal than before, and he knows it. They are silent again. Both turn their heads away from each other and gaze out the window as the sun sinks before the oncoming evening.

Finally, she clears her throat as if to signal a change in the conversation, "Do you have children, Jewels?"

He quickly responds, relieved by the swing in the exchange. "Yes, I do, from three different wives I live with now." He sees her confusion, so he clarifies with a smile of conviction. "In my culture it is permitted to have multiple wives."

"Oh yes, I understand. Do you love your wives? You must love your children."

"Oh," continuing with a smile of buoyancy, "my children are my jewels!" He pauses to reflect on the impact of the next thought. "I did not marry out of what you Westerners call passion. The marriages were arranged. I gained much prestige from these contracts." Once again, he is embarrassed by his emphasis on prestige and influence. Still, he can further his agenda here. "But the women also have gained. I provide a good life for my wives, and I treat them with respect." He needs to say this to make it easier on her later. She does not need to know the far-reaching truth now.

As Jewels fixates on the half-emptied glass, Christine extends her hands across the table and captures his hands in hers. He is numbed by her touch. It had always been forbidden in his society for an unattached female to touch a man. She is too bold, wine or no wine! Yet, he does not pull away, for her palms are warm and soothing.

"It's just that I mourn the loss of my child, who never had a choice to be conceived because of the choices I made, and I feel so guilty about that."

He looks across the table. Gone is the silly playfulness. Her expression is somber. As he listens to this beautiful woman, he does not hear pretense. The directness of her words come from an open wound, bleeding the sadness of sincere longing. Her hurt nips the scab of his own lonely world. She holds his hands firmly as if to ask another question. It will deliver the sting from a different time and place, a sting that will finally pierce the hardened veneer of an indifferent fisherman. It will be a question evoking his irreprehensible decision from a month ago.

"Jewels, did you ever mourn the loss of someone dear to you because of a choice you had made?"

Her rambling whirlpools around the fishing pole. Flick, Swoosh! The fisherman's line no longer dances alone. He has become the acquiescent fish lured onto the irrevocable hook.

VI

JEWELS HAS NEVER BEEN a man of loose words. He is a formidable man, intimidating and impressive; his words are always daunting, dreadful, feared. He never anticipated the sovereignty of the uncharted land beyond the window. His hands curl into fists within the embrace of her palms. He leans across the table as if to silence her forever, for she has just trespassed into what was never to be mentioned again. In spite of her clutch he stands, impaling her with a portentous glare. However, he quickly reads her trusting expression. She does not know the wound she has just pierced. Instead of shaking her off, he webs his fingers between hers, first with suppressed ire before easing to just a secure grip. This is not the time to address his past. He needs to get back to business. He quickly composes himself; he is a business man, after all. He has lost focus in a time frame that was tight to begin with, and he is quite aware that she will not hold on much longer. They need to leave the restaurant!

She is unsteady as he pulls her from the table. Fearing this would happen, he brings her tightly into his hip. Unfortunately, Jewels spies Dale guarding the front entrance with that edgy posture of concern. He knows that this compromised female must stand on her own volition if they are to leave together without suspicion. A revised plan is needed for a credible departure. Perhaps they can slip out the back of the restaurant. If not, then with some outside air, she might revive enough to exit out the front. He slides his arm casually around her waist and grips her bare arms in an attempt to brace the swaying body. It is a posture that conveys unassuming familiarity, the appearance of unobtrusive acceptability. He begins maneuvering her toward the glass doors, which lead to the outside rear dining and the opposite direction from the blocked front portico. They shuffle along, leaving the inside restaurant onto the open-air upper deck.

Strings of petite lights drape the overhanging rafters, winking at the oncoming twilight. The sun has sunk behind the treetops to the west, diffusing a pall over the greenery. The lower sundecks cascade in levels to a secluded part of the restaurant, and now in the early evening hours, they are vacant. It is an area in which they will have privacy, if not a possible outlet to the street. In the dimming light he moves her downward; her inebriated body is cumbersome in spite of how closely he presses her into him. Because she is fraying, he decides they need to rest on one of the lower platforms before going on—a temporary haven obscured from meddlers.

It is a jetty, which protrudes next to the distinctive pine embracing the vibrant orange sapling, the one which Christine had fixated on earlier. The platform is just slightly above the waterfall where the surge tumbles over boulders scattered in its path. Yet, because of the pronounced, flat incline of the falls, the gush peters out quickly into calming swirls in which a family of ducks gently lull. A duck nudges its young away from the harsh spray above, their innocent demeanor oblivious to callous nature.

This is a place where time and nature twist in a junction for understanding. By this waterfall, under the onset of twilight, his thoughts of life and death duel. The recent events from his homeland whirl around him. He has suppressed the incident from a month ago into the darkened hollow of night, keeping the account under a veil of pretentious activities. However, this woman has conjured up that distant darkness. He shakes his head as if to shake the thoughts away. He looks into the dark cavities of the forest and its meandering network of twisted limbs. He rethinks the operation. She could easily be disposed of there and never found. *How much allegiance do I have to the client, anyway?* But when he returns to her the darkness is gone, replaced by the light of her face.

On a whim he entertains a new thought. *Yes…she is certainly alluring. Maybe, I should take her for myself?* He props Christine against the wooden guard rail so that she faces the falls. He stands directly behind and wraps her in his arms, pressing his body intimately into hers. His fury is displaced by lust. He squeezes her still harder as if she can bestow redemption from those distant shadows. She grunts. And he snaps out of his self-gratification and madness.

"Are you okay, Christine?" He did not want to hurt her.

Misconstruing his question from physical to theoretical, she exhales, "I'm not okay. I'm some kind of mishap of nature. I'm a female still asleep, a female who has never been touched." Her legs weaken, but he quickly braces her tighter. He has become her scaffolding in spite of himself.

"Christine…Christine…" No answer, yet he demands an answer, and gently shakes her to remain conscious. "Christine!"

She cannot handle much more, so he eases the pressure. "You'll feel better in a little while." He, of course, is lying. He is still physically drawn to her.

"No, I won't be fine. Nature has turned her back on me! I have lost time. I'm no longer feminine."

"What are you saying? You are an exquisite woman! Any man can see that!"

"Not the right man!"

Again, Jewels aches for her. "Why is that, Christine? Why not the right man?" He presses harder against her, becoming more aroused.

She does not respond at first, then her response sizzles into the air. "The thieves of time have stolen my female spirit."

It is not that Jewels is brutally implacable, too callous and insensitive to see that she is hurting. It is just that he has to become a man of intuitive judgment, an indifferent man in an indifferent world, a business man of detachment. He pauses to reflect on how he was raised to feel this way, of how he has struggled not to become this way—the kind of man he is now. Is he just another thief come to steal her away into another night? He tries to shake this thought away, too. He can't. Instead he lowers his head and buries his face into her hair, trying to forget. She is enchanting; her scent is reminiscent of another woman in his life.

The memories return, the irreparable choices of his life, and the recent decision that had brought him before this woman. Oh, but her hair is so soft, her body so inviting, his desire so evident. He had not had these touches for quite some time. In fact, like her, he had resigned himself to a life without them. Yet, here she is, wrapped in his embrace. He looks beyond her shoulder. His desire has become humiliated by her clarity and her trust as she sinks into his ruthless arms. Jewels resigns to a breath of civility and then softly murmurs, "In the course of time, Christine, it will all come together…in the course of time."

Suddenly a sliver of light pierces the darkened greenery. It is that brilliant burst at sundown when the slowly descending orb finally reaches the last moment before its demise, pausing momentarily on the horizon before exploding and sinking into oblivion. As the blade of light slashes through the darkened greenery, the shadows of memories dissipate. And in that instant, he recognizes his mission…that this woman must survive, for her salvation is linked with his. He embraces her femininity with a gentler intimacy.

As Jewels gazes into the scenery he spies the vibrant sapling wrapped in the graceful limbs of the evergreen. He ponders how such a world is endowed to all that is living, in fact, endowed by birthright. Each species knows instinctively what is expected of it. Here, there are no governments to institute nepotistic laws, no religions to mold compliant adherents, no ancestors to insure merciless honor. It is an ecosystem in which life is not defined by doctrine, where the burden of carrying "the sins of the father" should not be lived out through the son. Here is a place where correct choices can be made, and guilt does not haunt in shrouded mirages. Christine and he are like the sapling and the evergreen. They are different breeds. He must shed the shadows of lost possibilities. What he is thinking would be scorned as heresy. There will be ramifications, but he will deal with that later, not now, not under the grace of nature's waterfall, where thoughts are allowed to be unpredictable, significant, timeless.

"Christine, listen. Can you hear the words of wisdom from the ancient shadows? I can. They are telling you…me…us…that the past is gone. We never have to acknowledge that it ever existed at all. It is time to even forgive ourselves. It is time for us to embrace what Nature has intended for us, Christine. And what we do from here will depend on nothing!"

As she feels his warm breath at the back of her neck, she revives. Jewels is jolted back from his solitary world. She twists in his arms, turning to face him. His chest rises and falls against her breasts. They draw their heads toward each other, and he passionately kisses her. He is deeply moved by her, but he pulls back. This is not the time or place to pursue such pleasures. Furthermore, it is questionable whether she is sober enough to recall what he just said, for her eyes are closed. When he makes love to her, he wants her to be able to enjoy him fully and remember their love making. That is not now. He will wait until after next Saturday. He stiffens to renew the toughness of his resolve; he must stay focused. Now is the time to finish business. It is time to leave the greenery.

Unfortunately, when he looks for a downward pathway, he realizes there is no outlet to the street. They will need to go through the restaurant to exit. Carefully holding her in his arms, he guides her back up the wooden stairs, leaving the natural radiance of the garden, returning to the artificial lights of the restaurant. Perhaps the inconceivable is about to become the possible.

♠ Chapter 4: The River ♠

The Card of No Return:
The dealer places the exposed card on the felt. It is the last community card.
The silent gambler stares into space, and the others become wary. He might
have the nuts. But too much has been invested by all to fold, and besides, there
is always the possibility of a twilight win. Certainly, when the pot is this huge,
it is worth the risk. All hands check.

I

THE DIMINISHING LIGHT hinders their movement as they trudge up the
layered wooden decks that lead back to the restaurant's glass doors. Too much
time has passed. Blending with the darkened shadows, the wide wooden slats
of the steps have lost definition, making him apprehensive that she might fall.
He clutches her waist firmly. She bows her head slightly and sinks into the
warmth of his chest. Their pace is unhurried but deliberate. However, her
unsteady gait is no longer a burden to Jewels. It is a new commitment to what
he has just pledged.

They arrive under the structure, which holds the strands of lights,
twinkling like the distant stars. Visibility returns and they pause before
returning to a world in which they no longer belong but must address. It might
never be as gracious as the natural world under the cleansing waterfalls, for
they must face inflexible attitudes. If they possess the courage to shed their
callous pasts, their actions will become their legacy, far outreaching even their
own existences. As Jewels is about to reenter the insensitive world, he
recognizes that it will be difficult. He has underestimated just how difficult.

The glass double doors from the decks leading into the dining area are
enclosed by a windowed wall allowing an unhindered view of the entire room.
Jewels scans the scene on the other side of the glass. It has significantly
changed from the somewhat unoccupied one they had left. The room is now

congested with a substantial dinner crowd. Unforgiving lights blaze above patrons conversing with punctuated intonations and emphatic gesticulations. As Jewels' fingers grip the cold metal door handle, he hesitates, uneasy. Finally, he twists the knob. An offensive muddle of voices blares out its discordant symphony of chatter. Embracing as one symbiotic body, Christine and Jewels enter the fray.

Once inside, Jewels decides not to return to their table, situated inconveniently at the far side of the room. He wants to leave the premises quickly and inconspicuously, but he still scans their table. *Nothing has been touched.* Upon the pale linen tablecloth, her half-emptied, golden wine glass reflects its longing. He realizes that he has not paid the bill. In spite of his initial intent, they must head toward the table, weaving precariously through the crammed maze of diners.

Jewels glues his precious Christine to his waist. They brush around protruding elbows, obtrusive legs, and probing eyes, all questioning the intention of the dark-skinned, sophisticated male with this fair, obviously compromised female. Jewels captures the blatant commentary painted on the faces. The scowls reflect attitudes of suspicion. He wants to lash back at their haughty smirks; that has always been the nature of this primal beast. Conversely, he longs to explain the newfound meaning in his life that has become the nature of his cerebral soul. But the deep tint of his skin and the Middle Eastern features of his face will never give him the chance to be heard. Weary eyed, the naked Adam and Eve, in clutching fidelity, trudge through the smoldering forest of rigidity.

In the laborious trek, Jewels must maneuver a frail Christine around an obstructing table where a gathering of couples is so packed that arms and legs extend into the aisle. As they lumber around the tables, Jewels catches the woman's smothered, but quite cheeky snip. "They're all over...can't get away from them...now look, they're taking over our women!" As if to give credence to the remark, her husband flips his hand upward in disgust. Unfortunately, this abrupt action spooks Christine, who happens to be directly in the pervasive arm's path. She stumbles backward, slipping away from Jewel's grip. Her hand knocks into a glass of red wine by the table's edge. The contents swish above the table like twisted ruby ribbon before plummeting red splattering onto Christine's off-white pencil skirt. Unruly brushstrokes smear down her exposed legs as the glass crashes against the hard floor. Miraculously the glass remains intact. But its alert is intrusive enough to breach all conversation. Fixed stares dart toward the incongruent couple. After a detectable pause, the startled moment transcends into dismayed heads confirming their predictable suspicions of immorality.

"Please excuse us. We're so sorry for the inconvenience. Did any of the contents spill on you, madam?" In spite of no other apparent spillage, Jewels tries to regain his composure as he politely addresses the indignant woman.

She, of course, will never accept an apology from such odious vermin; under her breath she sizzles, "Why don't you people watch where you're going?"

Brushing aside her insolence, Jewels attempts to redeem the situation; he is hardened to such voiced prejudices against his culture. As Christine slips a bit more from his already tenuous grip, he looks to the woman for assistance. Getting another evasive snub of distain, he resolves not to waste any more time with such haughty malevolence, not when he has inherited the possibility of Christine's benevolence.

He resumes channeling Christine over to the table by the blind window and gingerly lowers her into her chair. Then he performs an act that questions his cultural nature as a man. He retrieves a clean cloth napkin from their table and reverently kneels on one knee before her. With an unflinching promise to institute change, he clasps her calf and tenderly wipes her reddened legs, first one and then the other. The restaurant eyes watch in stunned silence. They do not recognize this as an act of compassion, nor as a deliberate act of courage in an attempt to break canon shackles. To those eyes, it is nothing more than a vulgar violation by a foreigner.

Meanwhile, alert to the commotion, Dale slashes a path through the crowded room toward the table in question. His somber presence reassures the patrons that matters are under control, and they may pick up where they left off in their chit chat.

"Ms. Christine, are you okay?" Immediately, Dale assesses the situation and reacts predictably, snatching still more napkins. Like Jewels, he squats before her. The two men's shoulders press up against each other as Dale flounders with indecision. Is it appropriate for him to stroke her? He bows his head and makes a choice, silently handing the cloth napkins to Jewels. There is an immediate understanding between the men. Jewels stares at the penitent man momentarily and accepts the offering. Dale retires his indecision with a breathy sigh.

Christine's legs are stained like stratums of reddened earth, and Jewels knows it is impossible to do much more for her here. He looks upward. Her head bobs to one side and then flops to the other. With admirable fortitude, she has attempted to remain coherent as long as possible, but her escalating weariness is quite clear to Jewels, and he is acutely aware of the reason. The immediacy of removing Christine from the premises is evident.

"Christine, we are going to leave now. Let me help you up." Jewels peruses her face to see if she understands: Her head remains slumped. He begins to raise her, bracing one of her arms, and Dale jumps in to assist by gently taking hold of the other. The two men stare at each other, again wrestling over decorum. Jewels gives Dale a respectful nod of thanks. Dale looks away and bites his upper lip as he folds Christine into Jewel's arms. Quickly snatching Christine's handbag, Dale hands it to Jewels, a statement of concession. Then, with portentous pomp of urgency in attending to his other duties, Dale turns his back on the couple and briskly walks toward the restaurant's entrance. Keeping his head upright, Dale refuses to display any more conflicted regret before this interloper.

Jewels hugs Christine in a firm embrace, placing an open palm gently against the back of her head. It hangs over his shoulder like a rag doll. He reaches into his trousers and withdraws five pristine, hundred dollar bills from a 24-karat gold money clip. He places the money next to the half-emptied bottle of golden wine on the pale-yellow linen—certainly, more than enough compensation. They move away from the table, half dragging, half shuffling Christine in twilight consciousness. As she snuggles her chin upon his shoulder, she is able to view what is behind them. At first her vision is blurred. Then, the abandoned table faintly begins to crystallize, and she refocuses on the bills lying slightly askew next to the wine bottle. The clarity of her sight sharpens. She is baffled by how her wine glass sits hauntingly less than half-emptied when its mate glistens completely full. Why was his left untouched? Her insides buckle in shadowy misgivings. She raises her eyes to the dim greenery beyond the window for answers. It tosses her a goodnight kiss as it fades into its own blurred shadows.

As the two pariahs exit the room, fleeting looks carry on their insular commentary. Jewels knows there will be other formidable eyes of scrutiny to get by. They must pass Dale again, who sentries the restaurant's entrance with folded arms in stiff confrontation, attempting to control his capitulation. Dale has been instructed to never interfere with the personal affairs of the clientele, but he is uncomfortable with this protocol, because he cannot prevent Christine from leaving with this stranger. Moving past the sentinel, Jewels ignores the obvious grimace. After a few steps he turns back to Dale. They look intently at each other but say nothing. Dale remains deadpan. Jewels continues to remove Christine from the world of rebuff to a vehicle of submission. The car had been stationed in front of the restaurant since early afternoon. Inside the sedan the restless inhabitant awakens.

II

THE ROAD HAS BEEN DEVOID of activity for the past hour or so, allowing the black sedan to inconspicuously doze on the other side of the street from the restaurant's steps. Its occupant has been waiting since the afternoon as the drama unfolded inside the restaurant. The phantom within the sedan had been well aware of what was occurring behind the wooden door, or he thought he knew, for he was usually the main actor in such a scenario. However, this time he is the understudy, the one who must watch and wait from the curtain's wings. He does not like this role; the squirming has been out of boredom. But there is another underlining reason that he dares not openly admit.

Time had trickled by in the stillness of the moment like lingering droplets of rain on his windshield refusing to fall. He had stared endlessly from the side window at the rainwater spray that had collected by the curb from whizzing vehicles in the afternoon…at the stray dogs that had roamed into alleys in the early evening…at the amorous couples who had huddled in porticos away from approaching car lights during the shadows of night. And, of course, he perused every face that had departed through the restaurant's wooden door. He repeatedly chastised himself that he needed to remain indifferent. Decisions were made, and that was that! There would be no retreat; the tedious silence in the black interior became the testimony of resignation. Finally the wooden door opens and the two emerge into a darkened mist.

Cameron fixates on the wilted woman in Jewels' arms; his waterproof bravado unravels like the broken beads of rain on the windshield. He grips the steering wheel until his fingertips numb. Then, in an impulsive spasm, he whips the door open and bolts from the Mercedes, keeping his fists firmly on the door's handle. He dare not let go without further directives.

When Jewels reaches the front of the car, he is so exhausted that he leans against the hood ornament, immobile, his booty tightly in his embrace. He signals Cameron to assist with the slumped Christine. Cameron moves and hugs the lifeless figure. But Jewels is resistant to letting her go.

"Be careful! Be careful with her!" Jewels barks. Cameron is stunned. Jewels has never exhibited such unreserved deportment with any of the others. Cameron doesn't understand that like himself, the man before him is losing control. Of course, the woman will not recall this exchange. The powder that was clandestinely slipped into her wine glass made sure of that. This knowledge troubles Jewels. He knows such an act is a violation of trust even when he handed her the glass she had so unquestioningly accepted.

"I got her!" Cameron assertively reassures the frazzled man and waits for Jewels to relinquish the woman into his care. The kingpin finally releases her to his subordinate.

Cameron slides Christine's body across the leather back seat and views the figure posed on the other side of the car. It is the same slumped ghostly figure that Cameron saw on the beach the prior night. Jewels had been struggling with something even then. Cameron had feared that Jewels suspects his disintegrating loyalty. From Jewels' peculiar behavior, Cameron detects something more critical. This woman is not as important to the operation as she is to Jewels personally. Could Jewels' strangeness be connected to something else? Even at the concert, Cameron had strong suspicions about why Jewels was particularly drawn to this woman. If his instinct is correct, then, unfortunately, there will be consequences, especially in light of his own recent affinity for her. If it is a question of his allegiance, the consequences will not just be complicated, they will be dire. Cameron has to know for sure. This is the reason he assumed the role of understudy in this afternoon's drama. He has to know for sure so that he will know how to proceed. Now as he watches Jewels, he still does not have a firm answer.

"Where's the guy?" Jewels' aggressive growl articulates his attempt to maintain control in an out-of-control situation. The recent turn of events in the restaurant has generated that change. Jewels fears that if Cameron is privy to what was promised behind the door it might undermine his authority. So, he overcompensates in his inquiry. "Where is he? Where's the guy?"

"Don't worry; the boy is out of the picture…at least for the moment."

Jewels is troubled, not from hearing these words, but by the reckless delivery of them. "I told you not to harm him! We may need him!"

"Rest assured, he's still breathing. But, he's not happy."

Jewels is well aware of Walt's threat to the operation. Initially, Walt had been a vital element in securing Christine, now he might be even more relevant in getting her to be committed to him. But Walt is a loose cannon, too unpredictable to calculate the odds.

When Cameron sensed Jewels was beginning to doubt his competence, he revised the protocol for retrieving the woman. By arranging for Jewels to become involved, two issues would be put to rest: a man's impatience and a madman's conscience. This is how Cameron has come to view the enigmatic Jewels. The first was being addressed; the other matter would have to wait. Nevertheless, Cameron feels he must stay close to the woman, so he has assumed the role of penitent driver and passed the issue of what to do with Walt onto a brute in the organization, a henchman without a conscience.

"Take her to the boat!" Jewels' tone is even more agitated than before. He turns and struts away from the Mercedes, the inference being that his role at curbside has concluded. This affected posturing is only for appearance. When Jewels gets to the car that has been hibernating in an abandoned alley a short distance away, he will have to think over the events of the afternoon and how they affect his situation. For now, Cameron and the woman will travel to Sandy Hook where Jewels' yacht is docked. Jewels will continue down the Garden State Parkway back to the casino in Atlantic City. There, he must address the now unfinished business, as well as redesign his plans for Christine before Saturday. He can wait. Yes, he can wait until Saturday. He need not give any more thought to ending his life. Perhaps his luck has changed like the flip of the cards. He never thought that his imminent demise in Atlantic City would be altered to a forthcoming renewal of his life.

As Cameron watches Jewels dissolve into the shadows under the street lamps, he is well aware of how precarious his relationship is to this man. Tonight, Jewels seems even more ambiguous. Cameron removes any empathy he has for him and looks at the beautiful woman lying across the back seat, unconscious and unaware of her present circumstances, or what is about to happen to her. He is saddened by the thought that he has been an inadvertent participant in her ruin. He bends into the sedan's back seat to maneuver her body into a more comfortable position. Cradling her head and back, he gently lifts her, then readjusts her skirt, which has twisted awkwardly around her waist. He removes his jacket, rolling it into a bundle, and gingerly places it under her head. He returns to the driver's seat. For a moment, he is a frozen figure. Staring through the misty windshield, his fists clench tightly around the steering wheel. Cameron shifts his vision onto the rearview mirror above the console and stares at the reflection. He wants to lie next to her, kiss her, but his will is not his own. The vapor beyond the windshield pitter patters "let her go!" He starts the ignition and turns on the wipers. The blades squeal and swish away another missed opportunity.

These thoughts continue to invade his psyche as he drives into the darkness toward Jewels' yacht. He squirms in his seat; the Mercedes inches down the street. As it passes under each antique lamplight, water beads burst against the black sedan's hood like pregnant teardrops sobbing into watery tributaries on the glass. There will be no escape for her. Her destiny was sealed even before he saw her, because of who she is and who he is.

The Mercedes crawls past the abandoned alley; a lone figure hunches with his hands jammed deeply in his pockets, his jacket collar still up. He continues to watch until the sedan's tail lights lose their definition in the mist. Then he inadvertently smiles. It is difficult to discern if it is a tenuous expression of satisfaction or a momentary startle of apprehension. Jewels turns and walks deeper into the alleyway to a different destination.

III

AFTER THE LONG DRIVE from the restaurant, the early morning light peeks over the darkened horizon. Cameron carries Christine from the Mercedes, her limp body draped over his arms. He boards the yacht and notices none of the sparse crew is on deck. He carries the comatose woman directly into her designated stateroom and places her gently onto the bed, carefully sliding the pillow under her head. He scans her body. She is even more beautiful in this serene state. Her auburn hair flares upon the white pillowcase, exposing her delicate neck. The white blouse is half unbuttoned, and her soiled skirt is twisted about her thighs. Ironically, her legs lie tightly against each other, as if instinctively protecting her vulnerability. He is aware that his desire must be constrained, so he turns from the disheveled body. Another, waiting outside the stateroom, will take care of the rest.

When he reaches the door he pauses, thinking that maybe he can still rescue her. His worst fear is that this emerging desire does not matter anyway. Does he have enough courage to believe he can challenge fate? He twists the knob and allows foreboding fate to enter. His duty is done. He must remain on the other side of the door to wait for the message.

His palms clutch the damp railing from the oncoming morning mist as he tries to block the scene on the other side of the door, but cannot, because he has witnessed it before—too many times. He envisions Christine carefully being undressed, undisturbed in her drugged state. He knows she will remain unconscious at least until late morning. Perhaps it is better that way; perhaps it is best she remains shaded from the cruelties imposed by society. Better that she not know what is being done to her. After the exam a white sheet will be draped over the naked woman's body.

Finally, the heavy door to the stateroom opens, the task completed. The other emerges, ready to impart her findings to be relayed to Jewels. Cameron ignores her presence. He continues to peer at the vast ocean rather than admit his implication in the deed. He dreads what is about to be disclosed, yet, conversely, craves to know for that knowledge could determine Christine's redemption or renunciation. However, he knows that whatever is imparted to him, his ability to save Christine will become even more tenuous.

They both lean against the railing, Cameron and the specter, in a momentary pause before the distortion of truth. Following the proper protocol of her station, for a menial as well as a female, she must wait for permission to speak. Finally, Cameron, knowing that he can no longer prolong the inevitable, shifts his head sideways, sweeping a glance past her eyes. He commands his eyesight to ignore her message and to resume glaring out across the water beyond her. However, she misinterprets his action as a signal to proceed. She looks directly in his direction and gives a nod, no words, just a single nod. Her gesture is ambiguous. He is unsure of its intention, yet he does not prod her for clarity. He does not want to be engaged with this creature any further than necessary. He affirms her message with his own equivocal nod, pretending that he has understood her. A mirage of truth sometimes is enough. Dismissed, the woman dissipates into the early morning gray. What Cameron did not see was the subtle but satisfied sneer on the old woman's face as she walked away.

If a man has surrendered his humanity so long ago that he can no longer remember having had it, is he incapable of ever retrieving that humanity? This is the ache within Cameron's empty soul as he leans alone against the damp railing. He wanted to be inside protecting her, holding her, making passionate love to her. But he can only grip the rail tighter. It is not that he is incapable of taking command of the situation; it is just that he is unfamiliar with these new sensations stirring within him.

If he does not act on these urges, it will only be another lost opportunity, another notch in the Old West Colt 45. And just like those infamous gunslingers who refrained from human embrace as they sauntered along the dusty paths of their solitary lives, he, too, has allowed opportunities to slip away so easily throughout the passage of his own time. He longs for this woman. She holds the lure of a pristine world in which he can begin his life over. He would make different choices if she were by his side! Sometimes even a gunslinger can become a captive in a contrived truth.

He lifts his face for the early morning sun, waiting to implore forgiveness. His tightened fists ease around the rail, but the coldness of the metal sends shivers through him. The unresolved writhes away from the vanquished night as it sinks behind a blind sunrise.

IV

SO, IT HAD BEEN A DREAM, I think even before I open my eyes. Branches gently sway among shadows like arms mesmerized in a slow dance, the limbs wrap around my body, pulling me downward in a tender rhythm. The shimmering greenery of the forest blends into an undulating blue of the sea as the wooded melody transformed into a siren's song. At first the singing is just above a whisper; then it surges. The high-pitched lyrics are in a language I cannot recognize. Nevertheless, the tone is beguiling. The siren might sing to forlorn sailors, but her stories are about women. As a woman, bearing naked breasts above the unrelenting seas, her voice becomes their voice. It wails about their plight; it is her plight, too. She sings to the passing ships of men sailing the seven seas in search of some meaning in their lives just as she sings to justify her own existence. For her function as a female is to sooth their delirious passions and give them hope that one day their thirst will be satisfied. She tempts them with her obsessed embrace, lures them to their impending fate as she quietly drowns their insanity into the inescapable depths of their souls. It is no wonder that men have feared women throughout the ages. Even Adam was doomed by Eve's song. If men were to control their own destiny, they had to make sure that women would never possess them. That is why the beautiful siren must relinquish her sweet song beneath the sea, so that her voice is forever silenced above it.

This is the song that plays within my dream. Of course, I am a different breed. I am an American woman. A child born from the ashes of the Sixties, my femininity articulated by the women of that decade. They hewed hope from the fallen tree of male domination, and the feminine mystique emerged. This is what I was told. But now I am a female in my forties, and I doubt what it means to be a female.

The blare of a distant fog horn nudges me awake into a haze of diffused lights. Small moons smudge the inside of my eyelids. I try to open my eyes. But strangely, realize they are already open. I drift into the haze. Perhaps I am still dreaming. My stomach stirs for an answer. It is an answer of hunger, not of food, but of a different sustenance. The rumblings in my bowels churn again. Bile seethes deeply in my throat, an answer wanting to be spewed, but too constipated for release. I am a captive in some elusive shadow of truth.

This is a strange place and I am completely naked, trapped in my own madness! I try to ignore that thought. I tremble. For some time, I tremble. The sensation subsides into gentle shivers. A whiff of salted air caresses my prone body. It is warm, but not soothing. The warmth molds beads of dread above my brows. Sweat tickles from my forehead, down my cheek, behind my neck, and collects in dampness on my pillow. Another breeze drifts into the room. It is cooler. Its chill triggers another solitary tremor. The shockwave reverberates into convulsive upheavals and this time, I cannot harness them. I twist my head over the side of the bed and purge my guts in an endless spew of vomit onto the floor.

When there is nothing left and the dry heaves have finally subsided, I return my head to the pillow and peer upward again. I lie motionless and fixate on the painted ceiling of alabaster white. Rectangular inlays of darkened wood interrupt its starkness. I find the contrast artistically pleasing, and my breathing regulates. The tremors have dissipated. Overhead spotlights are scattered throughout the low ceiling. Yes, these must be the small moons, casting their eyes downward at me. They appear so close it feels that if I was able to reach up, I could touch them. However, I am still motionless from the neck down, a sensation brought about by a reluctance to move in this world of bright moons. But this is not the only light.

Flickering sunlight blends with salty breezes, and ribbons over me again. I turn my head sideways to discover the source. Beams are filtering through slats of wooden blinds. The thin slats try to restrain the imposing sunlight but cannot halt its fluttering rays. The humidity seeps through and presses against my skin, shackling me into a deeper sense of apathy. I remain where I am and listen for what lies beyond the blinds: a chorus of familiar sounds. The flapping of waves, the squawk of sea birds, the gentle hum of a boat motor wash away the residue of bile. Once again, I drift. My head refuses to leave the security of the pillow, so I allow my eyes to roam.

Three of the walls are covered in wooden cabinetry, flaunting countless petite drawers buttoned with shiny brass knobs. The wood is the same highly polished teak as the rectangular inlay on the ceiling. On two adjacent walls alcoves interrupt the layers of drawers. In one niche fresh flowers drape gracefully over the edges of a colossal, multicolored cut-glass vase. In the other recess there is a painting of a fair skinned mermaid. It piques my curiosity, and I linger on the picture.

A female figure rises from a blue green ocean, her slender arms twisting upward in a longing reach toward an unblemished, powder blue sky. She looks as if she is levitating into the heavens. It is a curious painting. However, it is not the only canvas in the room.

I shift my attention to the opposite wall. Three massive abstracts hang, smeared aggressively with primary nautical colors. The brash compositions provide uplift for a compartment that seems to fold into itself from the excessive teak wood and low ceiling. It is a cabin designed with detail and luxury, yet foreign, and remote.

My vulnerability is entombed in ludicrousness. I bring my body up to a sitting position; the room whirls in a sudden sickening rotation. I plop back down to the haven of the pillow, uneasy about any recurring bouts with my stomach juices. I just want the merry-go-round to stop. Finally, it does.

I decide not to make any more sudden moves but commit my body to its vegetative existence. Perhaps if I lie very, very still, my fractured brain will regain enough sensibility to figure out how I came to be in such a state.

I am drawn back to the ocean sounds beyond the open window. Although still veiled behind the closed slats of blinds, I envision a lone seagull within the flapping of the waves. Its squawking seems to summon up another distant memory, the squeal of a hawk hovering over a waterfall. Squinting further into tunnel vision, I snake through a haze of a smoky room and muffled voices to a pale-yellow tablecloth. An open wine bottle is in close proximity to twin wine glasses, one half empty, the other untouched. Near the table's edge are five one hundred dollar bills, hopelessly neglected. Yes, I now know where I had been and with whom I had shared that wine. His name was Jewels.

Aware of a subtle rocking motion, I look down at my nakedness and surmise just where and with whom I had been last night. Uncertainty swindles that possibility, for how could such a kind man take advantage of me? I am caught between wavering truth and stark assumptions. Here I lie, interrogating my naked predicament. Explanation hints with the caw of the seagull beyond the blinds. It mingles with a song of the inescapable plight of the siren who so easily relinquished her body. She had been a solitary siren, lustfully singing to the inevitable fate of men. But are not both men and woman doomed in the same watery arena? Can there be redemption for either?

An insistent knocking from the other side of the cabin's metal door ruptures my probing and severs these ambiguities. I partially sit up and grab the thin blanket to cover my exposed body in a vain attempt to shield my vulnerability. Whatever could I be thinking, that a flimsy sheet could protect me from the demons of the unknown?

"Who's there?" In spite of an effort to sound compelling, my voice is hoarse and feeble. I am not up for any further assault on my person.

The door squeals open and an ancient, disfigured specter enters. "Good afternoon, misses, can I be of assistance?" It certainly is not what I had feared. The voice is solicitous enough with a gracious foreign accent. But most important, it is the voice of a female. I relax.

Immediately, I am aware of the stench of vomit emitting from the side of the bed. Whoever this person is, I need to harness my pride and fear to regain mobility.

"I do need some help getting washed…" then, realizing my self-absorbed ingratitude, I add, "Thank you."

The hunched figure moves further into the room. She is dressed in Middle Eastern garb and wears a head covering, yet her face is fully exposed. I can see that it is deeply lined, blemished with darkened blotches and timeworn scares, a face markedly unnatural—menacing. But, in spite of this, her voice remains receptive and comforting, and I am quite grateful for her presence. She flutters about the stateroom, quickly pulls away the covers, and firmly embraces my waist to lift me from the clutches of the bed and my wretchedness. I surrender into her custody. Together, we shuffle over a polished wooden floor to an adjoining bathroom. She glides my body into a shower stall and gingerly places me onto a wooden plank seat. Reaching past me, she twists the spigot. The gentle spray rains down upon my bowed head and drapes a vapor of warmth, rinsing away not only the sweat and vomit, but the soiled confusion of my soul. I bathe in an ageless stream of sustenance. When I am finally able to look beyond myself, I see through the misty glass door that she is gone.

Eventually, I turn off the water, but remain seated, drifting further in lost time. It isn't until I begin shivering that I decide to leave the shower stall. The strange woman is there, obediently waiting with a dry towel over her forearm. She drapes it around me and lightly begins to pat my body dry. I am perplexed. Why would a stranger be so attentive?

"Who are you?" I cannot constrain that question any longer.

"I'm Jewels' wife," she replies unassumingly.

V

AFTER THE OLD WOMAN had attended to the pressing tasks in the stateroom, she returns to the bathroom. She stands back a few feet from the shower, trying to avoid peeking through the steamy glass at the nude figure. She understands why Jewels is drawn to her. The American is not slim, but has fine, feminine lines. The deciding feature is her skin, the alabaster white a thin layer of fragile whiteness. The translucent face is as flawless as the surface on a china doll. The specter is drawn to this woman's beauty, accentuated by her long wavy hair, a deep auburn that gives even more contrast to the purity of the blanched skin tone. Perusing the rest of the body, she sees a well-developed female flourishing with maturity. The coppery lushness continues its sensuality in her pubic hair and coffee-tinted nipples. The older woman tries to recall when she, too, was so sensual. Unfortunately, that memory has faded. She bows her head with jealous reverence, but the occasional glimpses remain. Snatching a rolled, sea green bath towel off the shelf, she stoops in servile attendance and waits with resigned obedience. She has acquiesced to this position in her life long ago, in spite of the veiled anguish within her.

When the door of the stall swings opens the ancient woman slides the towel off her arm and begins to dry the alabaster nude. As she brushes off the moisture, she tries to brush away the naked privilege allotted to those with such distinctive skin tone. Her own complexion is a deep, muddy brown.

The innocent victim senses the animosity as the initial gentle touch becomes a brisk rubdown. This is what prompts the question: a question not asked out of idle chitchat, but from some forbidden peculiarity. "Who are you?"

The answer is delivered with solemn directness, divulging that she, indeed is Jewel's wife.

The naked woman takes a step back in denial and bunches the edge of the towel in a twisting grip. It slips slightly off one shoulder and embarrassingly she covers herself in a gesture that suggests she is finally conscious of her nakedness. The specter knows the American woman has questions, *why was she here…naked…Jewels…her?* But she will not appease those uncertainties, at least not now. For some time, the two say nothing to each other. Finally, the pensive woman slithered past the old woman, returning into the stateroom. The other follows.

The American approaches the edge of the bed and gazes at it. *What is happening?* The bed has been made; its fitted beige coverlet snuggly tucked into the mattress, pillows fluffed and arranged as if they have never been lain upon. The offensive odor of vomit is also gone, replaced with a pleasant whiff of lavender. Lying on top of the coverlet are the woman's clothes, clean and pressed. Without turning around, the woman asks, "Did you do this?"

As before, the reply was simply, "Yes."

"When?"

"When you were in the shower."

"I couldn't have been in there that long!"

"You were. You must have lost track of time."

After pausing momentarily to digest that comment, the woman clears her hoarse throat and whispers, "Thank you."

Perhaps the old woman could have liked this person in another time and place, but now that can never happen. This beautiful woman is her arch rival, so there can never be any alliance; she is a reminder of everything that the older one loathes about herself, about her life, about her existence as a female, about the man who has denounced her. She will do everything in her power to destroy this American woman. Already she has begun the process. Now that she knows what Jewels wants the plan is simple. The old fires that still smolder within her will finally be quelled. It is the only power the pillager can claim as her own. Unfortunately, when the unsuspecting woman thanks her, there is some remorse for what she did last night as well as the consequences that will befall from such action. But that thought is short-lived.

Approaching the outside door, the old woman turns and gives a slight bow, not the customary dismissal of respect, but a hidden vow of defiance. And with this final gesture the ancient woman leaves the not much younger woman alone.

VI

I DRESS QUICKLY, feeling a disquieting urgency to leave the stateroom; something evil seems to be lurking within. This unnerving sensation is exacerbated when the old woman tells me who she is. *Jewel's wife? Jewel's wife!* That seems implausible. I cannot accept that Jewels was ever involved with such a woman. She is hideously forbidding. In fact, it is still difficult to believe that Jewels would be involved in any licentious act with me. Yes, it is true that I do not really know this Jewels, a stranger. But somehow during our casual encounter at Dante's Restaurant, I felt a bonding in spite of my drunken state. Do we really need to know someone a long time to connect? We both seem to have unresolved issues in our lives, and by sharing those sentiments as strangers, the burden was temporarily lifted for each of us; we were no longer alone. No, I cannot accept that Jewels would harm me. However, I also cannot negate that I am missing some vital information. Could I have been violated last night by Jewels? I cannot recall anything after the restaurant, except the dream of the mermaid with naked breasts sweetly ensnaring wandering sailors. Did I, too, become a desensitized siren of the night? The unforgiving answer to that question is lost in blind memory. I leave the room, its truths and its lies.

Outside, the yacht is just as exquisite as the stateroom is inside. The polished teak captures the brilliant sheen of the afternoon sun. The luster is everywhere, on the buffed deck and railings, on the vinyl threads and flotation cushions, on the riggings and triangular flags. I move to the stern of the sizable vessel and lean over the edge of the guard rail, clutching it tightly. The wake is not intense, just a continuous whitening foam trailing behind like long strands of hair splitting in half. The white froth churns upon the sea as engines drone in a steady hum; I am mesmerized. The marriage of the visual and the vibration releases the unsettled thoughts from the stateroom.

Within the vast, darkened blue of the ocean an array of diamonds pepper the water's surface like sparkling voices. Their mirrored reflections yearn to sing to me, and I feel privileged to witness such beauty. I imagine mermaids under those sparkles. Did their golden hair sway with the water currents under the surface as my hair wisps in the wind? Did I belong to the same sisterhood? I grip the wooden guard rail at the stern of the yacht, viewing what has been. Or, are those kidnapped sirens not just mirages, but foreboding voices of what truth lies ahead? In spite of a momentary chill, the low autumn sun warms my backbone as it penetrates my white linen blouse. I tilt my head back to bask in the rays' caress.

"Entrancing, isn't it?" An invasive sunbeam stabs through the fragile harmony, and I spin around. A dizzy sway thickens inside my head, and I shut my eyes to catch my balance. Grabbing for the railing, I seize an arm instead, and immediately I am in a firm embrace. I know this man in spite of my closed lids. He scaffolds his body into mine so that we face each other and presses me tightly into the guard railing. A slight pain shoots through my backbone, and I squint into the glaring sunlight. I see only a fragmented head blocking out the ball of fire, his hair blazed like a sunburst. It is not the man I thought. The disjointed face is Cameron's. My mind is as disconnected as the strands of his hair wildly flicking in the restless sea breezes. He tightens his arms and draws me further into him. The whiff of his aftershave is the same as at the concert, affirming that this is indeed Cameron and not Jewels. That realization eases my anxiety. Pulling me from the railing and its frothy backdrop, he guides me under the shelter of a nearby canopy. No words are exchanged; another language is in play. I acquiesce under Cameron's touch. Words must wait. Although we are now out of the harsh wind, the edges of the awning continue to flutter nervously, a reminder of the inescapable volatility of nature.

Under the covering a table has been prepared: dried fruit, hard flatbreads, and various marmalades. All are in heavy white bowls, pigeonholed within a low nautical counter top. There is also a glass filled with a red liquid. He positions me on the low circular lounge in front of this stunted table. I grimace at the food.

"Cameron, I'm not so sure I can eat any of this." My insides are definitely empty, but still very much unsettled.

"Christine, this is exactly what you need." He lifts the tomato juice to my lips. I sip its contents. He spreads some deep purple mixture onto the dry toast and feeds that to me, too. I don't resist; I am in need of tenderness. As Cameron gently feeds me, I see his effort is not only to replenish me with food, but to grace me with a hope that tomorrow is worth saving. But I cannot negate the underlining incongruity of this situation. Was he not the one who manhandled me in the hotel room? For what reason? Should I trust him now? His presence on this yacht is unfathomable. How has he materialized here?

"Cameron, why are you here?" I stare into his eyes to emphasize the importance of my question.

His response is a prolonged silence.

"Cameron, you have to answer me! Did you sleep with me last night?"

"No." His response is crisp. He looks away to avoid the follow-up.

"Did Jewels sleep with me?"

He turns to face me. "No." This time, his response has a vicious tone. Nevertheless, I will not allow his abrupt attitude change damper my questioning.

"Then why is Jewels' wife on this boat?" I am becoming agitated by his laconic answers.

Once more he hesitates, as if calculating a reply. "Because Jewels owns this yacht." I give him a look to show that I will be relentless in my inquiry.

"He felt that you needed some rest from your inebriated state last night. So, he asked me to take you back to his yacht."

There is a pause in the conversation.

"Then Jewels is not here?"

"No, Jewels never came on board. He went back to Atlantic City. He'll be there till Saturday."

That information should have been enough, but it retrieved the ghostly conversation between Cameron and Walt that I had overheard from the hotel room's closet. The pivotal word was "Saturday." Saturday was brought up as some designated date for me. Walt was supposed to fill in the whole story during our meeting at Dante's. But Walt was a no-show! And I am on a yacht in the middle of who-knows-where. Am I again being kidnapped? Is Cameron my kidnapper? How does Cameron know Jewels? Is Walt looking for me?

"Cameron, do you know where Walt is?" If he does know, that means that Walt may also have been abducted and will further confirm that there will be no one to save me.

"Yes, I know exactly where he is."

My apprehension becomes my nightmare. We sit in silence, avoiding looking at each other.

VII

CAMERON STANDS AND MOVES beyond the canopy into the twilight of the setting sun. His resiliency is fading. He presses his chest into the guard rail just as she had. Like her, he is captivated by the hypnotic splitting in the yacht's wake. And like her, he scans the ocean. He hopes that she does not call him back for more questions. He needs to forestall the unspeakable, but he knows that more questions will come; she is too perceptive. How long can he keep her at bay? Any conversation will bring her closer to the unspeakable. How can he possibly explain the events that led her to this yacht? This momentary separation from her gives him the time to either devise a plausible fabrication or divulge the truth.

Remaining at the stern, he places his elbows on top of the guard rail and clasps his palms to mull over his options. He is expected to follow orders. There has never been a problem before, but he is not a man who adheres to loyalty defined by another. That is why he has survived in this unforgiving business. The only allegiance he has is unswervingly to himself. He learned long ago to be self-reliant, to serve his own selfish interests. Yet, now, it is that very selfishness that challenges him. He can never allow her to be possessed by another man. She must be his alone.

This type of thinking is in direct contradiction to self-preservation. Jewels is not a man to be pushed aside. Jewels is formidable, with extensive resources affording him the luxury to get what he wants. And right now, Cameron suspects that Jewels wants this woman not for a client anymore, but for himself. Such a conflict will certainly be a game of wills, for Jewels is both relentless and ruthless. The only trump card Cameron presently holds is that Jewels has no idea how Cameron feels about her. He digests this thought, flinging it into the twilight's breezes. He turns and faces her. And like men's mutinous desires throughout time, he deserts his survival and surrenders to the lure of rapture.

Her unkempt auburn hair swishes in the updrafts. The delicate wisps brush against the lifted collar of her white blouse and straggle across her bare neck. She rubs the sleeves of the blouse, running her hands briskly up and down her arms. Apparently, she is chilly, perhaps scared. He fixates on her exposed throat; it is pale, vulnerable. He is beguiled. He walks deliberately before her. His fingers wrap around her exposed neck. She rises, absorbed by his touch. He moves into her as if wanting a kiss. It is an action of desire, nonetheless, still startling. Her eyes widen. Two luminous pearls mirror back to him, and he understands how they have captured Jewels as well. They are like the blue green waters of a siren's eyes in search of truth. Suddenly, her expression alters into suspicion. Pushing him away, her voice becomes insistent.

"Cameron, you better tell me what this is all about!"

He withdraws from her magnetism by releasing his hand on her neck and moves under the canopy to the opposite side of the prepared table. Some distance is needed for him to recollect his thoughts. Although he knows that it is time to explain, he is hesitant how much she can handle. Initially, she was to believe the problem concerned Walt. Maybe this is how he should start. That will mislead her before addressing that the problem is really her.

Inhaling deeply, he begins. "Walt got himself into trouble." He pauses to see if she is accepting that. She nods, confirming her own lingering suspicions. "Walt owes a tremendous debt for losing in a poker game. You know, just bad luck."

Disbelief returns to Christine's face; Cameron recognizes that she will not accept any of this without further explanation of what is really at stake. He must convince her that Walt is in a very precarious, if not dire predicament. Her doubt about Walt's luck, of course, stems from the fact that she knows him all too well. Walt is too good a poker player to place himself in a no-way-out corner. Cameron knows this, too, just as he knows the nature of Jewels. There is an uncanny similarity between the two men.

VIII

CAMERON PICKED THAT UP the first time he watched Walt in action two weeks ago during the preliminary tables of the tournament. After a week of elimination, the easy marks were siphoned off, leaving only the best poker players.

Remarkably enough, the East coast was the site for the arena this year. Usually Vegas or some well-known gamblers' paradise in Europe was the venue of choice. But because of a tidal wave of Asian interest, mixed with Middle Eastern sovereigns, an unlimited number of players entered the buy-in at this year's Atlantic City coveted tournament, making it the debut for numerous newcomers to the game.

Walt was an amateur, certainly not well-known. He was from the old school of poker, bred in dingy, smoked-filled rooms with dubious characters in the tough back alleys of Newark and Philadelphia. Schooled on the streets as a boy, he crafted his instinct of *when to hold and when to fold*. He was a player of intuition rather than rehearsed moves. That made him a very dangerous poker player. No one could second guess him because he was unpredictable. Because his survival depended on his performance in poker, he made sure that he was never greedy or stupid, thus enjoying an unassuming lifestyle over the years. In many ways, Cameron and Walt were kindred spirits. Walt knew how to survive at the tables, just as Cameron knew how to survive away from them. Perhaps it was this imbedded self-preservation that allowed Cameron to quickly spot one of his own kind. Cameron knew that this gambler would never be in the final round of the main tournament. Instead, he would have a personal invitation to sit at a more exclusive table. He would be one of the hand-picked poker men to cut the deck in a private parlor at the casino, a table arranged by an anonymous benefactor. This private game would commence on Friday and continue until the showdown of last man standing. Few would be privy to the existence of such a gathering.

Why would Walt be attracted to this closeted event? This "under the radar" poker player had a much different motivation than most gamblers. For Walt, poker was not only an arena to make money or display his skill. It was not just a game of wits against others, it was a game against himself. It defined his existence. Poker is indiscriminate in allowing men from all walks of life to sit together as equals. It validated worth for a street kid like Walt, who had endured too many hard knocks in his life. Ironically, it provided a similar lure for Jewels, who in spite of a silver spoon existence, also needed a sense of self-worth. Regardless of different backgrounds and skills, these two men had one commonality: They lived vacant and disconnected personal lives. Poker gave them the legitimacy for their rebellious retaliation against that society.

Although Cameron understood the rebellious spirit that brought these two men to Atlantic City, Christine's grumbling over Walt's loss was for a different reason. Cameron is aware that if he is to get through this operation, he has to quell her prodding.

"Look, Christine, I know you and Walt go way back. He is definitely a shrewd poker player, I must admit…you see, it was just a bad shuffle of the cards…his luck just gave out."

Her head twists into a skeptical tilt; she sees through his rambling. "Cameron, I don't know exactly what's going on here, but one thing I do know for certain: Walt never plays poker with luck. The only time Walt depended on luck was when he was afraid, and that only happened once in his life…when he was eight years old. If Walt is in trouble with a gambling debt, it is not because his luck gave out." Suddenly she recalls Walt's recent penetrating wail in the hotel room. She decides not to reveal that because Cameron has no knowledge that she had overheard that cry of fear from her closet sanctuary.

Even though it is late afternoon, a darkening ether palls the sky. The seams on the yacht's planks lose their demarcation like the lines drawn between him and this woman. *How much should he reveal to her?* He turns to flip on the deck lights. When he looks back, he sees the radiance of her beauty under the soft hues. And the seams fade even more.

"Look, Cameron, apparently, you know the truth. Just tell me."

But the truth will devastate her, or perhaps worse, he will lose her and that will devastate him. Perhaps he will be able to spare her the intolerable hurt if he conveys just enough to appease her. He continues by briefing her on the background.

"Okay, Christine, Walt made it through the first couple of rounds during the week in the main tournament. Then, last Friday he was invited to play at a private poker party. This happens all the time. Personal gaming tables are set up apart from the main event because poker is played all day, all night, anywhere, especially if the stakes and players are attractive. And during that poker game, Walt miscalculated his final hand…and he lost… big."

"How big?"

"More than he should have bet." His words are fainter than before. And like the blurring of the wooden seams, his intention to defraud her vanishes. He will unveil what has brought her to this moment. He steps toward her, resolved to continue his narrative.

Suddenly, there is a low squeal behind them. Cameron turns and spies the figure lurking just beyond the deck lights. She slithers out of the darkness, a specter materializing from dim recesses of memory, misplaced, yet never expunged. It is the deformed woman from the stateroom, Jewels' wife. For some time, the woman had been clandestinely absorbing their conversation. She deems her duty in life to be the eyes and ears of her husband. Yet, in reality, she has not just been spying for Jewels, but waiting for the moment to seal an unquenchable vengeance against him.

She emerges from the crevice clutching a tray with two cups and a coffee urn, the plausible basis for her presence. She places the tray onto the table and unscrews the urn. A slow ghost of steam emits from the nozzle like that seductive tango between Cameron and Christine in their playful bantering on the hotel's terrace. Now he is engaging in a different joust, a more reprehensible one, which will bring about grim consequences for Christine, and for him if he is not careful. He snatches the urn and pours the liquid into the cups, rudely ignoring the deformed woman's service. It is his attempt to send her an incontestable signal of dismissal. She understands his snub. Yes, she will go. However, before departing, she imparts her own intimidation. Her glare warns him not to transgress into unforgiveable waters. Even though he knows he is, he no longer cares. He despises this woman and all that she embodies. Impatient, his words are blunt. "That will be all from you! Leave us alone!"

The specter does leave, but her stench remains, an insidious reminder of his duty to his superior. It is an odor that sinks him back into the silence of an irreversible rogue wave. So, instead of continuing to address Christine, he moves to the stern of the yacht. With his back to her he leans over the railing, his integrity grappling for words. He is aware that Christine is pensively waiting for him to divulge why she is there. He wants to answer her completely instead of just giving her fringes to the truth. He gazes into the yacht's wake, seeking how to begin. Jewels' wife has flustered him, and he cannot hold his thoughts together. They dissolve in the wake of the yacht, parting seas, pushing back the layers of lies. What he wants to say aloud, he can only speak silently to her…

IX

YOU ARE AN INTELLIGENT WOMAN. Surely, you can recognize a ruse. Do you even know when and where this all began? You know. Don't just look to me for the answers! If I give you enough time, you can figure this out for yourself. And then I need not worry about misleading you anymore. You know that it began on Friday evening…

…about midnight when I noticed you leaning against the door to the private poker room. I could not determine if you looked like a demure school girl, hesitant to enter a classroom, or an overconfident prostitute, eyeing her prey…caught in some passageway between approval and denial. And there you remained, tugging on your lower lip as you were about to enter, squinting through the cigar smoke, the residue from the five gamblers, who reposed on their cushioned chairs throughout the evening like languid Cheshire cats, licking short-lived victories or rationalizing hasty retreats. Just before your arrival, three of the felines had left the nest with shattered pride. Only two gamblers remained.

How did you ever wander into this remote area of the hotel without being stopped? It is restricted for the financially snobbish clientele. It is exclusive not like the main poker room, where you probably started the evening in search of your friend? Did you think that he had abandoned you? Let me assure you that main room was not for him. He needed a more private place where his suggestive repartee could flit with cigar smoke. Bawdy innuendos about the finer sex could be embellished in exclusive privacy. A place where yarns about conquests, fueled by the seismic bosoms that paraded in and out of closed doors satisfy manly thirsts—firm and quite alluring bosoms. Was that the reason you were hesitant to enter, trying to determine if you were the schoolgirl or the prostitute?

You missed the earlier hours, the prelude to your entrance, even though you eventually became the main event. I was there from the beginning, standing on the sidelines, an invisible conspirator. I witnessed the hands of poker that led to the insanity.

The action really began about ten o'clock when the five players were still sizing each other up. As I watched them, amusing myself by labeling each gambler by the disposition of each man's play. These labels have been around a long time among gamblers. The old timers used them to intimidate their opponents. The "lion" was Carl Mann, one of the bigwigs of the casino, very skilled at poker and very tough to beat. Charles Rich, the "elephant," was also a well-known player on the circuit. Unfortunately, his reputation preceded his play, a reputation of playing too many hands and remaining in the game beyond when he should. He seldom made it to the final faceoff. Then there was the old navy seaman, Captain Frank Massey, the "mouse." Too conservative, too timid with his bets, therefore never a big winner. Then there was the "jackal," unknown to the others, but not to me, his demeanor as crazy and unpredictable as his playing. The fifth hand was also an unknown, a foreigner, the "invisible specter" of the feast. He seldom spoke, or even looked up from his cards. Such a group should be boring to watch. However, that was not the case at that table. If you had been present, your ears would have burned because our jackal made enough fire for the entire bunch.

On the yacht Cameron looks back and spies Christine staring beyond the side rail, hypnotized by the diminishing light upon the disheveled waves. He returns his gaze to the receding wake as he reflects on this firebrand, continuing to speak to her in his head...

The jackal was not only an erratic gambler, but a captivating one. Even his attire was an ambiguous statement. Over the back of his chair he slung a blue vintage jacket that matched his washed-out jeans. Although in his forties, this slapstick look gave him a youthful appearance despite the receding hairline. Instead of the finely pressed, button-down tailored shirt and casual slacks apropos to this level player, he added a black t-shirt with an iridescent green "St. Patrick's Day from Savannah, Georgia" logo, in spite of its being November in the Northeast. Every so often, he would vigorously rub the design on his chest for good luck, boasting, "The second biggest St. Patrick's Day Parade in the country!" It was obviously an act of intimidation.

Nevertheless, he remained within thin lines of decency on one matter. This was New Jersey, just a stone's throw away from New York City. Although he was crass on other subjects, he was sensitive to the dust from the Twin Towers. He spoke of being raised in Newark, just across the Hudson River from the 9/11 hallowed ground. He struck a chord with the others at the table when he spoke about 9/11 as a time when impenetrable buildings crumbled, invincible friends perished, impervious beliefs shattered…and nothing would ever be the same again. Yes, this unbridled jackal had an ambiguous nature. He was arrogant and cocky during the entire game. He had the gift of gab. The dude never shut up! He jabbered over each play. I knew it was only a tactic to gain advantage by distracting a player's concentration or intimidating a weaker one to drop out. Without a doubt, he knew his poker, and in spite of his antics and gutter language, he never underestimated his opponents. He easily detected vulnerabilities in others. And only once did he move beyond the bounds into offensiveness.

"Oh!" he said in a high-pitched intonation, "Oh my, hardly a trickle, and on deuces!' Of course, it was to remind all that the pot was too scanty. Then in the following hand he recited a nursery rhyme using curse words. This behavior seemed to spook the mouse into folding his hand prematurely. Maybe it revealed something within the verse. However, I knew that he was only bluffing. No matter, he took the pot and slouched into his chair with a haughty smirk. His unkempt curls draped over his eyes in a lazy look of mischievous confidence.

Yet, there was more to this jackal, another side to this gambler. I caught it in the watch he wore. His Rolex covertly was turned inward on his wrist. If a man's timepiece reflects the man who wears it, this timepiece was the only exposure of who he was. The rim was etched, "Go All In" and "Stay Off Tilt." Could an owner of such a watch be taken seriously? To the other players' demise, they saw only a hotshot who never took anything seriously. I saw him differently. When he played, he took the term "Off Limits" literary, and the larger the stakes, the more tilted his play. I recall the last couple of hands…

"Big Blind, ten thousand…Small Blind, five thousand," a sum in stark contrast to the jackal's casual demeanor. With each shuffle of the cards, the prominent dealer chip marked who would have the advantage in this richly played game.

With each new hand, the jackal positioned his right shoulder in his low, exaggerated lean over the table's ridge and aligned the two dealt cards in cupped palms. Then he would flip up the corners of the layered cards with his thumb for an imperceptible peek. Quickly, he would jerk upright, flinging one arm impudently over the back of his chair and pose, plopping his head in a tilt as if to instigate the start of play.

"Let's do it!" he snapped as if in drunken impatience. He appeared to always be in an alcoholic stupor. Ironically even though there were always filled tumblers in his cup tray, he covertly passed them back to the hostess, untouched, whenever his opponents were preoccupied. If he needed to sidetrack further, he did so with his blatant prodding and licentious yarns, the language invasive enough to stir any male chauvinism or offend any female intolerance. Even the croupier, who tried to ignore the lewd intimations with lowered eyes, often wore a slight grin in understated applause. On the table was the flop: a deuce, a seven, a jack. All hearts. The turn brought a queen, also hearts.

"Well, lookie' at all those hearts! I'm in love again!" the jackal's voice thundered.

"Can I help anyone here?" the waitress inquired.

"Hum, yes, mamma," moaned the jackal moving his glare from the cards on the table to the bosoms, which ballooned from her black, skimpy outfit. It was an obvious reference directed to the waitress's question and not the exposed cards. He ordered a scotch and soda, which, of course, would never be touched.

The betting became furious in spite of one last card to be drawn. The dealer's chip, which lay in front of the jackal, meant he controlled the betting. It was time to take advantage of that position. He knew each player drooled over all those red hearts lying naked on the green. He raised with his usual fanfare. The foreigner folded and kept his head lowered. Strangely, the jackal momentarily ceased his babbling and squinted at the foreigner—just squinted.

The last card was turned over, the river card, which darkened the field on the green. It was a black spade, the notorious Queen of Spades. The jackal was not naïve to the high probability of someone holding a flush or a full house, or even three of a kind, all strong hands. Up to this point, the jackal had held back on any significant betting. He was more than ready to go in for the kill; the pot was enticing. But, this river card, the Queen of Spades, has history among gamblers, a forbidding reputation as a spoiler. Was it time to challenge fate? At that moment, I came to understand that this jackal was superstitious, a gambler who takes omens seriously. Nevertheless, I saw the decision he made. But first he wanted to have a little more fun.

"Oh, I'm in love with all the heartthrobs in my life!" He whined his innuendo as the waitress returning to the table with a Sprite for the elephant. She stood directly across from the jackal. As he stared at her, he quietly said, "I should call...but... maybe I should call on you first, Babe?" The waitress glared back at him. Making his eyelids roll into a lazy droop, his eyes sank to her riveting breasts, and he moaned, "I do love those voluptuous queens." All caught the lewd interpretation. Surprisingly, instead of calling the hand, the jackal winced at his hidden cards and then, face down, tossed them away to the dealer. "I fold." He looked up and caught the foreigner looking at him. An instant connection was made. The jackal, like the foreigner, was out of this game. The betting was over, leaving the other three men to eye the sizable winnings in the center of the table.

"Let's see 'em, gentlemen," the croupier directed. The players turned over their cards one at a time cursing their loss to the final opponent, Carl Mann, the skilled lion.

"Well, I'll be damned! Didn't see that coming!" the lion tried to sound humble as he piled his winnings into obscene stacks of color chips before him. He turns his head slightly to the jackal. "So, buddy, what were you holding before you dropped out?"

"Nothin', just bluffin'."

"Yeah! Well, I really thought you had something going."

The jackal smiled back. I suspect he was well aware that he had the winning hand probably with pocket queens, making four of a kind. The foreigner also surmised the jackal's hand after the comment of "all those voluptuous queens" followed by the dubious stare. These theatrics would never be allowed in the main casino, but this private game stretched the limits. By the end of the evening, those limits would be tested beyond anyone's fancy.

Finally, Carl Mann said, 'So, buddy, don't think I caught your name."

The jackal turned to him and nonchalantly said, "Walt."
I, of course, knew the guy's name but didn't speak up because there was only one other gambler who really mattered. And he already knew it, too.

Throughout the evening, the reserved foreigner from Pakistan remained unmoved by Walt's chatter. He gave a nod or slight tap on the green for his checks and folds. His silent signaling was crisp and never misinterpreted. He tolerated Walt's boisterous routs because Walt never was a threat to him in terms of making any sizable losses. Moreover, this foreign gentleman recognized talent, and understood that these antics, along with calculated meager winnings, were nothing more than a ploy to give the other players a false sense of confidence. Therefore, the foreigner remained above the fray, waiting, too. Besides, Walt's entertainment made the hours more digestible. The three other men not only laughed, but often encouraged his innuendos.

Shortly after the "Witching Hour" of twelve o'clock, something changed. At first it was only a subtle stirring, perceptible to just two of the players. A new hand began. Each player received their two holding cards. The mouse raised before the flop, a strong indication that he was concealing formidable picture cards. Of course, he became very talkative, parading his auspicious cards even more. Then the flop laid a deuce, a three, a five, all hearts; unfortunately, a low-level flop, and certainly not a good flop for the off-suited power cards held by the mouse. I watched the mouse grimace and become "quiet as a mouse," after he checked. In spite of the low cards on the table, they were all hearts and teased a possible flush, not a bad hand to start the betting. The players looked at their cards again… all except Walt. I'm sure the other players were thinking the same as I, because they joined the mouse and just checked. It was to be a waiting game.

When the turn showed another three, and not another heart, the elephant raised, followed by the lion's re-raise. The foreigner and Walt stayed quietly even. However, because of the heavy betting on such low exposed cards, the mouse spooked and folded. No surprise there. Four players remained.

The river brought out the second five, the last non-heart card. Someone most likely held a full house. It was only a matter of who held the larger "boat" as we say in poker.

The elephant finally had his boat, a full house, only a small craft. The lion's self-righteous sneer sniffed a feisty meal. The foreigner and the jackal still were quite subdued, making the lion suspiciously silent.

The lion fixated on Walt, who looked like a drunken chimpanzee, swinging and smirking in the chair. The lion saw an arrogant chimp who was probably bluffing again. The lion decided that it was time to press the jackal.

"Well, Mr. Walt, I have to tell you that I find all of your bedtime stories quite entertaining, but I do think it's time for you to go to bed. First, let me send you off properly. I raise."

The pot was sizable. The lion was hungry, ready to go in for the kill. Although the foreigner had enough to cover the new bet and had already committed a large chunk of his chips in the pot, he folded. He pushed his chair slightly back from the table as if to gain a different perspective of the scene. He believed that he understood this jackal, who only shot from the hip when he was sure that his gun was loaded. Yes, the foreigner would be patient and quietly watch. This unsettled Walt. He could not figure what made this foreigner tick.

When the foreigner folded, the elephant's confidence unraveled. The elephant peered at the flop as if in a trance, trying to recall all the cards that had been played. Of course, it was an impossibility because every precaution had been taken to prevent cheating, but he tried anyway. He looked at his threadbare chips and felt he had been blindsided. The croupier prodded him to make a decision. In spite of a good hand, he realized he had probably lost. He pushed the remaining chips into the center and abruptly stood, tossing his cards on the table to expose his full house with threes as high cards. After a moment he exhaled, "It's been a pleasure, but I think it's time for something stronger than Sprite." He moved away, not waiting for the outcome.

Then came the last hand just before you showed up, Christine. Two gamblers remained at the table, Walt and Carl Mann, the lion. Walt still had not responded to the lion's raise. It was time to make his debut.

"Well," Walt said, "You boys have been teasing me to a point that I'm not sure if I'm the king of the jungle, the Elephant man, or just Mickey

Mouse!"

I'm sure that these men were acquainted with the poker types. The mouse squirmed uncomfortably in his chair; the lion smiled regally from his throne. Walt sidestepped, bringing the Pakistani into this mix. His voice was not as boisterous as before, but it was just as impious as ever. "So, as my daddy used to say to me, 'Boy, if you find yourself getting tired, then either pull it out, or put it all in.'"

He paused to give a lewd smirk toward the waitress, who gawked at him for a second, then turned away. "And so, I'm goin' be a good son and follow my daddy's advice."

It was the make-or-break moment of the night. Shortly after that remark, Walt counted his chips and pushed over enough to cover the lion's bet. "It seems that I'm almost all in," he said as he slouched in his chair, one arm swinging recklessly behind. He had to get rid of the lion.

"Well, my man, Mr. Mann, I'm not sleepy enough for bed yet. So, I would like to re-raise you."

The lion snickered. "What with, the crumbs you have in front of you, Mr. Walt?" The others stared at the few chips before the condemned man. They foresaw the jackal's looming demise.

Walt ignored their stares and turned to the croupier in a somber, unfamiliar demeanor, and asked to sign for a marker. "If that's all right with everybody!" he added with abrasive aloofness.

There was a stiffened pause of uncertainty. The pot was sizable, this was a private game with no limits that included not only what was on the table. Someone would have to approve such a request.

Walt caught the quick eye exchange from the croupier to me, and then from me to the Pakistani. I'm sure that was when Walt understood who was the benefactor of this private event. He also realized who would be his main adversary at the end of the evening. The loan was granted, and the play continued.

Thinking over that moment, I saw that this was a calculated move, what Walt wanted to know throughout the evening: *Who is this foreigner and what is the real prize of the night.* The lion seemed oblivious to what had just occurred. He glared at his victim. "Well, Mr. Walt, it's time to expose yourself," he said, then snickered at his own lewd audacity, "And spare us from any literal translations, please!" Walt paused dramatically to savor the remark.

The betting completed, Carl Mann turned over his cards with lionized satisfaction, "I believe those fives make such a pretty foursome, don't you, Mr. Walt?"

Walt said nothing. He just leaned over the table in his familiar slouch and neatly stacked cards. The top card was a four of hearts. The lion sniffled, "Don't tell me that the other card is a six! You know that you would have to have a six of heart to beat my four of a kind, and those odds are rather slim."

"No, no six of hearts, not even a six," Walt said with pretentious resignation.

Walt continued to look down at his own cards. Then in his teasing fashion, he slid the bottom card into view. There lay the ace of hearts. "I believe that's called a wrap."

"No, it's called a wheel!" injected the mouse.

"No. That's called a straight flush wheel!" choked the lion.

Walt lowered his chin and raised his bedroom eyes upwards to the lion's, who had his glued on Walt's cards in disbelief. The Pakistani saw that Walt had really won at the flop and had been drawing them all into his sting. The foreigner learned what he needed to know…*this jackal does not bluff when the stakes are high.*

The lion had enough to play a couple more hands, but Walt had broken him. The lion was done.

X

SOME OF THE BEST POKER PLAYERS in town had toppled like pawns on a chess board, leaving only two for the final showdown. The reserved Pakistani was who Walt was most concerned about, a matter solidified during the marker request. The real game of the evening was about to begin. Walt was up against a different opponent. And, because this mysterious man was the benefactor of the game, a formidable man of means, he must not be a man who should be taken lightly. As Walt deliberated on this, his nemesis was watching him.

After a short recess, the two men returned to the final table, the American gunslinger and the Pakistani backer, just as Cameron had predicted. They were about to play a different game of poker. The stakes were not just financial. This game of bluff would penetrate the soul of each man.

Prior to resuming play, Walt decided he needed to know more about this quiet gambler. Continuing with his casual demeanor, he extended his open palm toward the foreigner in a handshake of courtesy. The Pakistani responded with a detached nod, an extension of the foreigner's impenetrable icy-cold armor. This did not seem to throw Walt who believed that nothing is so absolute when engaging with human brittleness. One just needs to find the Achilles' vulnerable site. He must slingshot the right size pebble to get "Mr. Ice's" attention. He resorted to his old standby, sexual repartee. However, with each distasteful potshot, there was still no response from the Pakistani. Walt realized that if he was to provoke this man of frost, he might have to be even more impervious than his opponent. He needed to do some insensitive fly-fishing in these waters. Like all good storytellers throughout the ages, he knew that if you tell an off-color story and sprinkle it with inappropriate insults against one's ethnicity, even icy-cold fish might bite. To be "culturally incorrect" might work. Walt began to talk about virgins.

"Let me ask you, Mohammad, do you have to wait until you die to meet up with all those virgins? That must be some kind of a bad love-in, man. I'll tell you, man, I can really dig it, you know."

Suddenly the foreigner stirred. It was only a slight shiver of his shoulder as if to flick away a fly, but Walt caught it. Finally, after a few uncomfortable seconds, the Pakistani nonchalantly replied. "All my wives were virgins when I married them." Then to clarify further, or to perhaps gain equal footing in this tenuous conversation, the foreigner continued, "It is expected of our women." Then clearing his throat. "By the way, my name is Jewels."

"Jewels, yeah, got it, Jewels, nice…real nice. You're a real gem."

Walt sensed there was nibbling on his line; he needed to poke the rod a little more. "So, Jewels, you say all your wives are virgins? What do you do, ruin them, then throw them away?" Walt felt that if he continued to be crude, it might throw this player off balance since nothing else seemed to faze him.

"Oh, no, I'm still married to all of them."

Time to do some reeling in, "Really! How very boring. Most American women are expected to be experienced before they get married; that's how we American men like it…nothing better than being with a real woman…if you know what I mean."

Jewels did not respond to the insult. He looked past Walt to the figure leaning against the door frame. Her image was like a mirage, and he questioned the legitimacy of his state of mind. It had been a long evening, and without a doubt he was tired. Yet, as he stared, this vision crystalized.

She was delicately layered in a muted, beige and violet, soft chiffon dress with short, sheer sleeves. Her auburn hair fell upon her shoulders accentuating her bare slender arms and pale naked neck. Unruly wisps tumbled downward to the pronounced crevice of her breasts. Without pretense, she was alluring, not alluring with a paltry naiveté of an attractive debutante, but with the poised confidence of a sophisticated woman. He was excited by the sight of her. Yet, she seemed to be oblivious to his reaction of her.

Because Walt's back was to the door, a situation he often avoided when playing cards, he did not see what Jewels saw. However, he did grasp the change in his opponent and immediately knew that whatever was behind his back would finally bare the exposed Achilles' heel of Jewels. That was also the first time Cameron caught a glimpse of Christine before the concert.

The flapping of the canopy catches a waft of sea breezes coming up from the western horizon. The approaching bleakness smokes toward the yacht, locking everything in suspended gray. The chill harasses me, and I twitch from an uncontrollable shiver. Even the warmth from the coffee cup that I have wrapped my fingers around is no consolation. Cameron poured it for me before he retreated to the railing at the stern, a short distance from where I am still seated. He is allowing time and space for me to digest our interchange about Walt. Yet, somehow, I really do not believe that we were just discussing Walt.

I have always thought of myself as a clear thinker, someone with the ability to collect the pieces of a puzzle and deduce a logical understanding of what is happening. So why am I so uneasy before this man? I am drawn to him. When I get back to my desk, probably overloaded by now with articles for the up-coming issue of *Women's Monthly*, I will do some inquiries on this Jewels character and this man who is connected to him in some way. But what day is it? It cannot be the weekend anymore. Could it be Saturday, yet? No! However, it must be close to Saturday! Time has become as lost as I am.

The thought of time poses more pertinent questions. If I don't show for work this week, will I be missed? I have been given leeway to come and go as I please in my office. I have never been pressured to punch a clock. That means no one has ever questioned my absence. No one will question my absence now. No one will come looking for me. And where would they look, anyway...here on this unassuming yacht...somewhere on a vast sea...beyond any visible harbor? And if found, how could I have any plausible explanation of what has happened to me? I look for answers as I try to peer into the mind of the stranger with his back to me. Hanging onto the railing he is motionless, frozen in the ominous mist which envelopes the yacht. I want to speak to him, to ask the questions spinning about me. Yet, perhaps I need to remain silent, to regain some sanity of my situation.

Can answers lie in the recurring songs of sirens' distant voices? I allow myself to sink into the lullaby of the ocean's cantos. The songs are about Walt. And about me. The voices chant, "Where is Walt?" And I ask the same question about me. I drift with the waves beyond the railing as I sort through the strange occurrences. If I can recall past events, I might be able to gain some understanding of what is happening. Replenished by the small morsels of food that I had ingested with Cameron's prodding, I am more committed to unraveling those thoughts. The answers must be connected to this man before me. The coincidence of Cameron's presence weaving in and out of the days might be the thread to lead toward a semblance of truth. But I cannot approach him...not yet. How will I know if he is telling me the truth unless I can remember some vital details myself? Cameron leans farther over the railing. He, too, seems unresolved, as if grappling for answers in the ocean depths.

Is my life in some balancing act with his? I delve into Cameron's comments about Walt; his words lacked accuracy. Throughout our lives, Walt and I have been entwined in unquestionable truthfulness, always forthright with each other. Sure, I was not always privy to his daily encounters, the details of his precarious situations. Some things are left better unsaid. However, on the important stuff we never held back. We sought each other's advice. That is why Cameron's comments about Walt's gambling problem sounded so hollow. Walt would never lose big in a poker game. He is too shrewd. Therefore, I am missing some cornerstone of this puzzle. I see the vacant space on this chessboard. *"Where is Walt?"* is the haunting song from the deep. The clues lie with this man before me. I watch him as untamed strands from the back of his hairline fling about in the breeze.

The boat's engines have stopped. The crew has begun to secure the yacht for the oncoming storm. I look over my left shoulder. Under the reach of the floodlights, white crests glisten on the black water. They twist in sensual dances, beckoning me to sink further within my memory, crooked fingers luring me deeper into the unknown. Lightening halos the rims of the distant cloud formations, followed by a solemn boom. Under the oncoming night's cloak, a cocoon of rainclouds wraps around Cameron and me, severing us from the rest of the world. The breezes electrify the wisps of my hair, caressing my cheeks. I try to rise, however, I cannot find my balance in the rocking yacht, I grab the table's edge, and immediately sit back down. My advantage is slipping away from me. I look over to Cameron, still clutching the railing.

It is obvious that he is hedging from telling me what has happened to Walt, and what is happening to me. I push back time and look deeper into the sea. Disjointed images float to the water's edge like flotsam, and I hear its modulating intonations. I recall the woozy woman awakening naked this morning in the stateroom as sirens from the deep wail and moan outside her porthole.

I remember the firmness of a disfigured woman's hands as I regained some inner fortitude to rise and return to the world. She was Jewels' wife, Jewels, the stranger who caught my attention at the restaurant. Although I thought I had met him before last night, I still cannot recall where or when. He, too, held me firmly in his arms as I collapsed onto his shoulders, seeing the wine glasses before a vanishing, wooded vista. His words threaded the trees, like the swish of red wine flinging in space. Jewels was grappling for meaning in the gaps of his life. He seemed to be yearning for some new breath.

I, too, was at the edge of breath. That was why I was at the restaurant. Walt was going to tell me something important…something that concerned why I was held against my will in the hotel room in Atlantic City.

But Walt didn't show up at the restaurant! That was not so very unusual, but the fact that he did not get back to me was significant. Maybe Walt was hurt! No, that is not it. Walt can never get hurt! My entire life has been cosseted by my unconditional faith that Walt is strong enough for both of us. He made a promise to always watch over me. Are not gods invincible? But Walt is only a man, and even gods have frailties. Perhaps naïve childhood oaths must be broken when challenged by irreversible actions.

Cameron seems to know where Walt is. So why is Walt not here with me? And who is Cameron? What is his connection to Walt? It was Cameron who held me against my will in the hotel room, who grabbed me in some thwarted embrace—an embrace that felt terrifying like a displaced hunger! But then there was the quarrel I overheard as I hid in the hotel closet. Cameron and Walt were discussing something covert about next Saturday. Something that involves me. Whatever it is, it is connected to that hotel room and its casino.

The waves no longer give gentle slaps. The floodlights strain to remain lit, then flicker as from some inexcusable shame. Cameron turns and faces me. Behind him, I can no longer distinguish the line of demarcation between the darkened sky with its highlighted, turbulent clouds, and the black ocean with its stringy, lacey froth. All fade into a backdrop beyond his silhouette. He rests his back against the railing and braces himself, wrapping his elbows around the railing's bars. He is unapproachable. He leans back and tilts his head, his eyes on mine. It is as if he knows that I can figure it all out if he gives me more time.

Okay…okay, Cameron! I am resolved to figure this out!

Cameron said something about Walt making it to the finals for the poker tournament. The casino was holding the tournament for two weeks, and Walt had been there for the first week without me. But when I arrived at the hotel during the second week, I couldn't find Walt in the tournament section of the casino. That was late Friday night. I had registered with the hotel and brought my luggage up to his empty room and freshened up. Walt told me that I could stay with him after I told him of my breakup earlier that day. Of course, there were separate beds. If Walt needed to satisfy any male urges, he just had to go elsewhere. Walt had enticed me to join him on this junket two weeks ago when he bought two concert tickets for a performance this weekend. He said to me, "Well, Babe"—Walt always called me "Babe" when he knew he had made a good decision about something. (On the other hand, he called every girl "Babe.".) "Well, Babe, we will hit two birds with one stone; you will go see this singer of yours, and I will make a lot of loot at the same time!"

I knew that he had been preparing himself for the big poker bash. It seemed like an auspicious weekend. But when my date bailed, I lost any will to attend. "Oh, Babe, forget the bastard! I'll take you to the concert…I'll make it worth your while…Just pack a few tidings and come on down to A.C.! I'll leave you an extra key at the front desk…get yourself settled…Come look for me…I'll be at some poker table." These words are the same ones that had played and replayed in my mind. There must be more, something I'm missing!

XI

ON FRIDAY AFTER I PICKED UP the guest key, I showered and put on something attractive to restore my soul and my femininity as well. Then I ventured out to find my friend. Walt has always been an enchanter at the restoration of lost souls. But I could not find "Walt Babe." I searched the casino floor where the tournament was being held. When I could not find him, my first thoughts were that he was just carousing. Although this was a usual occurrence, I was miffed. He should have left me a note of where he would be, especially knowing how fragile I was from my ordeal of the morning.

It was about midnight, and my sense of time and space had become muddled as I wandered aimlessly through more remote sections of the complex. Finally, I had enough and decided to retire. It seemed useless to search for him at that hour anyway. As I strolled back to the main elevators that would bring me to the room, boisterous laughter came from an open door down a vacant, side hallway. I had been worn-out by the day, but I still retained that unsettled curiosity to see what was causing the commotion.

When I came to the doorway, I saw a vast but dimly lit room with about ten men milling inside. Some of the men huddled around a couple of waitresses brokering for trysts for the night. Although rather large, the room had a sense of congestion about it, not only from the swirling cigar smoke and suggestive snickering, but also from the scattering of vacant poker tables and chairs which laid dormant and close to the walls, like lost souls out of their element. I, too, felt like a lost soul. And viewing the scantily dressed women with the men, I knew that I was definitely out of my element. I was about to leave when I suddenly caught something familiar within the dimness. Under a subdued light there was an isolated poker table in play. Although he had his back to me, I instantaneously recognized the infamous slouch and curly hair. It was "Walt Babe" sprawling in his seat in all his glory. There was only one other gambler at the table, but I couldn't see clearly enough from this vantage point. I did spot the croupier, which would suggest that the final showdown was either in process or about to convene. I was intrigued by the scene. It was like some secret society of men where women—respectable women—were barred. So, if not a respectable woman, but a curious one, I decided to remain by the door.

I would never intrude when Walt was involved in a poker game. I understood how seriously Walt played, and made sure that I would not be a distraction. So, I leaned against the door's edge and watched and waited. I knew poker decorum; that a respectable distance from the table must be maintained when a game is in play. Although I never participated, Walt had taught me that little detail a long time ago, as well as other incidentals of gambling. However, when he swiveled around in his seat and saw me standing there, he discarded that protocol and vigorously waved for me to join him. I thought that maybe he was out of sorts and needed me, so I left custom and respectability behind, and approached. When I was standing next to him, he wrapped his arm around me and strangely remarked, "Here's my girl!" He had never been so familiar with me, not during a poker game, endgame, or any other game in life. And, I certainly was not his girl! But I chucked this causal familiarity up to a bigger picture. Walt was never casual in anything that involved poker, so I figured that this pretentious show was part of his game plan. Because this was really beyond my scope, I just went with the flow.

Yet now, as I analyze the events that led up to this stormy evening on Jewels' yacht, I can see that my scope was not just shortsighted, but perhaps blind. Reemerging from these thoughts back to Cameron's glare, the convoluted puzzle begins to crystalize.

That was when I saw him! It was just a glimpse, but enough for me to see how compelling he was. And I understood that he had been staring at me since I leaned against the doorway. As I drew nearer to the table, he continued his stare, a stare that was piercing. His glare was not disrespectful, nor unwanted, for I felt a flush of flattery at being noticed. However, his eyes would not let go of me, even when I demurely looked away. But when I glimpsed back, I still saw his eyes pressing into me. I froze. What should I do? Walt squeezed my waist stronger to reaffirmed that I was playing my part just right in this little melodrama. The stranger gave a slight nod as if confirming his decision, and then turned his face away from me. That disarming man was Jewels.

Shouting above the clamor of the bellowing waves, my voice is more pronounced, "Cameron, last Friday it was Jewels who was sitting across from Walt at the poker table…right?"

"Christine?" Cameron breaks from his reverie with a question and repeats, "Christine?"

"Jewels was at the poker table," I repeat, no longer as a question, but a revealing statement.

He nods, just nods that I finally got it.

"Okay…okay!" getting my second wind. "So, what has that to do with Walt?" Cameron continues his stare. I am no longer shouting; however, I am adamant in my probing. "What does that have to do with Walt's debt?" He still does not move his eyes off me. "And why am I on this yacht?"

He does not answer me. He does not answer any of the questions I am throwing at him. He does not have to. The answers are refocusing with the clarity of the aperture of a camera's lens.

Apparently, Jewels is the one to whom Walt owes a debt! How could this be connected to me?

Walt interpreted the glare of his opponent. And as he pulled himself around to discover the source of his epiphany, Walt saw what had captured the interest of this impenetrable man. As Christine adorned the rim of the doorway, he realized the bait needed to finally bring the beast down. However, at that moment he did not comprehend the full impact of his action. Walt waved her to approach the game.

XII

AND NOW IN THE APPROACHING STORM comes Cameron's silent answer; from mid-air Christine snatches Walt's betrayal. She slowly rises, pushing her volatile body from her seat and moves beyond the edge of the canopy. She faces Cameron in disbelief. Just above her head the fringe on the covering convulses in the uncertain ocean gusts. Another shriek of lightning flashes and its trailing thunder reverberates in deafening aggression.

She shudders but remains where she is. The floodlights on the yacht falter, go off, return momentarily, and then extinguish completely. The yacht holds its breath within obscurity. Another flash, she blinks and snapshots Cameron at the railing. Then all is blind again. In the next flash he reappears just inches from her, but only for a second, as if reality has magically snapped its finger, he is there before her, then gone. All is suspended in muted blackness. Gently, very gently, in distinctive plunks, beads of rain smack the vinyl cushions on the deck chairs in slow, discordant notes. The symphony riffs into a pitter patter upon the wooden deck, escalating into a rushing crescendo. Still within night's mask, she asks plainly:

"Cameron, what was the debt?"

Although darkness still drapes them, her sight returns through the touch of his hands as they stroke her arms. He, too, can only see her through his fingers as they smear the cool wetness over her silken skin.

The flashes return indiscriminately, allowing them to view each other as if in a series of still frames in a filmstrip. *Frame one:* Rivulets of rain kidnap wisps of her auburn hair and plaster a few soaked strands across her forehead. "Cameron, what do you want from…" It is another unfinished question. *Frame two:* Cameron's face is so close that his breathing seems to siphon her question and replace it with his. *Frame three:* The sunken caverns of his eyes search her face, scanning for the answer to what he just asked. *Frame four:* Her teeth clench in hesitant thought before darkness returns, a pause to allow desire. *Last frame:* Her lips form the muted word, *yes.*

He cups his hands behind her head and firmly draws her to him. He presses his cheek against hers and her eyes close. He slides his lips upon hers. The tingling intensifies as he brushes over those lips, back and forth, back and forth, as the rain continues to lash out in relentless whips. With only sensations to guide them, their impatient limbs explore curves as desire deepens into an intimate reservoir where rational thought ceases. They pause to release the tension. He glides his palms down her limp arms to her hands. Their fingers intertwine to form a language of their own. Still in darkness, he takes a step backwards, then another, and then another, squeezing tighter to reassure her. They shuffle through uncharted corridors of the deck as their arms stretch like a suspension bridge under the shadows of deliberate intent. When they turn the last corner before her stateroom, they pause again. Another bolt of lightning glowers over them. He asks his soundless question once again, and in the split second, she gives him the same soundless answer.

It is in the pause when we are lured into the anticipation of breath. There, time halts, replenishing sensibilities of our humanity. Passions are not to be traded or denied. They are the fulfillment of our lives. Throughout this day, Cameron leaned over the guard railings looking for an answer to justify his life. As he stared endlessly across the ocean at the horizon, he realized there was nothing out there. There was no answer to his questioning. He was a man who had lived his entire life negating personal feelings. That was why he was so effective at his work. He had been immune to human degeneration. To him, the faces were not human faces. The faces were not faces of desires, or even fears. The impersonal faces were only commodities. He was only a man hired to get the job done. But something had changed when he saw her face as she leaned against the doorway to the poker room, dressed in her beige and violet chiffon.

He opens the door to her stateroom and guides Christine out of the drenched night. Inside, he stands facing her. Within the tint of moonlight, she is captivating. He desires her more than anything or anyone in his life. He does not quite know how to respond. He takes a couple of deep breaths. These are different breaths: breaths of promise, but also breaths of regret, for he must have enough courage to tell her the truth before he embraces her any further. He drops his arms quickly and moves away, startling Christine. "Cameron?"

He quickly returns to her and presses her tightly into his chest. "I'm so sorry, Christine. No...No...it's not you. I want you to know that I want you...I want you very much...right now." He hesitates; after a moment, he continues. "But there is something that you need to know. And I need to tell you...because after you hear what I'm about to tell you...you may not want me to make love to you."

"That I'm Walt's debt to Jewels?"

"No,"

"Good, because that's what I thought and that's crazy!"

"No, not just that." He quickly looks away. "More than that."

Christine's confusion quickly becomes another foreboding. Cameron takes her hand and brings her to the bed. She sits on the edge. He situates himself next to her, close, yet not touching.

"Cameron, I'm so cold." He feels the uncontrollable shivering, and he knows what has to be done. He reaches for the blanket and drapes it around her shoulders. Slipping his hand underneath, he removes her drenched blouse. She assists in removing the rest of her clothes. He wraps the blanket tightly around her. He is moved by how willingly she acquiesces, in spite of whatever he is going to impart. Suddenly the floodlights come on outside the stateroom. The light slivers through the slats of the shutters, which cover the porthole windows, imprinting bars of illumination across the blanket, and onto her face. Because the rain has removed her makeup, he can see how her skin is like silken sand, unblemished in fragile purity. Her wet, matted hair, even darker now, has a reddish sheen that brings out the unusual hue of her blue-green eyes. He cannot release his gaze and takes a deep breath of awe. As the rain continues to pelt against the shutters, the blustering wind snaps him back to his task. He begins by telling her what had happened at the poker game, the night he first saw her.

XIII

ALTHOUGH OUTSIDE THE STATEROOM the world batters itself with reckless onslaught, inside this apprehensive man and this perplexed woman sit patiently at the edge of the bed, clasping hands in a promise of truth. Cameron keeps his eyes on her face. Even if he should discern a pang of fear, he is committed to continue his narrative until he has finished. He leans his shoulders close to hers, so close that he can feel the brush of her breathing, a gentle wisp. She waits. He speaks softly in that private space between two people that wraps both deeper into that space of intimacy. "Christine, do you remember the night of the poker game in the private room at the hotel?"

"Friday night...very late Friday night?" Her quick reply suggests that she wants him to understand that she, too, is committed to candidness, however, her sudden eagerness also suggests how fragile is her reluctance.

"That's right...this past weekend." Cameron is still trying to unravel what had caused her to be ensnared in the plot. She examines his stumbling eyes as he peruses her face. She can see he is trying to speak about something that is very important. She needs to allow him to continue without interruption. He catches the intent of her silence and nods.

Cameron inhales and begins in a matter-of-fact tone. "This was the same poker game that was in play since three thirty that afternoon. The game started with five men, but by the time you arrived after midnight, it was in the last stage...only two men were left."

"The showdown!" She interjects, but immediately admonishes herself for speaking, wanting to retrieve her words and not break his commentary.

He, however, is impressed by her poker vernacular. "Yes, the showdown!" He gives her an inquisitive smile. "It was Jewels and Walt facing off. And, you know, Christine, I knew it would all come down that way, even before the game began." He caught the wince of her twisting brow, a query that perhaps this game might have been tampered with. He arrests her questioning look. "Oh, everything was on the up and up. The promoter insisted on that."

"So, you're not the promoter?" Even though she is about to make love to this man, a stranger, someone she knows so little, it doesn't matter. This thought surprises her.

He pauses and decides that she needs to understand who he is in the scheme of things. "No, Christine, I am not the promoter. I'm too poor to provide the kind of financial backing to have a private poker game at a prestigious casino. I'm merely the person who provides the incentives, the one the promoter needs to grease the palms that need to be greased to make things happen. I made the arrangements, and it was my responsibility to ensure that this was an honest game. I made sure of it...and I take my responsibility quite seriously." He stares deeply into her eyes to see if she understands what he means. She seems to. He continues his explanation, "I know what level of player Jewels is, and I saw Walt in action the week before in the casino's main room tournament. I knew these two were in a different class than the others." She nods her head in agreement for she has always known that Walt's poker flair is unmatched.

"You know some poker players are just a special breed: self-assured...deeply layered...intelligent. They have an insatiable appetite and will satisfy it at any cost. Unfortunately, these also are the men who crave the game of poker because it feeds not only their greed, but their ego. They live on the fringes of illegality because their boundaries go unchecked. They never join traditional society, even though they have a smooth enough veneer to look respectable. But the most significant, and perhaps most dangerous characteristic of this type of man, is that he really cannot fully distinguish what is honest from what is dishonest in or out of the poker game. And that is the man I had known for years; that is Jewels."

She understands that he is also describing Walt and is impressed by how adept Cameron is in grasping human motivation. An uncomfortable silence follows. Like a whiff from a shadow, she senses his reticence about her resiliency in coping with whatever is gnawing at him.

"Cameron, it's okay…it's okay. You can speak to me…I can handle it." A subtle pang of concern clinks within her, but she ignores it. "It cannot be that bad!"

He stands and moves away from her, then turns around. Although these were the words he needed to hear, he is still in angst. His pitch rises. "Jewels is not only a successful poker player, he is also a successful business man…quite a successful business man! Ironically, Jewels came to A.C. on some other business, and poker was to be a small diversion. But that diversion became the main event." Cameron's precarious commentary becomes the trek of Sisyphus pushing an endless boulder up the side of a mountain toward a shadowy precipice. And within his own myth, he fears that this will lead to his own demise. He does not want his life to end this way, nor does he want it to be her fate either, for he is moved by this woman. She is different, much different than any other creatures he has known, exquisitely different. He vows to intervene in this downward spiral of impending fate. He pushes the mythical boulder upward. "Jewels' business might not be legitimate, but I assure you, he is well-recognized in his country; his business is not only lucrative, it has made him a very powerful man, and…"

He halts in mid-sentence.

Christine senses that Cameron's hesitancy is that he is transgressing into some compromising area, and she wants to rush to him and throw her arms around him, embracing his fears away. "If you do not want to tell me Jewels' line of work, that's okay, Cameron."

"No, no. I need to tell you…Christine, you need to know."

Her pang rises into a vile panic. "Why do I need to know about Jewels?"

Although Cameron hears the faltering in her voice, he drives the boulder further up the mountain and avoids her question.

"Jewels inherited the business from his father. He did not have any option but to follow in the old man's footsteps, although, there are times I think he regrets the life for which he was predestined." Cameron realizes what he has said, and momentarily sinks into a similar reflection of his own life. He wants to believe that what he is doing now might be the first time he is rising above that void. She, however, sits motionless. Whatever panic slithers within her veins, its molten lava renders her immobile. Her breathing falls into his. The truth wavers somewhere in the silent spaces.

He takes a deep breath and spews words into those spaces. "Jewels arranges trafficking for female exchange."

"What?" A reddened ember flicks out from her veins.

"He buys and sells women for men."

Christine just stares at him for a moment; she can only react with a flat voice. "Prostitution?"

"No, not prostitution." He falters but needs to explain the rationale of such practices; she must harness that strength to endure what is to come.

"Throughout the Middle East particular women are in demand, and wealthy men will pay exorbitantly to be satisfied. In many cases it is really a win/win situation. Some of these women would only live barren, impoverished lives if they were not married off to these wealthy men, and in return these men gain beautiful women who bear them children to carry on their legacy. So, a legal contract is drawn up when a woman is chosen. Most of time the woman is well taken care of. That is…that is…" He abruptly stops speaking.

"That is…what is?"

The dragon, which has slumbered dormant in its lair throughout his life, has just raised its ugly head over the edge of the mountain. Cameron's lower lip slightly protrudes and begins to quiver. He has never displayed such emotion. But now the monster is about to unleash its deadly fumes, and the seething evil slithers in Cameron's unfinished sentence, "That is…unless she is not a virgin."

"Virgin?" Her perplexed squinting prods him to go further into the beast's lair of inhumanity; she is about to follow him.

Bluntly, perhaps too bluntly, he rattles. "In certain cultures it is of utmost importance that a bride be cleansed of the impurity of another man's body." He pauses, no longer looking at her. "When the contract for the exchange is made, it is unequivocally understood that she must arrive intact…untouched." He looks at her to punctuate his point. "You understand what I mean?"

Christine squints, then nods in affirmation. Cameron continues as if giving a dissertation. "Most of the time, there is no problem because in that part of the world these females are quite young and have been under the watchful eyes of their mothers and sisters. Because poor families can earn a sizable income from their female offspring in this fashion, it is a serious business to keep these commodities pure." Cameron caught the cringe on Christine's face at the word "commodities." It is a look not receptive to women being referred to as "commodities." He rationalizes. "It's really not personal, it's just business, and in some cases, survival...survival in a part of the world where survival is always on the precipice of extinction."

Christine's stomach begins a lowly rumble of uncontrollable shivers. How are these degrading acts connected to her, an American woman, and this man, whom she still desires? "So, what happens if after the exchange is made...and, Cameron, let's be clear here, don't you really mean money for a woman's body...that it is discovered that she is not a virgin?"

From those initial encounters with her, Cameron knows that Christine possesses an astute aptitude for delving into the heart of a matter. When she asks this question, he is not surprised, he just regrets that he must answer her. The weight of Sisyphus' boulder has become heavier than ever, but he persists in the futile push up his mountain of despair. "It's not just that money has been exchanged, but that the honor of the husband has been compromised. In such cultures, it is the law to marry only virgins. This is how governments control the morality of local cultural norms. If the bride is determined not to be a virgin, this is serious, so serious that it is considered a crime."

"A crime! Well, it's a good thing, I'm not going to such a place!" she snaps with droll sarcasm. And then she glances at Cameron to see if he caught her understatement.

"Yes, Christine, I am not naïve. I realize that you are an American woman, who lives in a free society immune to these practices."

His remark should have appeased any quivering inside her. But it doesn't. There must be more to her involvement than just her experiences. Her eyes twitch.

He ignores the trembling because there is more, much more. "However, sometimes poorer families still go ahead with the exchange even though they suspect that their daughter is not intact. They hope that they can get away with it. After all, if this is the truth about their daughter, then it is thought that she is really only dirty baggage and of no further use to them...so why not at least try to make an attempt to gain a profit? You see, Christine, deep within this tradition, women are considered only property of the owner. Whether it be her father or her husband, that man has the right to do whatever he pleases with that property. And, property, according to the law, can be bought, sold, traded, or destroyed." At the word "destroyed," Cameron's struggle is more evident.

Christine focuses on his lips and repeats her question more emphatically. "Cameron, what happens if she is found not to be a virgin?"

No answer. She pelts her stare upwards from his lips to his eyes, relentless in wanting the truth.

He addresses it, for he has no choice. "Justice must be upheld. If a bride is torn, or even if she does not bleed during the couple's first intercourse, she has dishonored her family and her husband. This is so frightening that some women have secret operations to reattach their hymen prior to their nuptial bed so that they can appear to still be virgins. But even if she is a virgin and bleeds, or if her husband suspects that she is not "clean," even without proof, he can declare that he has been shamed."

"Cameron, how could any wealthy, civilized person buy into this? No civilized country with enlightened citizens could believe this!"

"Not only do they believe it, the act of being dishonored might not end there. Her husband just annuls the marriage, and she becomes an outcast in her community. She lives out the rest of her life alone, or as a prostitute. But if the dishonor is pursued further, the crime must be exonerated by her family to salvage the honor of the husband.

Christine does not want to hear any more. She grips her fingers on the sheets of the bed and gathers the folds in tighten fists. "Cameron, if you do not want to go on…you do not have to. Then veering away from him…"Don't go on!"

But he has now reached the precipice, and the boulder is about to roll back down from whence it came. He blurts out in high resonance, "I saw it done…I saw it done, many times."

"What done? What was…done?"

His response is a gasp, but it audible enough for her to hear. "Honor Killings."

She had never heard that term before, but whatever it means, it is the twisted scalpel that is dismembering this man's innards. It punches her into silence. A numbing curtain drapes her.

His eyes can no longer stay on her but widen into a stare. His voice plummets to a low drone. "I saw a girl dragged through the streets by her hair. A crowd followed to be the witnesses, older, younger, sometimes other women, sometimes young girls…mostly men. I saw this scene repeated many times. Sometimes the girl is dragged by her father, sometimes by a brother, or another male relative. At first these girls do not resist; they have already succumbed to their fate. Sometimes the crowd clamors, 'Stronger, stronger, pull stronger!' and they clap their hands, shouting out that the father or the brother is a hero for what he was doing…and what he was about to do to restore the family honor. Then the moment arrives…it always arrives…no matter how stoic the girl has been, she begins to lose faith…lose her courage to keep silent…and she begins to whimper. They all reach that moment, and they all crumble. It starts when the young boys, then older men, begin to throw stones at her, as older women of the town flutter tongues into high-pitched sirens' shrieks. That is when her whimpering escalates into screams. And the screams become terrifying wails because the reality of the situation grips her. Her worst fears stem from the tales she has heard. That is probably what terrifies her the most, more than the physical pain of being dragged. It is what keeps most females in cultural bondage, imposes their willingness to be submissive."

"This is horrible...this is just horror—" She cannot finish the word.

Cameron swallows and then again swallows the word, "Horror...yes...horror! This macabre ceremony becomes even more gruesome when they reach her parents' house. As she is yanked into the place, everyone follows like shadows from hell. The women and some older men, who have seen this before, remain in the kitchen while her mother hosts them with something to eat and a warm drink of tea. Meanwhile, as the others continue into an adjoining room, the girl thrashes wildly under the tenacious grip of her slayer. Soon her hoarse voice bleeds into soundless terror."

Flayed by these words, Christine tries to abate from the truth, "So, she dies from fright?"

"Only if she is lucky!" And with arrogant single-mindedness, "Sometimes she is killed before she even has reached this stage when the offended husband just outright kills her as soon as he suspects that she has come to him impure...or the stoning in the streets is frenzied enough to slaughter her."

"Isn't there a law...to stop these barbaric acts?"

"Of course, but this is a morality based on the tribal culture, which decides what is acceptable. And in many cases, the law just looks the other way, indifference within a captive truth."

Neither speaks. Cameron is tormented as he watches Christine hunch over on the bed, clutching the blanket around her naked body. He presses his fists together and brings them up to his mouth. Although he has lost the words of prayer long ago, he now mutters for the strength to finish his description of this horrific event. He has to be vividly truthful if he is to save Christine. He fixes his eyes on her, waiting for hers to raise. An invisible thread of trust strings them together. Their breathing might be more labored, but it is symbiotic. They are becoming one mind, one understanding. He says the rest without lifting his eyes from her. The dragon rears on its hind legs and its nostrils disgorge the fiery evil.

"Then the honor of her disfigurement begins. This task is usually given to either her father or her brother because they are family, and they must prove beyond doubt their duty. The knife...the knife is large enough for all to see as the gathering, mostly men, lean over each other's shoulders for a better view.

Her clothes are ripped from her body. She is pinned down, legs separated, her ankles secured in the grips of men's fists. If she has not already died of sheer fright, which sometimes does happen, she is shaken by someone so that she doesn't become unconscious during the procedure. Then she is sliced, a number of times she is cut, and re-cut. The cutting continues with a gush of spurting red and mangled skin which paint her thighs. Then the knife goes to her face to imprint her crime there as well. When it is over, she is left to bleed alone.

The words are grueling, and he does not speak for a couple of seconds. "If she does not die, she is disowned from her family, never to be married, subjected to live an improvised, desolate existence bearing the disfigurement of shame not only by her intimate scaring but also through the testimony of her facial scaring. Because blood has splattered everywhere, men return to the other room wearing the splotches like badges of honor. And throughout this event, a casual gathering of cordiality continues in the kitchen. Now that the deed has been completed, those witnesses sit down and join the others for food and tea."

His eyes swell, but the tears do not flow. They are stuck in a hollow reservoir of emptiness. She continues to peer into him, trying hard not to ask her next question. He reads her stare, and knows what the question is, and he knows he cannot hide from it anymore. "Yes, Christine, I saw this because I made the arrangements, and I was responsible for the goods. And if the goods were soiled, I made further arrangements." He pauses. "Like I said, I take my responsibility very seriously."

Like a gush of lava flinging wildly into the air, a cry of despair vomits from her throat. She collapses on the bed and cradles into a fetal position. He rushes to her. Collapsing his body over her, he whispers, "I did not ever touch the knife...I never would do that." But those words are not enough. He has to finish telling her the truth as she shakes uncontrollably in his arms. "I did something worse than that...I stood in the corner of the room and watched...and felt nothing...and did nothing to stop this horrific act, caught in my own indifference."

He bows his head on her forehead. He cannot carry the burden of these memories alone any longer. These acts cannot be changed or ever rectified. It is too late for that. He sinks in the resignation that he has lost her, too. The "boulder" has just rolled over him, and everything in his life was for nothing. She was his last spark for living. He closes his eyes.

She releases herself from under his hold and slides away. He falls onto the bed supplanting his body for hers. The only evidence he has that she was real is the warmth left on the sheets where her body has lain.

The blanket slips off her as she drifts before the port window. Slivers, imprinted from the floodlights outside, imprison her face as she stares into the blinds. She stands naked before the light. Rain beads pepper the outside glass like anonymous tears and embed their shadows on her cheeks. She is like those tears, lamenting what has gone before, moaning about what has been, shivering about what cannot be. What happens to a woman who is never ready to dispel the shadows of her past, as this stranger has? What happens to a woman who tries to veil her passions into immobility, as this stranger no longer can? What happens to a woman who will not risk the possibility of change, like the ache of this stranger? What happens to such a woman at forty, who has lived desensitized to intimacy? Can she ignore these questionings any longer? Is there more to what she is, to what she can be? Or is it too late to matter anymore, but only to remain in a captive truth of her own?

XIV

AT FIRST, SHE BARELY HEARS the voices. The singing is distant, almost too remote to believe that it exists at all. She empties her mind and gently closes her eyelids. The sound of the waves kissing the keel is no longer harsh, just defined. She sways with the rhythm of female voices blending in overlapping arias in an ongoing opera embedded in the ocean waves. They are songs that have been sung from the beginning of life on earth. Women have always loved to sing beautiful music. It has been an integral part of their essence, just like forgiveness. The beauty of this singing has always been there for any listener who appreciates it. The layers of voices entangle and separate so that each voice can be heard distinctively. As a woman, she sings for herself and she sings for other women. She now needs to sing for men. The tragedy lies is that her sweet music will fall on deaf ears.

Walt watched and did nothing as she was violated by his father when she was a child. She watched Walt carry that guilt within him, letting that one act shackle him throughout his life without allowing himself to be absolved from his father's sins. That night in her grandmother's bed, she, too, became shackled, wearing her badge of shame for the rest of her life. From that moment she never allowed herself to feel desire in intimacy; sex was asphyxiated in the pretense of passion.

She recalls her first sexual experience in a pickup truck close to midnight after drinking at Old Man Mackey's rabbit farm. The darkness and the onslaught of rain concealed the boy and girl cocooned for endless possibilities, negating possibilities into a place where words didn't matter anymore.

Now as Christine stands naked in the light, she stands before another possibility. She can reject this tarnished man with his inexcusable past, or she can forgive him. She can reject the tarnished memory of her own inexcusable past, or she can forgive herself. It is time to extinguish the unremitting honor killing she has imposed on herself throughout the years and allow the unmitigated ache for passion back into her life. Christine softly speaks her thoughts aloud, not to Cameron, but to herself.

"No one should have dominion over anyone's intimacy, man or woman, family or society. Defining our passion is ours alone. It is our birthright." The judgment for her now is not what has been lost, but what more could be lost. The tragedy lies with indifference to that truth.

Those who remain unmoved by horrific acts of inhumanity mask their own humanity under the guise of cultural definition. Their yoke forever becomes a perverted delusion of truth. They are men drowning under the sirens' wailing. But he is different.

Christine knows what she must do; she is ready to sing her song, and he is ready to listen to her sweet music. She turns and faces him. He is not the man he was when those horrors occurred. His struggle has returned his integrity and humanity through tears of compassion. His request for redemption has worth. He is too important to discard, too important to be another lost opportunity. She is witness to the change in his life. Her function as a woman is to embrace this man now; then perhaps the fragile survival of humanity, for women as well as men, can be preserved. They are strangers, yet, each can value the other without requiring that they are the same. "Cameron." His chin lies lifeless against his chest. "Cameron, look at me."

He shifts his neck and lifts his head in her direction. Her silhouette is brazened in a halo of shimmering threads of light. The cilia engulf her and energize his breathing. He closes his eyes, then slowly brings his eyesight back to her image, questioning whether she is a mirage before him. Pushing up from the bed he stands for a moment by its edge. He approaches her. Standing pensively before her, he scans her naked body and becomes aroused. Embracing her hands with his palms, he lifts her hands to his cheeks and rubs them over the dried stains of tears. He opens her palms and tenderly kisses them. Her shoulders fall into his chest. He wraps his arms around her back, cupping her head in one of his hands. Threading his fingers through the strands of her hair, he assures himself that she is real. He needs to hear her name out loud, "Christine...Christine. I'm so sorry...so very sorry for everything in my life."

She places her index finger across his lips, but he continues his sunken words, moving his lips behind her finger. "It's just that there is no one else to say this to." She nods, absorbing his words and his pain. A transformation rivets them. She senses that he wants to speak further, that not all has been said. There still are so many questions, sitting like unanswered cards on the poker table. But enough words have been spoken for the moment.

XV

I BURY MY HEAD on his chest. The dampness on his shirt mingles with the fabric and his sweat, and I sniff that same masculine scent I caught when I first became aware of him sitting next to me at the concert. Imagine! That was only Friday night, not even a week ago; time floating without distance. I recall how I had yearned to fold into his arms. It was what I wanted but had never allowed myself.

I had resigned to a half-life existence. I had convinced myself that life was a series of conquests. I was that self-reliant female, accomplished but without feelings. I journeyed on a solitary pathway, denying intimacy. What I had ignored all these years were the warning signs that this trek was a conspiracy. I fell into the deception of always reaching for an elusive destination, the elusive right person to share my life. Whenever I attempted to take a chance in a relationship it was only a mirage of what I wanted to believe. I only went half the distance of desire by pretending desire, a mirage of passion. I convinced myself that I could handle this charade, that I didn't need to experience real passion. The irony was that I continued to negate that truth as I took up new quests, further beyond my reach, enticing me again. I would fall into the ruse once more, endlessly repeating the process, yet a little less confident than before, a little more solitary than before, always walking halfway into someone's arms, but never really arriving.

Truth can be defined in how I understand this night. There have been moments when I have watched a new mother rub her palms reverently over her enlarged belly, caressing her unborn. In those caresses she vows a promise of love forever. But reality defies that truth with its wretched statistics that haunt the daily news, coldly reporting the incomprehensible stories of the unwanted, the uncared, the abused children. What happens to a mother's promise? My irrevocable truth is that I will never carry out such caresses. My function as a female has deluded me halfway through my life as my time of bearing a child slowly diminishes. Am I capable of giving a promise of love to any man at this half point in my existence, when even a mother's love becomes questionable? As Cameron and I have unraveled our fears tonight, have we allowed ourselves to embrace a different time and place? Or is this only another half-truth? Can this intimate place inside this insulated stateroom dissolve the rest of the world and the half-truths of our past? Can we begin again? I shudder, wary, that this precarious moment can be snatched away as quickly as it was promised.

Protecting the fragility of our relationship, I press my shoulders further into his chest, sinking into his breath as it rises and falls. And with each breath, the shadows of the past dissipate. Each stroke on my hair, replaces a warm flow of renewed sensations riveting deeper into me. Perhaps it doesn't matter if the mirage is true or not. My thighs quiver, and I panic that I am about to fall, that I can no longer support myself or my precious truths. But he is intuitive and catches me, tightening his embrace in a hold that assures me, *I won't let you fall, Christine. I will carry you beyond the halfway point of existence.*

Blindly we take a chance, wanting to believe that this time it is not another mirage. This is what gives us the hope to continue. As the darkened room encases us, he pronounces my name. It reverberates back to me like an unfamiliar word, yet I know it belongs to me. He wants to speak more, but this is not the time for words. I gently place my finger over his lips.

He holds me because he is scared, too. We will be each other's light in the middle of this night. He commits to the risk of a beginning. He places his hands on my shoulders and squeezes gently but firmly. Then maintaining his grip, he pushes me back, so that he can fully view my exposed body. He slowly scans me intimately, lingeringly, and then returns his look back to my face to capture any qualms I harbor. He does not allow my eyes to leave his. Our truth must emerge out of trust in each other. He tilts his head in a soft questioning position and smiles a gentle smile, sliding into that familiar sideways lift. I easily mirror it. It is a language without words but with indisputable understanding. He receives his answer. He releases his grip and begins to unbutton his shirt. As he twists the buttons carefully through the holes, his eyes are still pinned to mine. I lower my stare and watch his fingers maneuver each button. As he finishes, he yanks his shirt out of his trousers, tails open and loose.

The mellow silence ingratiates the stateroom as the eerie turbulence continues to hover outside. It is a duality of existence. Its fury will continue to reign upon the natural order, whatever we say or do in here. Inside, however, silence flushes over me and I become lightheaded. He quickly lifts and cradles me in his arms. I fling mine around his neck, a gesture of my commitment to embrace the risk. As he carries me across the room coolness feathers over my bare skin. I shiver. He clutches me tighter. The soft hairs on his chest brush against my nipples. My forehead droops onto his cheek. He slides his lips over my brow and tenderly kisses it. His lips are warm and moist and leave a whisper of deliciousness. He tenderly lowers me upon the ruffled sheets gathered recklessly on the bed. Their chill penetrates my spine and I shiver again. Cupping my head in his palm, he lifts it and maneuvers the cotton pillow under it. He moves away. My quivering continues. He reappears but does not cover me with a blanket; he gently drapes his naked body over me, and his skin envelops me in warmth. Together we tumble sideways. He draws me into his chest. Our limbs dance in an endless waltz as legs entangle and arms explore.

After a moment he pulls slightly away, repositioning me on my back. He moves his face directly above mine. His mouth is so close that the warmth of his breath consoles the residue of my trembling. He speaks softly to me. "Christine, I wanted you...from the first moment I saw you."

He kisses my forehead, my eyelids, first one, and then the other, his eyes vigilant. But when his lips reach my mouth, his teeth tug my lower lip. Then in a fury of passion, he bears down, separating my lips, flicking his tongue, relentlessly thrusting. I am engulfed in his fury and my own rising panic. He presses his body firmly against me, his hardness against my thigh. I push against his shoulders in a contradiction of rejection and befuddled desire.

"Cameron, I have done this throughout my life with many men, and I never was able to feel anything. I just went through the actions of being satisfied. Cameron, please...I don't want to pretend anymore. And I'm not so sure that I cannot pretend, now."

He stiffens his shoulders, as if reflecting on some unfinished business. "Okay, I get it. Before I receive my pleasure, I must give you yours...the pleasure you deserve, as you had said that pleasure that is your birthright."

The moment halts in resigned suppositions. He looks intently for my response. Our stares shift away from each other and back, begging for a union to the promising ardor.

"I realize, Cameron, that this is not just about me. You have a birthright, too."

"Then, Christine, help me. I need to do this for you...but I need to do this for me, too."

I understand the grace behind these words, the history behind his meaning. It is the same grace and history I heard in the velvety singing within the waves, where the fluttering voices of unrequited desires from women as well as men were never given a chance to be heard. I lean into him and gently kiss his lips.

With all the reverence that a man can give to a woman, he strokes my cheek. His forefinger tenderly glides over my lips, lingering there. "Christine, will you allow me to kiss you?" I can feel my desire rising. He brushes his lips across mine. My lips tingle. "Let me kiss you, Christine...can I kiss you?" My breath swells; I am now moved that he asks permission to be intimate. I nod.

He nudges his forehead under my chin and gives my neck repetitive pecks. I comply and stretch my head back for him. His kisses gradually continue downward. He cuddles one breast and reverently kisses my nipple. Then he repeats the same movement with my other. I recall how he struggled when he groped me in the darkness of the impersonal hotel room and could not express such tenderness. Now he has no inhibition. He easily displays his desire. And without pausing in that desire, his relentless kissing lengthens onto my belly.

Suddenly he repositions himself, straddling his chest between my legs. He snuggles, comfortably, wedging himself. He then lifts his head like a turtle looking up from its shell. I glance down at him and snicker from the ludicrousness of the sight; I need to release some pending burp inside me. I tighten up, yet I certainly don't want him to stop.

"Christine?" He calls my name with patience. "Christine, it's okay." He knows that I need this reassurance. "Relax…lie back, relax, Christine…I'll be very gentle." And with these words he reaches for my knotted hands, clutching the gathered edges of the sheets. My fists have been pinned to my sides. He places his palms over my hands to steady them, intertwining his fingers with my pensive ones. His grip is firm and comforting. As my tension releases, I sense that he is aware of that unleashing too.

His head lowers. He hovers and then brings his mouth onto me. His breathing comes in waves of warmth. Each breath brings me to a higher level of anticipation. The dance begins. I envision the puckered lips of a fish opening and closing in hesitant approaches to the delicious bait. His tongue flicks like an elongated flame, twisting, stroking, sucking. My eyelids drowse and lift, waning within the sweet sensations as my pelvis rises and descends like sheer linen wafting in a gentle breeze. He squeezes my clenched fingers, asking permission for deeper intimacy. I squeeze back my response. His palms move away and cradle my butt. I gasp. With each jab I try to catch my breath in unbearable rapture.

Suddenly, he pulls away from me, panting, "Not yet." He flips onto his back and stays very still. After a second, he shimmies his body up next to mine so that we are both lying parallel on our backs, our shoulders slightly touching. Comically, our heads flop toward each other, and we share a smile. He murmurs, "I need a short break."

"Well, Cameron, can't take it, huh?" I tease him with flirting relish.

Playfully, he flings an arm over my chest and pins me like a wrestler on the mats. "Who said I'm done? I just started."

"Well, that's a relief! I thought that was all you had!"

He grins.

We don't move for a couple of minutes, at ease in each other's embrace inside the cabin, as the winds still whiff around the yacht's bulkhead. Within, the shimmering shadows on the walls are more mischievous than ever. He watches my eyes scan the stateroom. The painting of the mermaid hanging in the built-in cubby catches my attention. She is so delicately beautiful, the pinnacle of nature's mythical treasure, her arms extending toward the sky.

Cameron follows my glance, and he, too, stares at her. Finally, he asks a peculiar question, "What do you think she is reaching for? There doesn't seem to be anything within her grasp."

I glare back at him. "Cameron, she's a mermaid; mermaids reach for drowning men." He shudders.

We exchange glances. "Christine?"

I allow a moment to drink in his question. I am ready for this man. I want him as much as he wants me.

He tilts his head so that he will be able to watch my expression. His hand deliberately resumes its movement over my stomach, reaching further downward to my thighs. They involuntarily quiver again, this time from tenacity, not timidity. He slides his hand between my inner thighs. His touch asks that they be separated. I acquiesce. He strokes; I gasp. "Christine, it's okay. I'm in no rush...you deserve this."

I reposition my hand over his and press his fingers into the tender sensations quietly beginning to seethe. As he fondles, his fingertips explore over, around, and into the most intimate places within me, physically and spiritually. I swoon into his touch. With guided pressure and tempo, he moves onto me. He becomes an apt lover. Time trickles without measurement. I am abundantly silken. This place no longer exists. I turn my neck toward the port window and my head slumps willingly on the soft, cotton pillow.

I lapse into vacant pauses of sound. The sweet songs lull intermittently somewhere in the distances of the evening. I wander within their refrains. They escalate as they move closer, and then subside, rising again, like the ebbing of the ocean's waves stroking the shoreline. My eyelids drowse, and I transcend to that place beyond the porthole. Somewhere, a lone seagull hovers above the ocean and glides in flight, upward, hovering into the clouds, upward, reaching with its wing span...reaching and gliding without moving a feather, hovering, gliding, reaching.

Suddenly the gull stalls in midair, captured in a pregnant updraft... sustaining itself in a solitary pause in midflight. Without realizing how I arrived, I halt in suspended ecstasy...catatonic, but aware of the impending crescendo that is about to peak, and I relinquish my will to the rush.

Delirious sensations feverishly erupt upward from my loins. Primal gasps convulsively burst from my throat and my half-life existence shatters into repetitive seizures...wave upon wave wrack frantically in heaves of delight as undertows of endless arias grip me downward into irretrievable fulfillment. I pull him deeper into my silk. As he finds his own rhythm, he groans and groans, again. I passionately hold onto him and feel the release of his own gratification. Finally spent, we lie still. Quenched in the contentment of our intimacy, we wane into the receding tide of sleep.

XVI

WHEN HE OPENS HIS EYES, he can only discern faint threads of flickering light upon the far wall. The stateroom is still swathed in darkness, and he feels a comfort in that. It is not morning yet. But as he focuses in the dim light, there is enough visibility from the stateroom's porthole for him to see the auburn highlights shimmering in her hair, its scent, intoxicating. He is careful not to make any overt movements that will awaken this woman, sheathed in his arms under the sheets. He wants Christine to rest. She will need to be strong for what is to come tonight. Ironically, he does not realize how strong both of them must become. For now, he adores how serenely she poses as he swaddles her from behind. They lie together like a pair of fitted question marks, a statement of the night. His arm drapes over her torso, and his palm rests on her belly. His hand breathes with it in peaceful symmetry.

He bathes in her sweet fragrance as he continues to burrow into the back of her neck. She is real, not a mirage. He cannot refrain from giving her a slight hug. She stirs. His eyelids fold, and Cameron drifts back into the delicious sensations of their love-making. He dreams himself away, believing that this moment will remain forever.

Suddenly, a skirmish of cold sweeps across the tops of his exposed shoulder blades, alerting him to once again be realistic. Soon he must wake her. Too many unanswered questions wait for her to ask, and he must address them, the ones that were left behind earlier. That was his unfinished business. She has to hear the entire truth because selective omissions of truth are still only a mirage of truth. And that would negate that promised trust they gave each other. For now, one promise he silently murmurs to himself is that whatever happens, he will never abandon her, even if it costs him his life.

She stirs again, perhaps from that sixth sense innate to females. "Cameron?" she beckons to him with whispered femininity.

"Christine, I'm here." She turns over, and he pulls her to him. Instinctively, she cuddles even closer. As they lean into each other, their lips savor a charmed ballet. Once again, they fold into the enchantment of making love. This time their passion is unfathomable and more eloquent. When they have exhausted themselves of every ounce of bliss, they still clutch each other in that unwavering embrace that affirms their promise of never letting go.

XVII

THE ECHOES OF THE STORM are prevalent, just not as unsettling as before. The two lovers lie in contented grace, a place to speak softly. It is a moment wrapped in silken ribbon, a place where questions can be asked. But, this time, it is not Cameron who initiates the unraveling.

"Cameron, why was it so important that I know Jewels' profession?" Her question directly threads the eye of the needle. He holds her tighter. He sears his answer directly into her eyes so that there is no doubt about the truth of his words. "You are Jewels'…commodity."

She swallows. That word is even more difficult now, but she grasps its full meaning. "He wants to sell me to another man?"

Averting his eyes, Cameron says, "I'm not so sure. He may want you for himself…to become his wife." He peruses her expression as he continues with Jewels' plan. "He is leaving Saturday…and he believes that you will accompany him back to Pakistan."

She does not move. Time smothers all movement. And within the interlude, she sifts through what Cameron had told her about Jewels' world. She swallows harder. Without further hesitation she emphatically asserts, "Cameron, there is no way that I'm getting on that plane on Saturday! You know that!"

"Yes," he calmly understates.

Christine is not satisfied with his laconic answer, which suggests much more insidious consequences…consequences that affect them both. She trembles but plunges further into the fated cave, "Cameron, what will happen if I refuse to go?"

In its darkened cavern, the sleeping dragon whips its head and exhales as Cameron discharges the fire within its belly. "Walt is being held as a hostage to make sure you do not renege." Anticipating her refusal to accept this reality, Cameron sucks in his breath, "He will be killed."

"Killed! No…no, Jewels would not do that!" Her voice and expression show her aversion to such a possibility. After a moment she continues, "Would Jewels do such a thing?"

Cameron doesn't speak. Both are silent. A spurt of bile from the depths of her soul rushes into her throat. "Cameron, what will happen to you?"

He does not respond to that question either.

She knows the answer. She knows the answer to both of her questions.

She draws in a deep breath, like the dragon summoning fire back into its belly in one sucking breath. Decisively flicking her head with haughty self-assurance, she heartily declares, "Well, that does it! I always wanted to see Pakistan!"

He doesn't laugh. He just stares at her. Neither move, neither speak. Then, Cameron begins to chuckle. His chuckle rivets into a burst of laughter. Christine scrunches her brows together and squints back at him. His laugh wrings into convulsive hysteria as his eyes tear and his body contorts wildly. Suddenly, she is drawn into his boisterous insanity. Like the comparable moment in the hotel room, the lunacy of the situation rocks them back to some sensibility. And within their humor, truth becomes secure. They subside and collapse onto their backs, bathed in the same exhaustion as the aftermath of their passion. The ceiling's inlaid rectangles calm them further as their watery eyes clear.

"Christine, have I told you that I can really go for you?"

"No. As a matter of fact, I don't believe you have."

Minutes pass more easily now. They have learned not to fear the pauses of their silences. Without looking away from the ceiling, Cameron gently says, "I can really go for you."

She doesn't move, but echoes, "I can go for you, too."

More silence, and then she jabbers, "Well, Olli, this is another fine mess we got ourselves into!"

This jolts them into another fit of laughter, but they subside much quicker this time, and punctuate this episode by embracing. Their nakedness soothes the frazzled truth.

"Christine?"

"Yes."

"Christine, I'll never let you go. I'll always be here for you. Can you trust me?"

"Yes." After a second, she rethinks the situation, "Cameron, so you have a plan?"

"Well...I'm in the process of figuring one out."

Playfully, she retorts, "I was afraid you were going to say that." He returns a smile, that same sidewinder smile she loves so much. Her tone turns serious. "I have a sobering thought." He knew this realization would finally come. "Because Jewels believes that Walt sold me to him, and because I am only a commodity, then I can be bought, sold, or even..." He winces, but she concludes, "...or even destroyed." She stares into his eyes. "Cameron, does Jewels believe that I'm a virgin?"

He pauses, and his answer to her question is a quiet, "He might."

"You're kidding! A woman...my age? Where would he get that crazy idea?"

Cameron does not answer her; he doesn't have to.

She says only one word, "Walt?"

Cameron looks down and nods.

Now, her fury erupts, "I'm going to kill him...when I get my hands on Walt...I'm going to..." she halts from the reality of the situation. "...that is, if Jewels doesn't kill him first. In fact, on second thought, maybe that's what I should tell Jewels to do!" After she subdues her preposterous madness, she attempts to minimize that possibility, "Okay, okay, I know Jewels is not capable of killing anyone he loves with his own hands!"

Cameron allows her to rant. He will have to convey more, and he is not sure how she will digest it.

She realizes that Cameron is not intervening, and his humor is not evident anymore. She becomes wary, but they are stronger than before, no longer harnessed by their pasts. They have transcended to a promise of faith. Soberly she turns to him, "Cameron, tell me."

He lowers his voice to that same drone he used to describe the honor killings. "When Jewels' father died this past year, Jewels had to take on the burden of making sure that the business would stay solvent. It's not the kind of business that is audited, if you get my drift." He gives her a quick glance, and then continues. "To preserve the transfer of power, he had to be above reproach in his ability to walk in his father's shoes. His father was a very influential man, who many revered...and feared."

Cameron slides off the bed to remove himself from Christine. He walks to the port window and remains motionless, peering beyond to whatever calls to him out there. She is not about to allow him to be pulled back into the funnel of that whirlpool again. No siren will drown this man. She rises from her bed and goes to him. She hugs him from behind, tightly embracing with all the love that she can emit with her arms. He turns around in her hold. He looks down into her face, and he knows where his love for her began. He now has the courage to finish. "Jewels' judgment day came last month. He had a niece, whom he had adored since her birth, when her mother, Jewels' younger sister, died in childbirth shortly after bearing this niece. Jewels and his only sister were not just siblings sharing the same household, but they were each other's salvation. Throughout their childhood together, they were able to keep all that was decent in the world out of their father's clutches. So, when his sister died, Jewels was devastated. On her death bed, he promised her that he would always take care of her daughter. And he did that with all of his love and joy. He watched over his niece better than her father, who died just a couple of years ago. The girl was sixteen at the time. For the past two years, Jewels made sure that she was cultivated to become a lovely and suitable young lady for marriage. And recently, he found the perfect husband for her."

Christine already surmised where Cameron was leading. But she knew that she had to allow him to finish.

He continued. "The marriage ceremony was set, and no expense was spared. It was to be the event of the year. The night before the wedding, the husband-to-be is told that his future wife had been soiled. She will come to him the next night, broken, not pure. She had lost her virginity to another."

He wanted to stop but Christine helps him get through as she prods him on. "So, Jewels had to exonerate the family name?"

He answers her by the continuous flow of words. "Jewels contacted me for advice. We had known each other through our business dealings, and we had developed an understanding of each other. In many ways, our lives were similar even though we grew up in different hemispheres." Cameron looks to see if Christine is still resolute in hearing the rest. He sees her strength. "I told him to see if he could buy off the man by having him pretend that this situation with his niece was not true. But somehow the information leaked out into the community. All eyes were on the Old Man's son. Would he be worthy of their allegiance? The townspeople all had stakes in his decision because throughout the years, they had had to honor the code laid down by his father for such a crime. Many had hardships from such judgments. Now, the House of Jewels must also own up to its duty. Jewels had no choice. Besides, there were those who watched from the sidelines...waiting for this very moment...hoping this would be the final ruin of his family's power...watchful eyes that hungered to usurp the lucrative business.

"Cameron, Jewels had a choice. We all have a choice when it comes to defending what is the right thing to do—the right truth."

This evening has allowed Cameron to come to terms that she was right, but that thought had not occurred a month ago. Not only had Jewels tarnished the promise he gave his beloved sister, he had stained the innocence of humanity. Cameron barely is able to utter the rest. "I watched Jewels drag his niece through the streets. I watched him remain expressionless as he crossed the entrance to his house with her clutched in his sweltering fists. I watched how he didn't flinch as he withdrew the knife and brought it down upon the only one he loved more than his own life." He pauses. "She didn't survive the night. And in another sense, he hasn't survived since either. He lost interest in everything: his wives, his children, his business. He has no energy for anything except drinking and poker. His life was over when he did that act. It was over, that is, until he saw you in the casino on Friday night, and Walt told him that you were a virgin. Some lost spark flickered in his soul."

"Because I was a virgin! Cameron, Jewels is an intelligent man. How could he really believe that?" Christine's voice trembles to a concept that seems so incredible to her.

"We believe what we want to believe, what we need to believe, even if it is only a mirage of truth!" Cameron pauses. "But there is more... it's not only that."

"Really! Then what else? Whatever could the reason be for this madness!"

"Because you resemble his sister. However, I'm not sure if Jewels has made that connection yet. But he will. Even though many years have passed since her death, the appearance is uncanny. I knew his sister, and I caught that similarity when you first showed up on Friday. I had to see you closer, so that is why I sat next to you at the concert. I had to confirm my suspicions."

Christine glares at him. She does not know how to respond to this, and she shakes her head in disbelief. "Cameron, I don't have the same skin tone of a Pakistani!"

"Jewels' mother was British and had the most delicate and fair skin coloring. Her daughter inherited her mother's beauty, the pale skin tone, and brilliant auburn hair. Unfortunately, as his mother slowly discovered her husband's profession, she became unfaithful." He pauses. "That was Jewels' father's first honor killing. There were many others." He ponders how such an act would have affected any son's life. "After that, the Old Man just about tolerated Jewels. He blamed his young son who had absorbed all of his wife's love and attention. The Old Man was jealous and saw this as the reason for his wife's aloof attitude toward him. What Jewels' father negated was that it was his own behavior that drove her to dishonor. The Old Man was ruthless in his duty!"

"Cameron, you are telling me that Jewels would carry out his guilt onto me...to do the same honor killing to me, too!"

"Maybe...maybe not. Christine, it really doesn't matter because he will never get near you. I'll see to that...even if I have to kill him."

"Cameron! Oh, Cameron! No...You can't do that! You are different than Jewels. You never killed like that! You just were some man standing on the sidelines."

"I never held the knife, but blood permanently stained these hands from all those scenes I witnessed. I know about killing because I know about honor. When I was a boy, I once saw a priest kill a man...because of honor...the honor of the cloth, he told me at the time. The justification for death is determined by the destroyer who sees the world selfishly. We all harbor the potential of each other's destruction. And, now that I have found something pure and truthful in my life, I won't hesitate to do the same...I will kill for the honor of preserving my love for you!"

"Cameron, that kind of honor is a contrivance. That is how contradictions become accepted truths, the thwarted justification of such acts." Christine gazes at Cameron, unafraid, but still amazed that he can speak so easily of destroying another person.

One last unanswered question vacillates on the thread.

"Cameron, do you know who spread that horrific rumor about the niece?"

He straightens his posture. "Yes, I know who it was." He is no longer afraid of such questions. He can answer this woman with the candor she deserved. "It was Jewels' wife, the woman on this yacht...the woman who...so that Jewels would know for sure...examined you, as you lay in this stateroom, naked and drugged."

Christine's mouth gapes and her eyes widen. The pieces of enigmatic dust become specks of lucid light. The mirage lifts, but one more false impression shadows their love.

"And I bent over the deck railing just outside your stateroom, retching my silence overboard while she did that to you." Tears river his cheeks like holy water. He does not wipe them away. For the first time in his life he feels good about himself as he cries.

She kisses him, and kisses him again, and again, and takes him back to bed where they make love until they fall into the slumber of forgiveness, where truth is allowed to gently weep.

♠ Chapter 5: The Showdown ♠

The Player's Live Hand
This poker standoff is not just a game of probability, but one of possibility. For in one last desperate "play of the hand," if they can release the passionate grasp of their deluded quests, they can emerge from the mirage.

I

LIKE LINEN WAFTING ON A CLOTHESLINE, sheets of morning light drowse in her gentle breath. For Christine, evening's breath of love now causes reality to hibernate in satisfied sleep. In contrast, Cameron struggles with distant rumblings of uncertainty. Behind closed but twitching eyelids, he commands his disturbed vision to awaken and see if morning has arrived yet. He must remain vigilant, more now than ever. His lids rise. His eyes swing from side to side, scouting for any indiscretion that dares to skulk within the sanctity of the stateroom.

"Christine." He needs to speak her name. It lingers in the air like auburn honey. She does not hear his voice. He turns his head toward her while she sleeps peacefully. He is pulled into the hypnotic motion of her doze, where life becomes a natural process. Why should life be so difficult? He senses his own mortality. Cameron shuts his eyes and embosses her profile into his mind. His eyes reopen to gaze on her. Her skin is translucent in the beckoning light. He brushes his cheek against the pillow and imagines that he is softly caressing his cheek against hers. He takes in her sweet fragrance, but decides, in spite of his desire to touch her, that he will not awaken her. He must let her rest.

Suddenly, his body snaps as if he is groping to regain his balance from a fall. He resumes his scanning. He has never given much attention to the room's opulent timelessness: the patterns of teak in the ceiling, the rows of drawers embedded in the walls, the array of flowers in one niche, the painting of the mermaid transcending her world in the other. He focuses on the painting. It can be seen clearly as the morning's haze seeps through the wooden blind that obscures the outside world beyond the port window. Yes, within this world of the stateroom all appears to be what it is supposed to be. Still, he cannot negate the shadowy nagging at him. He blinks. Something is amiss, but what...but where? Once again, his eyes search in grid-like maneuvers above, around, and within every crevice of the stateroom, scrutinizing for any flaw. Finally, exhausted, he turns his attention back to Christina's profile and releases his uncertainty into her gentle snooze. He is about to join her reverie when, on the jagged edge of a sideways glimpse, he snags it.

There it is! There! With laser perspicacity, he bayonets the blemish in a gap between the slats of the wooden blinds...the wooden blinds that obscure the outside world beyond the port window. He spies a pair of fiendish eyes, shadowed by darkened smudges, darting with a profane stare through the slats. He knows to whom they belong. With primitive acuity Cameron swiftly shields Christine by draping his body over hers to conceal her from the creature's sight. Animalistic ire surges through his veins, and his back heaves. Instinctively, he maneuvers with frantic defense as he bolts off the bed and skids along the rug, drawing the hunter's eyes away from the vulnerable nest. He willingly will sacrifice himself to preserve her. With a fleeting look back he checks on Christine. In spite of the commotion, she remains oblivious to the danger, safe in the warm haven of deep sleep.

But for Cameron, the warmth of his love bed has vanished as coldness assaults his bare skin. He shivers, crouching low on the floor, improvising a strategy to face the enemy. The line of attack stings back with rug burns on his exposed knees, the smarting inconsequential. He gropes for his trousers, struggles into them. Dressed enough to go on deck, he must arrest the looming threat just beyond the port window. Shirtless and shoeless, he flees the stateroom to slay the dragon.

The stateroom door is heavy and difficult to open, especially against the outside driving winds. But he pushes harder against it, and then shuts it, charily, almost inaudibly. The morning air whacks his resolve, and he becomes pragmatic about how defenseless he is. He has come on deck without any armor or weapon. Perhaps it would make little difference. Foreboding shrouds his thinking; it might already be too late. Nonetheless, he will spar with the imaginary windmill.

Out on deck cold gales are the unrelenting residue of last night's storms within the squeamish morning; its hangover must be reckoned with. He holds onto the guard rail to steady himself as the yacht sways in its stupor. The ocean's spray soaks his trousers to a darkened stain, and beads of salt water mat his exposed body hairs into frazzled, twisted strains. As if out of nowhere a brazen shadow sweeps down above his head and startles him. A lone seagull plummets into the ocean a few feet off the port railing. It smacks the sea's surface, and its bedraggled wingtips spread haphazardly as it floats lopsidedly in the turbulent ebbing froth. Cameron grips the railing tighter to steady his nerves. The metal is cold and impersonal. As he stares downward at the winged beast of prey, his chest heaves. He cannot shake the image of the other ominous specter still looming somewhere on the yacht. He swallows hard, resolved to continue his hunt to ferret out this infection that will kill without remorse. He looks outward over the sea.

The pale gray covering of the morning casts a lifeless melancholy. The sky and ocean blend into the wash, making the horizon almost indistinguishable. In the far distance, a tint of sickly yellow emerges, forming a faint demarcation of dreaming and waking. The tinge of yellow diffuses visibility enough so that Cameron can detect any unsettling forms on the deck. His movements are slow, calculated, fearful. He quivers from the cold and wet onslaughts of the harsh elements but also from the yellow shadow of possibly losing Christine. She is the one who finally penetrated this mercenary's heart. Before her, his life was a rental of arrogant indifference where dreams were lost to the disillusioned, desires were lost to the inconsequential, and passions were lost to impotent intimacy. He was a man devoid of imagination, a man defined by others, lost. Without her, he might never regain the man he always thought he would be. But like the shadowy winged bird that flew above his head, some ancient human beast of prey, camouflaged within the dreary gray, still hovers just beyond his reach, predisposed to snatch her from him.

He continues his search. His bare feet slip beneath him on the slick teak boards. His balance is compromised by the elements, his exhaustion, and his doubt. He leans forward to secure a better footing as his head angles downward to drive through the onslaught. Suddenly, the yacht jars from a renegade wave, tipping the deck sideways and tossing Cameron onto a beehive-like pile of deck ropes. His composure unraveled, he pushes his body up from the tangled webbing. He stands firmly and looks back down at the disheveled rigging. That is when he sees her. Three feet away, slouching in a cranny between two sideboards, his adversary, cringing like a rodent gnawing with callous teeth. At first, Jewels' wife recoils, then releases a righteous smirk. She has been waiting for this moment; he has stumbled into her lair. But Cameron will not give her satisfaction. He will bring down the first blow.

"What are you doing there, woman?" Cameron emboldens his voice to gain commanding leverage over the obvious, impending confrontation.

She is not intimidated. "Don't you address me with such disrespect!"

She clumsily stands, rearranging the cumbersome black cloth that wraps around her in endless folds. She is brazen enough to uncover her face and raise her eyes to this man in a challenging stare. With obvious insolence she drives another stake into his heart. "You must know that you and your woman are doomed."

Cameron is muzzled by the blow. He knows the extended arm of Jewels' reprisals. This daunting creature has the advantage over him, for she has Jewels' ear. He knows how dangerous this predator is at manipulating confidential information for her own agenda. He painfully recalls how skillful she destroyed Jewels' niece. He must immediately extinguish her vicious propensity if he, and more importantly, Christine are to prevail.

"You know that this woman belongs to me now." Cameron takes her head on.

"Yes, I know." The creature's response is too overtly casual. Her nonchalant attitude is offensive and confounding. Has she already devised something menacing? Is he, naively, falling further into her snare?

He strikes again to secure his position. "You are powerless on this yacht. Whatever you tell Jewels, I will deny. He will not believe a woman, and more so, an old woman, over me."

"You forget one thing. She does not belong to you, and Jewels will never allow you to leave this yacht with her."

This is true, and he knows it is true. There has always been only a limited, if not pessimistic, recourse for them at best. Even if he and Christine clandestinely leave together, Jewels will unrelentingly ferret them out. There will be nowhere to hide, and he will be unforgiving when he finds them.

Her next jab would be the most sinister. She licks her lips as she mockingly fantasizes, "And when Jewels discovers that you have bed her, he will seek justice for the dishonor you have shown to him. I'm sure you will be…," she pauses to emphasize, "…well rewarded…that is after he takes care of his business with her first! He may even allow you to watch!"

Cameron pounces on her like an angry tiger, ensnaring his fists tightly around the veil, which no longer covers her dark hair but sags around her throat. She gags. However, the abundant cloth buffers her from being strangled. She is able to snake her hand under the folds of her chador and extracts a folded paper. Repetitively she smacks his face with it to break his dire hold. "Look!" she gasps. He regains momentary sanity and slightly releases his grip. "Look!" she wheezes again. They spew daggers of twisted ire, trying to intimidate each other. He rivets his wrath, boring it into her pupils in an attempt to dominate her. However, what he sees is not cowering, but perseverance. He is startled by such resolve. Ripping his hands off her, he collapses backwards onto the scattered ropes. On the soaked deck, she also becomes entangled among the disheveled rigging.

"What do you have, woman? What is that paper?" Is this some incriminating evidence that will hold Christine and him hostage to her evil?

"This is my note, which Jewels will receive when we dock tomorrow. It contains the findings of my examination of his commodity, his precious woman, your woman!"

"So, you are informing him that Christine is not a virgin?"

"Even though the possibility of her virginity is preposterous, I wrote that she was still intact for him. You see, it really matters little what the truth is. What matters is what Jewels wants to believe. I wrote that this virgin will bring a sizable bounty into his coffers from any wealthy man who longs for an unsoiled, attractive female with other special qualities. Because of Jewels' obsessive weakness for purity, he might even save her for himself. But whoever has her, the truth will be uncovered. Jewels will have been deceived again, and this time the stakes will not be dissolved so easily especially when he finds out your involvement in the matter." She smirks in self-gratification of her ruse.

Cameron stares at her, trying to grasp her intent for misleading Jewels. "Why would you do such a thing? I know that you want Christine destroyed, and you want me destroyed, but this lie would also ruin Jewels, your husband, who still has not recovered from what he did to his niece last month."

She leers into his eyes and calculatingly scoffs, "I know."

Cameron suddenly realizes how insidious her revenge is, not just for him or for Christine, but for Jewels. He tries to fit the puzzle pieces together. She is using Christine as bate to hurt Jewels? But why?

Christine has helped Cameron realize that he is blinded, so consumed in the moment, that he sometimes fails to pick up what truly defines a situation. So, instead of inflaming his ire toward this woman again, he pauses and reexamines the old woman's face. That is when he sees, perhaps for the first time, the deep scars embedded in her cratered cheeks and her twisted upper lip. Calculated slashes have viciously disfigured her. The cleft on her lip was obviously formed by some horrific ripping at the edges of her mouth. He has seen such cuttings before. He is well-aware how society responds to such markings. He continues to scan her face and see for the first time how she has borne such difficulties. As he continues to probe her disfigurement, her eyelids droop in regret. He had thought of her as an old lady because of her hunched shoulders and limping gait. Now, as he studies her more intently, he realizes that she is probably the same age as Christine. Underneath the violations, there once was a beautiful woman. The slashes had driven her into ugliness; the scars not only marred her physically, but destroyed the very spirit of her womanhood.

As he gawks, she elucidates upon what he has unearthed. "Jewels gave me a choice for my dishonor, either my body or my face. I told him to allow me to wear my dishonor for all to see, and to bear my own penance of what would never be seen again." She pauses before she nods to Cameron. "He is a just man, no?" Her tone is of a woman scorned.

Cameron flinches as he digests the pain that this woman endured a lifetime ago, perhaps prior to Jewels' subsequent marriages. Although Cameron cannot condone her recent actions, he sympathizes with what drove her to become such a woman. Christine has opened him to this. When Christine gave her unwavering love, she bestowed upon him the ability to imagine. Christine kissed his eyes open. He could not look into the eyes of another's pain without seeing his own. The scars of life, either outward or inward, destroy or define our humanity. He rises, and gently taking the old woman's fragile wrists, he assists her to stand. He has become a man who will define his own life because he now has the ability to love another woman. He addresses her with conviction, yet empathy, "I will not allow Jewels or you to harm Christine."

Although she senses his pity, she snaps with a hollow retort, "It's too late!"

"It's never too late. Give me that paper." She crushes the note tightly into her fist and backs away from him. She does not turn and thus cannot see what is behind her. "Give me the paper!" His voice is more insistent, yet he wants her to believe that his words are without pretense. He extends his arm solicitously, beckoning her to hand over the paper.

She remains impetuous to the absurdity. "Jewels will believe what is on this note." He tries to snatch it away, but she jolts back and stuffs it into her mouth, swallowing it. The wretched act done, she smirks with contentment. "Don't worry. The duplicate copy has been given to the captain for safekeeping. He will not change what was given to him. You cannot reverse what is to come. I am also powerless to change what has been done." She digests this last comment and how it brought her to her present predicament. She laments, "Besides, if Jewels ever finds out that I had falsified the contents in the note, his vengeance will be merciless." She pauses once again. The contented smile reverses into a draining frown. "I can never bear such consequences again!"

Her fear of Jewels is not an idle threat; Cameron has witnessed Jewels' uncompromising retribution firsthand. But he needs to pacify her and convince her to believe in him. "Well, that's perfect, you see! Do not worry. You have destroyed the evidence, right? I will never tell Jewels of our discussion here. The captain might have a copy, but I will convince him to give it to me. I will help you, just as Christine has helped me to resolve my past. Woman, give me your hand! I promise that you will be spared any dishonorable reprisal."

At first, she entertains the possibilities of his comments, but quickly reverts back to her intractable mind. Lifting her chin in arrogance not only to him, but also to what life had inflicted on her, she snaps back, "How can you promise something over which you have no power? You have defiled Jewels as your woman has! I will finally get my revenge, and I will tell Jewels what he does not want to believe, my-so-called truth, which will destroy him! We are all doomed!" Her stare diminishes into a vacant gaze. But Cameron cannot relent. He moves closer to her. Her eyes shift from side to side, and her head swivels in vehement denial, "No! No! No!"

Suddenly there is a surge of fury within the ocean. The yacht rolls, and as the crippled woman continues to back step, she loses her balance as her foot tangles in the unraveled rope on deck. Another wave swells and she tumbles backwards, falling over the railing and plunging into the angry water. Like the seagull, she momentarily floats on its surface. The loose black cloth of her garment spreads outward on the water's surface like the gull's frazzled wingtips, its blackness in distinct contrast to the snowy turbulence of the sea. She is frantic and flaps helplessly, becoming more ensnared in the cloth and rope. The darkened sheet continues to swirl around her, forming an inescapable picture frame. Suddenly, she stops moving and surrenders to the dance of the waves. Like a detached head placed in the center of a sinking funnel, she looks up at him as he gawks down from the railing. Without releasing her gaze, her head succumbs to the inky sinkhole of the veil. The disheveled, darkened mass follows, purging itself within the white froth.

Cameron is frozen, locked in indecision. Should he take no action, allow her to drown, and be rid of her for good? Will that save Christine? How can that save him? He is no longer capable of watching another life drown without making an attempt to save a life.

Some slithering monster scrapes against his forearm, and he is spooked. He looks down at the deck and watches the disheveled rigging unravel. The line is snaking over the railing and into the sea. Following its path into the turbulent eyes of the angry water, he realizes that the doomed woman is attached to the other end. He clutches the hissing rope; it burns his palms. Frantically, he still continues to grip the unbridled serpent, but it will not be restrained. It has become the controller of her fate and his as well as it entanglement about his bare ankles, ensnaring him within its clutches. He kicks it away and hurls himself over the cold railing, falling into the steaming sea just like the lone seagull, screaming out the name of his beloved, knowing that there is only a slim chance of saving her or him.

II

IN A FLUSH OF PANIC doubt palls his judgment. He wants to reverse his decision, but it is too late; he is already committed. Suspended momentarily in midair, his legs frantically scissor as if they have been deceived by the realization that they might never touch solid ground again. He squeezes his eyes tightly, envisioning that he is only in some short-lived nightmare. He imagines waking into the arms of Christine, shaken and soaked with fearful sweat. He prays. His prayer is to be in any other place than here, falling in midair. But as the bottom of his bare feet smack the heartless waves, the ocean's sting pierces this absurdity back to harsh reality. Cameron plummets, slashing blindly through the white froth, shredding it like tissue paper.

He does not remain under for long; his head quickly emerges. As he bobs to the surface, his first impulse is a gasp of breath. The cold, with its unforgiving knives, jabs into every inch of his exposed skin. Even his legs prickle in spite of the khaki trousers that cling like saran wrap. He whips his body in rotating spins, desperately scoping for sight of the deformed woman. As he rises to the crest of each wave, the ocean's vastness conceals any evidence that she ever existed. The morning's gray has sucked all life from the sky and the water, leaving only a vacant wasteland of despair. Even the looming hull of the white yacht washes into the colorless plaster. It towers near him like an impenetrable mountain, the point of no return. It is insensitive to his plight. The surf backlashes against its side, hewing it with muscular waves just like the ones that presently strong-armed him within the surf. He is helpless under their dominance. Suddenly he spies the beckoning lifeline; it is now taut. He follows where it has entered the ocean and swims toward it. When he is close enough, he draws in a deep breath and dives under the surface to find her.

The belligerent slashing above becomes a serene muffling below as he enters the silent world. He pries his eyes open, unable to assemble any images as the congested silt clouds the angry sea. Unexpectedly from above, a strong morning ray of light emerges over the distant horizon and scurries across the water, penetrating downward into the haze below the surface. Shapes become more distinct. Unfortunately, this clarity also has renewed the misconception that he is invincible enough to save her. He always was a strong swimmer. Instinctively he kicks...kicks with conviction, propelling himself deeper into the depths of his delusion. In this silent world, reason no longer matters and thinking reverts to primitive instinct. He commits himself to moving ever downward, hand over hand on the rope, descending to a place devoid of past history, driven by one thought...that he must reach her. He grapples with senseless motions, trying to hook any definable form. Another fragment of morning light pierces the mire and threads its path into the ocean's depths. He focuses on the illumination as he snags the lifeline and follows it downward. That is when he sees her. She is swerving in a slow, ghostly dance like a stringed puppet.

Recklessly releasing the rope, he aims his body toward her. But as he approaches her, the silt flares and fractures his vision. He becomes disoriented, and she vanishes into the ocean dust like a mirage. He is frantic, groping for the line, twisting for her image, fearing the end. Suddenly, in the chaos of the unknown he makes an arbitrary turn and bumps into a vague mass, coming face to face with her. He is startled. He does not recognize her at such close proximity. Her hair has escaped the cloth and wisps about her head in long, black strands like Medusa's untamed serpents swaying sinuously in the undercurrent. Her darkened, wide-eyed glare amplifies the two solid black pupils, now stunned and monstrous. She reaches for him. He wraps his arms around her, touching the silkiness of her skin. She is alluring. The cloth has fallen from her shoulders, and her torso exposes her bare breasts. The fabric wraps around her waist in a twisted snarl, fishtailing around her legs. It has snagged onto something below, harnessing her in an impenetrable trap. Believing that it must be from the rigging, he finds the end of the rope about her body and quickly unties it. But he is duped. When he tries to pull her upward, she is still anchored. She is caught in the twisted, black garment. It will not release. He realizes her predicament and tears at the cloth about her waist to free her. However, the more he grapples, the tighter the cloth becomes. She tries hysterically to squirm out of its deadly snare in a desperate, futile struggle. He digs his fingernails into her skin to get underneath the material, again and again, to gain her freedom. His ripping fingers cause her blood to smoke through the water like tired spools of thread.

He releases his grip. He is about to swim to a lower depth to find the source of the unforgiving hook, but she stops him. Instead, she clasps her hands about one of his ankles preventing him from going downward. Then, using her powerful arms, she jerks him up toward her face. She looks into his eyes and shakes her head. It's too late; she cannot hold on any longer. Her face relaxes with a euphoric expression, and she nods to him. In one last breath of life she opens her mouth. Unlocking her arms, she heaves his body away from her, propelling him upwards toward the light.

He has no will to leave her behind. He swiftly maneuvers himself about to dive down again. Suddenly he is gripped by the rope that has strapped itself around his ankle. It jettisons him away from her. Inverted, his arms extend toward her, but he is powerless to return…he has to leave her behind. As he rises, he watches her diminish into the depths. Her hair feathers in slow motion…her arms stretch out toward him, her fingers in a fragile farewell ballet. Her body bows with defeated grace, yet, her bare breasts remain firmly alluring above the black cloth, which curls downward from her waist like a siren's elongated fin, irreverently rising and falling in the current.

His lungs burn. He is fire in the icy water. Before his eyes is Christine's naked body emblazoned in cilia of light threads. He cannot resist her. She is calling to him. He commands his body to move closer to her. He reaches for her. Her face is near his. He wants to kiss her lips. A graying net covers his vision as its lattice meshes into a fading night. And like the shutter on an aperture, it imprisons him in darkness.

III

NOW IN THE SOLITUDE OF MY STATEROOM, I pile layers of blanket over my lover as doubts continue to swell. Yet I cannot quell his uncontrollable shivering—or mine. Before leaving us alone in the room, the captain draped a robe about my shoulders. Perhaps he recognized that we would need some time to come to terms with this untenable act of Cameron's attempted suicide. As I sit vigilantly on the edge of the bed, I cannot imagine why someone who finally has found a reason to live would snuff out breath forever. Why would Cameron want to end his life and our love? However, I do not address this question to him. We both remain mute, he frozen from the cold sea, I frozen from disbelief. He attempts to speak every so often, but cannot convey any coherent meaning. Instead, his eyes ask for my commitment to him. I cannot return his stare.

A short while ago I had heard my name and awoke with a start, realizing that Cameron was no longer in bed or even in the stateroom. My shouts became progressively louder as I frantically left the room and scurried on deck. The captain materialized from around the corner to see me, naked, frantically screaming for help. He was clothed in an undershirt and a dark pair of pants held up by a solitary suspender, its mate tagging impertinently behind. His expression quickly turned from startled to grave.

There was a grinding sound, and he sighted the rigging scattered on the teak deck in its unraveling chatter. He peered over the railing, grabbed the wild rope reeling down the side of the yacht from an unruly coil, and began yanking it back out of the sea, hand over hand, his muscular arms bulging under his white tee shirt, stretching the tattoo of the naked mermaids into distorted images. Suddenly, hauled from the sea, like some lifeless fish at the end of the line, Cameron's body dangled in the twisting rigging, which was wrapped about one foot and his neck. His body swiveled in the stiff surface wind, banging senselessly against the side of the hull. The sight of this horror sent my screams howling as I desperately groped for the swinging rope. I couldn't reach him! The captain shoved me aside, and I slipped backwards onto the deck, probably an action that saved my life because I, too, would have fallen victim to the merciless sea. I slipped again and again in a frantic effort to get back to the railing. However, the captain was adept at retrieving Cameron's body and heaved him over the railing, flopping onto the wet deck like a beaten mackerel. Still not able to regain my footing on the soaked surface, I slithered frantically on my belly, inching closer to Cameron as he lay on his back. I grabbed the rope loosely collaring his neck and body, pulling it, unscrambling it, trying to fight back the unspeakable thoughts: *Why would Cameron want to end his life? Why now when we found something to live for?* My arms clutched his chest, but I felt no breath. "No! No! God! No! Please, God! No! God, please, please!"

The captain straddled Cameron and systematically pumped his palms onto his chest, interjecting a quick puff of air into his mouth. Meanwhile, I sprawled helplessly, clinging to Cameron and incessantly rubbing his arms, praying that this captain would miraculously blow life back into this precious man. Suddenly a slew of noxious seawater hurdled out of Cameron's mouth, and his eyes popped open. I could not stop my arms from hugging and my lips from kissing. Cameron's eyes found mine, and he faintly smiled that sideways smile of his, and I knew my prayers had been heard. Finally, I regained enough composure to realize that the captain was standing over us, scrutinizing not only my nudity, but my blatant affection for some man other than the one to whom I had been promised. I looked up, wanting my eyes to thank him and to apologize for the precarious predicament in which I had just placed him. He was employed by Jewels. His duty, unquestionably, was to his employer, but now he was privy to information that could be lethal to all of us. However, he recognized that how he would handle this situation was not an immediate concern. He reluctantly tightened his lips and folded his brows into a grimace. Then he bent over and picked up Cameron with ease, enclosing the frozen man in muscular arms, tattoos stretching and distorting. I insisted that the captain take Cameron to my stateroom. He gave me another tarnished scowl, but silently nodded. I held the door ajar as Cameron was brought in and lowered onto my bed. He helped me remove Cameron's soaked trousers, and I threw blankets over his shivering body. With empathy, the captain gently draped a terrycloth robe over my shoulders.

Cameron was still agitated in spite of our efforts to comfort him. He pulled the captain's arm to him in a weak but insistent grip. Attempting to speak, only a gasping breath emitted from his blue lips. The captain leaned over and tilted his head closer to Cameron's mouth. As Cameron made another attempt to speak, the captain's eyes widened to the message. He jolted from the stateroom, flinging the door back with a bang. It wobbled on its hinges from the aggressive wind before finally shutting.

So, I sit on the edge of the bed, barely able to keep myself from falling off. One of my fists tightly ensnarls the sheet, the other lamely caresses his forehead. This ambiguity is an attempt to veil the pensive desperation in defining what our love meant to him. Unfortunately, in his present condition, I cannot ask. I dare not look into his eyes. From the edge of the bed, I wonder if our love was a mirage. As my palm brushes his forehead, I glare at the blue veins that protrude from the back of my hand, reminders of the passage of time. I am getting older; I cannot deny that any more. Is this why he doesn't want me? I can neither quell his quivering nor the thought of sustaining another tenuous love affair— this is the crux of my paradox.

I have always acted as if nothing in life is sacred, including love. I am such a pretentious realist. Whenever I have had to face unbearable choices throughout my life, I have defaulted to cowardice. That is how I broached love: hoping that through the promise of passion, everlasting love would come. It never did. One lover after another vanished from my life, the last kiss always concluding with the pat line, "I guess I don't feel about you the same way you feel about me." This never made sense, because I was never asked how I felt in the first place. No one seemed to care what I might want. I allowed the lovers to silently slip away, like sand through indifferent fingers. Was this the reason I never felt anything during intimacy? That I always suspected that rejection would be forthcoming? Of course, my lovers never knew this. I was skilled at intimate deception. But this man, by whose bedside I vigilantly sit now, has changed all that. He woke the sleeping princess inside me. This was my Cinderella story where I finally became the woman who deserved to be loved.

Yet how could he leave our sweet bed for the sirens of the sea and the solitary guitarist strumming another sad song? What should I do about all this as I sit quietly over a man I do not want to let go, yet distrust? Is it better to have not loved and consequently not experienced loss, rather than to love, but still lose? The pragmatic answer to that question again is that I have no choice. Doubt doesn't matter, for truth doesn't matter when I cannot allow this man to vanish like all the others.

Suddenly, there is an abrasive knocking at the stateroom door. "Missy! Missy Christine!" It is the husky voice of the captain.

IV

WITH THE CAPTAIN'S URGENT KNOCKS, I knew that his return would bring not only Cameron's message, but hopefully a supply a sympathetic understanding of our circumstances. From the other side of the door, the captain shouts, "Missy! Missy Christine! Jewels is on his way!

I leave the bed, tightening the belt of the white terrycloth robe before opening the door. I am not prepared for what I see: his matted hair is soaked from seawater as he stands rigid before me, a deflated man. "Cameron told me Jewels' wife...still down there." Thoughts whirl in my head. Was this suicide, murder, or some other truth?

The captain found Jewels' wife floating near the hull of the yacht. Her body was brought back to her stateroom. He has immediately called Jewels with the grave news, and Jewels informed the captain that he will take a helicopter and would arrive on board within hours. Jewels is on his way.

Wanting to know more about what he has said to Jewels about my intimacy with Cameron, I walk him to the door. But we exchange only silence. I am about to thank him when he wedges his foot in the door frame. I thought he was about to destroy whatever hope I had for salvaging my love. I misjudge his intent.

He shoves his hand into his pocket and withdraws an enclosed medicinal vial. "Here, your man might need this to rest better. Give him a couple of these pills, two will do; he will not wake until tomorrow." He pauses in a moment of indecision, and then adds, "This is what Jewels used on you." I squint back at him. Timidly, I take the orange-tinted vial and place it in the center of my palm. I am nauseated by its insidious implication. I cannot release my gaze from it, nor can I look at the captain. Without knowing what else may have been told to Jewels, I gently close the door and return to Cameron.

All the blankets piled about him have done little to cease his shaking. But his eyes are still alert, even though they have a watery, glazed covering. He is not aware of my exchange with the captain.

I move away from the bed and walk to the port window to inspect the horizon. There is no invasive smear on the expansive gray skies yet. When the blotch arrives, it will bring havoc into our lives. I turn to look at Cameron. He is in no shape to confront the inimitable dragon. Even if he should regain some resiliency, I fear the fallout from any confrontation. I recall Cameron's vow to never allow Jewels to get near me, as well as his vow to defend the honor of our love, even if it meant that he would kill. I cannot place Cameron in that situation; he is too precious to lose. I am resolute as to who will defend the honor of our love. My fist tightly grips the vial in my palm. I walk into the bathroom and fill a glass with water. I return to the bedside, put the glass down on the nightstand, and carefully place the vial behind it. Cameron's face has an icy, bluish sheen. I bend over him and kiss his face reverently. Although he does not move his body, his response is apparent in his signature smile. He tries to speak again. I discourage him, "Save your energy, love."

But he feels compelled to speak. I accommodate him by positioning my head to hear him. As I brush my warm cheek over his frigid one, my earlobe poses just above his lips.

"I tried, Christine, I tried to save her. I didn't just watch this time." I withdraw slightly so that our eyes look into each other. I understand what he meant; he was referring to Jewels' wife. His almost drowning was not a suicide, but an attempted salvation. He had emerged from the mirage of indifference. And because of his courage, I am ready to begin my journey out of my own mirage. We are not only pretentious realists, but endangered dreamers.

I lean over him draping my arms over the heap of blankets vigorously trying to rub the cold from his body, my face directly above his. I glide the back of my palms gently across his cheek, then pull back the edge of the sheet where my fists had twisted a short time ago. I make out a stain left from when we had bathed ardently in each other's body during the night. I turn back to Cameron. "I'm very proud of you. And I love you, Cameron."

I hear the returning murmur, "…love you."

Suddenly there is an invasive noise from beyond the port window, the distant summoning of a soldier to battle. If I do not take charge of the situation, Cameron and Jewels will face off in an irreconcilable battle—and all of us will lose the war. Within the midst of this dilemma is another summoning. *When Jewels lands his helicopter on deck, he will be expecting me to be there.* And I will deal with Jewels after I summon my courage for Cameron. I gaze at my lover again. His lips are still so blue, his skin still so icy, his eyes still so trusting. I pray for the courage to carry out the deception. I reach for the vial and unscrew the top. I shake two pills onto my palm. Carefully, I place my other hand behind his neck and tenderly raise his head. "Cameron, take this, it will help you rest." He readily opens his mouth, and I place the pills on his tongue. I retrieve the glass of water from the end table. Then I move the rim of the glass to his lips. He sips and swallows. After replacing the glass, I bend over and kiss his lips. I press my resolute lips onto his vulnerable ones, and gracefully we conceive a propitious child of faith. I pull away from him and remove my robe. I slide under the blankets and fold my bare body over his. I wrap my legs and arms about him tightly. They remain that way until his shivering stops, and his breathing undulates in a gentle repose.

Cocooned within the bed sheets like those swaddled questions marks, she becomes the one to cradle him from behind. This time the familiar embrace dissolves any residue of doubt about their love. In contented grace, Christine drapes her arm over Cameron's bare shoulder and caresses his upper chest.

His wavy hairs tickle her open palm as she reverently curls the ringlets. Her eyelids drowse in sync with the tender swirling, savoring the moment, for she is aware that this nourishing interlude will be brief. From the distance of the gray morn, impending doom seeps in. The delicate hairs on her forearms electrify and stiffen like wavering cilia. The warning is so subtle that her dozing lover does not detect the invasion of the dragon. But Christine hears it. Her gentle breathing changes into gaunt puffs in an imaginary attempt to extinguish its looming ferocious fumes. As the far-off huffing becomes more distinct, her hard-pressed panting becomes even more irregular. It is Jewels' helicopter.

Her rising apprehension goads her into leaving the warm bed. She leans into his back and wedges her lips between the crevices of his shoulder blades for one prolonged kiss. Then she gingerly unravels her body from Cameron, not wanting to disturb his doze. Oh, but the parting aches, and Christine forlornly shivers. In spite of this, she is convinced that she alone must battle the approaching beast. Cameron instinctively moans and reaches for her. His movement alerts her, and she freezes in conjecture of the possible consequences of his awakening. But he is too saturated from his ordeal and the impact of the sedatives to reverse their captivity, and sinks back into slumber. Relieved, Christine quickly exchanges defenseless nudity for the appropriate attire to face their nemesis. The outfit she had worn at the restaurant when she first met Jewels is her chain mail to embolden her resolve.

V

DIRECTLY ABOVE THE YACHT the despicable helicopter flaunts its blatant presence with a risqué swagger. Its dance spins out a pervasive shuddering that rattles the port windows. They chatter in confused bewilderment, and the bluster of the panes intensifies her terror. She pensively looks back at Cameron; at least he remains still.

The monster perches upon the top deck of the yacht. In the slow descent, the rotary blades thrash gusts of insane wind whipping against the teak deck. Finally, there is one stabbing jolt...a tinseling clang...then suddenly...silence. The engines have halted. A pause lingers. She is petrified.

The fold-down ladder of the helicopter snaps against the deck and ruptures the suspended stillness. Jewels emerges from its cavern and decisively moves from the helicopter even before the blades have finished winding down from their final rotation. He walks with his familiar, anxious gait, always at the edge of urgency, somehow receiving energy from this posture. This quick, angular movement reflects his quick, receptive mind as he immediately surveys and prioritizes any situation. Ironically his present priority is not his deceased wife, though that was why he was summoned, but

Christine, the reason he came.

It is not that Jewels is indifferent to his wife's death. When he was notified about the tragedy he felt an immediate pang of regret, but it was not for the loss of this woman, but for the long-lost bereavement of a vacant love, that once had auspicious beginnings. The demise of their love was set into motion when she was unfaithful to him. They had been childless in spite of their passionate love making. He yearned for a life with her, but most of all he yearned for the proliferation of his name. She had watched his disheartening expression with the onset of each month's menses. So, she devised a plan. Born from her endearing love, nevertheless, it was a plan of forbidden risk. Perhaps another's seed could be disguised for his, thus reverse his growing disenchantment. She believed that he would never know the ruse, or that he was deficient in his manly duties. Their love would perpetuate with her being with child. There was only one problem in this deception…Jewels was relentless in always knowing the truth. When he uncovered the duplicity, he was ruthless in his humiliation. Her twisting of the truth was unforgivable. That one occurrence snuffed out all passion within him, not only for her, but for those who would follow in his marriage bed. Ironically, with his two subsequent wives he was able to seed two children, but never out of love, and only from a one time, detached sexual act to consummate their wedding nights. His only love, his first wife, never gave him a child.

He had suppressed his desire to love again, that is, until he became guardian to his sister's child. However, he vowed that no adult woman would ever capture his soul as his first wife had. He did allow his first wife to remain within his household in spite of her visual disfigurement, perhaps as a reminder to the others of the consequences of imprudent infidelity. Ignored by Jewels and snubbed by all other members of his family, she had become a displaced woman in his residence. In spite of this she remained a prominent figure in the House of Jewels because of her business acuity and her insular discretion, which was the reason for her presence on his yacht.

The fall from grace had gnawed at her sanity. Her hours became a cancer of revenge, and she waited for the right time to implement payback. This retaliation against Jewels finally began last month when the disfigured woman leaked the vindictive rumor about his niece. Cameron had known about the old woman's betrayal, but had kept the instigator's identity from Jewels, who was sinking into deeper depression over the broken promise to his sister, her daughter's death, and the tribal Elders' waning confidence in his leadership. It was when Cameron waited outside Christine's stateroom during the old woman's obscene examination that he had finally decided that he would disclose to Jewels the old woman's betrayal. Whether this decision came from his own guilt, his intense ire for this creature, or his personal rivalry with Jewels mattered little, it was thwarted when the woman fell into the icy seas.

VI

JEWELS STEPS ONTO THE TEAK PLANKS and scans the deck for Christine. His intense passion for this mystifying woman can no longer be disregarded. Jewels' dead wife remains unattended in her darkened stateroom.

However, the person who appears from the lower deck to receive him is not Christine, but the captain. Jewels' jaw contorts with dismay. The captain notices his scowl, but approaches anyway, slouching instinctively, not to avoid the swinging helicopter blades, but from a submissive allegiance to his boss. He takes Jewels' briefcase and leads him off the upper level of the yacht. As the two men descend to the next deck, the captain vaguely spies through the darkened port windows, Christine's shadowy figure fluttering inside the main galley quarters. She is moving toward the doors that lead to where they now stand.

Christine, too, catches sight of the two men. They stand close together, their frames a dark silhouette against the gray, cloudless sky, like one monster with two bobbing heads, immersed in a heart-to-heart discussion. The proximity of their guarded stance conveys an impression that some provocative exchange is in progress, making Christine even more pensive. The initial self-confidence she had with Cameron drains to a pallor of misgivings. Could the captain be disclosing her unforgivable conduct into Jewels' ear? Her thoughts flutter in colliding ripostes. If she can hustle to the outside deck, she might be able to salvage any damaging account of the morning's events, which the captain might be relaying. But once she arrives at the threshold to the outer deck, she hesitates, faltering in self-doubt.

The dialogue between the two men abruptly ceases as Jewels glances up and sees Christine. His eyes squint into slivers of scrutiny, and this impassable stare never wavers. Christine attempts to decode his gaze but cannot. Is Jewels now privy to her relationship with Cameron? A silent scream of terror shrieks through her. She turns away, wanting to retreat back inside where memories lie blessed and secure. Her fleeting glance over her shoulder recaptures the vision of Cameron concealed beneath the bed sheets, and it is that image that emboldens her. She swallows her misgivings. Her only recourse is to blindly charge the dragon and sabotage captain's message.

She turns to face the beast, shoving the captain aside with an abrasive swing of her arm, giving him not even the slightest opportunity to clarify what has been spoken. Her rapid approach floods Jewels' senses into an intense arousal of desire. He bends his angular demeanor toward her.

Without losing step, she rotates her right shoulder as far back as it can go, and slaps him. His head jars sideways, his mouth feebly drops, and his eyes widen, the sting disconnecting coherent thinking.

"That...is for me!" Her voice nips the consonants.

The second hit is immediate. "This...is for your wife!" She delivers this whack with even more intensity. Although Christine is presently aware that Jewels had drugged her in the restaurant to inter her on his yacht, she is unaware that the offensive examination was not a directive from Jewels, but initiated independently by the dead woman. Ironically, Christine also is misinformed about the dead woman's final act of atonement. Because of his incapacitated state, Cameron was unable to reveal what had transpired below the ocean's surface. Christine does not know that the wicked woman had attempted to save Cameron's life in spite of the dreadful reckoning of her own demise. Christine is deluded by a mirage of what she wants to believe.

Jewels, too, is paralyzed by a mirage of meanings from the two attacks. His unresponsive retaliation bolsters Christine's most poignant blow, the one that should directly pierce the heart of the dragon. She, however, underestimates Jewels' resiliency, if not his mercilessness. Again, she is about to be deluded.

"And this is for your niec...!" she cannot complete the illicit word because Jewels breaks from his daze and grabs her wrist in mid-flight. His clutch tightens around her stunned hand, and he compresses an unrestrained ire into that grip. Christine's allusion to the dead niece is a reprehensible transgression. His eyes blaze. The swelling under his reddening fingers scorches a terrifying alarm. She realizes that he is out of control, and that she has gone too far. Her bravado could have become her own demise. Her mind swirls. She shakes her head trying to keep herself coherent, but a series of darkening hues halo her eyesight. Jewels' reasoning has vanished as he glowers directly in her face.

Suddenly, a stream of late morning light sneaks through the gray haze, washing the yacht in a buttery pallor. A soft illumination casts a façade upon Christine's face. Perhaps it is his thwarted conscience, however, whatever the rationale for the coincidence, the features of Jewels' beloved sister superimpose over Christina's face. Jewels squints at the illusion. The similarity of the two women is uncanny. Although Cameron had detected this similarity, Jewels had never noticed the resemblance before this moment; the correlation is unsettling. How could he have missed this obvious connection when he first saw Christine at the casino? Was it this likeness and not her beauty that attracted him? Is this the very reason for his obsession of her? In her tears, he sees the reflection of his insidious manifestation, and it spooks him. He never wanted it this way. He never wanted her to be afraid of him. He is not a beast; he is only a man. He veers from this hidden struggle, and his grip loosens. Her knees fold as she collapses. He catches her. Strapping his arms around her head and waist, he cradles her fragile body. In a suspension of time they momentarily pose like two Grecian statues frozen in their own tragic flaws. He slowly lifts her to a standing position as her back arches in a pliant curve. Still cupping her head in one of his palms, he studies her features intently. He threads his fingers through the strands of her hair straggling down her neck. Twisting the loose hairs, his fingers wrap around her neck, and he slowly draws her head into his chest. His eyelids drowse in a seductive urge. Her scent entices him into squeezing her even more tightly.

The captain breaks the spell with a timid cough and moves toward them with a pretense of extending assistance. "Let me help you with her!" Startled by the blunt presence of another person, Jewels shakes his head and signals with a flicking finger for the captain's dismissal. The captain doesn't move.

Perturbed that his order is being questioned, Jewels tightens his fingers into a fist and snaps, "That will be all, Captain...I will handle this...myself." Although it is quite obvious that the captain is reticent to leave her alone with Jewels, he knows well enough not to challenge this man's commands. He squints, nods, and briskly turns. As he departs, the captain's disturbed eyes look downward. They probe the impartial crevices between the teak planks of the deck for clemency for he knows that he should have remained to protect her instead of walking away.

The yacht rocks in a sway of duplicity. Some barbaric presence seesaws within a rational one. It is a deception concealing betrayal within the sphere of madness. They are left alone to either unveil the truth or continue the betrayal.

VII

EMBOLDENED IN HIS DESIRE, Jewels releases his hand from her neck and moves it to her bare shoulder, lingering momentarily before beginning to massage the bony blade. He slowly turns over his palm and drags the back of his fingernails down her bare arm from her shoulder to the inside crevice of her elbow. He repeats this movement in a deliberate suggestive slithering. Although she is now conscious enough to follow his intention, her arm hangs in a submissive trance. Finally, her wilted limb slowly rises as if commanded by some hypnotic plea. Her hand closes around his palm, appealing him to stop. He grunts and aggressively seizes her wrist again. He twists her petitioning limb behind her lower back. And like the furious tentacle of a sea serpent, locks her in an irrevocable clamp, an act of uncompromising intimidation. There will be no appeal. They remain motionless except for the throbbing of their breathing.

The flapping of ocean waves against the hull is a rhythmic narcotic for the ensuing terror. He begins to sway as he draws her waist harder into his.

She can only dangle like a rag doll in his inescapable hold. They rock and slowly revolve in a tight circle, two symbiotic bodies pivoting in an idiotic, sluggish dance. In the silent choreography she leans her head sideways against his chest, for she can only surrender to his madness. Yet this, too, is only a dance step of deception because he is unaware of her unfettered eyes frantically stalking the vast ocean beyond the railing. Within the dreariness, she seeks out any relief from her bleak fate, but the impersonal grayness only smothers her further in its abandoned gloom. Even the order of natural world remains unmoved by the petty petitions of humans. It merely winks at how humanity clashes against past and present moralities. It is a timeless sea in which ethics of decency and malice are nothing more than spraying licks from arbitrary waves beyond the railing, ardent in their initial intensity, but feeble in their debauchery as they dissipate back into the forgotten depths of a lackadaisical ocean.

So, it was with Christine's brazen attack on Jewels. Her petty condemnations were only self-indulgent floggings against his dominance. She had underestimated this man. She had thought that by aggressively confronting him she could deflect any ominous reprisals for loving another man. Instead, she can only allow her threadbare confidence to sink even further under his spell, futilely trying to postpone the inevitable. She is not sure what the captain had whispered into Jewels' ear. This uncertainty cannot be ignored much longer. She must exert her presence.

"Jewels, I know about Walt's poker bet with you." No response. The dance continues in its slow revolutions. She makes no further comment.

They turn…turn…and turn again without release, like the turning of an indifferent warp of time. The port window appears, disappears in the rotation, and then reappears. And in each passing, she probes the darkened windowpane for any saving grace: the captain, perhaps Cameron. Suddenly, a propitious prospect for being unshackled kindles as she detects a shadowy image shimmering behind the glass. But when she blinks, the apparition vanishes. She resigns herself to the fact that only her own sagacity will save her from a fated end.

"Jewels," she repeats his name, delicate enough to break the trance, "Jewels, I know that you want to believe that…you own me." He still does not respond. She becomes more direct and impales him, "…but, you don't!" Instantly she gulps, regretting the tone of her words, which ricochet back to her from the pointed silence of his response. They resume swaying in their dance.

Finally, he responds not with words but with coercion as his hand presses the side of her temple harder against his chest. The edges of her ear become numb. She hears the echo of his heart beating, vulgar reminder of delirious passion. The longing for her lover quagmires into the alluring rhythm of another's body. Sadly, the probability of ever feeling Cameron's touch again dwindles in swishing arias beyond the railing. An alien, resigning calm blushes over her as she drifts into the foreign lyrics. Yet strangely, this bizarre, melodious veil has become a respite from the stark reality of her vulnerability to Jewels' oppressive ballet. She swoons deeper into the delusion that makes the unbearable more bearable. Perhaps, this is similar to the fate of those women with vacant eyes, lifeless from stifling morality in domineering societies? These shells of women had to acquiesce the very womanhood endowed to them by nature. Thus, when one woman relinquishes what it means to be a female, she surrenders to the demise of all women.

Christine's constricted muscles submit to the dance, and this pleases him. He bows his head so that his chin lightly touches the top of her head. He brushes his jaw over her forehead in long, soothing swipes that entrench them both into the sweet sensations of an unexplainable serenity.

The harshness of his masculine voice breaks the moment. "Allah says in unequivocal terms that to kill an innocent is to kill humanity."

This utterance is not only displaced but disarming. She fixates on the word "kill" and frazzled by its possible intent to her own situation. Does this word pertain to what is forthcoming? She is helpless under his yoke; her head is bracketed sideways against his breast.

Like Saint George recklessly trying to slay the dragon, Christine forges blindly into its fiery breath, her saber of reason slicing through thin air, groping to make a connection. "Are you trying to justify what you did to your niece?"

This jab cuts deeply enough to make the dragon's head snap up. Jewels angrily snorts, "I cannot change my niece's death."

Christine has skewered open a wound. She has gashed the recent injury of what he very much wants to reverse but cannot. This lesion that refuses to heal harnesses Jewels into a grieving madness. Christine must decide if she will have compassion for his pain or maintain indifference to cripple him. Her abduction has forced her to contend with this insanity, if not the very definition of her own moral judgment as a woman.

"It is true, you cannot bring your niece back, or your sister." Christine immediately realized that was a slip of the tongue, for he had never mentioned his sister. Jewels doesn't miss that either. Christine rushes into the next comment. "But when you kidnapped me, Jewels, you chose to continue the destruction of another innocent. I am ensnared by a man who still adheres to the archaic belief of owning a woman, a belief that has lost relevance in a modern world. Most surprising, this is done by an enlightened man who not only knows this, but who can change this belief. Instead as you continue this insanity, you have contributed to the killing of humanity. What would your Allah say to that?"

He does not respond to her audacity but continues to dance. Yet, he is soaking up her words, fixating on the references to his sister and his niece. In the turning of the dance, uncertain queries gnaw at the surface of his skin. "How did you come to know so much about me…my sister…and my niece?"

Christine stiffens. Their dance comes to a standstill. They remain motionless for quite some time, digesting each other's silent commentary.

Jewels is uncomfortable in the pause. Impatient with the possibility that she will not answer him, he rocks again and answers for her. "Apparently, my deceased wife has spoken to you about these matters. I long suspected that she possessed a loose tongue." Christine still does not respond. She feels no remorse for the wife's despicable configuration as a female. Jewels is not aware that the niece's incident and his wife's role were relayed to her by Cameron, not his dead wife. The wife is now gone, and so is her loose tongue! But Cameron is very much alive! Christine decides to set up a thicker smoke screen to divert Jewels even further from that truth. Maybe, just maybe, Jewels is also ignorant about what else had occurred on the yacht. Maybe the captain said nothing about her relationship with Cameron. She decides to change the discourse further. "Your wife is dead. You should have more reverence for the dead!"

His tone flattens and becomes even more estranged than before, and Christine's "maybe's" diminish. "Neither can I reverse my wife's death, nor the murder of the child that woman briefly carried in her womb from another's seed." He lingers on that thought, then concludes, "Yet her infidelity has been addressed. Unfortunately, other betrayals against the innocent are still outstanding, and there is more justice to be done! Unfinished business. No?" Christine's eyes widen. The scared woman's disfigured body had once carried a child, an unborn child of tears! Its mother's slashed face riddled those tears. Had such a woman become so entrapped in the delusion of this man's justice that she allowed him to take the life of a child? As Christine looks at Jewels, she senses her own entrapment. Is he resurrecting a similar judgment on her because he knows about her relationship with Cameron? She asks herself again, *Is this what the captain had imparted to Jewels when she watched them in their clandestine discussion beyond the window?*

Unfortunately, Christine has misinterpreted Jewels' reference to justice. It was the wife who had inflicted her own self-mutilation and child's abortion to atone for her infidelity. The unfinished business Jewels referred to concerns the betrayal of a promise to his beloved sister to protect her innocent daughter. Christine is also blind-sighted by the whispers between the captain and

Jewels. The conversation between the two men was about the wicked wife's true executioner, the unforgiving ocean swallowing the deviant woman into its depths, an act of nature cleansing of another impurity from the earth. This was Nature's retribution for the wife's inhumanity. His atonement still waits in another court of humanity. Her feet stall again in the dance. Jewels, however, is committed to the waltz, still adhering her body to his and dragging her paralyzed legs beneath him. Because of this half-truth, she is his captive in the irretrievable mire of truth.

VIII

SHE TRIES TO PULL AWAY from him, but he grips her even tighter; he will not allow her to abandon him. "No!" He stops his dancing. He will not be forsaken. "I have brought you to my yacht, and I will not give you up!" He intensifies his hold and shakes her. She closes her eyes, wanting to deny what is happening. He shakes her more vigorously, like an animal jostling its prey between its teeth. "Look at me!" Her eyes roll without focus. "Look at me, Christine!" He grabs her hair and yanks it so that her head tilts up to his. His touch is brutal but his longing for her is unyielding. "I am a man disappearing! Open your eyes! You must see me!" He, too, is caught in his own irretrievable mire.

She peers into his face; it looks ancient. Could tears of human compassion ever have flowed from these hardened eyes? The cratered rivulets sunk in his cheeks are evidence of a different man. Her indifference begins to fade under the uncertainty of how she has defined this man. Her response to this overwhelming ambiguity is irrational. She kisses his lips.

Is it an act of immediacy, or is it an act of possibility? Certainly, it is an impulsive action, incomprehensible, not only to her but to him as well. But perhaps more pertinently, is it a kiss to condemn, or is it a kiss to atone? Humanity has struggled with the interpretation of such inexplicable kisses throughout history. Whatever its intent it becomes a kiss of mercy demonstrating the inexplicable compassion one human can extend to another, even to the beasts among us.

"Why...did you do that?" Jewels stutters, for Christine's incongruous kiss has finally sucked out his fiery breath.

"I didn't know what else to do." Her vague response sounded so nonchalant that it was almost as if his sister had spoken. He chuckles at its incongruity, but most of all from the familiarity of the words. The comment revived childhood memories when Jewels would banter with his sister and she would offhandedly give such casual comebacks to his overtly serious demeanor. His wonderful sister's playfulness always tickled his leaden spirit, bringing him back to rational thought during difficult situations. In fact, those were the exact words spoken by his sister on her death bed when he had asked why she had wanted him to be the guardian of her daughter. "I didn't know what else to do!" was her peculiar matter-of-fact reply. He releases his grip on Christine's hair. His palm glides across her cheek, and he tenderly cradles her chin. He raises it as he had done so many times with his sister throughout their lifetime together.

Entranced by his sister's memory, Jewels wants to release the ill feelings gripping him and Christine, so he tries to make amends. "I know why you kissed me. You knew that's exactly what I wanted you to do!" He winks to see if she catches not just the lewd, but lighthearted shift. He warms to the thought that his sister would have enjoyed such a remark.

He cannot dismiss Christine's face. He inhales, "You resemble my sister." He whispers more to himself than to her. Cameron's perception has finally surfaced. "You resemble the only person who was devoted to me, the only person who gave unquestionable fidelity to me...the only woman who ever loved me." Christine tucks this last comment away. It may be valuable later. Bowing his head, he flinches, "And, I broke my promise to take care of her daughter, my beautiful sister's daughter." He looks up. "And now I am drawn to you because you, too, are so beautiful!"

Christine knows that she is being pulled into the guilt of his past. "Are you really attracted to me or just the image of me?"

"Does it matter? In the end, Christine, does it really matter who we are, or what we want? When a man has become only a shell, does it really matter what image of a woman he needs to hold in the darkness of the night?"

Christine is deeply moved by his naked comment. She, too, has felt a similar emptiness under the unforgiving covers of the night. She quietly validates his words. "Maybe we are only a man and a woman out of sync with time and place."

"Maybe, Christine, we are a woman and a man colliding in a new time and place! I believe that some force has brought us together."

"Maybe, Jewels, that force of nature is just playing with us!"

"Well, I'm not playing here, Christine. When I first saw you in the casino last Friday, I knew that I could not let you disappear from my life. And now I know why." He peruses her face, savoring her features. The discerning faint lines of her eyes are receptive to what he has just said, and he continues. "I cannot undo the broken promise I had made to my sister...I cannot undo...any of that now..."

She knows that the entrenched rivulets chiseled in his cheeks are the memories of unforgiving guilt. She cuts him off. "The tragedy is not our inability to undo the past, but our inability to repair our lives after we have been broken."

"I cannot undo the past…because my entire life has been a lie. And for quite some time I really no longer cared about what I have become." He examines her face again. Christine follows his searching eyes. He sees his sister, but he also sees Christine's distinctive features. "I wanted forgiveness from my sister, but it is too late for that. Then you walked into the casino…and seeing you here on this yacht, I realize that you have given me a chance to apologize, not just to my deceased sister's memory, but to myself." With the back of his fingers, he brushes away the frazzled wisps from her forehead. Her body trembles from the sensation. Jewels feels the quiver. Both misinterpret the meaning, but that duplicity is no longer important because he wants her. "Christine, I need you in my life now."

Christine is apprehensive about where this is leading. They are too isolated on the yacht. She is not sure how to handle the outcome if she allows him to continue to believe that she would be his. "Jewels, I can never replace your sister. We're different…You and I are different…We come from different pasts that have made us distinctively…different."

His arm around her waist tightens, not in an aggressive embrace, but a longing one. He presses himself into her, and she feels his arousal. "Christine, you will be leaving with me on Saturday…to officially become my wife."

These words regurgitate with the insanity of their situation. It is an insanity that doubts probability, but not possibility. It is an insanity that unravels the life they had lived. But it is also where the insane actions of the present try to justify the lies of the past. They need to confront that possibility. Instead it is a possibility of doubt that drives her body to twirl insanely into a drunken stupor. Caught off guard by the sudden change in her demeanor, his relaxed grip allows her to wriggle free from his hold. She shoves him away, and he is momentarily stunned. As she staggers away from him, she glances behind her, snags his rejected gaze, and is pained by the sight. But her arm still swings around attempting to ward off any pursuit by him. Her fright is no longer what he can do to her right now on this yacht, but what she would allow him to do to her right now. Losing her footing, she stumbles. Swiftly he lunges for her extended arm and snatches her wrist. Catching her before she falls, he strongholds her, and she teeters on the dangling end of his grip.

"Christine, don't…don't move away from me," he breathes heavily. He shakes her roughly as if his commanding words and demanding tone will make her obey his will.

"Let go of me!" Her pitch is elevated and resolute. She insists that he listen to her. "You are hurting me!" He does not relent. She tries once more to make him understand, "You must let go of me!"

He needs for her to accept that her struggling is aimless, so he lowers his voice. "All this will not matter, anyway. You will leave with me on Saturday, and you will become my wife very shortly after that."

Although these words terrify Christine again, she harnesses the panic by mirroring his lowered tone with an emphatic whisper. "Jewels, I'm trying...to tell you...you do not...and you never will...own me!"

He stops yanking. Although he still has a hold on her wrist, he sees her alluring face even with its disheveled grimace. And the incongruity of her beauty and her denial of his longing humors him. He pauses, tilts his head, and smiles, for he cannot resist her. Perhaps some good old-fashioned American wit might console her enough to resume a more receptive attitude. "As they say in your Westerns, I won you 'fair and square,' girl. I own you!" He twists his lips in charming warmth as his eyebrows rise into his crinkled forehead in an attempt to punctuate the reality of her situation. "Sister, you're going nowhere, fast!"

Within the billows of terror and the gentle wafts of humor, possibilities engender probabilities, and she sniffs with a puff of amusement. His humorous remark shows a side of him that reveals some sanity. And this sliver of rationality opens the probability that she can get him to hear her message. She decides to piggyback on his humorous scenario. "Well, in this part of the country, Mister, we don't own people!" She punctuates that point in the reality of consequences. "I hate to tell you, partner...but there's a law!"

He is enjoying this repartee. Resuming the Western inflection, he continues the witticism. "Well, Sister, in my part of the country, we own people all the time. And by the way, there is a law there, too...I am the law...the only law!"

This bantering seems to be working, so she calculatingly shifts direction toward a possible resolution. "I thought you answer to another law...one of a higher authority!"

"You mean Allah?" Jewels slightly pauses, "I do."

"How soon we forget, out of convenience, perhaps?" She retorts with good old American snobbery. It is time to build her case. "Look, Jewels, maybe you're not as different to my world as you are to yours."

"Really!" he decides to follow her lead. "In what way...As a matter of convenience?"

"Perhaps! Look at you. You look different, you act different. You drink...you gamble...you have a sense of humor." She twists her lips in a consenting sneer. "You listen to a woman as an equal! You are the new Eastern Man!"

He mimics her playful sneer, realizing that he is not only drawn to her beauty, but to her fresh perspective on life. He caresses her with a play on words. "I am quite happy that you finally realize that I am a man, and as a man I have the needs of a man!" He thrusts his hips forward into a lewd position. His eyes once again drowse. He is enjoying this. What he does not recognize is that he has just allowed her the opportunity to toss down the gauntlet.

"And your needs as a man will be met if you play your cards right?" She inwardly flinches at such a thought, but proceeds with her strategy, for she knows that she must appear sincere if she is to survive the challenge. Her expression changes. It is now stern.

"Jewels, if I go with you on Saturday, I want you to know that you will never possess me. You might bed me, but you will never have me…you will never have my…devotion. In the dark of night, you will be making love to a corpse…your dead wife's corpse…your sister's corpse…in my body." Because he never released her wrist during their humorous exchange, Jewels now compresses his fingers, digging them into her skin. Christine flinches slightly, but then she merely glares down at her imprisoned wrist and continues in a matter-of-fact tone, "And by the way, your brutality will never change that fact." She pauses a second for emphasis. "Unless…"

He eases his clasp, but still is hinged to her. "Unless…what?"

She pauses again. It is important that she does not seem too anxious to answer.

He, however, by nature, is always anxious for answers, and he knows that she is purposely stalling. He shakes her arm, not too harshly, just enough to reiterate that he is still in control. She still does not speak. He realizes that he should not bully her any further because, in truth, he wants her to accept him, and he is curious about what she has to say. "What is it that you want?"

"First, let go of my wrist!"

He hesitates. He has never taken orders from anyone, particularly not a woman, and an American woman at that. He acquiesces. Why not? They are on his yacht, and she is not going anywhere without his consent. Furthermore, he amuses himself with the idea that perhaps he can be a new Eastern Man, so he drops his arms to his side, releasing her, but staying within reach. He repeats, "What is it that you want?"

Christine leads him out of the mirage of probabilities and into the truth of possibilities, "Another chance."

Confused, "Another chance? At what?" Jewels squints.

"At my freedom."

He stares at her, trying to come to terms with not only her words but her audacity. His pause is broken by a quick yelp, followed by a string of snickers. Finally, he subsides back into singular sardonic grunts. "Your freedom!" Grunts. "You American women are an interesting lot!" Grunts again.

Christine is silent but determined. She continues to look intently at him, facing him squarely, standing brazenly erect.

He returns her stare. "As they say in your movies, 'Honey, maybe you didn't get the memo, I won...Walt lost...It's pay up time. The game is over! You're mine! Is that not so?"

"Then play another game!"

"And I should do this because...?" He tilts his head in charming eloquence, eyes slightly askew.

Christine waits a moment to allow him to digest the next thought. "Because I was never asked if I wanted to be part of the game. You never asked my permission. I never gave you my consent. You never asked me what I could offer you." She hesitates, but closes with "...Is that not so?"

Grunt! "What can you offer me that I don't have, or for that matter can't buy?" Jewels responds in a haughty tone. Christine puts off that question. Instead she decides that she will outline the revised scenario.

"You will have a rematch game of poker with Walt. You set the rules. Change the rules if you want. Just be transparent and fair. If Walt wins, then you will release me from this former bet, and you will never have any contact with me, or for that matter, anyone else I choose to be involved with."

Jewels grunts, assuring himself that this will never come to pass. But he is charmed by her, and how she is interacting with him, so he plays along. After all, she is so alluring, and he does want her to love him. Jewels has never been able to walk away from any interesting wager, and this one is quite intriguing. "And if I win, what do I get that I don't already have?"

Christine smiles and quietly says, "You get me."

He reflexes on this remark. "But I already have you. Is that not so?" He mimics her inflection. Yet he is curious over her intent of the words *...get me.*

She waits momentarily, for she wants him to grasp that she is about to offer a serious proposal. "You don't 'just' get me physically. You get something more valuable. If, and only if, you happen to win, I will become not only a wife, but your devoted wife. A wife giving you unlimited passion, a wife who will take care of you. Most of all, I will be a wife who will give you unequivocal fidelity. In other words, maybe at first, I will not love you. But, in time I will learn to love you. Unconditionally...and forever."

Jewels does not immediately respond. He fixates on her face. For quite some time, he does not move. Finally, he turns from her, walks over to the railing and looks out across the gray ocean. This type of commitment has never been given to him by anyone, not from the wives of his impersonal arranged marriages, not even from the one who had professed love, but weakened to disloyalty. This was the one factor that all his money and power could never buy. He realizes that this was no longer just a poker wager, but the possibility of having what he always wanted to have, and perhaps needs to have. What Christine is offering would not only reconcile those broken promises but would salvage his broken life.

Yet, suddenly, denial of such a reality veers its ugly head, and doubt seeps in. He mulls this over, trying to decipher if her motives are honorable. His eyes tighten. It is obvious that Christine is privy to more of his fragmented past than he had assumed, yet in spite of that, she does not seem frightened to become his faithful wife. He cannot deny any of his past. Somehow, he doesn't want to deny who he is anymore, not to this woman. Instead, he wants to tell her who he wants to become…this woman who has captured his heart…who has given him the potential for meaning in his life. That can never happen if they are not truthful with each other. If she will give him a chance, she might be able to forgive him…and he might be able to forgive himself. A probability could become a possibility. But he must affirm her commitment to what she has just presented to him. He turns around and faces her.

"Christine, if I win, which by the way I will, I will hold you to this promise. And if you break it, I will consider it a dishonor to me." He walks up to her and sternly peers into her eyes. "Do you understand what the consequences are when an Eastern man is dishonored by a woman, even an American woman?"

He continues to stare directly into her face. This thought sends a chilling echo through her. She glares into eyes that might no longer be distant but are quite adamant. And she punctures those eyes. "Yes, I am fully aware of what is done during an Honor Killing!"

He conceals his wince. Instead, to test her resolve, Jewels clarifies. "And I will personally make sure that it will be done…and done without mercy."

Christine cannot speak but just nods her head to confirm the agreement.

He, too, nods to solidify the accord. As he continues to regard her face, he has a pang of regret that such a wager was made at all. But if this is what it takes to win this woman, then so be it. As he sinks into her beauty, he descends into the satisfaction of his bet. Of course, he tries to push the impossibility out of his mind that he might not win, and she could be lost to him forever. But when he recalls how easily he had won over Walt, his confidence returns. He decides to flaunt his upcoming victory in his rematch with Walt. "I hate to give you the bad news now."

"What bad news?" Christine worries that she might have been too hasty in her proposal. When she formulated this spontaneous wager, she was confident that Walt could easily out-perform Jewels in any game of bluff. But could she have made a serious error in judgment? Didn't Walt lose before to this man?

"I hate to tell you, but your boy is not a good poker player!"

"What do you mean?" Christine's concern wavers even more.

"Well, when I played Walt on the last hand, I was quite surprised he lost like a beginner after showing how adept he was prior to that."

She becomes outwardly pensive with this new information. Jewels is delighted to see her concern. He continues to drive his point. "Strangely, he kept betting right up to the showdown."

"Why was that strange?"

"Because when Walt finally showed his cards, he had had nothing right from the beginning."

Christine needs more information. "What was the Flop?"

"Two aces and an eight. And because I already held another ace in my hand, I was in good position. Then when the Turn brought another eight, I probably won the hand at that point with a Full House."

Something was definitely strange. But something was also very familiar. "Jewels, what were the suits?"

"Nothing with the same suits, just four lone cards lying forlornly on the green felt. Just four black cards. Silly man, your Walt, he surely knew he had lost! Then he did the most foolish move I ever saw after the last card was drawn."

"What?"

"He raised the bet."

"Raised the bet! You're kidding!" *This does not seem like Walt. Not only has he always been a shrewd player, who knows when to walk away from the table, he also would never bet with such a beginning hand. Never!* After digesting this, she quietly pursued the questioning. "Jewels, is that when he bet me?

"Yes. You."

"Me," Christine repeats quietly.

"That's when your man put into the pot that he would deliver you to me next Saturday. I would own you and you would leave the country with me. That is, if he lost the hand, which he certainly was going to."

"That's insane! Walt has never hurt me like this! And, why would you want me without knowing me? No man with any style, or for that matter, with morals, would do that!"

"True, but I had caught sight of you, and to be quite honest, I liked what I saw. Sorry I didn't ask your permission. But that's my style and my morality!"

Christine is perplexed. This does not make sense. "And he made a bet knowing full well that he would lose?"

"He certainly did, and with your so called 'freedom' at stake!"

Christine tries to make sense of what Walt was thinking. Why would Walt bet with such a hand? Some piece of the puzzle is missing. "Jewels, what was the kicker card before the final bet?"

"The last card? The last card was really "bloody" inconsequential because I already won. Oh Yes...the last card was a "bloody" Queen of Spades!"

Suddenly, Christine understands what Walt had intended through the brushoff slur, "bloody" of Jewels' vernacular. She is saddened by Walt's reason, but she also knows that Jewels' self-confidence is compromised by knowing only half of the truth. Nevertheless, the design of their fates has been set in motion and either Christine or Jewels will become the recipient of that 'half-truth.' Perhaps, their pact is an Eastern and Western gesture of probability.

He turns his palm upward and sweeps his arm in the direction of the helicopter. "It is time to go to the poker table. It waits with Walt and a solitary seat, my seat."

Christine panics. She does not want to be alone with this man, especially on a helicopter or any isolated destination.

"Look, Jewels. You are not to take advantage of me on your helicopter. Or for that matter, bring me to some back-alley warehouse. If this arrangement is happening, it must be held where there are people around."

Jewels smiles at the image of being alone with her, but he knows that he must remain patient if he is to get his ultimate reward. "Christine, you need not worry about me keeping my zipper up. Your virtue is safe with me for the time being." He gives her a knowing leer. "So, do you have a place in mind that would fit into your agenda?"

Unsettled by his suggestive comment, she hastens to address the other matter. "Atlantic City...at the same casino you played poker with Walt...in the same room." There would be enough activity and people to watch over her there.

He ponders how to make this work. Normally, he would have Cameron make the arrangements. But when Jewels emerged from the helicopter, the Captain had informed Jewels that Cameron, in trying to save his wife, was now lying incapacitated somewhere on the yacht. Jewels would need to rely on his other henchmen, who were already in Atlantic City. Furthermore, it was close to where his yacht would be docked for Saturday's departure. Yes, he could make it work!

"Sound's good to me. It's a deal!" Jewels sweeps his arm toward the helicopter.

She still doesn't move. She needs to tell Cameron the plan. Unfortunately, he is back in her stateroom under a cocoon of blankets. "Look, Jewels, I have to go back to my stateroom."

Jewels immediately becomes guarded. Is she is stalling? "For what reason?"

Christine picks up his concern, but it is essential that she get back to that stateroom. In a causal tone, she tries again to persuade him. "I need a jacket and my purse."

"I can buy you a jacket, and I'll send for your purse. You will not need anything in it. I can provide for everything."

She does not respond, but notices that her hesitation is making him more uneasy. He looks over his shoulder to the darkened port window and turns as if he is about to proceed into the interior of the yacht. However, the captain suddenly emerges from inside, hustling directly to Jewels. "There is a report of an impending storm quickly approaching. Do you want me to bring the ship further out to sea or go inland?"

Jewels gives a glance past the captain's shoulders toward the port window. Rethinking his decision, he shifts his direction and gives his directive to the captain, "Prepare the helicopter. The American woman and I will immediately be leaving for Atlantic City. You will remain on board and take the vessel out to sea to wait out the storm. When you can, steer the yacht south and pick us up at the same dock I had secured by the casino. Be prepared to depart early Saturday morning."

Christine has run out of tactics. From here on she must improvise cautiously. A half-truth might not guarantee her survival. Without speaking she turns and walks deliberately toward the ladder leading to the upper deck where the helicopter waits indifferently. Hopefully, he will take her lead. Rubbing his hand over his mouth, Jewels watches her. Then, jamming his fists into his jacket pockets, he follows behind. He, too, is improvising. Are they only a man and a woman trying to rise from under the veil of righteousness imposed by their societies? Perhaps their story is a statement of masculine and feminine forces colliding to exist in a modern world in spite of how they have been defined by the past.

Throughout his life, the captain has weathered the precarious winds of the ocean, and he has learned not to be presumptuous before their propensities. He brushes his chin over his shoulder to glance inadvertently back at the port window. The captain understands that her lover might lie securely in her stateroom now, but such a man cannot be shielded from the foolhardy trials of providence.

IX

THEIR RIDE FROM THE YACHT to the casino is uneventful. As soon as she boards the aircraft, Christine heads to a seat positioned next to the last small, oval, pressurized window opposite the doorway. She withdraws a red cashmere blanket from the overhead compartment. When Jewels enters the cabin, preoccupied by her body language, he almost knocks his head against the low overhang. In an overt motion of turning from him, she plops onto the leather seat, twisting her body within the blanket, slouching toward the window. It is a deliberate statement that there will be no more discussion between them.

Jewels sits on the other side of the aisle toward the front of the craft near the cockpit, a significant distance of separation, giving them the space both need. However, he still refuses to sever the connection completely. He swivels his chair around so that he directly faces her. There he remains for the entire trip, his eyes never wavering.

Any amateur poker player could have easily read the rejection, but he simply chooses to ignore her antics and fastens his seatbelt. Nevertheless, when he finally is situated in the plush captain's chair, his intertwining fingers pensively tugging on his lower lip are a more accurate gauge of his response to her rebuff. He stares in her direction, reviewing their wager. It certainly is demeaning for him to be shunned this way, yet he knows enough about her determination to accept the fact that she will not change her attitude. She will not submit to him until he has won the rematch. Although this is the type of position in which Jewels never likes to be placed, he will relinquish his pride on this occasion because he wants to believe she is finally his, or at least almost his. He replays her comments about his sister and his niece, and grimaces from distant rumblings of the possible fallout that might ensnare him again in madness. The bitter bile of infidelity rises. Shaking this heinous conjecture from his mind, he redirects his focus to Christine.

The thud of the blades whips intermittently, intensifying into whirls of ferocious woofing. She continues to maneuver the red woolen blanket over her chin in a halfhearted attempt to hold on to her dwindling security. As the helicopter hovers above the launch pad of the yacht, the late morning sun departs with a life of its own. Vagrant rays slither between colliding clouds, piercing through her side window. A lattice of sunbeams imprints itself upon the blanket, becoming twisting lines in its folds, much like the twisted webbing of her thoughts. However, Jewels is viewing the scene quite differently. He is captivated by how the radiant network falls on her auburn hair, turning selected strands into exquisite burnt highlights. The sight beckons him to leave his distant seat and embrace her in a pardoning declaration of his love. Instead, he remains stationary. In the confines of his deference, Jewels silently vows again that he will never let go of this woman.

Geometric lines crisscross the window pane before a submissive backdrop. Christine huddles closer to the glass. As the helicopter rises, the horizontal deck railing glides across the frame before tilting and slipping out of view. She peers downward and tracks the vessel sinking away, riveted to a specific port window on the yacht. As the distance increases, the reality of that window sinks, too. She questions if her unseen lover has ever existed at all. Soon the yacht is so minuscule that it loses its distinctive form. She squints and imagines that the solitary white vessel has transformed into a diminutive seagull, wading in its own lonely pretense upon the vast ghostly ocean. The helicopter veers a sharp angular left, and a piercing ray of light blinds Christine. She turns from the window and catches Jewel's stare. Abruptly, she falls back into the padded seat and grips the blanket tighter, pulling it over her head. Under its cover, she prays that she has made the right decision.

The limousine ride from the Atlantic City airport to the casino is also muted in trepidation for her. On the other hand, conversing in foreign tongue, Jewels uses his cell phone for a series of communiques, arrangements that need immediate attention. Not understanding the language, Christine merely gazes out the side window of the limo, watching the landscape whiz by in an array of endless insignificance.

During the helicopter ride, Jewels began to construct those arrangements in his mind: He will give Christine time to refresh herself when they arrive in Atlantic City. She will have her own suite at the casino to rest for the remainder of this day and the next, prior to the poker game, which is set for nine o'clock tomorrow evening, the night before they are to leave the country. He, too, needs his rest. His people would inform the casino that his personal suite should not be far from hers. She will be under the care of "selected gentlemen" from his party while he recoups, meaning that she will not be able to leave the room without his knowledge or permission.

The directives are given with unequivocal, if not unquestionable, understanding. He makes sure that his handlers will reach out to his contacts at the hotel to secure the specific private gaming room for the upcoming poker night. He certainly has enough clout to ward off any problems. Yes, he had his plan in place.

X

CHRISTINE IS ESCORTED to her hotel suite and enters the room alone. She is so exhausted, physically and mentality, that she collapses onto the king-sized mattress fully clothed and remains in almost the same position until late morning of the following day. She has lost all sense of time, because the suite's blackout curtains are drawn, minimizing any waking sunlight in the room.

As mid-morning arrives, Christine forces her eyelids to separate to discern her whereabouts. She shifts her head sideways; the red, iridescent digital clock on the bedside nightstand illuminates the 11:24 a.m. time.

Christine never looks away until 11:32 a.m. appears when she is finally able to process her situation. She still does not get up from the bed. She twists onto her side, pulling one of the soft pillows into her chest. She cradles it, imagining that she is clutching Cameron, reconstructing the curves of his body. This thought momentarily sustains her. But just as suddenly, the sting of his vacant frame returns her back to the dark reality of the hollow room. She releases her embrace, and the pillow teeter totters, faltering like her resilience, before dropping to the floor.

With the pretense of rising from the bed, Christine whips her legs over the side of the mattress. Her feet scuff the pillow lying aimlessly below. She sits erect for a moment, pushing the blanket off her thighs. A sobering thought grips her. Last night when she fell upon the bed, overwhelmed by weariness, she hadn't been covered with a blanket. Inspecting this blanket now bunched beside her, she recognizes that this is a small accessory throw, the one that is usually rolled up on a shelf in a hotel closet. Apparently, someone has draped it over her...someone has been in this room as she slept.

She feels violated by the unknown. Scanning the interior, she searches for any other evidence of an intruder. Hanging meticulously over the wooden valet next to the dresser is a V-neck, shoulder sleeved, red chiffon dress. It is an eloquent, yet somewhat overstated, tea length dress. Directly below the hanger are a pair of black stilettos with limping ankle straps. The finishing touch to the intrigue lies on top of the dresser where a small, rose velveteen jewelry box serenely waits to be opened. Christine understands this is her ceremonial attire for this evening's event. However, for Christine's immediate needs, what is sorely missing from the room is some nourishment to prevent her from collapsing before the evening's life altering event! She reaches for the house phone. There is no dial tone. It has been disconnected. Of course! She must not be allowed to communicate with the outside world, even if she perishes from malnutrition. She inspects the room for exits, hurtling off the bed and strutting directly to the blackout drapery. Shoving the heavy material back, the light assaults her sight from the sliding glass door. Unfortunately, when she attempts to open the latch, she discovers that it, too, has been mercilessly locked. This exit has obviously been secured from any possible escape. Dismissing this waste of her precious energy, she whirls around and charges for the exit door to the hall. Surprisingly, it opens. She exhales relief. But this, too, is only a deception. Directly across from the threshold, in an eloquent chaise, sits a bulky man with a buzz-cut hairstyle. He slouches with outstretched legs just casually enough so that the cuffs of his tailored, dark pin-striped suit only slightly sag on the floor. Accentuating his meticulously pressed, white, dress shirt is a thin, canary yellow tie with a gold collar bar and matching tie clasp. As soon as the door is wide enough for direct eye contact, he smiles and cordially addresses her in a thick, graveled voice.

"Good morning. Actually, I should say...good afternoon...almost."

Christine is startled. "Afternoon...Uh? Hum...hum..."

Extending unassuming courtesy in spite of his ill-bred speech and crass mannerisms, he alleviates her stuttering. "You must be hungry. Would you like some nice breakfast, or maybe you would want some nice lunch instead?" He politely pauses for her to respond. He smiles.

Christine finally mumbles "lunch would be fine."

He rises from his chair and approaches the partially open door. Christine backs away. He stops and smiles again. "I'll make sure that something nice is immediately sent up from the kitchen." He reaches for the knob and gently shuts the door, leaving Christine inside, facing the closed door, powerless and abandoned once again.

XI

IN SPITE OF THE ARRAY OF FOOD brought into the suite by the man outside her door, Christine's hunger has abated, her nibbling, meager. She makes no further attempts to leave. There is nowhere for her to escape anyway. She must remain and play out the hand dealt her. At least now she is no longer ignorant of whom the players are, what cards are on the table, and what is at stake: Her freedom, if not her very life.

The afternoon dwindles as she gazes out the secured sliding glass door from the fifth floor. She sits directly in front of it, sprawled in a padded chaise, one leg dangling aimlessly over an armrest. From this perch she sips in the panoramic view of the Atlantic Ocean, an intoxicated sentinel for the sundry vessels moving in slow motion across the horizon from right to left, from left to right. Every so often, she fixates on those stationary sea crafts that appear to be pinned to the blue sheet, like insects on flypaper. When the distant horizon becomes too mundane, she diverts her attention to a closer vista and drift into episodic spells as the hypnotic waves break the shoreline.

The afternoon empties into the infinity of the vast ocean of her mind. Vagrant thoughts about her predicament drift like those nomadic sea vessels. Like a lone vessel, Christine has been tossed in the torrent of an unforgiving tide. Women throughout time have been caught in this undertow, veiled under the helms of the passing ships of men. On the beach Walt tried to warn her. But he could not speak the truth...not then. Now his voice counsels her. Walt lost in a card game on a predictable hand. There had to be more involved in this blunder. Walt is not a bad poker player, he is a good one. He would never throw a game unless he had a reason. And, he would never bet on that particular hand. This was what Christine realized when Jewels had asserted

Walt's incompetence. Jewels was shortsighted.

Christine resumes scanning the vista. She watches the vessels move in predicable directions over the sea. The encounters with these three men were predicable, too. Unfortunately, Christine was so immersed in the currents of her disillusions that she had been shortsighted, too.

"Certainly, there is no immunity for poor eyesight, Christine! What you need is a good dose of insight!" She addresses herself and leans her head back on the cushioned chair to reconstruct her thoughts of the weekend.

What lies beneath this afternoon's confinement began with the distraction she had caused at Friday night's poker game, which then continued with the clandestine rendezvous at the concert Saturday night. Her convenient seat next to Cameron was actually a covert meeting between Cameron and Walt. That is when the kidnap was solidified. The sale of her soul was made the prior night on the river card during a poker game when Walt purposely threw the hand. Her soul was bartered on the Queen of Spades.

"What made Walt believe he had the right to broker my life?" Could the answer be found in his incoherent babbling on the beach? She looks back through the glass door and the afternoon's solitude. The vessels bob in and out of waves, sinking in and out of muddled sunlight as childhood memories fade in and out. She recalls how the two of them would bask in their games of pretend, especially their imaginary cowboy and Indian exploits of the Old West. She played the earthy frontier cowgirl, and Walt developed his instinctive Native American sense of survival. The illusionary realism imprinted itself upon the innocence of two children who believed that they could confront any evil in the world. It became their rite of passage through the insanity of their fragmented lives, for they were only children and were no match for worldly malice.

Walt would carry the sinful albatross of his father's violation of her like the crucifix that permanently hung on the gold chain around his neck. This unbearable guilt changed into an obsessive vigilance, not just to take care of her, but to protect her unconditionally. He became the self-appointed sentinel whose duty was to keep all that was vulgar at bay. She needed Walt's acuity and shrewdness, so she entrusted him with an almost unrestricted license to make pivotal decisions concerning her life. That myopic commitment made in childhood had far reaching consequences as adults.

Ironically, although these two childhood friends were never romantic, they deciphered each other's hidden thoughts, latent desires, and vulnerable fragilities…they were lovers without sex. She knew that she was attractive to men, but her casual lovers only saw her physical beauty, using her for their own whims and then leaving her. Of course, she was aware of Walt's over-active imaginative mind and his male inclinations toward her. But he saw her differently. Maybe Walt was just waiting for the right time to make a move. But that move never materialized because he could not see through the haze of guilt. Maybe he finally came to the realization that it would never materialize with him.

As Christine continues to unfold Walt's night of poker, she understands why he made his decision, based on the River's Queen. She was Walt's Queen . If he could not have her, maybe a wealthy, sophisticated man could. At first Walt had not seen the lair in which Jewels slept, or the unforgiving consequences of that lair. That last drawn card was not as inconsequential as Jewels had thought. Now Christine envisions a different card, not just a Queen, but a depiction of the notorious Queen of Spades stained red from the blood of women by the avarice of men. It is a captive truth of inhumanity.

Cameron allowed himself to change as he released the chains that defined his past. Now she must make a change. She feels a sense of shame over how she has chosen to live. Now she sits before a detached window and puts together the pattern of cards in her life. She turns from the ocean's impersonal vastness and approaches the bathroom to prepare for the endgame. She makes it as far as the corner of the bed when her eyes moisten. The tears flow slowly at first. But within seconds they rupture into an irreparable torrent, riveting her body into convulsive quaking. Clasping the corner of the bed she falls to her knees. Her palms gather the bed covering into twisting knots. The tears are an unbridled release of a violated eight-year-old, a childless woman, a hollow female. The release becomes tears of self-vindication, essential for her survival this night. When the bout subsides, she refocuses her composure on the bureau clock next to the bed. The red iridescent numbers on the digital face have patiently been waiting for her; the numbers glower 6:32 p.m. She must prepare for the final showdown. She has time for a long shower.

The steady stream immerses her in the sweet warmth of water caressing her body. It cleanses and baptizes her, returning her to the purity of her humanity. Finally, saturated with its goodness, she leaves the shower stall and sits on the bed, tightly wrapping the plush towel around her. It soothes her, and she finds it difficult to relinquish its hold. But she is a realist. She glances about the room. It is a room indifferent with trivialities. She spies some unfinished business on the far wall. She rises; the towel slides off her. She steps away from the disarray and walks to the dresser where the closed red velvet box remains untouched. She opens it gingerly. The fading afternoon light sizzles on the clear stones. She leans into the lamp and switches it on for closer inspection. She removes two hanging earrings from the white velveteen cushion. They drool eloquently from her delicate fingertips. The strings of diamonds appear like dew drops, shimmering in flawless transparency. She is mesmerized by their brilliance. She cannot even begin to surmise their worth. Jewels wants her to understand the bounty of his devotion to her. She gently returns the earnings to the box and closes the lid. She knows that she will never open it again. The time to dress, and undress her real self, has arrived.

XII

THE REFLECTION IN THE MIRROR captures the evidence that an exquisite woman, although in midlife, still does exist. Ironically, it also is a flawless manifestation of a daunted female. As Christine gazes at herself in the mirror, she knows full well that both descriptions belong to her. She finds humor with the thought that this brittle image of beauty has beguiled so many men. Certainly, she is more than she appears to be in this mirror, but they only saw what they wanted to see, for fragile loveliness truly does rest in the eye of the beholder. Tonight she will play that trump card. Tonight she will portray two women: the virginal damsel and the hardened dame. She will placate and cultivate the façade. Why? Because this might extract her from the quagmire in which Walt has brazenly placed her. But there is another reason for fanning the delusion of appearance. She needs to believe that her life will change. The stars have finally aligned themselves to release her from what has defined her throughout her life, and she no longer wants to be a woman defined by circumstances. As she dresses for the showdown, she hums the familiar melody, and softly stutters over its lyrics.

Strange, when you come to doubt your sanity,
When vision makes the tangible translucent,
And you can only focus on indiscriminate haunting;
When hearing makes words stutter,
And interim pauses collect meanings of incongruities;
When speaking only makes billows of breath,
Lovers' lies,
Lurking within mirages of truth.

She scans the figure in the mirror. Will this image be able to lure the indomitable Jewels into the mirage? Her appearance must be perfect tonight for that to happen. She inspects more closely.

The gown's airy chiffon against her flawless, pale skin gives her the appearance of a fairy tale princess, pleasant, and virtuous. The V-shaped neckline elongates her bare upper torso, shouldering her delicate arms into a stately posture, gracious, and refined. However, duplicity is there as well. The V-shape funnel leads to pronounced cleavage suggesting voluptuous breasts, substantial, and generous. The netted fabric wraps her midriff like a Victorian corset, accentuating the slim waist and lifting those bosoms to bawdy vulgarity. The tea-length hemline, cut high on the right thigh, allows one bare leg to peek profanely. Black patent leather stilettos with slender straps crisscross seductively across naked ankles. Without a doubt, there is duplicity in the image she wants to convey. She swirls, watching the chiffon sway this way and that as she pretends that she is a princess. Yet, her evening dress is not white purity, but scarlet seduction. With each swagger, she comes closer not to the image of a blushing princess but that of a crimson queen ready to dethrone the king. The deception is set!

Now for the final touch. She flicks back her auburn hair as she had always done when she had wanted a fluff of delicate wisps to cascade alluringly over her earlobes and shoulders. This time the façade must be addressed differently to accommodate her conquest. She rearranges her hair, fingering any fragrant strands and twisting them into an upsweep away from her face. Completed, she inspects her work and is satisfied; her naked earlobes will rightly expose her "intended" affection for Jewels. Her sea blue eyes delight in that decision. Yet suddenly they are clouded with regret. She is not totally insensitive, for she cannot ignore Jewels' desire to please her. He is just a man yearning for something more in his life.

"Christine!" She scolds the image before her. "Ignore such thoughts! You must remain steadfast!" She inhales deeply to solidify her thoughts. "Jewels is just another man misguided by his past. He has underestimated the scourge of a younger female's plight and must deal with a season woman's wrath." Although the image in the mirror is convinced by the pledge, the woman standing outside that mirror is not. She flinches in shame that she is capable of such hard-bitten words. Again, she inhales a prolonged breath to strengthen her resolve, nodding her camaraderie to that woman still caught inside the glass.

With pretentious self-assurance she leans in closer and puckers. Ostentatiously, she sweeps a crimson red lipstick repeatedly over her lips, trying to embalm a more steadfast plan with each stoke. Nevertheless, as she pinches the cylinder harder, she cannot dismiss the subtle quiver in her fingertips. She pulls the lipstick away, and it inadvertently slips onto the bureau, breaking apart. The cap wobbles onto the carpet. The lipstick is destroyed. Could this inconsequential mishap foreshadow another tenuous outcome for tonight?

A rap on the door assaults her already fragile composure. Another quick rap follows. Christine draws in a deep breath, pivots on her stilettos, and clip clops across the entrance hall to the door, away from the image in the mirror and the discarded lipstick. Her initial exuberance quickly falters; as she reaches for the doorknob her hand trembles. She commands it to stop, and finally her flailing composure is arrested. She is ready. She is in control of her destiny. She opens the door, smiles and murmurs to herself,

Doubt is a forsaken promise;
Passion is its deluded quest.

On the other side of the entrance the familiar, bulky sentry is cemented in his signature, eagle-spread stance. He is wearing a tailored dark suit that casts a bluish iridescent sheen, projecting a figure more assuming than he is. His massive arms fold in on themselves like two boa constrictors nestling across his chest. With an irreverent pause, his massive neck tilts as his eyes slowly scan her from the slick, twisted hair to her polished stilettos. His arms melt to his sides as his suggestive grin sprawls from what he has just savored. He thinks he knows this type of woman who is before him. They are two of a kind, so-to-speak. She knows that too, and she will use this understanding to her advantage.

"You look very nice, Missy Christine." He addresses her with quasi formality in a lusty tone. Christine is not insulted. She finds his guttural admiration comforting. Flaunting sexuality from years of experience, she acknowledges his discerning eye with a tilted nod. He does a short back step, displaying gentlemanly protocol for her to proceed before him. She flips a quick glance back into the room, sighting the velveteen jewelry box, still closed, next to the broken crimson lipstick, still uncapped on the bureau, the remains of mislaid desires. She turns away from these vanquished items and with savoir-faire vacates the room, never to return. He closes the door quietly and escorts her from behind. They proceed down a long corridor toward the elevator without further discussion; everything that needed to be said has been said. As she leads the way, Christine senses the burn of his stare on her derriere as well as the music that probably is playing in his head as he rocks with her rhythm. She increases her swagger to accentuate the elusive chant.

The brief trek to the elevator continues in a contented naughtiness. When they reach the elevator doors, he leans past her, purposely brushing his suit sleeve across her breasts. He leans into her bosoms as he presses the down button. She does not move away from the provocative touch, but instead remains motionless, preoccupied by distant scenarios. When she moves her sight to him, his eyes glower back. It is a knowing, silent exchange. He smiles; she smiles. Yes, the pact is confirmed.

The ding announces the arrival of the elevator and the door slides back, beckoning her attention away from his fragrant male urges. She walks deliberately into the opening and swivels on her stilettos to face him.

However, the sentry does not follow, and she is confused. "Aren't you coming?"

He responds with a grunt, a grin that droops to a sliver of regret over another interpretation of her question. He quickly retrieves his expression with professional discipline. "No...no...at least...not now." After a slight reflection of wishful desire, he tells her again, "You look very nice, Missy Christine."

But he has one last remark to impart. "By the way, the Captain from Jewels' yacht gives his regards to you. He is a long-time buddy of mine. We had a nice chat this morning by phone." With that comment, the opaque door sweeps close, temporarily effacing the implication of that comment, its messenger, and their intimate bond. His ambiguous aside could cause plans to go astray. However, she turns away from the impenetrable door of the unknown. She scans the greenery through her sinking glass cage.

The brief interlude concludes, and the impervious elevator door slithers back to discharge her. Her plan will work only if she can convey it to her partner in crime. Presently, he is nowhere to be found. However, as the door opens, its obscure exposé stuns Christine, and she slams her palm emphatically against the console to freeze the frame beyond the cavity.

"Well, baby, you didn't think I'd leave you behind?" The voice is a bit off its usual wit, but the gist is unmistaken. Certainly, Walt's chaffing is undaunted.

Still, Christine's immediate retort is as sharp. "Isn't that exactly what you did?"

Walt slouches in sheepish submission. "Ah, Baby...what do you mean?" He looks away, rotating his neck over his left shoulder as if it was engaged in some covert surveillance.

"Don't you be coy with me, Mister! I've been through enough! Starting with your babbling on the beach, followed ceremoniously by the knockout drug injected into me, to the wonderful realization that I was kidnapped, not once, but twice! And there is much more, which I don't want to talk about ever again. So, don't be coy with me!"

"Okay, I won't." His lackluster remark is too placating, not at all Walt's style. Christine peers into his eyes and detects a stab of smarting. Apparently, he, too, has been through an ordeal.

She tries to soften her tone, mainly because she needs him to fill in the gaps, but also because she senses there might be something more daunting to address. "How are you, Walt?"

His eyelids limp ironically with stiffened pretense. After a thoughtful pause, he lifts his gaze and truthfully answers her. "I could be better."

Christine surmises the possible implication. "Are you hurt?"

His jaw juts in a dislocated twitch. He considers how much of the truth to reveal to her. "I'll be okay."

Walt has always been a tough son-of-a-bitch. However, he is obviously masking a more profane agony than he is presently revealing. She cannot disregard his comment. "Can I help?" She pauses to see if he will tell her more. He doesn't. His silence confirms the ruthlessness Jewels inflicted on him. She doesn't know how to respond. She wants to delve further but is wary about pushing him if he is not ready to talk. And if it was that bad, he might distort the truth to protect her. She can only say, "I'm sorry."

These are the only words he needs to hear. He allows them to lick his surface wounds; unfortunately, the truly grievous damage remains buried. After an uneasy moment, he tumbles over his words, "I'm…sorry, too, Baby." He gulps in a breath. "Well, I guess I messed up…big time."

Christine reflects on her ordeal. "Yes, you did…big time."

"Sorry, Christine, I'm so sorry…so very sorry." Walt twitches his neck, and scopes over his shoulder again. Then he blurts out with a discordant disgusted breath, "I lost!"

Christine releases the elevator hold button and vacates the elevator, walking directly within inches of Walt's face. With his last remark, her compassion is compromised; she has had enough of the charade. "Like hell, you lost!" The elevator door skids closed and snaps with a clunk. "You threw that poker game!"

"No, Baby, no!" Walt's whine is pretentious again, and both know it. He avoids her eyes.

"Oh, yes you did!"

This time he doesn't answer her with words. Instead, he shrugs a shoulder hoping a stifled answer will be enough.

Christine is not finished. "Since when do you bet on 'Dead-Man's Hand?'"

Walt pastes on that "caught-your-hand-in-the-cookie-jar" expression, an all-too-familiar expression whenever she had caught him in a lie as a child. And as he had done as a child, he clings to a posturing that might allow him to weasel out of this corner. Conceding that she knows him too well, he half-heartedly drivels, "I would bet on that hand."

"No, you wouldn't! And certainly not with the Queen of Spades!"

"You're too damn superstitious!" Christine moves in for the kill. She is so close to his face that she can smell his breath. It is rank. In fact, he reeks of body odor. Certainly, this is not Walt's style, either. He probably has not bathed the entire week.

"Walt, I know." He stares at her. She lowers her voice, allowing him the opportunity to enter a place where both might finally have an honest exchange. "I know...I know why you threw the game, and why you allowed Cameron to drug me." She must hear it from his lips, and she will push him if she has to. "You lied to me on the beach!"

"You know?" He looks sheepishly at her and twists his head in a reticent arch. He always recognized her ability to see the bigger picture. "You figured it out?" She nods. "Christine, you watch me too well. You are probably the only one I was never able to bluff."

"Maybe." She lowers her voice to a whisper. "And you always were watching over me." He does not speak. Christine knows why. It might be too late, but this must be addressed. "You always watched over me...took care of me...but you could never have me. So, it was time to let me go. Isn't that, right?"

He tries to justify himself, "It was finally time for me to act instead of letting life just happen to you."

"Walt, you must release this insane guilt of the past. You didn't do anything wrong."

"Yes, I did!"

"No, you didn't do any wrong. Sometimes incidents in our life are beyond our understanding, beyond our control."

"It's just that I didn't even try, Chris. From that moment in grandma's bedroom, you went to a life of unhappiness."

"The life I chose to live was because of my own decisions, not yours!"

Walt wraps his arms around her. "It's not just that, Christine. It's that...I love you."

"I know you love me." She contemplates whether to finally admit her thoughts.

He tilts his head. "I didn't know that."

She brings her hand up to his forehead and brushes back a strand of hair. Her words convey the same tenderness, "Here's another something new for you, Walter. I love you, too."

He looks at her intently. His eyes glaze over, and his eyelids drowse into a seductive tease. "Well, this is a fine time to tell me this, Baby!"

Christine brings the moment back with a more poignant comment. "This is what we should have talked about on the beach last Sunday instead of lying to each other."

He smiles perceptively. He should have known better than to keep this from her.

"And the reason you lost to Jewels was so that he would believe that he won me. Then he was to take me back to his country, and I would live the rest of my life in wealth and blissful delirium. Was that how it was supposed to play out, Mister Walter?" She waits for his response.

"Yes."

"Why? Why didn't you ask me what I wanted? After all the years, after all we've been through, why did you not tell me the truth?"

"Because, Christine, I thought that you couldn't handle it. I have been watching you lately. You seemed so befuddled, trying to make some sense of your life. So, when I saw the possible solution of making your life better, I took it. As I played poker with Jewels, I saw a man who could give you a better life, so I made the call, Babe."

"That was a reckless call, Babe! You tried to be the puppeteer of my life! You had no right to do that. What went through that brain of yours to believe that this man would fall for this...fall for me?"

"Well, it was a spur of the moment deal. When you interrupted the poker game, I saw how this Jewels could not take his eyes off you. Then we got onto topics about chicks, and I discovered his weakness, this guy is competitive, real competitive. He doesn't like to lose anything, his money, his pride, his women. That's when I got the idea. If you married this man, you would be set. But Jewels is also suspicious, and not the kind to be told what to do. It had to seem like he made the deal, not me. The poker table was the perfect cover. I knew I could pull it off. All I had to do was to hook him into believing that he won you. All it took was just one look, and he was hooked. He would never be the wiser, nor would you. But you were wiser, weren't you?"

Christine gives him an incredulous look. She takes a deep breath and continues. "That lamebrain scheme of yours would have worked, except that you couldn't go through with it, right? On the beach you got cold feet. That's when I was supposed to be handed over to Jewels. Right?"

Walt silently nods.

"And when we returned to the hotel, and you saw Cameron as we were getting off the elevator, you got thrown off your game. Right, Walt? You realized that I had made some connection with Cameron, and that threw you even more. Right?"

"Right! That's right, Chris! That's when the kidnapping had to be moved up."

"And then I lost consciousness because Cameron drugged me. When I awoke in the hotel room, you were not there because you were trying to renegotiate the bet with Jewels."

"I found out more about this man's background, and I knew I made a mistake, a big mistake. By the way, how do you know all this?"

"Cameron told me some of it. I figured out the rest when I overheard your conversation with him in the hotel room. Actually, I overheard your entire fight with him."

"You heard everything?"

"Yes, along with everyone else in a two-mile radius!"

He winces in recollection.

"Let me surmise what happened when you approached the wealthy Middle Eastern man, who never gives back a bet. He was not very receptive?"

Walt hesitates, and then exhales, "That's an understatement!" The bruises swell in grated memories. "You got the right picture of this charmer, all right."

"You see, Walt, I think I know what drives Jewels. And one thing I came to realize over the last couple of days is that he is not an easy man to persuade, especially when he does not want to give up something he wants…in this case, me."

Walt shakes his head concurring. "Over the week as his 'house guest,'" Walt's words become a suppressed whimper, "I thought about what gives with this dude. I figured that his fascination for you was more than that just the fact that you are one hot chick."

Christine chuckles. "You think so, Walt? You still think I'm hot even though I'm getting on in years, as they say?"

"Oh, yeah, Baby." Walt knows she enjoys his flattery. It has always gotten her out of her funk during even the most difficult boyfriend breakups. But he becomes more serious as he reflects on their possible breakup tonight. He might never see her again.

"Christine, I did not want you to be hurt. You know that I have always tried to watch over you through your life. And I came to realize that you deserved a better life…a life I was never able to give you. Sorry, I made a reckless mistake."

"I figured that was the reason, Walt. You were always reckless. This time, however, you were just recklessly vigilant."

"I'm sorry. I tried to undo the damage, but…this Jewels…is a cruel man."

Christine flinches. "Walt, what did Jewels do to you?"

He twitches his chin over his shoulder. He does not answer for some time. She will allow him as much time as he needs to answer. Finally, Walt responds. "Well, let's say that I don't ever have to worry about having children anymore."

They peer into each other's eyes and into each other's lost opportunities. Now it is Christine's turn to be honest. "I know what that means. I don't ever have to worry about that either. I'm so sorry, Walt. I'm sorry for both of us."

"Yes, I guess that it's just too late for us."

Christine can no longer hold back the gentle thread of her love for him. She embraces him. "Maybe…maybe not!"

Walt catches the glimmer of hope. It is the kind of hope that flaunts before desperate men drowning in a callous undertow. "Well, Baby, what do you think we should do to this man?"

"Well, Walt, I have devised a possible plan. I really didn't know if I would have an opportunity to talk to you before now, so I put a marker in place to cover all bets. And by the way, why are you here now?"

"Funny that you ask that question. I asked that very question myself just a little while ago! I thought that I would never see you again, or ever see the light of day again, for that matter. I thought that Jewels had every intention of just putting you on a plane or a boat, and that would be that. And I knew my life would end soon after. But then I was politely summoned to get it on with him in another poker game."

"Summoned? Summoned from where?"

"As I said, I have been a 'house guest,' so to speak, in some hole in the wall warehouse, somewhere near here, still in A.C. I tried to escape a number of times, but Jewels' man was quite convincing that I should stay." Walt pauses to digest the reality he had undergone during the week. "The henchman finally was assured that I was rendered helpless enough not to go anywhere. I thought I was a dead man. But he was only toying with me. I suspect I was being saved for some twisted reason. Then a couple of hours ago, Jewels just entered the place and told me that I was to play a hand of poker with him, again, like we were old card buddies or something. I figured that it involved you in some way, especially when he informed me that I was to meet you at this main elevator and escort you to the same private poker room as before. Strange, huh? He knew I wouldn't split."

"Yes, he would be confident about what you would do, because he knew what I would not do. You see, it's not about you, Walt; it's really about me. And he is certain that I won't split either."

Walt nods. "When it involves you, he is deliberate. I caught that at the gaming table on the first night. Without a doubt, he is a damn good poker player. He sees everything, misses nothing. He is a calculating bastard who never wants surprises. Funny, how you became his surprise last Friday. But tonight, Christine, do you know what this is all about?"

"Yes, I do. I'm the one who suggested the rematch."

"Rematch! Why?"

"So, you could win me back!"

There was a long pause before Walt responds. "Chris, oh no!" with a resigning moan. "I'm not so sure I could do that…not now…not in my condition. That's a big gamble, and I'm not sure I'm up for it anymore. He is an invincible dragon!" Suddenly he snags her underlining displeasure in him and is ashamed. "But, listen, Chris, I'll give it a good ol' Yankee try!"

A hint of a smile emerges on her expression. Walt calms down and becomes more receptive to what she has to say. They have been able to communicate without words throughout their lives. And, yes, Walt knows that subtle grin. It is a grin that means she has something cooking. Christine is emboldened again, "Well, Mister Yankee, I know how to slay this dragon!" Her smile widens.

He gives her a quizzical look. "How?"

"By allowing him to be a very good poker player." Christine pauses and then adds, "There's something I read in a beginner's rule book on how to win at poker. Sometimes, to win a poker player needs to be patient and not just play the cards or his opponent's...sometimes a poker player needs to play position. But most importantly, sometimes a poker player must size up what's at stake and just play the pot." Yes, she has gotten his attention. "Well, Walt, I'm the pot, and you are in prime position against a man who misses nothing."

Walt smiles back.

Christine's expression becomes more serious; she does not want him to be reckless again. "And this time, don't lose!"

As they turn and proceed to the poker room, Christine notices the injured gait that Walt is desperately trying to downplay. She allows his pride to remain intact and makes no comment. If he loses tonight, he will lose more than his masculinity. They bend close to each other, locking arms, whispering subtle communiqués on the possibility of probabilities.

XIII

THE PASSAGE TO THE SECLUDED GAME ROOM crisscrosses over several pathways of the hotel where each day throngs of humanity weave in and out of their intimate maneuverings of life. As Christine and Walt entwine on their own pathway toward the private poker room, they press closer to each other, sinking into their own intimate whispers of intrigue.

Suddenly Christine halts in mid-sentence. She has caught a vagrant puzzle piece in flight. Slightly to their right and just above the Starbuck's coffee convenience stand, is an HD plasma wide screen TV. It hangs like a suspended flat mirror of the world. The sound has been muted so as not to be an annoyance to the casual passersby, who might be preoccupied with more personal concerns and does not want to address mundane nuisances. It is not the sound, but the visual images that assault Christine, numbing her by their frightening, no...haunting depictions.

A news broadcast is in progress with split screen reporting, cut into three rectangular frames—two vertical, one horizontal. In one of the vertical rectangles, a news reporter, blond, thirtyish, attempting to appear cosmopolitan chic, bobs her head in sophisticated seriousness to punctuate the talking points, capitalizing on the gravity of her report as the pinnacle of the news of the day, yet attempting to maintain objective professionalism as she delivers her commentary devoid of any real passion.

An adjacent second vertical frame complements the newscaster's report. It endlessly repeats an on-the-scene visual clip of moving figures. With each playback, the images are recaptured for further scrutiny, restated images as if caught in an echo.

Fading into a sooty camera lens eleven gaunt, young men shift slowly from one leg to another in sluggish aimlessness. They have unkempt, coarse, dark hair. Their short sleeved, buttoned down, off-white rumpled shirts are untucked over gray, wrinkled trousers. They stand in the middle of a fractured street before a backdrop of crumbled cement buildings. The entire screen appears in shades of a chalky haze that folds in upon itself. As if on cue, the young men turn their heads in unison and peer toward the camera. The lens zooms in for a closeup. Darkened eyes fixate like hollow caverns sunken from protruding cheekbones. Then zooming slightly out, the camera transmits more of the emaciated faces where sparse beards paste cindered chins below dumbfounded lips. The eye of camera alludes to the testimony of their backstory.

In the coffee alcove, few patrons looked up from their immediate matters to catch the scrolling sentences, all, that is, except Christine. She is riveted and continues to probe the last insert on the screen.

The third elongated horizontal frame lies below the other two verticals. The image is motionless: a massive lump, draped in muddied rags, sprawls upon the broken pavement. In the right-hand corner of this frame a smaller inlaid portrait of a pretty, young girl with long, dark hair. She appears to be in her late teens or early twenties. What unleashes Christine's tears is the arresting, unassuming pose of the girl with her faint smile.

Like all those who nonchalantly amble past this screen throughout the day, Christine, too, would not have seen any of this if it had not been for the bold headline: "HONOR KILLING—Girl stoned to death in Pakistan." The line is a continuous scroll across the bottom of the screen, emerging from the right disappearing to the left in its relentless spew. Christine relates this broadcast to her present situation and its foreboding consequences. After the deadening moment, she abruptly turns away from the screen and its portents, resuming her trek down the hall, clutching Walt's forearm even tighter.

XIV

AS THEY TURN THE CORNER of the last hallway, the looming door to the private room comes into view. Surprisingly, only one of Jewels' sentries is dutifully stationed by the opened entrance, and Christine worries, wondering if Jewels has arrived yet. If he is inside and sees Christine embracing Walt, he might become jealous and cancel the game, casting the two into precarious consequences. She releases her arm from Walt's. If her plan has any possibility of succeeding, she must appear to be disconnected from him. Yet, as she draws closer to the entrance, she is perplexed about why Jewels would have arranged for them to have any brief interlude together through the hotel corridors without supervision. Certainly, he would speculate that they would attempt to concoct a quick plan of defense before reaching the room. As she brushes the edge of the doorframe with her shoulder, she tries to fend off these misgivings, for her plan is already in play, and there is no turning back. However, this uncertainty deteriorates again when she sees Jewels.

In the dim light stale air currents waft throughout the room as colliding dust particles fall in funnels of florescent beams over the poker table. He is alone without his bodyguards, except for the lone dealer, who is already seated in the designated croupier position. Jewels stands at the far end of the table, glazing downward as if mesmerized by the sound of the dealer's shuffling of cards. As soon as Christine appears at the entrance, Walt following closely behind, Jewels breaks from his reverie and jettisons over to her, clearly ignoring Walt. He approaches with rigid, angular formality, like a stiff toy soldier, never releasing his eyes from her. His expression is a receptive smile, for he is pleased to see her and approves of her appearance.

"Christine, you are beautiful tonight." He bends into her, kissing each cheek reverently and is immediately warmed by the intimate contact with her skin. However, it does not take him long to realize that she is not wearing his earrings. As he pulls back to gaze into her face, he displays no disenchantment, his eyes are unwavering. Without as much as an indecipherable blink, he repeats his greeting, "Christine, you are beautiful, tonight." Yet, with this reiteration she now knows that he is aware of the missing jewelry and has felt the stinging rejection. Now she, too, can play a game of pretense. She returns a slightly twisted smile, making no mention of his gift. The poker game has just begun. Christine is in a prime position; her misgivings have just melted away. She knows her plan will work, for he misses nothing.

Ignoring this obvious rebuff, Jewels tenderly cradles Christine's forearm and guides her to the side of the table where a lone chair is positioned about five feet from the table's edge, opposite the seated dealer. It is a straight-back chair, rigid, but not totally uncomfortable because of the cushioned seat and a throw pillow placed against the back rungs to make her more at ease. However, this comfort is not afforded to the two combatants who will be stationed opposite of each other. Two vacant, utilitarian chairs face off at the far ends of the oval table. This is purely business, and there is no need to give attention to creature comforts. Jewels has no intention of remaining at this table any longer than need be.

After Jewels escorts Christine to her seat with gentle civility, he turns to Walt, who had been purposely disregarded. He gives an off-hand flick of a wrist to indicate that Walt should sit in the chair closest to the entrance. Walt does not move immediately but glares back at Jewels with arrogant solemnity. If Walt sits in the chair Jewels has designated, his back will face the door, thus spiking a stake in Walt's delicate, superstitious disposition.

"I'll just take this other one, my man!" Walt condescendingly ignores the directive and walks deliberately to the chair farthest from the door, directly facing the room's entrance. Jewels watches this maneuver with unresponsive scrutiny. Walt's strut suggests not that there will be no quibbling about his seating choice; this is an obvious display of defiance. Jewels is down two points, and Walt's confidence is bolstered.

Typically, Jewels would lash out with swift vengeance in reaction to such insolence. But restraining his retaliation in front of Christine will show that he possesses disciplined civility, an attribute he absolutely wants her to believe he has embraced. He will take care of these flagrant insults later, in his own way, out of sight from any witnesses. And as for Christine's subtle insurrection with the earrings, he will be tolerant because he is focused on a more relevant matter: making sure Christine will be his at the end of this evening.

Instead of reprisal, he gathers Christine's hands and cups them in his palms. After a couple of seconds, he brings the back of her hands up to his lips and tenderly kisses them, first one, and then the other in a gesture of his devotion to her. It is also a statement accepting her challenge regarding the earrings.

Each participant recognizes that these theatrics are nothing more than the prelude to the upcoming performance. Emboldened by his display of self-control, Jewels is more certain about the outcome of the night. He releases her hands, turns, saunters toward the table, and casually maneuvers onto the vacant chair that Walt refused to occupy.

Both combatants finally situated, Jewels swivels his neck toward the dealer and gives his nod for the game to commence. Jewels' back is to the door.

During the pre-game prelude, Christine observes Jewels closely. She examines his expression, trying to discern any evidence that he will renege on the agreement made on the yacht. Throughout the past day she has been apprehensive about whether Jewels was forthright about their handshake to procure her release if Walt won the game. It was her spur-of-the-moment plan devised on the deck to forestall Jewels from absconding with her there and then, and perhaps it might have been a bit shortsighted. Furthermore, she had to divert Jewels from going head-to-head with her unconscious lover, lying naked in her bed. Cameron's animosity toward Jewels is a dangerous rivalry, not only for him, but for her as well. She is relieved that Cameron is conveniently out of harms' way on the far-off yacht. She tries to envision the moment after she gains her freedom when she will be able to rejoin Cameron, and together they will live out their lives without the stains of their pasts. It is an auspicious thought that keeps her from crumbling before this dragon.

However, this thought is only an illusion of hope. Jewels is only appeasing her under the guise of accommodation; he has no intention of fulfilling such a contract. He will never let her go! He feigns the motions of the poker game because he wants her to do something that he is well aware that she does not want to do. If she can be more pliable with his terms prior to their scheduled departure tomorrow morning, perhaps with more time, he might be able to nurture a more endearing commitment to him. This is the true reason he devised this charade. He had never been able to exert such patience in any other relationship, but she is worth the effort. He releases his indoctrinated rigidity, and with new found vigor, justifies his actions under the shadow of truth.

The croupier does not appear to be a timid man. The manner in which he palms the deck shows how adept he is at his craft. Yet, in spite of his expertise, both Jewels and Walt pick up on the tick just above his left eye, a subtle tick...a pensive tick...no, more than that...a foreboding tick. Perhaps he is apprehensive not just about the game, but about his personal well-being. Both players ignore his affectation.

What has made this a precarious situation for this croupier is not only the insidious rumors surrounding this Eastern man's reputation, but the unorthodox rules of this poker match. Jewels, of course, had to alter the rules of the game to conclusively secure Christine as his prize. He is aware of the immorality of what he was doing, but rationalizes his deception with the fact that Christine initiated the game. He is just going to hold Christine to the gauntlet that she, herself, had laid before him on the yacht. She granted him unconditional autonomy to formulate the rules for this poker showdown, and he has done just that: devised the rules with his, not her final end in mind.

Jewels realized that modification of the game's rules will only succeed if Christine does not realize that the deck is loaded in Jewels' favor. If she had any inkling, she will never fulfill her promise of unconditional loyalty when he takes her back to Pakistan. So, Jewels only disclosed the tweaked rules covertly to Walt prior to her being escorted to the private room. It was made clear to Walt that he is not to tell Christine about the setup of the game. Walt has experienced firsthand the serious intent of Jewels' threats, and this directive not only concerns his own welfare, but Christine's. Walt has no intention of jeopardizing Christine's life any further than he has already, so he unwillingly complied. He is resigned to the fact that the only way to secure Christine's freedom lies in his skills as a poker shark.

Walt possesses street smart savvy and resilience to physical discomfort. Jewels' brutal indoctrination was an incentive for Walt to fire up his latent, cocky attitude. When Walt was informed of the rematch, he was more determined than ever to annihilate his tormentor. *I will beat this scum bag, even if I die doing it!* Of course, this thought was only based on stark will power and no real strategy. However, when Walt heard Christine's plan, he was convinced that their partnership might slay the dragon. So, he refrained from telling Christine all the details that Jewels laid out. Walt is sure he can save Christine without alarming her any further. It is this thought that bolstered Walt's confidence as he entered the poker room. *I'm going to make this beast eat his own vicious rules!*

XV

THE GAME WOULD STILL BE SEVEN CARD POKER, except that it was to be a shortened game, a very shortened game with not only variations, but unusual incentives. There would be only one round played between the two players. Play would begin with each player receiving two dealt cards, face down. The players would be allowed to look at their concealed cards and decide if they wanted to keep their hand. If neither player wanted to play the cards they were dealt, both would be forced to discard their hand. Even if the other player wanted to retain his cards, he still had to relinquish them. Either player could determine if the cards would be discarded, but Walt would always initiate the decision. It would appear that Jewels was giving Walt the advantage, of course, this was only posturing in order to mislead Christine. If the cards were surrendered, the dealer would reshuffle the deck and deal two fresh cards to both players. This process would continue until both players were satisfied with their opening hand. Once both accepted their holding cards, play would resume.

The second change occurred with the Flop. Three exposed, or "face-up" cards would be placed in the center of the table. Each player would have the option to check, meaning that play would continue, or fold, meaning that all play would stop, and the game would be over. Whoever folded first would lose the hand, the game, and, consequently, Christine. However, if both agreed to check, another exposed card would be placed next in the Flop, the

Turn card. Again, either player could fold, meaning that the game had ended and a winner would be determined. If the Turn card was accepted, then the game would resume once more with the final exposed card. The dealer would place this fifth card, the River card, next to the other four turned up cards on the table. As with the Flop, the Turn, and the River cards, the dealer would ask each player if they wanted to fold or continue to the showdown. Because no more cards could be put into play, the players would show their concealed hand, and the winner would be called by the dealer. Walt would be the first to turn over his cards, and then Jewels would expose his hand. When all cards were shown, the hand with the best combination, according to poker rules, would win the game. However, in the Showdown, either player could have the option not to show his cards at all and just fold, giving the win to the opponent by default. This slight variation of the rules seemed fairly straight forward, that is, until a rider condition was attached to the game.

This altered form of poker was strange enough, but Jewels was to deviate further. He wanted this mock-up poker match to be finished as soon as possible, for it was only a charade for Christine's capitulation to him anyway. So, he contrived an addendum to entice Walt to drop out of the game without prolonged delay, but it had to be a plausible defeat in Christine's eyes. For this to transpire, Jewels would utilize the tools of his trade: money and fear.

If Walt chose to fold immediately after the Flop, he would receive one million dollars. Not a bad incentive to get things over quickly. However, if Walt continued with the play, this offering would diminish. For every card after the flop, the amount would be cut in half. If Walt did stay in the game after all five cards were placed on the table, he would only retain a quarter of a million by the showdown, but only if he folded at that point. Yet, if he remained in the game to the end and won the match, he would, of course, win the most coveted prize, Christine's freedom. Walt would not only be up against a dwindling pot, but the possibility that if his hand was weaker than Jewels' in the showdown, he would lose everything. Jewels took into account that Walt might still fight for Christine to the bitter end no matter what was on the table. So, if this foolish man would not fold in spite of the shrinking monetary incentives, then perhaps a more merciless incentive would damper his gallantry. Jewels caustically conveyed to Walt that if he was unremitting to the end of the match and had a defeated hand, he would not only forfeit all the money and lose Christine's freedom, but he would lose his life as well. This was no idle threat. Walt knew the stakes. He had intimately been exposed to Jewels' vengeance throughout the past week. There was no limit to how this brute would settle a score. Of course, Christine would never know about this last component, nor would she be privy to the financial incentives.

These unorthodox poker initiatives to throw the game were unfolded to

Walt just prior to retrieving Christine. Jewels was aware that Walt would keep this to himself to protect Christine. When Walt finally saw her by the elevator, he had wanted to blurt everything out to her. But he refrained. If he did, Jewels would forgo the game and just cart her away. Besides, Walt knew that if Christine was aware of this ghoulish betting, she would quickly concede to any of Jewels' demands to protect Walt. So, paradoxically, not wanting to burden her with this grim reality, Walt carried these rules to the gaming room silently.

Instead, during the short moments he had with her, he allowed her to disclose her plan. It wasn't a bad plan, just a very treacherous one. If it worked, perhaps the outcome of the poker game wouldn't matter anyway. To be safe, Walt would try to merge both plans. The dealer was only told the rules of the game, not the side-bar initiatives. Both opponents knew what was at stake, or in this case, who was on the stake. And although the dealer was kept in the dark about the real pot, he surmised that this was a high stakes game. And the subtle tick under his eye confirmed that.

Jewels had bent the rules without compassion. He'd never cared much for Walt anyway. He felt he was a weaseling, liver-bellied weakling, a pesky fly he would rather swat away than contend with down the road. But for some reason, Christine regarded this nuisance as important in her life. So, for now, this insect was not expendable. However, after exploiting Walt during this poker game, Jewels had no qualms about Walt's demise, whoever was victorious. Jewels' other justification for conniving in this match was that he upheld the outcome of the first match, the one in which Christine rightfully was won by him. For Jewels, perhaps the most poignant motive was that a loss in this second game would be calamitous to him personally. He had made a connection with this woman, a vital connection, and there would be no recourse for him if he lost her.

The dealer announces, "What's your pleasure, gentlemen?" Although the winner was already determined in each of their minds, ironically, no one in the room had any inkling who that would be.

XVI

MOST OF THE ROOM IS OBSCURED by shadows. In contrast, recessed light fixtures, sparsely positioned throughout the ceiling, funnel shafts of light downward like ethereal vapors from some distant past, fraudulent memories of our lives. The scene could have been a smoked-filled Western saloon. The background fades inward toward the poker table in the center of the room. It is quite distinct, flooded with concentrated illumination from the crystal Tiffany lamp suspended directly over the field of play. It casts an unearthly, chalky paste on the hollowed faces of three men. Christine, from her grandstand seat, gazes in frigid pensiveness at this bizarre tableau, slightly removed from the table, but close enough to still be considered another opponent, for she is not only the bystander, she is the booty, and, unbeknown to Jewels, she is also the bait. The four apparitions lean forward envisaging their imminent conquests.

The croupier shuffles two cards to both players. Walt arranges the cards so that the one lies on top of the other. He cups his palms to conceal his hand, and as always, using his thumb, flips only a smidgen of the left corners to snatch a peek of what he has been dealt—a jack of spades covers a red six of diamonds, weak cards.

Walt stalls, deliberating on what line of attack to use. If he is to have any leverage, he must devise a different approach than his usual game plan. *Lousy hand*, he mutely converses with himself. He looks up, but there is something out of whack. He cannot ignore Jewels' behavior, or rather, lack of it. *This guy hasn't picked up his cards!* Walt is leery about why Jewels' cards are still sprawled on the green felt just as the croupier had dealt them. Walt gnaws on a hardened piece of skin from the edge of his left thumb and mulls over this incongruity. *He's not committing. This wise guy must figure that he can't make a move until I decide if I want to keep my hand.* Although this seemed the likely reason for Jewels' conduct, Walt is still uneasy because he is suspicious about the crazy rules of this God forsaken game. He is also bothered by something even more menacing. He is keenly aware of Jewels' incessant stare, not at the cards, but directly at Walt. *This son of a bitch is trying to freak me out! Okay, Man, if you want to play that game, I'll play.*

As Jewels wields his glare at his opponent, Walt decides that he must begin the overture. He speaks up in a taunting tone, "No need to rush. Isn't that right, man?" Jewels continues to stare. "After all, you set the rules. And you—you the man!" Although Jewels shows no outward reaction to Walt's impertinence, he inwardly is bemused that Walt can maintain any drollness after what he has gone through this past week. He does not realize that his adversary is not the broken pistol he has surmised, but, instead, a very loose cannon. Walt continues to jeer. "Let's make it more interesting, huh, Bud! Let's mix it up a bit!" Walt discards his undisclosed weak hand, flipping his cards irreverently back toward the dealer. The orphaned cards lie face down on the felt.

The croupier fans an open palm toward Jewels to relinquish his hand, according to the rules set down by the man, himself. Without a sound, Jewels pushes his unseen cards toward the croupier. The cards are collected, reshuffled, and two new cards are divvied out. This time Walt does not immediately examine his cards. *I'm goin' give this wise ass a moment or two to check out if he's goin' look at those damn cards of his.* Walt senses that some other game is in play, the real game of the evening. Finally, he tires of watching the fossilized man, for Jewels has continued to retain his aloof posture. Walt peeks at his own hand, an ace of hearts covers an eight of hearts. Although Walt quickly reads his cards, *still not a great hand,* he pauses before speaking. He pivots his head as if cranking his thoughts, holds onto one of them, and then darts a hard look back at Jewels. Walt has finally formulated a strategy that does not deviate too far from the original one he had devised with Christine in the corridor. He recognizes that the churlish stare of this impenetrable man might, in fact, make her plan work better.

Glowering back at his opponent across the table, Walt crisply announces to the croupier, "I will keep these!" Then Walt's head flops sideways in an audacious tilt as if goading Jewels to finally look at his cards. Jewels, however, remains disengaged. Walt's lips slither in a pout; *yes,* he tells himself, *I'm going in for the kill.*

After a few minutes of muted inertia as the two men eyeball each other, the croupier nervously requests, "Do you wish to keep your cards, Mr. Jewels?" The croupier addresses him in this manner because he has never learned Jewels' last name. And because Jewels is the promoter of this card game, the dealer feels obligated to speak to him with a more decorous demeanor than necessary. In fact, that is not Jewels' name at all, given or surname.

As a child, he was called "Jiles" by his mother. He was born in a comely rural town just outside of Tewkesbury, England, his mother's town. His Pakistani father named him Jamal, but his mother affectionately thought that was too formal for such a little boy, thus "Jiles." When his parents relocated to Pakistan, his father's homeland, "Jiles" changed to "Jewels" when her husband's kin misunderstood her British accent. "Jiles, Jiles, my little Jiles," his mother addressed her little son. The misconstrued pronunciation became "Jewels, Jewels, my little Jewels." As an estranged woman in a foreign land, she gracefully acquiesced to this designation. She wanted to please her spouse's family and assimilate into her new environment, so her compliance with a name change seemed insignificant. Besides, this concession was not so thorny. The name "Jiles" was not even her first choice. In fact, the name was the final selection after a preponderance of ten other names. Unfortunately, in the process of surrendering to this point, she fell into a pattern of capitulations in this unforgiving society. Renouncing her son's identity was to become the inception of other surrenders she had to endure as a woman under her husband's roof. As time when on, she justified the name change because her son had become the only remaining jewel in her life. How ironic that this jewel turned out to be the blackened stone in the lives of so many other women.

The cards remain scattered haphazardly in front of Jewels as he still does not address the croupier or the cards. Walt conjectures what this silence means. *This asshole really has no intention of ever looking at his hand...and thus, a chink in Walt's armor!* Walt swallows the implication that Jewels is not sincere about this powwow. If this is so, then not only has Walt lost this poker game, or the so-called lucrative enticements, but even worse, and perhaps most unforgivable, Walt might have just lost Christine. The two men remain motionless for a very long time. The croupier drops his chin to his chest and waits.

Finally, the awkward silence is interrupted by words dripping with rigid formality, seasoned with condescending edginess. "I will keep these cards," Jewels utters effortlessly without even looking at them. In spite of his self-imposed folly of playing the game blindly, his glare and duplicitous tone seem to explicitly seal the fates of Walt and Christine. Should Walt fold after the flop, his million dollars intact. Of course, that means he will sacrifice the only woman he has ever cared about. He cringes that he even entertained such a greedy thought. Instinctively, he feigns a defensive posture. His lips tighten with a thirst for vengeance and his drooping eyelids squint with retaliation. As Christine watches, she observes the Walter from her childhood, who would stand stoic before the deranged demands of his father, in spite of the internal shattering of his spirit. Now, like the child ghost, Walt summons up a surreptitious bravado to suppress his waning confidence, No *way, man. You're goin' down!* In poker, as in life, an exposed weakness renders anyone irreparably vulnerable before the dragon, jeopardizing that inner strength needed for the final battle. This poignant lesson was learned from his father.

The croupier is relieved that someone has at least spoken, and he quickly deals the Flop. Three cards now lie exposed in the center of the table, a black ace of spades, a black eight of spades, and a black eight of clubs. The dealer refrains from speaking, giving the combatants a moment to digest their positions. Although Walt's brittle confidence is bolstered by his full house; he is spooked that Jewels has not looked at his cards. *God only knows what this asshole has!* Neither releases their gaze from each other, it has become a waiting game, a game of who will flinch first and relinquish his venerated stakes.

Christine is becoming unhinged; she cannot quell the subtle quivering in her loins. She fears that Walt might not be able to handle the position in which she has placed him, for it is obvious that Jewels' intimidation is daunting. Her head becomes heavy with childhood memories saturated with unforgiving doubts. It throbs, *Walt might not be a boy anymore, but Walt is, after all, only a man! How can I expect him to stand up to someone so overwhelming?* She thought that she had shackled such qualms on the yacht when she had no idea of what had become of Walt and had to accept that her fate would be determined through her own resourcefulness. But when Walt resurfaced at the elevator, she had become empowered by the thought that together they would become that invincible, childhood duo again—she, the righteous cowboy, and he, her faithful Indian brother. But now as she watches Walt, her confidence faces stark reality. Perhaps she was mistaken. Maybe as we get older, it becomes impossible to believe that our past has prepared us to take on the future. Instead, with each passing year of our lives, we only become more entrenched, sinking further into a mire of our own making, holding onto what is no longer true,

To hide her trembling, Christine places her left clenched fist in the protection of her right palm. She squeezes hard, refusing to succumb to the impending calamity. Because of her position at the poker table, this action is her only solace. It will have to suffice. She needs to be more patient.

Shadows expand and retract like ghoulish phantoms as the door to the private poker room opens and quickly closes, allowing the hallway's illumination to sprawl into the dim interior momentarily. Sentries enter and leave as if in some ongoing rotation. Jewels' men are keeping some prearranged surveillance on the situation. He has things stacked in his favor. With each shifting of the guard, Christine shivers in a cold draft of probabilities wafted away by impossibilities.

Covering his eyebrow with his right palm, Walt snatches a concealed glance in Christine's direction, and he sees her hands. He has seen these hands wrung before and knows that her faith in him is diminishing. He tells himself that he must be strong for her. But he, too, quivers as he regurgitates the memory of the haunted childhood, when she had needed him, and he had caved under his father's stain.

The croupier does not raise his head but continues in a subservient bow before the flop on the green felt. He swallows his words, "Check or Fold?" Clearly this time he is soliciting Walt as his head tilts slightly to the left. Of course, this dealer is in the dark about the million-dollar incentive for Walt to fold at this point. For that matter, he also has no awareness of Jewels' fanatical quest to have that elusive promise of everlasting fidelity from a woman who happens to be the ante in this poker face-off. If he had known what was at stake, perhaps the croupier might have walked away from the game. Now, he remains in a state of pensive limbo, confused by all the irregularities, yet too much in his own denial to address some forbidden unknown.

An uncultivated poker player would never grasp the real action that is in progress. These two men are seasoned poker aficionados who have calculated possibilities from probabilities. Throughout their years of play, they have learned how to detect early winning hands not just through reason but through observation. Observing Jewels' aloofness suggests only one possibility to Walt. *It doesn't matter what I'm goin' do with the cards.* He concludes that any move on his part is insignificant in terms of the predetermined outcome; the deck was stacked before the game began. Even more foreboding, Walt concedes that he will probably become expendable shortly after this evening's play. *I'm already a dead man!*

Ironically, Walt does not realize that a different, yet just as precarious, uncertainty is playing havoc within Jewels, who is also caught in a web of pretense. Jewels must sustain the charade as long as possible for Christine to accept his determined outcome. Walt, on the other hand, must feign the legitimacy of the pretense, giving enough time for Christine's plan to work. Both men are captive in a thread of deception until the moment that truth is revealed. Emboldened, Walt heralds, "I check!"

The game senselessly continues. The million dollars has just been cut in half. Christine's freedom also has been severed. Jewels emits a sardonic snort of disbelief and curtly repeats, "Check!" Not folding on the Flop quashes Jewels' suspicions that Walt is scamming him. If Walt could not be induced to abscond with the baited money, leaving the girl behind, then perhaps Christine is more valuable to Walt than Jewels originally surmised. Jewels needed to know that, and now he does. Jewels shifts slightly in his seat as he prepares to reckon with an obviously more obstinate adversary. In their own manner, both seem to desire this woman more than their own life.

What the croupier desires is to have this game over with as soon as possible, so that he can remove himself from this undercurrent of madness. Although he was handsomely commissioned to deal for this private party, he is now regretting that he had accepted. He buries the next card, and then exposes the sequential Turn card next to the Flop. It is a black ace of clubs, and to keep the momentum, he immediately presses the play. "Check or fold?"

Walt knows that he has a strong winning hand, a full house, aces high. The hand does not matter anymore, for his qualms about his true loss overshadows any win. Although maintaining a façade of continuing the play will be difficult from this point, Walt knows that he must do so. In poker, there is always that unremitting delusion that fate is bluffing. Providence is fickle. Every poker player must come to terms with the truth that the cards have no memory. They are indifferent to unrequited requests or past offenses. Like time, they appear on the green felt, apathetic to man's triumph or man's collapse. Walt's function is to prolong the play a bit longer, so that whimsical providence can intervene.

"So, Jewels, man, one more card to go, and I see that you have decided to go blindly into the River. Now that's class, man. Gutsy move. But watch out, you might drown!" Walt punctuates his comment with a sneer. Jewels stares back.

Suddenly there is a stirring at the entrance. The intrusion is initially noticed only by Christine with her direct line of vision to the door, ardently waiting for providence to arrive. Quickly, the others become aware of this presence as well. A man enters the room, a cocky gun slinger. He is familiar. To Walt, he is the thug who possibly crippled him for life...to Jewels, he is his sentinel, an egotistical scoundrel reporting for duty...to Christine, he is the bodyguard outside her hotel door, whom she misled in order to salvage her life. He swaggers with brute adroitness across the room and plants himself in that spread-eagle stance, about five feet behind the croupier. He folds his bulky arms in his signature embrace. He stands directly facing Christine, however, he does not look at her. He stares into space as if he is reading tea leaves in the floating dust particles.

From stagecoach wheels and horses' hooves, a cloud of dust filters throughout the saloon, coating it in a haze. The finite particles of the past senselessly collide in random pathways in the funnels of the ceiling lights, and the sentry becomes preoccupied with the hovering dust, attempting to justify his actions. But such actions are irrelevant to why he is here. The bodyguard makes no more effort to look beyond what he can observe, blindly disregarding any intangible particles existing outside the light beams, for he is an uncomplicated man with uncomplicated motives; he is present at this card game not for a task expected from his boss, but for a hazy promise of a forthcoming tryst from Christine.

Of course, that promise was contrived by Christine, who has always been adept at manipulating, and exploiting, the truth. Throughout her life, she has easily fabricated contradictions, justifying that flirtatious conduct is only one aspect of being a woman. In the Old West she would have been called Belle, draping a delicate wrist over the shoulder blades of the invincible gunslinger. It would be a gesture that she was his woman, that she understood her function in the scheme of the game. She believed that time was a single thread of deception, which could be rectified later. Yet, in the solitude of night when she lain alone with the disregarded dust, she could not ignore the reality that she had ensnared herself in her own paradox, the contradiction of seeking to become someone she never wanted to be, a half-life existence.

Today, though women live more complex lives, they still struggle between two worlds of uncertainty: the virtuous female and the illicit woman. Sometimes, a woman catches these distinctions in subtle or blatant glances. Guarding her integrity, she deliberately looks away, fearing what consequences would unfold to how she would be defined: the good little girl, the faithful wife, the great lover, the other woman, divorced, available, sexy, loose, slut, bitch…

As the bodyguard postures himself before her, Christine clearly concedes how he has defined her. Yet, because of his myopic callousness, all components have been put in place for the ruse. As she deliberates on when to initiate her plan, for timing is crucial, she inhales the fleeting paradox that once again she must use her feminine charm to lure a man into believing that she will be his. She draws in a deep breath and berates herself for becoming entangled with another dissolute character. She scrutinizes the displaced bodyguard. With a twinge of sexual urgency overshadowed by constrained hesitancy, he shifts his weight from one leg to the other, at a loss about what is expected of him. And his cowboy spurs clang in lost memories. Exhaling the throbbing immediacy, she silently vows to herself, *"This will be the very last time that I will ever fall victim to this!"*

She casts her head backwards and gulps a handful of dust, suppressing a cough into the thought, …*this is the last time.* The words might be just another empty promise, said before, many times before, it might be too late for her to ever rise from the immoral mire of her gender. It has always been services handsomely paid for yet squalidly recompensed, devoid of that true intimacy needed to sustain a woman. The fallout has been that the substance of Christine's life has slowly vaporized in the discarded dust. She has watched herself slowly disappear like the dust from the Old West. Christine swallows the ascending phlegm, and the acidity burns her throat, searing a residue of her existence.

The shadow of the sentry further unnerves the croupier and his escalating concerns regarding the legitimacy of the game. This time the inevitable question carries an even more conspicuously strident delivery, "Check or fold?" The dealer again bends in the direction of Walt, daring him to continue this indefinable madness.

Walt is not thrown by such urgings. He is a gambler adept in utilizing unstated poker parlance. So, in spite of the apprehensive dealer and Jewels' tenacious eyes, he remains unyielding. Silently, he ricochets his own fixed stare back at Jewels as he patiently awaits the signal. *Come on, Christine, give me the signal! Come on, Baby! Let's do it!* Walt prods inaudibly, trying to connect with Christine through some mind meld.

It was the signal that they had discussed when he had escorted her to the poker room. She had scantily briefed him on his part of her plan. Because careful timing was needed for the dragon's downfall, Walt would be in an optimal position to set her plan in motion. They parted with the understanding that she would give him a signal when she was ready.

Walt believes he has detected some movement to his left; Christine seems restless. The dust has stirred, and an impending cough can no longer be suppressed. She turns her head and tries to muffle the sound. However, this time it is audible enough to initiate the plan. But this is not her intention.

Unfortunately, Walt construes this covered cough as the awaited sign. He has misread her meaning. She is attempting to convey that she wants to abort the mission, but it is too late. Her back-peddling began when she snatched a blur just beyond the doorway.

Walt has no inkling of her predicament, and loudly projects, "Check! Let's get to that River card!" He claps his hands irreverently, then overtly looks at his cards again. It is an ostentatious gesticulation, too gross a response for the moment, but enough of a distraction. His flamboyance lingers as he inspects his cards. He has not forgotten what his hand was. Oh no! In fact, his hand is quite irrelevant, and he knows that. He is making this blatant gesture of a second look for another reason.

The proposed strategy is for Walt to noticeably relax his concentration to allow Jewels a moment to break from his relentless stare. In that calculated pause, Jewels would steal a glance, perhaps a glance of doubt, toward the only one who really matters in the room to him…Christine. And so, within a momentary blink, Jewels would use this opportunity to look away from the game. He would divert his sight from Walt to her. And within that glimpse, become ensnared in her ploy, for Jewels misses nothing! However, Walt's premature unleashing of the plot makes Christine stall under the yoke of indecision. Jewels does not see what he was set up to see.

Earlier in her hotel room Christine devised a plan that she believes will release her from Jewel's invincible grip. She is his captive hummingbird, sipping the nectar of imagination. This brazen kidnapping is netted in an irrational primitive ideology. She understands that she must resort to drastic measures to open the claws of this invincible dragon. But how? Jewels is a man of unlimited financial means and a powerful entity with unchecked resources to carry out his desires. What St. George Dragon Slayer has the audacity to rattle bones outside the lair to confront such a beast? The only Achilles' heel of this impenetrable man is a weakness from within, an irreconcilable memory, the veil of guilt and doubt. Christine needs to convince Jewels that, like his niece, like his wife, like his mother, she also will eventually bring dishonor to him. The dishonor he fears the most: the dishonor of infidelity, a memory to suck him back into the mire of uncertainty.

Because she resembles his sister, Christine recognizes that Jewels' irrevocable grip on her has to do with equating both women as sacrosanct spirits, the only women in his life who epitomize purity. No matter what Christine says to convince him otherwise, he will only accept what he wants to believe, whether it is the truth or not. If she had told him that she was not that pure embodiment of perfection, but a tainted woman, so repulsive in his intractable psyche, he would never have listened for he has a distorted vision of what she is. Christine has concluded that if he is to accept the truth, he must observe it with his own eyes. Perhaps then, and only then, he might be convinced to release her from this insufferable bondage. He has to see firsthand that she is mocking him. This mocking is the defining poison arrow to pierce the vulnerable heel of the brute.

All she needed was a catalyst, someone amenable to doing something unorthodox, someone who was no stranger to a shameful lifestyle. That person was the bodyguard stationed outside her hotel room. They were of the same ilk. Inappropriately, Christine wooed this man into assuming that she was attracted to him. And he was a receptive candidate. She immediately knew this when he willingly succumbed to her risqué teasing. She was good…yes, she was very good at what she did. She had him believing that he was the one who had come on to her. The flirtations were very suggestive of what the future would hold for them. When she had asked him to join her in the poker room to continue where they left off, he hesitated, but gradually salivated with the likely possibilities of a covert encounter. By the time they left to go to the poker room, the proposed covenant might not have been set in stone, but it was definitely set in mud. He had not realized it, but the mud was actually quicksand.

Now, her sweetie sentry, the red herring, is positioned just behind the dealer, facing her. He appears anxious to get started but has no idea what to do. He has little realization that Christine's simple scheme is about to place him in an uncompromising situation.

She would begin with a suggestively shift sideways in her seat, exposing enough leg to allow the hem of her dress to rise, just a sliver of upper thigh. Her legs would slowly part. She had told him that she was not wearing any panties. Her eyelids would drool in lewd suggestions. She would fan his fantasies by seductively dragging the tip of her tongue across her upper lip. The portrayal, of course, was a superficial depiction from the repertoire of any streetwalker. Although Christine has never resorted to such crass behavior, she has observed these tainted exposés with men who acquiesced to lust. Besides, these antics were really not intended for the bodyguard at all. This performance was to be an exclusively for Jewels. She knew if Jewels could be distracted from the game long enough, he would catch her insulting vulgarity because Jewels misses nothing!

Earlier, when Christine watched the boats from her hotel window, formulating this plan, she knew that what she was about to do would hurt Jewels very much, even cripple him, not just beyond reprisal, but perhaps beyond repair. But this decision was one of survival.

She was determined to cut the shackles, but she was also anxious about how to make this promiscuous maneuver work. It is imperative that Jewels watch her antics at the precise moment and that she act plausibly enough to a man who is suspicious about everything. It must not appear contrived. Jewels is observant, she just needs some arbitrary impetus to initiate the foil. With Walt's help she might be able to pull it off. During the brief trek to the poker room, she told Walt to await her signal to coordinate the timing. When they entered the poker room, Walt immediately began to formulate his side of the game plan, distracting Jewels from his incessant stare. When given the go ahead by Christine, Walt would simply relax his intimidating look, allowing Jewels to refocus on Christine's blatant performance and realize that this woman will never be committed to him, never be loyal to him, and will eventually disgrace him. It is an insane tactic to release her from his insanity.

And this snare probably would have worked, except, like all spider webs, it sometimes snags more within its net than intended. In fact, sometimes the design of the thread is woven so faintly that it is invisible to even those who know it is there, and they become ensnared in their own blind misinterpretation of truth. Under funneled shafts of light, such a delicate weave now hovers over the contenders of this poker standoff. A mirage is about to descend upon four misplaced people before a gaming table. They must face why they have faltered in their lives. It was the sinking of a life...

...a reckless gambler, plummeting under the endless guilt of a father's sin,

...an antiquated man, falling under a fallacious faith into despicable brutality,

....an absent lover, drowning below indifferent seas,

...an incomplete woman, weeping for the forsaken unborn in the fallow fields of her womb.

> *Strange when you come to doubt your sanity;*
> *when vision makes the tangible translucent,*
> *and you can only focus on indiscriminate hauntings;*
> *when hearing makes words stutter,*
> *and interim pauses collect meanings of incongruities;*
> *when speaking becomes billows of breath that gasp into lies,*
> *lurking within a mirage of truth.*

These fragmented lives dangle on the tattered fringes of truth, not to hover, but to collide. So, although Walt misread the signal, he did his part, pretending distraction so that Jewels will catch what he is supposed to catch. Suddenly, the arbitrary element, the irrevocable turn of the cards, is about to unhinge Christine's ruse. In a wink of uncertainty four individuals are about to encounter the true possibility of change.

XVII

INSTEAD OF TURNING OVER the last card, the dealer hesitates long enough for the interruption at the door to halt the play and topple everyone's plans. Cameron's absence was the void in the mirage, but that is about to change. Exploding into the room, he hurtles the door against the wall so obtrusively that the sudden assault snaps the unsuspecting participants to attention. All breath comes to a standstill as Cameron assesses his options. He struts deliberately to the side of the croupier, and without any vocal directive, taps the dealer's shoulder, signaling that he is to be relieved and that there is to be a new broker, a man on a mission. Without hesitation, the croupier relinquishes his seat and walks quickly out of the room without looking back to see if this is acceptable to Jewels. Cameron replaces the dealer with his presence and his audacity. All are speechless.

Intertwining his fingers, Cameron rotates his wrists with an insidious crack: He has returned to the field of battle. He leans his elbows against the table's edge and palms the cards, cradling the face-down deck in his left hand. Slowly he lifts his head. He snatches the succinct look from Jewels.

"Cameron, I was told by the Captain that you tried to save my wife. I am surprised to see that you are feeling better so soon." Jewels gives a slight nod, a consent for Cameron's presence.

Cameron sweeps a glance toward Walt. He is uneasy about Walt's physical condition. Obviously, the brute has manhandled Walt beyond his directives during this past week. Walt squints back at Cameron and frowns at this man's intrusion.

With a slight bowing of his chin, Cameron discreetly lifts his eyes to Christine. Although he postures a deadpan expression, his gaze lingers on her briefly, just briefly, but briefly enough. And in that prudent split second their eyes kiss. Although she is beguiled by his presence, she ponders his recovery from his ordeal, as well as what implications his presence might provoke.

Confidently flipping his head backwards, he breaks the laden moment with a resounding, "Now, gentlemen, I believe we need the River card." Using the first three fingertips of his right hand, Cameron slips off the top card from the deck. With graceful dexterity, he flips it over, placing it next in line to the other four exposed cards.

All stare at the five cards, an ace of spades, an eight of spades, an eight of clubs, an ace of clubs, all black, and a red Queen of Hearts kicker. Momentarily, these players become different participants of another poker game suspended in a time warp to the Wild West. Walt breaks the spellbound group as he explodes with caustic glee, "Well, lookie' here, if it isn't Dead

Man's Hand raising its ugly head again…this time, saved by the heart of a lady!" All three men look toward Christine.

This deal cannot be coincidental; this is almost the same hand Walt lost last Friday night. In that game the kicker was a black Queen of Spades. She sits back in her seat and recalls the childhood saga of Wild Bill Hickok and his demise. It is an account, which engenders the moral that regardless of a notorious reputation, no man is invincible. Certainly, this poker room is not the saloon in the town of Deadwood, South Dakota, on the afternoon of August 2, 1876. Cameron is not wearing a waistcoat of the finest brocade, sixty-dollar calfskin boots or carting the infamous Colts 1851 Navy with ivory handles, imprinted with an eagle stretching its neck, grasping a Liberty scroll. But in an unexpected deceptive moment, providence has dangled the elusive threads of possibility with its connection to the past. Christine recognizes these woven filaments. They are similar to those cut from the wailing sinews of a man and woman who craved guileless passion in a world that no longer could distinguish between passionate ardor and dogmatic sin. Christine looks across the seas of time, an instant of a week, to her lover at the other side of the poker table.

A faded pallor shades Cameron behind a phantom screen of her imagination: Two lovers embrace in lost fervor. They press their naked bodies together and relinquish themselves to sensual splendor. Their exploring arms glide over their bodies in long drags of fragile strokes, pulling each other even closer, trying to absorb and be absorbed. In the ebbing of unbridled pleasure caressing fingers touch the most intimate places of their being in a frantic search for poignant truth. When they are spent, they burrow and drift downward. They bathe in each other's scent and are graced with a contented clarity that affirms that they do truly exist. As Christine clings to this image she vows that she will not vanish. Change is possible—and she can implement that change.

Suddenly, in a fragmented shard of light, Christine sees the snapshot of a young girl, an inlay on the screen of a news report about a recent Honor Killing. Another slice of impassioned light instantly pans over the citizens of the world, sipping cups of coffee as they meander in detached aloofness past the ghastly monitor. The young woman with her long, dark hair and a feigned smile twists in the rising steam of sensuality. She, too, perhaps had been caressed in the act of making love. Still another lightning bolt flashes; it is a bolt of vengeance, the punishment for her infidelity. And her fate becomes the fate of all women from the beginning of existence. For in her stoning, she was not only punished, she was denied the very right granted to her by Nature, the act of intimacy. Where is the outrage over this tragic fatality? Where are the voices of the discontented protesting this travesty? Who will be the slayers of injustice? Certainly not the eleven gaunt young men with unkempt course, dark hair, wearing short-sleeved, buttoned down, off-white shirts and gray, wrinkled trousers. They lolled with sluggish aimlessness on a nondescript street in front of a backdrop of crumbling buildings. They meander within the void of their own delusion. This is not only their crime, but a crime accepted by an indifferent world. Perhaps the only ones most apt to rise above the apathy of this crime against women are defenseless women. This pretentious game of chance is a fortuitous table of possibility, empowering an immoral woman with not just the foresight, but the opportunity to make a moral decision within the parameters of her own truth. Although Christine does not realize the impact of such thinking, she has not only saved herself, but she has been imbued with the ability to save humanity from the destruction of its own self-fulfilling prophesy.

Christine delves inside herself, pioneering groundbreaking courage. Her plan has gone astray. Yet, it can be salvaged. She needs to get back on track, for how can she now implement her provocative plot, posing flirtatiously to the fraudulent lover standing in a direct path behind her true lover? She tugs on the hem of her dress with both hands and drops her head, giving it a subtle shake to signal the sentry that all bets are now off. He might be a brute, but he is a street-smart brute who has learned to pick up on such subtle gestures. He quickly deciphers that there has been a turn of events. He unfolds his arms, turns, and begins to leave the premise.

Halfway to the door he halts in his stride, as if a misplaced thought has tugged him back, and he returns to clear up some unfinished business. He flings his massive frame around and walks deliberately up to the right side of Jewels, the side closer to Christine. He bends low, as if bowing before an emperor, so that his mouth is just a breath away from Jewels' ear. He whispers with a hissing sound. His concealed words make it difficult to determine if he will continue to be Christine's decoy, or if he will revert back to Jewel's right-hand man. To whom does a man like this give loyalty? Christine and Walt comingle concerned looks. Jewels remains unresponsive. When finished with his dubious counsel, the brute turns and resumes his departure from the room without any appearance of forethought. He is a soldier in the line of duty, who has long come to terms with letting go of unsubstantiated opportunities. Yet, just before his final departure, he hesitates. Without turning, an enigmatic smirk snakes upon his lips. He might be an insignificant gadfly, connected to nothing but his own arbitrary agenda, yet, he is the most dangerous vermin in existence: an entity devoid of imagination. He departs from the scene. There are no other bodyguards in the room.

Now behind closed doors, isolated in a remote area of the hotel, a woman and three men are no longer defined by society's precepts. Although they will partake differently in the conclusion of the game, they have the potential to redefine truth by their own moral compasses. The showdown has begun.

Cameron takes a deep breath and announces, "Well, gentlemen, let's see them! Turn them over!" It is time to reveal the hidden cards.

Walt exhales, knowing full well that this is a futile gesture. Fainthearted, he turns over his two cards. Christine's plan is botched, his life teeters in a balance of the inevitable. He never would win with the cards exposed on the table. Now he must place his faith in a different Lady Luck. Although she is committed, Christine is shaky from what she is about to do. Cameron's arrival has emboldened her, but it has also confronted her resolve to provoke fate. Cameron senses some struggle in the anxious shifting of her eyes. He calls Walt's exposed hand, "Full House, Aces high." Although Cameron is unaware of the rules or the incentives of the game, he realizes that this is the last hand of the night. He turns toward the Pakistani and addresses him. "Let's see 'em, Jewels."

When Jewels does not immediately comply, Cameron receives his answer...Jewels has lost the standoff. Jewels lowers his head and becomes transfixed on his unturned cards almost as if he is sinking into them, x-raying the obscure value of the cards that have been dealt him in life. To make it official Jewels must turn over his cards or pronounce that he has folded. Once again, Cameron not only prods, but provokes the Pakistani. "Are you not going to show your cards, Jewels?"

Like the showdown at the O.K. Corral in the old Westerns, all four are still, seized in a bated suspension of choices, ready to draw, wary to be the first. They are caught in a clouded mirage. The men must either resign that nothing will ever change for them in their lives and give up, or embrace that elusive lure of opportunity, that in spite of their ceaseless reality of disillusionment, change is possible. Jewels picks up only one of his cards as if that would direct his decision. Turning it over, he fixates on it before warily placing it over the red Queen of Hearts. It is the notorious black Queen of Spades, the card of avarice and the unpredictability of life.

Jewels jettisons up, flinging his chair ten feet across the room, startling all. No one moves to stop him. "Enough!" Jewels shouts. "This has gone on long enough!" He charges toward Christine and snatches her wrist. "Christine, you are coming with me!"

She tries to recoil, but his clasp is too tight. "Jewels, you are hurting me!" Walt vaults from his chair and wedges his fists between them, ripping into this indomitable vice. In his futile attempt to protect her from any further onslaught, Walt sees the futility of his ability to save her again and falls back into ineptitude. He curdles a desperate howl, like some wounded animal,

"Don't touch this woman! Don't hurt this woman!" With venomous grit, Walt mauls the dragon, frantic to dislodge Jewels' stronghold.

Jewels was prepared for this. He slithers his left hand deep into the flap of his opened jacket and withdraws a small pistol, his fingers wrapped tightly around the trigger. Extending his arm, he primes the weapon, aiming it directly between Walt's eyes. Walt freezes. Jewels knows that this will be short-lived. Walt can no longer be intimidated; he readily will martyr himself for this woman. Sensing the tight bond between the two friends, Jewels calculatingly retracts the gun and presses the barrel firmly against Christine's forehead. Walt raises his flattened palms to freeze the action and steps back. The stakes in the game have just escalated. He swallows his irrefutable resolve to annihilate the dragon and glowers, fearful of making any movement. Sometimes this is the only way to deal with insanity.

Without relinquishing his sight or his aim, Jewels coils his other arm around Christine's torso, drawing her into his body, bracketing her like his booty. Then he bows his chin over her scalp and brushes it lewdly on her hair. She turns her head sideways in rejection. For Jewels this charade is not an act of conquest, but one of defeat, for this capture is no longer a false claim. By obtaining her this way, he has lost her. But the whiff of her scent is so intoxicating that he refuses to relinquish the contrived future. Clinging to desperation, Jewels squeezes Christine's delicate waist.

"Jewels, you are hurting me!" she whispers into his chest so faintly that he is the only one to hear her words. Christine is aware that Walt's razor-sharp rage has arrived at a precipice of no return; she must defuse this standoff. The tone is effective. Jewels releases his grip, snapping back like a severed, coiled spring. Christine falls forward into the haven of Walt's arms. Jewels' arms wither. They swing limply at his sides like detached cable lines split by lightening. Yet still tethered in his fist is the renegade pistol, even more volatile now.

In his retreat Jewels glares down at the weapon and reconsiders its potential. He clutches its handle tighter and begins to sway. The release of Christine has discharged a different validation for his life. The swaggering becomes more pronounced. He is a drunk trying to snatch any thought of redemption. There is none. He whimpers; he cannot commit the act of taking his life with his own hand. It is not that he is a coward or an adherent to religion doctrine. He is only a man who earnestly wants to believe that there still might be a reason to live. Christine has been the purity he has sought his entire life. If he kills himself now, he slays the memory of that desire. It is that thought that has become too sacred to violate.

He hunches over. Everyone stares at the incredible sight, but they are also frozen. Oddly, a sound of mirth trickles from Jewels. It quickly discharges into bellows of hysteria. He twirls erratically, pivoting his neck as if he were deranged, as far back as it can go. He is seized by the lunacy of his situation.

Walt is wary of the looming aftershocks and places Christine behind him. She, stupefied by the absurdity, has had just about enough of the spectacle. Jewels' dramatics do not coincide with her perception of his strength. She pushes Walt aside, putting up a hand to halt Walt from restraining her, and confronts Jewels' bizarre antics, "And what is so funny?"

"This!" Jewels flings his arm about, haphazardly. His laughter rivets into a stupor of hilarity.

"Jewels, get a hold of yourself!" Christine is concerned that this madness is beyond retrieval. What she does not realize is that Jewels has just severed his twisted reality and is more rational than he has ever been.

He stops, looks at her, and stands erect, composing himself in that similar fashion whenever he needed to exude power over an adversary. He squares his shoulder blades and juts out his chin. This time, however, the adversary is not someone else; it is himself.

"Christine, I know!" His eyes are moist; she cannot decide whether from absurdity or pain. He lowers his voice and peers directly at her. "I know," he repeats more softly, "I know all about you...about who you are. I know."

Christine shivers. She is frightened by what these words imply. With a guarded response, she approaches Jewels. Walt reaches for her again, but she sidesteps further. She is hesitant as she sinks forward into the unknown. "Jewels, you know that I am not a...?" She chokes before completing the thought.

"Yes," he cuts her off, soothing her apprehension. As his chin lowers, his eyes rise into his forehead. "Yes, and a lot more. I've known since my wife's death." He draws a deep breath as if sipping through a straw. What he is inhaling is the reality of the past, allowing it to finally surface. "The captain told me." He glares, waiting for her to respond. She stands straight and wide-eyed. "And just a while ago, that stupid bodyguard thought he was telling me something new!"

Christine is suspended in a precarious moment. What specifics could the brute have whispered into Jewels' ear?

Jewels catches her concern but misinterprets it. "It doesn't matter. I still want you. It doesn't matter to me anymore, Christine. I am not the same man anymore. Because of you, I am different. You have given me a reason to become what I always wanted to become, but never was able to." And with these words, this archaic man has not only severed the insanity of his past but has re-entered the fold of the human race. He shrugs his shoulders as if chasing away inconsequential thoughts. He waits to give her a moment to digest what he has just said. It is important that she believe his words. She has pulled him out of his mire, and it is now his turn to pull her out of hers. He is about to say something more, something that needs to be said, but will not be given the opportunity to be said. The pause is interrupted by another presence.

For within the calmness of reason, a subtle click of a trigger jolts folly to resurface. All turn toward Cameron, who is pointing a long-barreled pistol at the ceiling. Another gunslinger has entered the saloon. The incongruity of this image is bizarre. During the commotion, the three players of this drama were sightless to the other character on stage. Patiently calculating his options, Cameron waited until Christine was safe enough for him to finally enter the scene. From years of practice, Cameron has cultivated patience and observation without interference, as well as the ability to discern the critical point of no return. Although the furious moments had been intense, Cameron saw the incensed players were only blustering in a paltry power struggle. Even when Jewels introduced the firearm, Cameron knew that he would never hurt Christine. The captain had updated Cameron on Christine's strength, especially noting how she cleverly spoke to Jewels.

Although Cameron appears to be in control, he has come to this poker game haphazardly in his own self-fulfilling prophesy. Seeing Cameron now clutching a gun, Christine is aware of his mission. He slowly lowers the weapon. It appears to be attached by an invisible crane beyond human constraint as his arm extends out of his shoulder blade, like the neck of a timid turtle, protruding from its shell. Cameron aims it directly at Jewels.

Jewels' eyes squint as he peers down the darkened cavity of the barrel. He remains unfettered, confused by this action, but it doesn't take him long to connect the incongruent puzzle pieces. Jewels swivels his neck back to Christine and snags the truth. Renewed fits of laughter reeve from him like an undercurrent of an ocean wave. He has been wary of Cameron's recent aloofness, and now he understands. His head swivels, twisting with the realization why she was never able to give herself to him freely. He had presumed that it was Walt who had her heart; he never suspected her heart belonged to Cameron. He squeals, "So!" It is an unsettling comment, not only to Christine and Walt, but to the man pointing a gun at him. Cameron's hand begins to quiver. The comment signals that there is no turning back. Jewels knows Cameron must fulfill his task. Sweat swelters into tiny pearls around Cameron's hairline. The moisture turns into rivulets, which scamper haphazardly down his arm and stream onto his palm, making the gun feel heavier. Cameron wants to squeeze the trigger. The metal is moist, cool, inviting. Yet, he cannot do it.

The showdown has not yet finished. Jewels will have his wish. Another man's hand will do what he is incapable of doing. In a final act of forgiveness,

Jewels twists his torso toward Christine. His right arm rises from his side like a sail wafting in a gentle breeze, allowing his fingertips to tenderly caress her cheek. Christine absorbs his touch as he affectionately strokes her. It is a goodbye caress.

Whirling himself about, the condemned man faces his executioner. He knows that Cameron is not bluffing. Cameron has come this evening to settle up for past sins. He is more than capable of killing. Cultivated by the sins of death, watching it from the sidelines like some voyeur, Cameron is no stranger to the ending of a human life. But, oddly enough, with each ticking second, the shaft of the pistol droops into more questioning reluctance.

"Come on! Come on! Give me your best shot!" The doomed man taunts.

Cameron snaps his pistol back up, saluting pretense away. As Jewels resigns to the reality of his demise, Cameron falters further away from his resolve. He had thought this finality of Jewels would demolish that final barrier of his insensitivity, paving the path to loving Christine. It was to be an act of emancipation, challenging fate by finalizing what should have been concluded long ago.

As Christine watches the renounced hunch of Jewels' shoulders, she is seized by an unmistakable paradox of choice. Cameron's action will never resurrect Jewels' niece! This action is senseless. She shrieks, "Cameron, don't do this! Please, Cameron, don't do this!"

Cameron's hand begins to shake violently. The muzzle sways in a wild swag. His eyes swim in blindness. Not only does his vision blur, but his determination has lost clarity as well.

"Come on, Cameron...Come on, man...Get on with this!" The words could have come from Jewels again, but this time the prodding comes from Walt. He shouts to Cameron, egging him on as if cheering a hometown sports team. However, the stakes of this provocation are not local pride but serve to bring about dire consequences.

From the darkened distances of the room another persistent echo slices through the haze of tears. "This is not who you are." Christine appeals for his insanity to be dissolved through reason. "Cameron, you are not a murderer..." She pauses for emphasis. "You have never been. Now you can choose life."

Cameron can feel the coldness of the trigger's metal pressing against his index finger. How easy it would be to squeeze it. Just a little more pressure, and choice is no longer a problem. The indecisive man answers her echo. "He's only a burden to our happiness, Christine. He must never be allowed to commit those horrible acts again."

Christine's persistent voice tries to pierce those words. "How can we ever be happy with this act over our heads?"

Cameron stiffly shakes his head, attempting to reject any thought of reason. "He is nothing less than a lifeless shell of a man, worthless to anyone, even himself. Who would care if this man who has brought so much unhappiness in other's lives was eliminated?"

Realizing that Cameron is on the brink of his own destruction, Christine inches toward Jewels. She places her body directly between the two condemned men, one with a weapon to his heart, the other with a weapon in his heart. Walt lunges to take her out of harm's way, but his arm whips the wind. He is too late. "Christine! What are you doing?" Walt's wail is a plea in a sea of hopelessness. "God! Don't let this be!"

Christine tries to arrest his prayer. "Walt, Wait!"

"I don't understand." Walt whirls toward her again. This time he connects and grips her lower arm.

Christine is now in the middle of the three men who not only love her but need to be released from her. She first must quell the panic in her best friend. She looks directly into Walt's confused eyes. "Walt, you have to let me go. It's time for you to let go of me." This remark, of course, goes beyond the present moment. Walt catches its deeper meaning. He had sold her in a poker game, not because he wanted to rid himself of childhood guilt, but because he wanted her to have a better life. And in that flicker, they both understood. "It will be okay, Walt. I'll be fine. I'm strong enough."

Walt releases his grip, his hand slipping away from her like silken sand. Still, he remains close.

Christine rotates to face Cameron, her body still in the line of fire. Cameron's face is flushed with exhaustion. His expression is a cavern of twisted crevices, lost in gullies of sweat. His other arm hangs like a wilted flower. The barrel of his gun aims downward, drooping still further with indecision. The scene is captured in a snapshot where dust is immobilized in the gap of time. Here, life is suspended, trying to come to terms with the integrity of a second thought. This is humanity at its finest moment.

XVIII

"CAMERON, IF YOU DO THIS, it will destroy us." Could this suggest the possibility of losing her? His hand trembles. "Cameron, you don't need to do this…there is another way." The barrel of the pistol tilts slightly lower.

"How, Christine? He will never let us be together." He snaps the pistol back to its target. "Move out of the way, Christine. I'm about to do the world a favor."

"No! No, you're not doing the world a favor!" She pauses to recoup her thoughts. She is about to propose the unbearable for Cameron, especially in his present state. "Cameron, you need to put the pistol down because I have something important to say to you. This is very important to me!"

His eyes squint back with a perplexing look. Christine softly says, "I want this man to live."

Cameron jerks the gun at the ceiling and pulls the trigger. The jolt recoils with astonished winces. "Christine, don't tell me that you have fallen for this man!" Christine spreads her arms, one to console Walt, the other to prevent Jewels from raising his pistol behind her back.

Emphatically, Christine proclaims, "No, I have not, nor will I ever! But this man is a powerful man, an influential man, a man of abundant means, who…if given a chance…can make right his wrongs." Jewels eases his guarded arm, and Christine feels the subtle release. Under her breath, just audible to Jewels, she murmurs, "You see, I heard what you said by the waterfall."

Jewels tilts his head. "I'd didn't think you were alert enough to understand my words."

"I heard the words trying to release remorse and the words trying to embrace life. And I have been mulling over those words throughout this entire day."

During this interchange her eyes are riveted on Cameron. She beseeches him, again. "Please, put the gun down." Her tone mellows further to soothe his fractured soul. "For me, please put down the gun. If you really do care to change,…put it down."

Cameron's expression relaxes, his head bends with fatigue. His arm drops to his side. The gun is still tight in his grasp, his finger welded to the trigger. He bows his head and softly speaks, "Christine, I do care."

"I know you do."

These caressing words should have brought finality to this confrontation, but they do not. Time in a mirage is provisional. Arbitrary interference always lingers with possibility and produces dissemblers of truth, for…doubt is a forsaken promise., and passion is its deluded quest.

Throughout his life, Walt had never sat with his back to the door during a poker game. It was just a silly superstition that never had any significance until now. And because of that ensconced practice, Walt is the first to see.

He whips his arm toward Christine, this time connecting. With a firm yank he rips her from Jewels' feeble embrace. Stalled in their sparring, Cameron and Jewels turn their heads toward Walt, who has thrown Christine to the floor and is now enveloping her with his body like an unsuspected, renegade ocean wave. And in a snapshot of a second, Cameron catches the implication of this action. He swivels his head back toward the door to discover the source of the calamity. Cameron still raises his pistol. He will not have the opportunity to recant his decision. Without firing a shot, he blacks out before his body hits the floor.

Christine pants a muted scream. She wrestles from under Walt, and dragging her stunned body, claws across the carpet, digging desperate fingernails into the pile for faster traction. Cameron's slumped body seems to be an unattainable distance under the yoke of interminable time. In what seems like slow motion, she finally reaches the figure and shakes him violently to awaken. He remains limp. She cuddles him in her lap, wrapping her arms around his head, pressing him into her. Her sobbing wavers between the certainty of improbability and the denial of possibility.

The bodyguard stands in his signature eagle stance, framing the threshold at the entrance. He is poised, forever a soldier in the line of duty. And because he is that entity who has misinterpreted his role, he is, forever, a man on the verge of truth without ever knowing the truth. When he heard the gunshot, he believed his boss was in harm's way. And, seeing Cameron's pistol dangling at the end of a wavering sleeve, there was no doubt but to shoot first and ask questions later. He targeted his mark and shot. However, as the aftermath scene unfolds, there is no mistaking the affection the brute is witnessing as Christine swoons over her obvious lover. His jilted manhood retraces the recent interplay he had with her just a short time ago. He realizes that he has been played a fool in her game of deception. She has used him without regard to his pride of manhood. This realization sears into another irrevocable decision.

With lingering determination, he lifts his pistol, aiming the crossfire with deadly accuracy, for he is an adroit marksman. The target imprints on the upper left temple of the tainted woman. A devious smirk slithers over his countenance as it did earlier, and he bathes in the melted honey of retaliation. Ever so slightly he compresses the trigger, and the moment is delicious. However, it must be said that he is a man who should never be allowed such satisfaction. In fact, he is that man who, even after such a deed, would never be completely satisfied. This is a man who is unable to comprehend the worth of a life because this is a man who has no moral compass.

Instinctively, Jewels withdraws the buried weapon still glued to his spurned hand, and with deadly vehemence turns to take out the vermin. Jewels would never have anyone harm his Christine! Jewels fires. Like two snakes waggling in a dance of death, each discharges its final breath of venom. Before his demise, the bodyguard releases the last shot from the chamber. The bullet's thud interns in Jewel's chest. Christine is unscathed. Jewels falls.

With the squeeze of senseless retaliation, an arbitrary act does not justify the truth. It only becomes a wild bullet within truth. The Queen of Spades lies face up on the floor. Blood paints it red.

XIX

WHEN MONEY IS NO OBJECT anything can be made to look right again. Walt makes all the arrangements to place the puzzle pieces back into their respective spaces on the puzzle board. The casino was easily coerced into accommodating. This type of unsavory notoriety would discredit their chaste reputation, impact their elite clientele, and ignite thorny interrogations. Clean up needed to be swift and thorough.

It took the Captain two months to bring Jewels back to Pakistan, the time needed for the warlord to recuperate enough to retain a formidable presence when he surfaced from his limousine, in spite of the bandaged sling swaddling from his neck. He was greeted with fanfare from his family and notable political aficionados of his village. His wives were inquisitive about the death of his older consort, who was given proper prayers even though her remains were buried at sea. Of course, no one knew the truth of the elder wife's death. That remained muted in suggestive glances between Jewels and the Captain.

Jewels lived a rather propitious life for next couple of years. Because he ruled with clarity and confidence, he became effective enough to procure sanctions from the village elders and enact a number of changes in his tribal community. He was particularly remarkable in diminishing some of the archaic customs that demeaned women. In particular, he made sure that the practice of Honor Killing was banished. However, although it might be possible to change the laws of the land, it is often difficult to change the spirit of the law, especially when it meddles with the traditions of its people. Yet, his reforms did instill a better standard of living for most and a period of tranquility.

One day, Jewels was in his garden, engaged in his favorite pastime and his daily respite from the demands of government. He was sitting before a canvas, painting a pastoral scene. This particular afternoon, the subject was a gentle waterfall, which cascaded over rock formations into a serene pond. The greenery encased a timeless portrait of a familiar distant place. A local lad approached him clutching a hidden object under his shirt. The boy was aware that Jewels did not like to be disturbed during this private activity except in matters of urgency. However, he had heard the rumors in the back alleys. This was a sensitive issue that would result in dire consequences that only a powerful man could address. It was a communique to be delivered covertly only by an innocent messenger, illiterate, and too young to understand such matters. Consequently, as the boy inched his way toward Jewels, he maintained a bowed head of deference.

Aware of a shift in the afternoon breeze, Jewels lifted his chin and found the youth standing to his right. He stared at the awkward stance of the child for a moment, then nodded his head slightly, a signal to permit audience. The youngster moved in closer but remained a polite distance from the seated man. His young head continued to bow in reverence.

"Lift your chin, lad. You need believe that you are not less than me."

The boy maintained his penitent stance.

"Do you hear? Why do you not lift your head? Speak!"

Gazing downwards, the boy responded. "My father has taught me to keep my head below a great man."

"Well, your father is right. However, I am not such a man. Therefore, lift your head so our eyes can meet, and we can speak about things that matter."

The young boy looked up, and when he spied Jewels' gentle grin, he mirrored back a trusting smile.

"Now, why is it that you have come into my garden?" The lad's countenance abruptly changed.

The boy's eyes once again wilted as he stammered, "I have a message to give you."

By the child's wavering behavior, Jewels realized that the message must be grave. "Tell me, young man, what I need to know."

"There is a young woman who requests an audience with you." With that, the tender hand pulled out a folded note from his garment and handed it to him. Jewels carefully opened it, thoughtfully perused the brief contents, and then delicately slid it into the pocket of his garment. After a second digesting his thoughts, he turned back to the timid courier. "Thank you. You may leave."

At first, the boy hesitated. But when he saw Jewels' reassuring nod, the boy relaxed and recovered his gentle smile. Two generations had just embraced the probability of change.

The note was from a young woman who lived in the outskirts of the valley, an area under tribal jurisdiction, as well as a dominion of the House of Jewels. Still, it was a territory where its people lived simpler lives in contrast with the more sophisticated inhabitants of town. These clannish dwellers existed much in the same manner as their forefathers. The only change came with the initiative of offering its youth—both men and women—an opportunity to study at the nearby university. Unfortunately, this young woman was caught in an archaic web.

She had been engaged to a handsome young man from her region for more than a year. Both had fallen in love when they attended the university. They lived a blessed life because they were the new, enlightened generation. And this is what she thought when she told him about the night that she had spent with a soldier the year before the arrangement of their marriage. She believed that her fiancée was contemporary enough to handle this information, for she had not wanted their marriage to be smothered in secrets.

She was wrong. He became senseless with what he called her "infidelity." It mattered little that she had not even known him during this time period. His rage not only drove him away from her but propelled him to her father's house. There, her fiancée demanded that honor be restored to his name. And he demanded that her father perform the rite.

Now, her father was a simple man and aware of such "Honor" practices during the reign of Jewels' father. His survival in the village was steeped in local tribal mores, and he had raised his daughter according to tradition. This insult was an affront to the Faithful, and he was wary about how the Elders would respond if he ignored his duty. Besides, the young man was quite adamant that if the father failed, he would step in.

The daughter was summoned from the university to her father's house and threatened to be disowned if she did not show. However before attending to her father's demands, the naïve girl was taken aside by an elderly aunt who secretly imparted her fate. The older woman had lived a long, arduous life and had witnessed this atrocity more times than one should. She could not stand by without intervening and directed the young woman not to go to her father's house, but to seek out Jewels instead. The seasoned woman had heard about his progressive stance on these matters. With no other recourse, the daughter wrote the note to Jewels. Because of his compassion, perhaps this powerful man would be able to help.

When Jewels saw the words "Honor Killing," he knew that he had to take immediate action. He summoned the father to his compound and emphatically stated that not only was this practice forbidden, but that he would personally penalize, with the full vengeance of the law, anyone who resurrected this barbaric act. And knowing how difficult it would be to uproot hardened dogmas from local obsessions, he also summoned the young woman and arranged for her passage to America. There she would continue her education and find a new life to become whatever she was to become without fear of reprisals.

And that would have been the end of it, except for the revenge of her slighted finance, who stole into Jewels' bedroom that evening and executed Jewels before committing his own death.

XX

CHRISTINE LEARNED ABOUT THIS from the young woman who had shown up at her doorstep. Jewels had given the girl the American address. "This woman in New Jersey has a story to tell you. Listen carefully."

After serving a cup of tea and retiring onto two cushioned chairs, Christine smiled at the young female and began telling her own story...

"An early morning sun smeared a soft haze across my windshield..."

When she finished, Christine related how deeply saddened she was by the senseless death of a man who had finally come to understand what really mattered in life. Before departing, the young woman hugged Christine, trying to console her with the thought that if it wasn't for Jewels' intervention, her own life would have been the one that would not have mattered.

XXI

THE HUM OF THE HELICOPTER dissipates into the distances of the late afternoon, buzzing like bees sweltering between the daffodils in the wallpaper of her bedroom. Christine looks at the photographs on her dresser. All the memories are still in place, pieces on a puzzle board, separate, but connected. Sunlight streams into the room. She follows the beam on the wallpaper. It seems as if the daffodils are bowing their reverent heads to her. Doubt is no longer a forsaken promise, nor passion a deluded quest.

She shifts her attention back toward the window. He has been standing there for some time, watching, waiting. The view is certainly captivating from this height. She's sure that he is watching the yachts far below. They must appear like toy boats, inching their way up and down the Hudson River. He looks back over his shoulder, and he gives her a sagacious smile that seems to punctuate his thoughts. It is a disarming smile, one difficult not to fold under his charm. It is a smile that had come to his defense in many a ticklish situation.

As he gazes back at her, he drinks in her thoughts. It has taken him a long time to come to terms with letting go. He always struggled with letting go throughout his life…letting go of his distrust…letting go of his guilt…and now letting go of a friend. Letting go has been just as difficult for her.

They finally realized that they were old enough, educated enough, compassionate enough not to be prosaic, predictable, or scripted. They were, after all, a man and a woman of substance, no longer midway in making an irreverent mistake. They would no longer be companions of the day nor lovers in the night. Letting go is not only an altruistic definition of love, it dissolves the residue that lingers in doubt. That is how to sustain the truth and not live in a captive mirage of it. She allows him to return to his vigilance, watching, waiting, listening to the songs in the distance. There will be more songs from the sirens. Perhaps they will sing about him next time. She exhales a billow of breath, and the mirage is gone.

XXII

CHRISTINE CAN NO LONGER IGNORE the cell phone. She reaches over the side of her bed and peers into its greenish screen. The message asks her to meet him at their usual restaurant at three o'clock. Wrapping her arms around her waist, she realizes that she is still wearing Walt's favorite sweatshirt, the one he would never allow anyone else to wear. It is damp and has the scent of sea water.